Martina Reilly, formerly writing as Tina Reilly, is the author of a number of bestselling novels, including the Impac-longlisted *Something Borrowed*. She is also the author of several award-winning teenage books. Martina has worked as a columnist for the *Irish Evening Herald* and does freelance columns for the *Irish Independent*. In her spare time she acts, teaches drama and writes plays.

For more information, please visit www.martinareilly.info

Praise for Martina Reilly

'Like Marian Keyes, Reilly takes a cracking story and adds sharp dialogue and buckets of originality' *Scottish Daily Record*

'Has all the elements of an excellent read: mystery, drama and romance' *Woman*

'A top holiday read' *Closer*

'Martina has the wonderful knack of combining sensitivity for a serious subject with a big dose of humour' *Irish Independent*

'Martina Reilly's characters are so well observed . . . a substantial read' *She*

'Hard to put down, laugh-out-loud funny . . . perfect holiday reading' *Woman's Way*

'Reilly is a star of the future' *Belfast Telegraph*

'[Will] have the most hard-hearted reader wiping tears – and not just of laughter – from their eyes' *Irish Evening Herald*

'Good, solid entertainment' *Irish Examiner*

'Reilly has a wonderful comic touch, both in the way she draws her characters and in her dialogue . . . a brilliant read' *U Magazine*

'Brilliant' *Liffey Champion*

The Wish List

MARTINA REILLY

Formerly writing as Tina Reilly

sphere

SPHERE

First published in Great Britain in 2009 by Sphere
This paperback edition published in 2010 by Sphere
Reprinted 2010

Typeset in Baskerville MT by
Palimpest Book Production Limited, Grangemouth, Stirlingshire
Printed and bound in Great Britain by
Clays Ltd, St Ives plc

Papers used by Sphere are natural, renewable and
recyclable products sourced from well-managed forests and certified
in accordance with the rules of the Forest Stewardship Council.

Mixed Sources
Product group from well-managed
forests and other controlled sources
www.fsc.org Cert no. SGS-COC-004081
© 1996 Forest Stewardship Council

Sphere
An imprint of
Little, Brown Book Group
100 Victoria Embankment
London EC4Y 0DY

An Hachette UK Company
www.hachette.co.uk

www.littlebrown.co.uk

For my two wishes come true – Conor and Caoimhe.

1

ALLIE COULD PINPOINT the exact moment her life with Tony changed. It was heralded by a ring on the doorbell at five o'clock on a mild Thursday afternoon in May. Tony was at work and Mark and Owen, their two sons, were playing football out the back garden. Owen stood in the goalmouth, sucking his thumb as Mark kicked the ball at him. Owen made no attempt to save it, much to Mark's delight.

'He's only a baby,' Allie had called as the ball whizzed dangerously close to Owen's face. 'Will you give him a chance, Mark?'

'I *am* giving him a chance,' Mark called back cheerily. 'He's just not making an effort.'

Allie laughed and then the doorbell rang.

A well-dressed man in a grey suit and shiny shoes stood on her doorstep. His hair was cut military-short so it was impossible to say what colour it was. His face was pale and lean; his eyes were blue. An ordinary face and instantly forgettable. Allie wondered idly what he was selling.

'Hi,' he said, his blue eyes meeting hers. 'I'm looking for Tony?'

'Tony?' She was puzzled. 'He's at work.'

'Oh,' the man casually put his foot just inside the door, 'can you give him a message from Larry?'

Looking at his shiny shoe, positioned so that she couldn't slam the door on him, Allie's legs grew suddenly weak. It was at that moment she knew that everything she'd tried to keep a lid on was going to blow up in her face. All the stuff she'd tried to ignore was coming to her doorstep at last.

'Larry?' she stammered, 'We don't know a Larry.'

'Tony does,' the man said, smiling at her, which made things worse.

Allie swallowed and didn't respond. She knew if she spoke her voice would shake. She was afraid, too, that she might say the wrong thing.

'So,' the man said, 'can you give him a message from Larry?'

Allie nodded.

'Tell him that unless he pays Larry what he owes by next week, he'll be minus a limb, OK?'

It took a moment before Allie digested the threat. She swallowed hard. 'What do you mean?' her voice trembled.

'Mammy!' Mark yelled, 'I hit Owen in the face with the ball!' Owen could be heard howling from out the back garden.

'Look after him, Mark,' Allie called back, without taking her eyes from the man in the suit. 'I'll be there in a second.'

Mark appeared in the hall. 'I don't know what to do, his nose is bleeding.'

'Go back outside,' Allie snapped. 'Go back outside and don't come in until I tell you, right?'

'But Owen—'

'MARK!'

She knew he jumped but she could sense him leaving.

'Cute kid,' the man said. 'You've two, is it?'

'That's not your business,' Allie said fiercely, forgetting her momentary terror. 'My children are not your business.'

The man gave a shrug. 'Everything is my business until I get paid.'

'What does he owe you?' Her voice was stronger, firmer. She had to know, to find out how bad things were. To sort this mess out and keep her family safe.

'Has he not told you?' The man raised an eyebrow. To the casual observer, he'd look as if he found something amusing.

'You tell me how much he owes or you leave right now,' Allie said.

The man's eyes narrowed and suddenly he didn't look so ordinary. 'Ooh,' he said, 'I won't be going anywhere until I get my money.' He smiled.

Allie recoiled as the smile only served to emphasise the coldness in his eyes. 'How much does he owe you?' Despite her best efforts, her voice trembled.

'Fifty thousand and I'll want it by next week.'

Allie felt the world begin to spin. She knew this man calling to the house was no accident. It was done to frighten them. If he knew Tony like he said, then he knew Tony had got work after losing his last few jobs. This was to show that he knew where Tony lived. That he could get to him if he wanted.

'You'll get it,' she said. 'I promise.'

'Good,' the man nodded. 'Next week.'

Allie watched him walk away, his hands casually tucked into the pockets of his suit. He hopped into a car and was gone.

She closed the door, her whole body shaking. Then she made two phone calls, speaking calmly into the receiver, before slumping to the hall floor, where, ten minutes later, her two kids found her.

2

Six weeks later

MARK WASN'T ASLEEP when his bedroom door was pushed open and the yellow gleam of the landing light fell across his bed. He didn't think he'd slept at all. He had lain awake for ages last night, staring up at the ceiling. The luminous stars his daddy had put up, spelling out his name right across the ceiling in big star letters, had made him feel a little sad. This was the second last time he would see those stars, though his daddy had promised that he would stick some more up when they moved to their new house. Mark wasn't sure if he believed him. His daddy promised a lot of things and then they just didn't happen. And when he reminded him, his daddy would get cross and then his mammy would tell his daddy not to get so cross. And sometimes they would fight and Mark would think it was his fault. Then his Granny Magda would arrive with Fintan and maybe roll her eyes and say things like, 'That's men for you, if they can't let you down they piss all over you,' and his mammy and Fintan would get cross and say that Magda should not be using such language in front of the child and his nana would—

'Hey, Marko, are you awake?'

His daddy's whisper broke into his thoughts. He hadn't heard him enter the room. Mark wondered if he'd get in trouble for being awake so early, but decided that he wasn't good at pretending to be asleep. He sat cautiously up in bed.

'Yeah. Hi, Daddy.' He noticed his mother standing there

4

too, and she gave him a little smile. His daddy had his arm about his mammy, so that was good. Mark liked it when they did things like that, though he knew kids at school who thought it was disgusting. Mark pretended that he did too, but he didn't. It was nice.

His daddy was dressed all nice for a change, in jeans and a shirt, and he had his brown leather jacket on. His daddy was really tall, at least six feet. And thin. Very thin at the moment. It was all the stress of moving house, Mark thought. He'd heard his mammy say that to his nana. His daddy dropped down on to the bed beside Mark and grinned at him. 'You all set for the big move, Buster?'

'Suppose,' Mark grinned back. He liked when his daddy called him that. This morning he seemed in a good mood. Though you could never really be certain.

'It'll be fun, sleeping in a new room, having loads of new mates on your new road.'

Mark wasn't too sure about that. He didn't have that many as it was. And his best friend never visited any more for some reason. 'Yeah.'

'Listen, Marko, I have a little bit of news for you.'

There was something in his dad's voice that made Mark's heart start to jump about a little. Mark glanced at his mammy in the doorway and she smiled at him again. So maybe it wasn't *bad* news.

'Is it good news?'

His dad made a funny sort of face and Mark giggled a little. His daddy could be very funny sometimes. His mammy always said that she loved when Daddy made her laugh. And Daddy always said back that if she looked in a mirror she'd laugh even harder. Mark thought that was hilarious.

'It's good and bad,' his daddy said.

'Oh.'

'The bad bit is that I've to go away on a business trip.' He paused. 'Again.'

'When?'

'Today. I've to be at the airport for about nine. It was a last minute thing.'

Mark's heart sank. His dad wasn't going to be there to dig up the back garden at the new house, which was a mess. He wouldn't be there to help load things into a van or put stars on his ceiling or anything. 'For how long? Is it only a short trip?'

Again a look passed between his parents.

'Eh—'

'We're not sure, Mark.' His mother came into the room now and placed her hand on his daddy's shoulder. 'It's to America. It could be for a good few weeks at least. We just have to see what happens.'

'But can you just say no?' Mark wanted to cry. His daddy was always going on business trips. Sometimes he didn't even tell Mark he was going away and then he'd come back and he'd always be in a bad mood because his boss worked him too hard.

'I wish I could.' His dad reached out and ruffled his hair. 'I really do, Mark.'

He sounded as if he meant it, which was something.

His mother crouched down beside the bed and took his hands. 'I know it's hard, Mark. But you and I will work together, won't we?'

Mark shrugged.

'And when I come back,' his daddy said, 'I'll have a lovely present for you and Owen and a big kiss for your mammy.'

'Ugh!' Mark made a face.

His daddy bent down, grabbed his mother around the waist and planted a big kiss on her lips.

His mammy laughed and so did his daddy and they looked into each other's eyes and Mark was suddenly happy.

Allie followed Tony downstairs. For someone who had been a master of deception, lying to his kids didn't seem to come that easily to him. It reassured her a little. At the bottom of the stairs he turned to her and hesitantly placed his hands on her shoulders. 'Thanks,' was all he said.

'I did it for Mark,' she said, shrugging him off. Ever since that man had come calling six weeks ago, she had this anger that she wasn't able to express properly. Oh, she'd given Tony hell at the time; she'd been packed and ready to go when he'd arrived home about ten that night. The kids had been bundled off to her mother's and she'd stood there in their cosy dining room, suitcase at her feet, waiting for him. He'd come in, oblivious as usual, and she'd quietly asked him about the fifty thousand pounds he owed. He'd paused, paled and initially denied it. So she'd picked up her case and walked to the front door. He'd said nothing as she opened it, then as she stepped outside he'd come running after her and begged her not to leave him, sworn that she and the kids were his whole world. Clasped her wrist so tightly that it had hurt. Finally, after he'd become more upset than she'd ever seen before and had blurted out everything to her, she'd agreed to give him this one last chance.

'I know you did it for Mark, but thanks anyway.' Tony turned away with a defeated look on his face. 'What time is your mother arriving to mind the kids?'

'In around ten minutes.'

'OK. D'you want a coffee?'

'Go on so.' Tony made great coffee. He'd bought an outrageously expensive machine a while ago and was the only one who could operate it. Allie watched him pull the coffee from the press and begin to mess about with the coffee maker. She never tired of looking at him. She loved the way the sunlight bounced off his jet black hair. Even though she was angry at him, sad at him, she still loved him so much that it hurt her heart to think about it. Truth was she didn't know if she could have left him that night. Even as she'd opened the door, part of her had known he'd come after her. And she knew he loved her too. They wouldn't still be here if she doubted it.

7

'I love you, Tony,' she said suddenly.

He paused in the act of flicking the machine on. Turning to face her, his dark eyes met hers. 'You are the only thing I ever did right, Allie. I dunno how I got so lucky.'

She didn't answer that. The memory of their first meeting, when he'd leaned out of a car and yelled a 'Hello gorgeous!' at her, had changed and twisted into something that didn't make her smile any more.

Tony bit his lip. 'I swear I'll—'

'Don't,' Allie said. 'No promises. Just come back, OK?'

'I will.'

The silence was shattered by a ring on the doorbell.

'It's Mam,' Allie said, breaking the moment by moving towards the front door to let her mother in.

Magda, in a bright pink tracksuit and sparkling-white trainers, bounced into the hallway, saw Tony and abruptly turned back to Allie. She adjusted her bright pink sweat band so that her hair wasn't clumping underneath it and asked, 'All packed for the big move?'

'Yeah, nearly.' Where had her mother got that tracksuit? Allie wondered, trying not to smile.

'D'you want a coffee Magda?' Tony called out. 'Allie and I were just going to have one.'

Magda eyed him in disdain. 'I never touch the stuff, Tony,' she said. 'Caffeine is a *drug*, so no thank you.' She turned back to Allie. 'Are the children still asleep?'

'Mark might be awake,' Allie said. 'You can go up to him if you like.'

'I will so. I've bought the nicest thing for his new room. He is going to love it. Fintan helped me choose it.' She turned back to the front door and peered up the street. 'He's just parking the car.'

Magda had met Fintan at Dietwatchers two years ago and they'd been inseparable ever since. Allie liked Fintan to a point, she just wasn't too happy about the way he seemed to be

8

replacing her own father in her mother's life. Magda had thrown Allie's dad out when Allie was fifteen for yet another infidelity, with yet another neighbour. And aside from a few birthday cards, they'd never heard from him again. Allie tried never to think of him, but when she saw Fintan and her mother together, she always did.

'Oh, here he is,' Magda cooed, waving wildly, 'my live-in lover!'

Behind her back, Allie rolled her eyes.

Fintan bounded up the path, all smiles and layered, flicked grey hair. He too was wearing a tracksuit, though his was a sober grey.

'Hello, Allie. Hello, Tony. All set?' he boomed as he entered the house, slamming the front door behind him. Allie reckoned in amusement that both her kids were probably now awake. Not waiting for an answer, Fintan loped after Magda up the stairs to the kids' rooms.

'Forget about the coffee,' Allie said, grabbing her coat. 'Let's go while they're distracted.'

Tony hesitated. 'I might just say goodbye to Owen.' He paused and swallowed. 'And maybe Mark again.'

Allie felt sorry for him. 'OK.' She shoved her arms into her rain jacket and zipped it up. 'Don't upset them, though.'

'I won't.'

She was driving as they only had the one car and she couldn't afford to be without it. Anyway, what good would it be sitting in a car park for a few weeks? Of course he could have taken a taxi, but she wanted to drive him there.

She heard him making Mark laugh upstairs and then Magda and Fintan brought the two boys down to wave their daddy off.

3

J EREMY PULLED ACROSS his lace curtain and peered out the window. Of course he didn't pull the lace curtains too much, because that would give the game away. He didn't want to be seen to be looking out the window because then he'd be labelled nosy by the woman and her two boys who seemed, as far as Jeremy could tell, to be moving into the house next door.

Jeremy, far from being nosy, just had a healthy interest in the comings and goings on his street. He liked to know who he was living beside. So many people nowadays didn't even know their neighbours and, while Jeremy had no intention of getting to know this young woman and her children, he at least liked to be aware of who lived next to him. You never knew when you would need your neighbours. Jeremy had a dread of falling down the stairs and not being able to ring anyone, or perhaps he might slip getting out of the bath, though he fervently hoped that the bath incident wouldn't happen. He didn't really want to be found naked by a young woman and her two boys. That would be humiliating. No, far better to fall down the stairs than slip coming out of the bath. He'd be very careful getting out of the bath in future. His son, Adam, had suggested on his last visit that Jeremy should get a shower installed, but Jeremy didn't like showers. Showers were for people in a hurry. Jeremy didn't have to hurry any more, he had nowhere to go. He spent a long time in the bath, it helped pass the time. He liked to think in the bath, to sort out his life, to think about his two sons, and of how very odd they were.

There was Adam, the eldest, thirty-three years of age and still gallivanting around the place. Oh, he had a job but it wasn't the sort of job Jeremy hoped he'd get. Adam had been a very bright boy, good in school, but he'd thrown it all away to become a children's television presenter. Every day, Adam dressed up as a pirate and interacted with a parrot that said rude things and made children laugh. Jeremy couldn't see what was so funny himself. He didn't watch Adam very much.

His other son, Joel, was thirty and married for the last eight years. He already had two children, a boy and a girl. In Jeremy's opinion Joel's children needed taking down a peg or two. They were very vocal and had opinions on everything, even on the fact that Jeremy smoked. His granddaughter, Jenny, told him it was bad for him and that he shouldn't smoke in the house. Jeremy had reminded her that it was his house and that he'd smoke if he wanted. Jenny had wrinkled up her little nose, a nose that reminded him of his dead wife's, and said in a piping voice that got on Jeremy's nerves, 'Well, it's your funeral, Granddad.'

The two children who were moving in next door were boys. Jeremy pulled at his overgrown white beard, trying to decide if he was pleased about that or not. Girls were annoying but at least they were quiet. Boys could be quite boisterous. One of the boys moving in seemed to be around eight years old. He was a fat sort of child, probably from eating too many sweets, and he had jet black hair and an eager, helpful look on his face. He was pulling things out of the boot of his mother's car and carrying them importantly into the house. He was dressed in a sports jersey and tracksuit bottoms. The other boy, smaller, stood to the side and looked a little bewildered. He seemed to be around two. His head moved back and forth, up and down the driveway as he watched his brother and mother unpack. Then he stuck his thumb in his mouth and began to suck on it vigorously. That would ruin his teeth for sure, Jeremy thought.

11

He scanned the vicinity for a sign of a father. To his dismay there didn't seem to be one. Maybe he was away or something. In Jeremy's opinion children needed a father. Boys especially. Mothers spoiled their sons. Look at what had happened with his own two: one a pirate and the other already a father of two. Jeremy hoped that the woman wasn't a single mother. The last thing he needed was her rapping on his door looking for him to fix things in her house. Women were not much good at DIY, he'd found. His own wife had tried to fix things a couple of times and ended up making them a whole lot worse. One time she had even managed, and to this day Jeremy didn't know how she'd done it, to cut out the electricity to the whole street. That had been very embarrassing. Nelly, though, hadn't found it embarrassing – she'd laughed at his mortification and made him laugh grudgingly in turn. Jeremy pushed the thought from his head, where it threatened to overtake his curiosity about the new people. He watched for another while as the family moved their belongings into the house. He was a little glad it was a family as the last crowd in that house had been students, and they'd been very noisy and had had a lot of loud parties. Jeremy had got sick of turning his own radio up full blast at seven in the morning to wake them up. Well, he reasoned, if they kept him up at night, he'd get them up in the morning. They'd taken to calling him 'The Incredible Sulk,' which hadn't been at all nice.

A little family might just be OK, he thought. Especially if they stayed out of his way until he needed them.

4

ALLIE STARED AT the boxes of stuff she had taken from the car and was glad that she'd listened to Mark and labelled each one. There was a box marked 'Kitchen' and another 'Bathroom' and so on. Normally she would never have thought of it, but Mark had seen a programme about moving house and told her that that's what the people on the show had done. She wondered sometimes how she and Tony had produced Mark. Eight years old and terribly sensible. It made Allie laugh sometimes when Mark talked about mortgages and bank loans. He'd even asked if they'd be able to move house in the current climate. But it was sad, too. She'd told him that she was the grown-up so it was her job to worry, but Mark still insisted on looking at the news. Allie was convinced that Mark somehow thought that if he looked at the news he could control things by knowing about them.

'Mammy?' Mark arrived in the kitchen. He had foraged a bag of sweets from somewhere and his mouth was full. 'Do you know where the stuff for my bedroom is?'

'Come here and gimme a hug.' Allie held out her arms and Mark came towards her, shoving his sweets into his pocket. 'D'you like your new house? Didn't we do well?'

Mark surveyed the tiny kitchen and the narrow hallway. 'It's not as big as our last house,' he acknowledged eventually. 'But at least we've still got a back garden where I can kick a football and practise my keepie uppies.'

'You can.' Allie hugged her eldest child tight against her and ruffled his dark hair, the same kind of hair Tony had.

'Will Daddy put up goal posts when he gets back like we had in our old house?'

'Course he will.'

'Will he know where the house is?'

Allie bent down to Mark's level and tipped her forehead off his. 'Yeah. Sure we all looked at it together, didn't we? And he helped me pack all the stuff – do you remember?'

'Daddy didn't help much. He just sat looking at the walls and you told us not to disturb him.'

Allie flinched and tried to make a joke about it. 'Yeah, he was a big lazy bones, wasn't he?'

'Yeah.' There was a pause then Mark asked quietly, 'Is Daddy coming back?'

'What?'

'You had a big row,' Mark's lip wobbled, 'and you said you'd leave him and now he's gone and even though he shouts and stuff, I love him and I was just thinking yesterday that maybe—'

'Oh honey pie,' Allie hugged him tighter, 'stop! Wipe your eyes, come on.' She looked about for a tissue but of course they were all in boxes so she took a tissue from her sleeve and attempted to dry his eyes.

Mark squirmed out of her arms. 'Ugh, I don't want your dirty hankies, Mammy.'

'It's not dirty, cheeky.' Allie pretended to tickle him and was rewarded with a laugh. Then, as he scrubbed his eyes with the palm of his hand, she said seriously, 'Mark, even though Daddy shouts, I love him too. And he is coming back, OK?'

He nodded.

'No more worrying, OK?' She hunkered down again to his level. 'Your daddy just has a big hard job to do, that's all.' It was partly the truth, she told herself.

'I wish he was here.'

Allie pushed his hair from his eyes. 'I wish the same,' she said. 'But sometimes you just can't have what you want so you have to settle for the best you can get. One day, we will be all together. When Daddy's boss is happy, he'll have more time to spend at home with you, me and Owen.' A thought struck her. 'Where is Owen?'

'He found some colours and took them into the front room.'

'Aw no!' Allie left Mark standing in the kitchen and was just in time to stop her youngest from colouring a big patch of the wall in blue.

Unfortunately she had been too late to stop the red, yellow and green.

'Well,' she said, hands on hips as the two boys looked at her, 'Daddy won't have to paint this room now.'

Mark and Owen thought that was really funny.

Later that night, after she'd put the two boys to bed, she began to sort the boxes out. Moving house had been a strange experience, packing away her whole life into brown cardboard boxes. She'd found things that years ago she'd put carefully away and never looked at again. Then, while packing, she'd suddenly unearthed them in the attic or under the bed or squirrelled away in the back of a wardrobe. She put all those memories into a box marked 'Miscellaneous'. She had a sudden urge to examine the stuff inside. She pulled off the tape and the top of the box flipped open. Allie opened it further and pulled out a handful of old cards. Valentine's cards that Tony had sent her when they had started going out together, and in the early days of their marriage. They were funny cards, typical of him. *Darling,* one of the cards read, *seven days spent with you makes one weak.* She smiled now looking at it.

Tony excelled in making her laugh. Unfortunately, he excelled in making her miserable too. One card that she pulled open had obviously been sent after a row. *OK,* he'd written in his neat script, *I admit I'm no saint, but would you really like me to stand naked on a pillar and flagellate myself? You, however, are the saintliest person I know . . .*

Allie laughed.

There were pictures of them on holiday. Tony, squinting into the sun, his hand shading his deep-set brown eyes, a lazy grin spread over his face, his body slightly slouched as his other arm rested lightly by his side. He was incredibly photogenic. Not that he wasn't good-looking in reality, but in photographs he had the ability to project an easiness that was missing in real life. Day to day, Tony could be tense and edgy. Manic, even. He only ever seemed to be happy around very old friends or with Allie and the kids. In all other situations, he appeared uncomfortable.

There were more photos in the box. There was one of the two of them, taken by some stranger. God, she thought as she examined it, she had looked pretty damn good herself. Her long brown hair was tied up with a bright red scarf and she was much thinner than she was now. She was staring up at Tony and he was grinning down at her, and they were so obviously in love that it brought a lump to her throat. She wished she could go back and change things. She wondered, even if she was given the chance, if she would have been able to do so.

'Stop it, Al,' she told herself firmly, 'you're luckier than some people.' She replaced the photos in the box and taped it back up. The only thing she left out was the funny apology card.

She hugged it to her as she climbed up the stairs to her new room.

The way the full moon shone through the window, a big slice of light cutting across the floor, sliding on to her bed and up the door, made her smile a little. There was something about this house that made her feel really positive. It was going to be great for the four of them here.

She knew it would.

16

5

JEREMY WAS OUT in his garden. It wasn't much of a garden really, not since his wife died. In the spring it was passable, as the daffodils she'd planted years ago came up, but now, in July, there was nothing. He had never got around to planting summer flowers and, if he were honest, he wasn't a man for flowers. He hated seeing them wither away and die. It gave him a sort of pain in his heart. However, as Adam kept telling him, everything died; it was the beauty it created when it was there that he should enjoy. Adam was a bit of a nuisance like that. Jeremy was convinced that Adam read all sorts of New Age, New Man books and trotted out useless pieces of information that he'd memorised. That was the sort of thing people in the media and the arts did. Though prancing about as a pretend pirate with a rude parrot on your shoulder could hardly be called art, could it? Jeremy really didn't think so.

The reason he was out was that he had noticed a bright red object down at the end of the garden. He'd been looking out his window and one moment there was nothing, then suddenly it was there. Jeremy didn't know what it could be. He strode towards it, feeling curious, when from across the wall a head bobbed up.

'Hey, mister?'

Jeremy jumped. The voice was loud and childish. The head had now disappeared but shot up again a second later. 'Hey, mister?'

Jeremy approached the wall cautiously. It was the new boy

from next door. The fat one. He didn't really want to talk to a child, especially one with a big loud voice. 'Yes?' he said, emphasising his well resonated diction for the benefit of the child. 'Are you calling me?'

'Can I get my ball back?'

The boy was jumping up and down, attempting to see over the wall. He was fatter close up.

Jeremy frowned. 'Pardon?' he said, squinting at the boy poking his head over the wall.

The boy gasped suddenly and took a step back. His mouth hung open. His eyes grew large as they raked over Jeremy. 'Wow,' he said.

'Excuse me?' Jeremy suddenly felt uneasy. He ran his hand over his beard, patted his head and felt the bare skin on his cheeks to make sure he hadn't got food or dirt on his face. There was something very strange in the way this boy was looking at him. 'What are you staring at?' he growled.

The boy gulped and still continued to stare.

'Well?' Jeremy demanded.

Now a sort of flush crept up the boy's face and an uncertain smile began at the corners of his mouth. He took a step nearer the wall and continued to gawk. 'Are you . . .' He gulped again. 'Well, are you . . .' His voice dipped. 'Are you Santa?' he breathed.

Jeremy took a step back. What? Was the child making fun of him? 'Pardon?' he said.

'You look like Santa,' the boy said, his eyes lighting up. 'You're fat and you've got a beard and a big red sort of face.'

'I am not fat,' Jeremy said crossly. 'I'm just wearing a big jumper, I get cold easily. I've got big bones.'

A grin split the boy's face. 'I won't tell,' he said breathlessly. 'I won't tell anyone if you are.'

There was a silence then the boy said again, 'I'm good at keeping secrets.'

Jeremy frowned, considering his options. This boy thought

he was Santa. If he told this boy he was Santa, he'd have to be a good boy, wouldn't he? Jeremy liked good children and if this boy was good, he'd have no problems from him. But was it a bit mean to pretend to be Santa when the boy would find out that there was no such person in a couple of years? That might cause trouble. But Jeremy could be dead by then. In all likelihood he might be and besides, Adam was always telling him to seize the moment.

'Yes, I am Santa,' Jeremy admitted, in what he considered a suitably grave voice. 'And if you tell anyone, I will not bring you any presents this year. And if you let your ball go into my garden, I will not bring you any presents this year either.'

The boy had come close to the wall now and was staring at him in awe. It was quite a nice feeling, Jeremy thought.

'Where is Rudolph?'

Jeremy managed a smile. He'd have to brush up on his Santa knowledge, he thought. His own children had been too intelligent to believe in Santa – they'd given him up as a bad idea at around five. This boy obviously had a lot of growing up to do. Jeremy sighed and answered carefully, 'Rudolph is resting for his big trip around the world on Christmas Eve.'

'How does he rest?'

'He has a lie down.'

'I didn't think reindeers could lie down.'

'Rudolph is a special reindeer. You should know that.'

'Oh. And is he in your shed?'

Jeremy winced. 'No, he is not. He is in a secret location in the North Pole. Now, you heard what I said, didn't you? No letting the ball into my garden or you'll have no presents.'

'I heard,' the boy said solemnly. 'Cross my heart I won't let it go in again. Can I have it now?'

'Right.' Jeremy picked the ball up. As he handed it over he said, 'And my name is Mr Lyons to you. You cannot call me Santa.'

'If I called you Santa everyone would know,' the boy said delightedly. 'I'm not stupid.'

Jeremy nodded, a faint smile on his lips. The poor kid didn't realise the irony of his statement. 'Good boy,' he said. He made to turn away.

'I'm Mark,' the boy said, then added, 'but you probably knew that.'

Jeremy didn't answer, just began to move off.

'Where is Mrs Claus?' the boy called after him.

Jeremy froze.

'Your wife?' the boy prompted. 'Where is she?'

Jeremy turned around and blinked a little too much. 'Eh, Mrs Claus, she's, eh,' his voice faltered, 'in the North Pole with the elves. Helping them make the toys.'

'I didn't know she helped.'

'Well, she does.'

'My daddy is away too with work. My mammy misses him. Do you miss Mrs Claus?'

'It's Mrs Lyons to you,' Jeremy said firmly. 'And, well, I'm used to, eh, Mrs Claus not being here any more.' He had to swallow a bit after he said that. 'Now, if you'll excuse me.' He was sweating as he walked away. There was perspiration on his upper lip and he licked it away.

'I love you!' the boy called after him and Jeremy winced.

He hoped none of the neighbours heard.

6

'WELL, WELL,' TESS said approvingly, as she deposited a large cake on Allie's counter top, 'you have made this place look nice and homely.'

'Thanks.'

'Hasn't she made it look nice and homely, John?'

John, Tony's younger brother at twenty-five years old, had no interest in homely. He grinned wryly at Allie and nodded. 'Very homely, Sister-in-law.'

Allie dipped her head. 'Thank you, Brother-in-law,' she said back.

Allie had been dreading the inevitable visit from Tony's mother. Ever since she'd heard the news about her son, she'd been in shock. She'd taken to bed for two weeks and, according to herself, had lived on vitamin drinks and vitamin tablets. 'Not a bite could pass my mouth,' she declared. Now, however, the shock had passed and she had arrived, bearing gifts and condolences. John had obviously decided to come with his mother to offer something other than mild hysterics. He was peering out the back window.

'Good size garden you've got,' he remarked in what he hoped was a positive voice.

'Yeah, it's a bit overgrown though.' Allie joined him, having put on the kettle. 'I'll have to get it cleared. Mark is dying to get some goal posts in.'

'I'll do it for you,' John offered.

'Oh God, I couldn't have you doing that!'

'Yes you can,' Tess spoke up. She was busy organising the cups for the tea and setting her enormous cake on to a plate, hacking great big slices off for them all to eat. 'John is – what was that nice expression you used, John?' She peered in mild disapproval at him. 'Oh yes, "between jobs" at the minute, so he can afford the time. It'll keep him off the streets.'

'Mam,' John snorted back some laughter, 'I'm twenty-five, hardly a teenager.'

'Well then,' Tess clicked her tongue, 'you should stop acting like one. Do you know any other men, Allie, who, at twenty-five, don't know what to do with their lives?'

Yeah, your other son, Allie felt like saying, but she didn't think Tess would take it as a joke. 'If you could do the garden, John, that'd be great. I'll find some way to pay you.'

'I don't need paying.' John shot a sly look at his mother, who was now pouring tea for them all. Tess had tried to work the coffee maker but had given up after Allie told her that Tony seemed to be the only one able to do it. Affecting a martyr's voice John sighed, 'I'll offer it up for all the holy souls in purgatory.'

'You should offer it up for your own soul, more like,' his mother tutted. 'Now,' she patted the table, 'sit down here, Allie. I've made a lovely cup of tea and wait until you taste that cake, it'll do you good, so it will. You're looking very thin altogether.'

'Thanks,' Allie said, grinning.

'I didn't mean it as a compliment,' Tess admonished.

'Where's the lads?' John asked.

'I think they're upstairs,' Allie said. 'I'm surprised they haven't come down yet. Mark!' she called. 'Come on and see who's here!'

In answer, they heard a clattering of feet above and then Mark pounded down the stairs with Owen following behind. 'It's John!' Mark shrieked as he hurled himself on his uncle.

22

John laughed and swung him around, almost knocking the ceramic duck from the countertop as Mark's feet skimmed by.

Owen held his arms up for a go.

'And up we go!' John yelled, oblivious to the narrowly averted disaster.

'Outside with them,' Tess ordered sternly as she hopped up to stop the duck hurtling to the floor as Owen knocked against it.

Owen started to cry. He hated loud voices.

'Aw Ma, you've upset the little fella now!'

'And you nearly broke one of Allie's ornaments.'

John hefted Owen up in his arms and said, 'Right lads, I'm going to be designing your back garden, so let's see what we're going to do with it.'

'Yeah!' Mark cheered. Then 'I want goal posts!' he said, following his uncle outside. 'Come on and I'll show you where I want them.'

Tess stared fondly after them. 'He's a terrible man.'

'The kids love him though.'

'They do.'

There was a silence. Allie was reluctant to break it, knowing that the next subject would be Tony, now that the kids were safely out of the way.

'So,' Tess said after a bit.

Allie smiled at her.

'How are you managing?'

'OK,' Allie wrapped her hands about her mug, 'I'm unpacking as you can see.' She indicated the half opened boxes that still lined the hallway. 'And I've all summer to settle in, so it's the best it can be I guess.'

'And Tony,' Tess' voice caught at the mention of her son's name, 'have you heard from him yet?'

'Nothing yet. I'm not sure if he's allowed any contact the first week or so.'

'Oh.' Tess sniffed loudly and began to fumble in her patent

black bag for a tissue. She eventually pulled out a large brilliant-white handkerchief. 'Oh, sorry,' she dabbed her eyes furiously, 'the last thing you need is me blubbering.'

'I need some paper!' Mark bounded in the back door and screeched to a halt at the sight of his nana crying. 'Are you crying?' he asked in horror.

'No, no, my eyes are just watering.' Tess attempted to smile at him.

'Does that happen when you get really old?' Mark came closer to have a gawk.

'There is paper up at the computer,' Allie suppressed a grin, 'and some pens.'

'We're designing the garden,' Mark said, forgetting about his gran's leaky eyes. 'John says we might be able to fit in a sandpit!'

'Oh no, you don't want a sandpit,' Tess said. 'Cats will do their business in it.'

'What business? Like daddy's business?'

'No,' Tess wrinkled up her nose, 'their poo.'

Mark rolled his eyes. 'Sure,' he said.

'You tell John there's to be no sandpits.'

Mark ignored her and raced out to get the paper.

'He'll turn your garden into a mess if you let him,' Tess said to Allie, still sniffing, 'so be firm with him. I wish he'd find a woman to settle him down, and then I won't have to worry about him any more. His dad would turn in his grave if he knew that he still hasn't managed to find a decent job.' She sniffed again. 'Tony was the sensible one. He made us so proud. And now . . .' Her voice trailed off. 'What on earth happened?'

Allie shrugged. 'Only he knows that,' she said. 'He has to figure that out for himself.'

Mark ran by them again and out the kitchen door. Tess finished dabbing her eyes. 'Well, I'm going to find out all I can about it,' she said determinedly, 'and I'll fill you in, Allie.

You look after those boys of yours and you know John and I are here if you need us.'

'John's going to see if we can get a roundabout in the garden!' Mark shrieked loudly.

'Well,' Tess smiled, rolling her eyes, 'I'm here at least.'

Allie laughed.

7

ADAM HAD RUNG that morning and announced that, as he was going to be in the area, he might as well visit. Jeremy didn't like the 'might as well' at all. It sounded as if his son viewed it as a chore, as something to be endured. But then Jeremy had to admit that he endured Adam's visits. His son seemed to think that everyone should be in good humour all the time: he was eternally bouncy, eternally smiling and eternally telling Jeremy what he should do to have a better life. He didn't like the way Jeremy spent his time alone in the house. He urged him to get out, to join clubs. Jeremy didn't like clubs, they were full of nosy people, nosy old people, and Jeremy was not ready to be declared old just yet. Seventy was the new fifty as far as he was concerned.

Still, if Adam was going to call it meant a shopping trip out to get some supplies. Adam liked bread and cheese. Not any old bread though, no; Adam liked the bread with the tomatoes in. The one that smelled and tasted funny. The expensive one. Jeremy wasn't going to buy a whole loaf of it; it would only go to waste. Adam would eat one or two slices and then leave. So that's all Jeremy bought – two slices of tomato bread in the local deli. The first time he had asked for it, they had looked at him as if he was mad. No, they'd told him, you have to buy the whole loaf. Jeremy had informed them that he didn't have to do anything like that at all. Then one of the cashiers had recognised him. She had made a 'nuts' sign, tapping her head with her index finger and rolling her eyes, and immediately he'd been able to purchase his two slices of bread. Jeremy didn't care if they thought he was nuts. If his mental status allowed him to be economical – well, it was worth it.

Jeremy peered out his front window. It was a nice day. That fat boy from next door was out, kicking his ball up and down. Some children were eyeing him from the other side of the road. They seemed to be laughing at him, though the boy didn't notice. Jeremy had grown quite fond of the boy. Well, maybe fond was wrong as he'd never actually talked to him since they'd first met, or really seen him, but that was why. The boy was keeping out of his way and that was good. Jeremy pulled on his coat and unlocked his front door. Stepping outside, he took a deep breath. The boy stopped kicking the ball and a kid on the other side of the street hissed, 'Here's Germy.' Someone laughed.

Jeremy bristled at the nickname they thought was so funny. He hated children.

'Hello, Mr Lyons!' the fat boy shouted.

Jeremy nodded briefly to him and ignored the stares of the other children as he strode up the street, his hands in the pockets of his coat, his face impassive.

Mark stared after Santa in awe. He'd been about to kick keepie uppie twenty-nine when Santa had come out of his house and messed it up on him. Still, twenty-eight was a good number. His dad would be pleased. Mark hopped on to his wall and watched as Santa strode up the street. He was a good actor, pretending to be really nasty when all the time he was planning to give the kids toys for Christmas. Mark felt honoured that he'd been told the secret, yet he worried that maybe he might let it slip to someone, or maybe shout it out in his sleep. Would Santa forgive that? It wasn't as if he could help it if he talked in his sleep.

'Hey you!' a big kid shouted from across the street. 'Fatso!'

Mark flinched. He didn't think they were talking to him, but maybe they were. He decided not to answer.

'Hey Fatso!'

Mark looked up; all the kids were peering at him. There were three big boys that he knew from his school. Robert, James and Peter. There were some girls, too. They were all grinning. Mark didn't say anything.

'How did you get so fat, Fatso?'

They were definitely talking to him. Mark swallowed hard. He didn't want to cry but being called Fatso was not very nice.

'Do you eat lots of sweets?'

Mark dug his hand into his pocket and it curled around some hard boiled sweets that his uncle John had given him. 'Do you want some?' he asked instead. 'I have some in my pocket.'

There was a silence from the other side of the street, then a murmuring.

'No,' Robert, the biggest boy, eventually called, 'you probably want them for yourself so you can get fatter.'

They all laughed and started to walk away.

Mark stared after them, stunned. He didn't feel in the mood for keepie uppies any more.

Jeremy watched as Adam pulled up in his red sports car. Adam liked to draw attention to himself; he'd always been like that. From his youngest days, Adam had sung and danced and acted. He'd starred in school plays and won talent competitions. Jeremy had been suspicious of the whole thing but his wife had encouraged her son to follow his heart. If it had been up to Jeremy, Adam would have learnt a trade or gone to college. But no, now his son drove around in flashy cars and wore colourful clothes and laughed loudly. Not the kind of son Jeremy had envisaged.

As usual, a crowd of kids gathered around Adam and his car. At first it had been the car that attracted them, but then one clever kid had recognised Adam as Jolly Roger and now every time he arrived kids crowded about, the younger ones with scraps of paper which Adam signed for them with his customary flourish. He crouched down to the kids' level and they laughed at whatever he was saying to them. He let the older boys peer inside his car and grinned at them as they fiddled with the radio, wincing as they turned it up full and the boom filled the whole street. Fifteen minutes after he'd pulled up with a screech, he managed to extricate himself from the kids and lope up the driveway. He was carrying a loaf of bread and a packet of biscuits.

Jeremy opened the door before he had time to ring.

'Hey Dad,' Adam grinned easily as he entered, 'how's tricks?'

Jeremy didn't answer. What sort of a question was that? He watched Adam as he walked towards the kitchen. Adam had his height, his once blond hair, but his mother's slenderness and lithe movement. 'This place looks good, have you been cleaning?'

'I always clean,' Jeremy said. 'There's no problem with my cleaning abilities. Now, would you like tea?'

'I'd prefer coffee.' Adam opened the fridge and peered inside. 'Oh goody, you've got cheese.' He pulled out the small block that his da had purchased that morning and then found a knife. 'I brought my own bread, and your favourite biscuits.'

'I bought you some bread.' Jeremy was annoyed. Had he braved the street for nothing? Had he almost tripped over a load of drinking, smoking teenagers in the park for nothing?

Adam hesitated. 'You did?' he said. 'Well, that was nice. I'll have your bread so.' His dad's bread was always stale and there were only ever two slices.

Jeremy felt he was being managed. Adam did that a lot: pandered to him. 'You don't have to,' he said, trying to sound as if he didn't care, 'I'm sure your bread is nicer.'

'I'll eat your bread, Dad,' Adam said patiently. 'Is it in the bread bin?'

'Yes. I'll put on the kettle, shall I?'

'Do that.' Adam turned to the bread bin and opened it. Two slices of bread sat there. They had gone hard because they hadn't been wrapped up. Adam sighed. Another half-stale sandwich to eat. He pulled the bread out and cut the cheese. His dad had no butter. 'Would you like a sandwich, Dad?'

'No, thank you. I don't tend to eat lunch.'

His dad ate very little for such a big man, Adam thought.

There was silence as Jeremy brewed the tea and Adam made his sandwich. Adam didn't speak until his dad was sitting opposite him, a cup of tea in front of them both. Obviously there was no coffee.

'I see someone has moved in next door,' Adam said. 'What are they like?'

His dad shrugged. 'Family. No father. I think he's away on business. Two children.'

'Have you talked to them yet? Are they nice?'

Jeremy gave a shrug. 'Sort of. They seem OK.'

Well that was good, Adam thought. At least it wasn't stressing his father out. 'My series has been commissioned for another year,' he offered. 'It topped the ratings for a children's programme.'

'Oh,' Jeremy smiled. 'That's marvellous.'

'Yes.'

More silence. Adam bit his lip. There had to be a way to say what he wanted to say. Each time he came here he had planned how to do it, and each time he found himself unable to. Thirty-three years old and still scared of his dad. He was pathetic. 'I, eh, visited Mum's grave last week,' he said instead. 'It looked well. I think Joel and the kids must have visited. There were flowers on it.'

Jeremy didn't respond. He stared into his tea.

'Petunias, hyacinths, daisies, pansies . . .' Adam trailed off. 'The flowers on Mum's grave,' he explained weakly.

'I'm not into flowers,' Jeremy said in a strangled sort of voice.

Adam paused. 'OK,' he rallied, attempting to sound upbeat, 'so what are you into these days, Dad? Done any more ice hockey? Rugby?'

His joke fell flat.

'I'm into reading my books, doing my crosswords. I walk in the park occasionally.'

'Have you thought any more of getting out and about?'

'No. You don't need to go out to read books or do crosswords. And I said that I walk in the park.'

'I was thinking of getting a man in to do the garden for you. Would you like that, Dad?'

'The garden is fine.'

'Yes, but to cut down the six-foot-high grass and plant flowers and tidy up the oak tree and weed it and—'

'I like grass. Green is my favourite colour.'

Adam sighed and bit into his stale sandwich. At least his dad remembered to get the sundried tomato bread. It didn't go great with cheddar cheese but the man had tried. He wondered if he just sat there and said nothing whether his dad would offer anything in the way of conversation. He thought he'd try it. He concentrated on eating his sandwich and drinking his tea whilst remaining shtoom. His dad slurped on his tea and after a few minutes of silence, glanced at him.

'Why aren't you talking?'

'I'm eating. You always told us it's rude to talk with your mouth full.'

'You never listened as far as I can remember.'

'Never too late.'

Jeremy rolled his eyes and scoffed, 'You always were the cheeky one. How many autographs did you sign today?'

The question caught him by surprise. 'I dunno. Ten? Fifteen?'

'Do you sign them by your own name?'

Adam grinned and shook his head. 'No, I don't. The kids want me to sign them Jolly Roger, so I do.'

For some reason, Jeremy felt oddly let down.

Mark sat on his bed, the side light on, a stubby pencil in his mouth and a sheet of paper in front of him. In the room next door he could hear his mother typing away, working. She worked at night a lot now because it was the summer holidays and he was at home and Owen was not at creche. Mark knew she could only afford one creche place so while he was at home she took Owen out too. Mark thought that this was very sensible as creche places were expensive.

Mark chewed on his pencil, wondering what to write. He wanted to give the right impression without sounding mean. Still, that was the good thing with writing, he supposed – if he made a mess of it, he could cross it out and start again.

Dear Santa,

I hope you dont mind me riteing to you early but I thaught that I would send my letter first and give you a head start on Christmas. And as you live next stoor it is easyr for me to post it dan if you lived in the North Pole. Can I plees have a TV for Christmas as my brodder keeps standing in deh way of our other one. And dat is all I want. And for my little brudder, he doesn't care so anything will do. Also some boys on dis road are mean and I will not tell you their names but you should watch out cause mayb dey will be on the bad list. And also can you make my daddy ring from America as he went away and has not rung yet and he is gone for six weeks so if you make him ring, it will be an early Christmas present if you can do magic outside Christmas.

Tanks from Mark (the boy next stoor)

Mark reread what he had written and was very proud of it. It was the longest thing he had ever written in his whole life. He folded it up and decided to post it early the next day.

8

ADDICTION TREATMENT CENTRE

T HE WORDS, EMBLAZONED on a sign opposite, were a major
slap in the face. Allie parked her Micra and sat for a
moment, unable to summon the energy to get out and walk
towards the hospital building. This was her life, she realised.
Visiting Tony in a treatment centre for drug addicts was now
an undeniable part of her existence. She supposed that on one
level it was a relief. Having Tony inside these walls, knowing
where he was and that he was being looked after and moni-
tored, was a huge weight off her shoulders. But him being
inside was acknowledging a truth that she had refused to face
for the last nine years of her marriage. How could she have
been so blind? How could she not have known? But she had
known, somewhere below the surface where she strove to keep
things on the road, she had known that there was something
wrong.

Tony was manic and fun one day, and deeply depressed the
next. He'd been aggressive and tender, loving and distant. And
finally, after she'd found tabs of valium in a discarded pair of
jeans, the penny had dropped. Her husband was on drugs. But
she'd rationalised it. Tony didn't hang about in alleyways like
other addicts. He never injected, and if he was moody and
grumpy and had a tendency to fly off the handle, well, so did
she. Cocaine wasn't addictive as such. When he'd lost his first
job she'd told herself that he was too good for it anyway.

When he'd taken money from their joint account without telling her or explaining where it had gone, she hadn't asked. After all, they were equal partners in this marriage and he never quizzed her on how she spent money. *Denial, denial, denial.* And then he'd started really shouting at the kids, shouting at her, coming in stoned and over-talkative and crashing into depression. He'd spent money he didn't have and now they'd been forced to sell their house – and Tony's car – and move. His dealer had been paid from the money but at a huge price for them. All they had left was a ten-year-old Micra on its last legs and a much smaller house. And they'd sold their old house cheaply to get the money fast. Allie had laid down the law: there were to be no deals, no promises; the money was to be paid and they were moving on with a clean slate.

But how clean would it be? Tony had agreed to treatment and he'd checked in for an assessment to this place. Lying to the kids. She hadn't liked lying, but how could an eight-year-old handle the truth? She'd been so upset at the trouble between her parents when she was young, she wasn't going to put Mark through that. And besides, Mark was used to his dad saying he was going away for work. Whenever Tony had gone AWOL before, she'd always lied and told them that it was a business trip.

Another car pulled up beside hers and Allie watched the female driver, who looked to be in her late twenties, lather on some bright pink lipstick before taking a few deep breaths. Then she hopped out and slammed the door, without realising that her coat was caught in it.

'Hey!' Allie yelled, getting out of the car, but it was too late. There was a ripping sound, followed by the woman hopping about on her black patent stilettos and saying, 'Shit, shit shit!'.

Allie winced. 'I did try to warn you,' she said.

The woman was examining the tear. She glanced up at Allie and grinned. 'Aw well, I always hated it anyway.' She took the coat off and threw it on the back seat of her car.

Allie smiled back, liking her at once. 'I'm Allie,' she said, sticking out her hand.

'Holly.'

They nodded to each other.

'You been—'

'You been—'

'You first,' Allie said. They had begun walking in the direction of the low-lying grey building. Holly's ability to stride along in her high footwear impressed Allie a lot, and momentarily distracted her from the fact that in a few minutes she was going to see Tony for the first time in a fortnight.

'You been here before?' Holly asked.

'No. First time. You?'

Holly made a comical face. 'Third,' she said. Then added jokingly, 'Three times a charm.'

Allie's heart sank. Three times. Christ. 'Does it not work?'

'Oh, sorry,' Holly groaned dramatically, rolling her black-mascara-ed eyes. 'What a fecking terrible thing to be telling you. Yes, yes it does work. Of course it works. My sister was clean for a whole year the last time.'

Allie winced. A year? After a whole year of hope for it all to come crashing down. If Tony was clean for that long, she'd think it was all over. Jesus.

'Unfortunately,' Holly continued wryly, 'she relapsed about two weeks ago when her boyfriend broke it off. Jesus, if I had him in front of me I'd wring his scrawny neck, so I would. So,' she gave a sort of self-deprecating grin, 'here I am again.'

'I'm sorry,' Allie said, falling into step with her. 'That must be hard.'

'Yes, it is. But she's alive so there's hope, I suppose.'

'It's my husband's first time in a place like this. I don't know what to expect.'

'It's pretty much like any hospital,' Holly explained. 'They can wander around, have coffee, go for walks. Did you not see it at the assessment?'

Allie nodded. 'I just hope it works.'

Holly cocked her head sideways. She paused for a second, before saying in a gentle voice that belied her brash exterior, 'A day at a time, Allie, that's all you can do.'

A day at a time? That didn't sound so great to Allie. How on earth could she live with a guy who could fall off the edge at any moment? How would she ever feel secure? At least when he was on drugs, it was the worst it could be. There was a security in that.

Holly pushed open the hospital door and the scent of fresh flowers assailed their nostrils. There was a huge vase of lilies at reception. It was cheery at least.

'Hi, Julie,' Holly grinned at the receptionist.

'Hi, you,' Julie smiled back. 'She's waiting for you. She's in a bit of a strop.'

'Well, there's a big surprise,' Holly laughed, not seeming too bothered. 'By the way,' she introduced Allie to Julie, adding, 'it's her first time here.'

'Hi,' Julie held out her hand, 'I think I remember you from assessment. Tony is your husband, right?'

'That's it,' Allie smiled. People tended to remember her husband.

'They're both in the day room,' Julie said. 'Holly will show you, Allie. You're in good hands there.'

Allie smiled, feeling more positive. At least it was a nice friendly place.

She followed Holly to the day room. It was deliberately cheery and calming. Various landscape paintings adorned the walls, greens and browns and pale yellows. Patients sat with their families at tables, some barely talking, others hugging each other hard. Holly waved at a tall, skinny, sullen-looking girl across the room and, touching Allie briefly on the arm, wished her luck. From the expression on Holly's sister's face, Allie got the feeling it was Holly who would need the luck. 'You too,' she said back.

Her eyes scanned the room for Tony. There he was, right at the back, watching her, his expression wary. She raised a hesitant hand to him and a grin lit his face, making her heart flip over.

'Hiya, Gorgeous,' he said, standing awkwardly in front of her.

Again she remembered his sunny smile the first time he'd said that to her. Hanging halfway out of a car window and laughing. So she said now what she'd said that day. 'Hi, Distinctly Average.'

His grin faltered at the old greeting and she knew he was remembering that day too. He'd laughed when she'd said that, not in the least offended, and told her that she needed her eyes checked. 'You should start by seeing me,' he'd bantered. Allie had snorted at his cockiness but had admired it too. Still, she was about to refuse when he'd rear ended the car in front because he'd been so busy trying to chat her up. His dismayed expression, like a bewildered kid who doesn't know why he's in trouble, had somehow won her heart. As he stepped out of his vehicle to give his insurance details to the guy whose car he'd hit, she'd waited beside him, feeling a little responsible. Then after the police had gone, she'd asked him if he could still afford to take her out. And as he'd gazed at her with those black-brown eyes, amusement sparkling in them, she'd been captivated. She sometimes looked back and wondered if he wasn't a little high at the time. And he'd told her, most sincerely, that of course he could.

'Thanks for coming,' Tony swallowed, breaking into her thoughts.

She wondered if he would hug her, but he didn't. He carefully maintained his distance, his hands half jammed into the pockets of his combats. It hurt but she made her voice deliberately bright. 'We've all missed you. How are you doing?'

He stared at the toes of his trainers. 'It's rotten in here. They like to talk about stuff.'

'Do they? Like what?'

Tony cast his eyes skywards. 'Just stuff about everyone's life and motivations and stuff. It's kinda stupid. Who really thinks about those things?'

'Well, if it helps you, it's worth it,' Allie said. She reached out and touched his hand.

He flinched before saying, 'D'you want to go for a walk?'

Allie tried to ignore the hurt she felt at his imperceptible drawing away from her. He was depressed, she could tell. 'Sure.'

They walked out of the room, through reception and into the grounds. Allie noticed that Tony's gaze was skimming left to right in quite a disconcerting way. He led her to a wooden picnic table and sat down. Allie got the impression that he spent quite a bit of time out here. She took a seat opposite him.

Tony looked all around, before thrusting his head towards her and whispering urgently, 'I shouldn't be here, Allie. It's a mistake. They're all worse than me.'

She was startled. Whatever she'd expected him to say, it hadn't been that. Even so it registered at the back of her mind that the counsellor had warned her this might happen – no one ever believed they were as bad as anyone else. She stalled for time. There was no way he was coming home, not unless she could be certain he was fit to stay. 'What do you mean?'

Tony took her hand in his and now it was she who flinched. She noticed the fear and paranoia in his eyes and she wondered if maybe he was right. Maybe they were all loopers in here. Maybe he was on a wrong ward or whatever.

'One of them, right, stole from his job. Money, Allie. He swindled his boss out of thousands to feed his habit. I've never done that. And there's this girl, she was a prostitute. And another one left her child outside her mother's house for her mother to mind and never went back for it. They're all talking about what they did and it does my head in. I swear. I've never stolen from work, never hurt the kids, nothing. It's recreational, that's all I do. Nothing like what they've done.' His voice had risen on the last few lines and a couple of people glanced over. 'And everyone listens to everyone else's conversations,' he said even more loudly, making Allie smile briefly.

He turned back to her. 'Allie, you have to let me come home.'

His expectant look made her feel sick. She stared into his face, her mind slowly tumbling in a panic. 'You agreed to come here, Tony.'

'And I did. But not to parade my faults in front of a bunch of losers.'

Her stomach rolled. 'But you do want to get better, don't you?'

'I am better.' He spoke to her as if it was obvious. 'Look. I'm clean. I miss you and the kids. I want to come home.'

'And I want you home but, Tony, I can't live with the uncertainty of you any more. I need your counsellor to say that he is happy to let you go.'

'They won't say that,' he hissed. 'They want to make money. They try to convince you that you need help.' He tapped his head. 'I know my own mind. I know I'm well. Please.'

She should have guessed that he'd hate it here. Tony, unless he was high, wasn't a great mixer. Being with a bunch of people he didn't know would freak him out. And being with the bizarre people he described was not going to be good for him.

'Maybe you're on a wrong ward. In with the wrong crowd.'

'They're all the wrong crowd,' Tony said desperately. 'They're the kind of people your mother warned you about.'

Her mother had warned her about Tony but she hadn't listened. 'What do you want?' she finally asked.

'To get out of this kip. You'd think with the money they charge they'd treat you better, but they don't. It's talking and talking and everyone jumping on everyone else for the things they say. It does my head in. And the things they say . . . it's depressing, Allie.'

Allie hesitated. She didn't believe he was OK to come home, but maybe she could have a word with his counsellor and see if there was a problem between Tony and the other patients. 'I'll talk to your counsellor.'

'No!' His shout made people nearby jump. 'No, he's in on it. He won't let me go. He keeps on asking me why I use. I tell him it makes me feel good and he goes on about why don't I normally feel good, it twists up my head, Allie. Please get me out.'

'Tony,' Allie said patiently, 'just let go my hand, will you, you're hurting me.'

'Sorry.' He disentangled his hand and looked imploringly at her. 'Allie, you have to believe me. I am fine.'

How many times had he said it to her before? How many times had he promised to stay clean and then let her down? Maybe she could have coped if it was just her, but she had Mark and Owen to think of. 'Tony,' she said patiently, 'a man called to our door demanding fifty thousand euro.'

His face darkened. 'I had that under control. I had a job, didn't I?'

'What? That paid you fifty grand a week?'

'No. I could have done a deal with him.'

'You lost that job.'

'They were downsizing. I could have got another one. You know I could have.'

'What? A different one that paid fifty thousand euro a week? He was giving you one week, Tony.'

'I would have sorted it. You wouldn't let me do a deal with him.'

His refusal to see what danger he had put them all in infuriated her. 'When will you cop on?' she snapped. People looked over again. Out of the corner of her eye she saw Holly wincing. She leant across the table at him and hissed, 'You weren't in a position to do any deals. Are you stupid? Do you care about us at all?'

'Is this going to be thrown up in my face every time we fight now?' He stood up.

'Is everything OK here?' A sort of security guard had come over.

'No, it's not OK, but no one cares.' Tony glared at Allie and stomped off.

'You bastard!' she shouted.

There was silence. Allie became aware that everyone was looking at her. 'Well, he is,' she said defiantly.

She asked at reception to speak to his counsellor and was shown to his office. As she waited, she let her gaze wander from the numerous certificates along the wall to the books on the shelves. She read the tongue-twisting titles on the spines and wondered if there was anything they could tell her about how to cope. She was so busy distracting herself with thoughts of flicking through the pages of a book called *Treating Addiction* that she failed to hear the counsellor as he entered.

'Mrs Dolan?'

Allie jumped, flushing, and took her hand from the book. 'Yes. Call me Allie.'

'Allie. Hi. We met at your husband's assessment. Sit down, do.'

Allie sat, perched on the edge of the chair. The counsellor, a tall, skinny man, took a seat opposite and nodded encouragingly. 'Well? What can I do for you?'

He had the longest face Allie had ever seen. 'It's Tony. He wants to come home. He thinks he shouldn't be here.'

There was a brief silence.

'And you?' The counsellor looked at her.

Allie swallowed hard. It was a betrayal of Tony to say to his counsellor what she really thought. She settled for, 'He can be bad sometimes.'

More silence. Then the counsellor began to speak, counting out Tony's misdeeds on his fingers. 'He has lost jobs, he has

41

spent money he didn't have to get drugs, he has lost friends and he has lived from fix to fix.' Pause. 'He is addicted, Allie. We know this from his assessment. Now, as he is my patient, I can't say much more. It is up to you. All I will advise is that this wanting to abandon treatment is common, and it will pass.' He studied her. 'He can check himself out if he likes, of course, but . . .' he let the sentence hang there.

Allie knew she had to make a decision.

'What do you want?' the counsellor pressed. 'What is it you think will be best?'

'I want him to stay,' she answered in a small voice. Her eyes filled up. Tony would hate her for that. 'I want him to stay and get better and stop putting us through what he's put us through.'

The counsellor nodded. 'I think it's the right decision,' he said gently. He added, 'Most cocaine users suffer from an under-lying depression. We need to see if that's the case with Tony. At the moment he's depressed because coming off cocaine, while it doesn't have the physical withdrawal symptoms that occur with other drugs, can lead to severe depression. He's not thinking straight.'

Allie lifted her eyes to look at him. His words reassured her.

'Tony will not check out unless he has your support. Don't enable him to do it if it's not what you want. As you know, we like family members to come along once a week to our family days. You'll learn a lot more there.'

Allie had planned to go. It would help to see what other people were going through. And, she thought, feeling a little guilty, it would also help to see if others were worse off than she was.

'I'll do that,' she said.

'And don't worry,' the counsellor nodded, 'he'll come around.'

She wished she could believe it.

'There is a support group for families of people with

addiction,' the counsellor said. 'You might find that helpful, too. I have the details here.'

She'd got the literature on that before but hadn't planned on going. Still, she let the counsellor search among his drawers until he found what he was looking for. 'Friday nights,' he read. 'Eight o'clock. Here you go.'

'Thanks,' Allie smiled at him and tucked it into her bag.

'He will come round to the idea of staying,' the counsellor said. 'Promise.'

9

JOHN, STRIPPED TO the waist, was busy digging Allie's back garden. As he was currently 'between jobs' he'd offered to babysit the boys while she visited his brother in hospital. At the same time, he said, he could make a start on the garden.

Allie, having just come in, watched out of sight of the window, as he ordered the boys to put all the rocks and stones in a wheelbarrow. Mark and Owen seemed to be competing with each other as to who could lift the heaviest rocks. Owen had just picked up the most enormous one and John, hands on hips, was laughing at him. 'Wow, way to go, big guy,' he chortled. Owen smiled gummily and with difficulty tried to walk across to the wheelbarrow. If he didn't watch it, the rock would take his toe off, Allie thought anxiously.

John didn't seem too bothered, however, and turned back to his digging. Allie wondered a little at the wisdom of having this overgrown child watching her two lads. Still, he'd done a lot of work since that morning. She rapped on the window and made a T sign with her fingers. John grinned and, wiping his hands on his jeans, dropped his shovel and came in to join her.

Mark and Owen followed him. Owen had abandoned the rock, Allie saw with relief. 'Ice creams for you two,' she said to her kids as she handed them a milky ice pop from the freezer. 'Now, outside and play and give John a rest.'

'Did you have a good time with your friend, Mammy?' Mark

asked as he tore the wrapper off his ice pop. 'Was it one of the ladies from your job?'

'Yes, yes it was,' Allie lied. 'Holly.'

'Did you go for coffee?'

'Yes. It was fun. Now out!'

The two wandered back outside, licking their ice pops furiously.

John waited for a second until they were out of earshot, before asking, 'How was it?'

Allie opened a packet of biscuits and John took a couple. As he munched she told him about Tony wanting to come home.

'My mother said that might happen,' John nodded.

'Tess? How does she know?'

John bit his lip and, half grinning, said, 'Well, it's not really funny but I'm going to laugh so don't get offended, OK?'

His effort at not smiling made Allie smile. 'What's not funny that it makes you laugh?' she teased slightly.

'My mother,' John began in mock seriousness, 'has become Ireland's leading authority on drugs. She has borrowed every book on the subject from our local library.'

'No way!'

'Uh-huh, and last week she got stopped by the cops for tax on her car and they saw all the books on her back seat and pulled her in for questioning.'

'They didn't!'

'They did, and she told them that if they were out doing their jobs properly her son would not be able to buy drugs and thus become a drug addict.'

Allie laughed. 'Jesus! Did they go mad?'

'They did not. They gave her some of their own leaflets and she's read them and now she's ploughing through the books. She'll be over advising you soon enough. I even caught her Googling the subject last night.'

'Great.'

They grinned at each other, then John said seriously, 'She'll torment you, Allie, but just try and understand that it's her way of coping. She likes to know all the facts.'

'I know.'

John glanced down at the table, before risking the question he'd wanted to ask since hearing about his brother. 'How long has he been using, Allie?' Before she could answer he said, 'And don't tell me it's only a few months, I know it's not.'

'How?' She stalled for time. Tony had begged her not to tell them the whole story.

'I just know. I mean, I never guessed before you told us, but looking back, Tony's moods were always a bit up and down.'

Allie gulped and looked at John's concerned face. She owed it to him to be honest, he was Tony's only brother, for God's sake. 'He's been using for years,' she confessed. 'Mainly cocaine. A bit of hash now and then. He was using a little heroin too, near the end, to help him come down.'

John looked as if she'd hit him. 'He's that bad? That far gone?'

'He's not injecting,' she said, trying, as she had done at the time, to look for brightness. 'But I dunno, John, it's like he's trying to run away from his life or something. He'll take anything, I reckon.' She closed her eyes. It was such a relief to tell someone. She'd glossed over the truth with her own mother and with Tess, but John was different. 'He's been using stuff for years.'

'Why?'

'Why does anyone? I don't know. But he says the feeling is great. His counseller thinks he might have been depressed or something.'

'And all the times he changed jobs?'

'Mostly he was let go for not turning up.'

There was a brief pause as John took it in, then he said with quiet intensity, 'You should have told us, Al.'

'We didn't think he had a problem. I dunno, it kind of crept up on us both.'

'He owed fifty grand, for Jaysus sake.'

'I know. I can't believe I was so stupid.'

'You weren't stupid, you just wanted to believe him.'

'I did.' Allie bit back the tears.

John bowed his head. He wasn't much good with all that emotional stuff. He could kill his brother for doing this to Allie and the kids. He indicated the back garden. 'I'll, eh, get back to work.' This was the only thing he could do, he thought.

'Thanks, John.'

'There's a large shrub out there,' John stood up and pointed out the kitchen window at a big plant covered in red blossoms, 'it's being choked with ivy. Do you want me to get rid of it for you?'

Allie looked. The shrub in question had blossomed despite being half strangled by the climbing plant. 'Naw, leave it. It looks nice.'

'OK. If I get a chance I'll transplant it and kill off the ivy. But for now I'll just work on getting the garden habitable.'

'Yeah. Thanks.'

He smiled at her and was relieved when she managed a smile back.

Jeremy watched from his bedroom window as that young chap and the two children resumed work on the back garden. He was a hard worker, that man. He'd started digging at around ten o'clock and had only stopped briefly around one when the mother came back. Once upon a time Jeremy might have been able to do that, but now, with his old body protesting every time he moved, he wasn't able to any more. Growing old was a curse. The chap had done a nice job of digging out the hard soil, his wife would have approved. Nelly had loved her garden.

Jeremy flinched as the fat child spotted him and waved

enthusiastically. Jeremy raised a hand in return. He was trying his best to avoid that child ever since he'd found the Santa letter lying on his hall carpet. Mark must have posted it when Jeremy was watching Ireland AM. When the programme finished Jeremy had come out of the room to make himself a cup of coffee, and the yellow envelope lying on his brown hall carpet had caught his eye. Initially Jeremy thought that it was a flyer from someone looking for old clothes and shoes and things, but no, it was addressed to Mr Lyons and a big picture of Santa was drawn alongside.

Jeremy had read it with a growing sense of horror. What had he started? He'd stared, mind freefalling as he'd read the text, the letters huge and looping. Then, unable to do anything else, he scrunched it up and put it in his bin. It was only July, he told himself. At least the kid had it out of his system now and wouldn't be posting any more. Jeremy was a little appalled at the spelling mistakes in the letter. His boys could spell properly at age eight. Schools weren't what they used to be, that was for sure.

His front doorbell rang and Jeremy frowned. He wasn't expecting any callers. Well, no one ever called. He sighed as he descended the stairs, hoping it wasn't some religious person trying to make him change his beliefs. He was a bit weary of asking them if they'd change theirs for him. The novelty of making them squirm wasn't what it used to be. Through the glass he saw a tall man and a woman. A little girl hopped up and down, all bouncy ringlets. A boy with a thunderous look on his face stood crossly beside her.

Jeremy groaned. Joel and his family were the last people he wanted to see. Jeremy didn't mind Joel on his own, but his family were hard to take. Lucy, his wife, never seemed to want to visit and his grandchildren, especially his granddaughter, seemed to have opinions on everything. Most of their opinions of him were pretty unfavourable. Reluctantly he opened the door to admit them.

'Hi, Dad,' Joel said, stepping into the hall. 'We were just passing.'

'I've nothing in the house,' Jeremy said as they all tramped past him. 'I didn't know you were going to call.'

'We didn't know ourselves,' Lucy, Joel's wife, said, shooting dagger looks at her husband. 'Joel thought it would be nice.'

'And we didn't,' piped up Jenny. She was busy looking around. 'Your house smells, Granddad. All smoky.'

'Jenny!' Joel admonished.

Jeremy noticed the smirk Lucy gave.

'It's not very nice to say someone's house is smelly,' Joel went on. He plugged in the kettle. 'We were just passing, Dad, and we decided to call in to see how you were. Was Adam up recently?'

'Last week. He's got a new contract for the show apparently.' Jeremy sat down, resigned to the fact that he'd have to put up with this invasion for the time being. He wasn't very good with his grandchildren, unfortunately. And though he grudgingly admired Jenny's spirit, he wished she would refrain from drawing attention to the fact that his house smelled of smoke. He pointed to a press, thinking that if there was one thing children liked it was food. 'Adam bought me some nice biscuits. You might as well take them out, I'll not eat them all.'

'Biscuits?' Now his grandson seemed to perk up. 'Where?'

'In the press there. Now don't be greedy and eat too many, you'll rot your teeth.'

Jenny had found the packet of Marietta and was making a face. 'Ugh.'

'They'll hardly rot their teeth on those,' Lucy observed dryly. She took the biscuits from her daughter and opened them for her. 'Want one, honey?'

'No. They're yucky.'

'Len?'

'I'd rather eat cabbage.'

Well, there was ungrateful, Jeremy thought, folding his arms

49

and glaring at his grandchildren. Honestly, what sort of kids were these? In his day they would have sawn their arms off for a biscuit. And Marietta were fine biscuits. Jeremy remembered that Joel used to love them. He'd butter one Marietta and place another on top. Then he'd squeeze hard and watch the butter come squishing out of the holes in the biscuits.

'All you need is a bit of butter and you're set,' Jeremy said. Jenny and Len didn't look convinced.

'Go on out and play,' Joel urged them. 'I'll buy you both something nice from the shops in a little while.'

The kids ran off out the back and were soon playing hide and seek in the long grass.

'Now Dad,' Joel laid a cup of tea before him, 'how have you been? Have you got out?'

'I don't go out. I like it in my house. You? Have you got out?'

'Well, eh, yes.'

'That's nice for you.'

Joel made no comment. He carried a cup of tea to the table for himself and sat opposite his dad. He had put on weight, Jeremy thought. Joel used to be all razor cheeks and jutting jaw. Now his face was red and round and jowly.

Lucy stood up. 'I'll just go and keep an eye on the kids.' Without glancing at either of them she left, slamming the back door behind her.

'Your wife doesn't like me,' Jeremy observed as he took a sip of tea. Joel knew how to make a good cuppa at least.

'Oh, she does,' Joel said. 'She's mad about you!'

His tone was so insincere that neither man could look at the other.

There was a silence, broken only by the shrieks of the kids outside. 'Look, Dad.' Joel leant towards him. His face was very red, and Jeremy reckoned his son suffered from high blood pressure. 'We're worried about you – me and Adam. Adam says that you have no life.'

It was lucky he wasn't drinking or he would have spluttered his tea out all over the table. 'I don't go swanning around in fancy cars, I don't go spending money like it's going out of fashion, I don't live a high flying life, but I do *have* a life.' Jeremy put his cup carefully down, his hand shaking a little, feeling hurt. 'I resent that. Now, if you came merely to insult me, then—'

'No, Dad, not at all. It's just we'd like to help you. How about starting with maybe getting someone in to clean for you?'

'I'm not having a cleaner poking in my drawers, thank you. I can clean my house myself. I don't need help.'

'How about we pay for someone to do the garden?'

'I already have.' The words were out before he realised that he'd said them. Joel looked sceptical. 'A young chap,' Jeremy went on. 'Once he's finished next door he'll come in here.'

Joel wasn't sure what to say. Somehow he doubted it was the truth and yet, if he said that, his dad would have a fit. Jeremy had been a hard man to grow up with. Sometimes Joel wondered why he bothered. Why did he drag his family here to see a man who seemed to have no interest in them? His father's apparent indifference to his sons' lives seemed to bounce off Adam, while it cut him to the quick. 'Well,' he eventually said, 'that's good. Well done, Dad.'

Jeremy nodded, only feeling a little guilty for deceiving Joel. But honestly, he didn't need his son's pity or his money. 'Thank you,' he said back and took another sip of his son's excellent tea.

There were kids in Santa's garden. Mark could hear them shrieking and having fun. He climbed up on a wooden crate that his mother had given him to play with and peeped over the wall.

There was a lady there. She was very pretty with long black hair tied in a ponytail and make-up on her face. She was smiling as a boy and a girl ran about trying to catch each other.

51

Santa had a cool garden. Really long grass with lots of rocks and weeds and a big tree too. The woman spotted him looking and smiled.

'Hello,' she said. 'What's your name?'

'Mark. I live here.' He indicated his garden.

The two children had stopped playing and were regarding him curiously. 'Did you only just move in?' the boy asked.

'Yep. How come you are in Sa— Mr Lyons' garden?'

The girl made a face. ''Cause our daddy wanted to come here and talk to him. We didn't. He's our granddad.'

Mark gawked at them. 'No way! You're so lucky!'

All three stared at him.

The girl was the first to recover. 'Well, we hate—'

'Jenny, why don't you ask the little boy to play?' Lucy cut in swiftly.

'Do you want to play?' Jenny asked.

Mark thought about it. It would be nice. None of the kids on the road would play with him, even though he had the coolest football of them all. And he had never promised Santa that *he* wouldn't go into his garden, just that he wouldn't kick his ball in. 'OK.'

'Well, tell your mammy first,' Lucy said, smiling.

'I will, I will.' Mark ran off.

Things had come to a halt in the kitchen and Joel, with something akin to relief, made the decision to leave. He stood up, his dad stood up and together they walked into the back garden to round up the kids.

'Hi, Mr Lyons!' a boy with jet black hair called out to his dad. 'How are you? I'm playing with your grandkids. Do they know?'

Much to Joel's surprise, his father flushed and started to cough and then to shake his head. He didn't yell at the boy though, which is what Joel expected.

'Do we know what?' Jenny asked.

'Nothing,' both Mark and Jeremy said together.

'Dad, what is the kid on about?' Joel asked, puzzled.

'I suppose he wants to know if I've told them about the gardener,' Jeremy spluttered. 'Something like that.' He shook his head at Mark. 'Not yet,' he said.

Mark nodded. 'Oh.'

Joel looked from the boy to his dad but said nothing. His father was acting quite strangely. 'Right, well, we'll be off so.'

'Hurray!' Jenny skipped up the garden and vanished into the house. 'Come on, Mark, come out the front way and you can wave us off.'

Jeremy watched in horror as the boy from next door gleefully ran into his house, followed by Len. Kids really didn't know their place at all these days.

'So when is this gardener starting?' Joel asked.

'I'm not sure. I have to have a chat with him,' Jeremy lied. 'Didn't you have to go now?'

'Yes, we do.' Lucy took Joel's arm and propelled him up and out. Jeremy heaved a sigh of relief.

Some hours later Allie sat at her computer screen, planning next term's English classes. She'd been putting off this job and now that the house was quiet, she felt able to tackle it. John had taken the kids for a sleepover to give her a break, and though she missed the sounds of them shifting under their duvets, it made it easier to work. She wondered if Owen and Mark had gone to bed in their nana's yet. She pictured them all snuggled up in the double bed they slept in when they were there. They were great for sleeping, she thought fondly. They took after their parents. There had never been any waking up in the middle of the night or climbing in between her and Tony. Once they were asleep they were asleep. Well, unless Mark had one of his nightmares, though even they seemed to be settling down.

Recently though, Allie had found herself wishing that she

could climb into their beds and snuggle up beside them, holding them tight as she drifted off, inhaling the scents only they had. Instead she now lay for hours in her own, her mind tumbling, refusing to switch off. It was easier to work until she was exhausted and then sleep on in the morning. She was putting the finishing touches to her school class plans for next year when the phone rang beside her. Wondering who it was, hoping that the kids were OK, she picked it up.

'Hello?'

'Hi.' Tony's voice sounding so contrite made her blink back relieved tears. 'I, eh, couldn't sleep,' he said hesitantly.

'Could you not?' She didn't want to sound too much of a pushover.

'Nope,' he said. There was a pause. 'I'm sorry about today, Al.'

'It's fine.'

'No, it's not,' he said, sounding desperate. 'You know I hate rowing with you. And I'm sorry for always having to say sorry.'

She couldn't speak, she just cradled the phone in her hands.

'I, eh, have to whisper. I'm not allowed make calls home just yet but a girl here, Veronica, gave me some money to call you. She said she knew what it was like.'

'That was nice of her.'

'Yeah, I guess.' Another pause before his words tumbled over themselves. 'Look, Al, I hadn't planned on asking you to get me out, but when I saw you I just wanted to be at home with you and the lads. It's awful here, you know.'

'Tony—'

'But I'm staying,' he interrupted. 'Even if it's just to prove to you that I'm not like these people.'

Allie smiled and took the risk of teasing him. 'Trust me, you are like no one else on this earth.'

'I'll take that as a compliment.' She knew he was grinning.

'I only want you to get better, that's all,' Allie said then. 'I just want a good life for the four of us, Tony.'

'Me too. I will come out clean, I promise.' He paused and she was startled when he admitted softly, 'My counsellor says it's a psychological addiction I have.'

'What's that?'

'I dunno. I think it means that mentally I crave it, but not physically. It's that way with cocaine, apparently.'

'Oh.' She didn't want to ask too much in case he'd pull back.

'Yep.'

There was a silence.

'Where are the lads? It all sounds really quiet in the background there.' He wasn't going to say any more about it, obviously.

'Your mother took them.'

'Damn. Trust me to be away when we have a free house.' Allie smiled.

'Oh shit,' Tony groaned.

'What?' Allie asked and then understood as a strident voice demanded to know what Tony was doing on the phone.

'Are you in trouble?' Allie asked.

'Story of my life,' Tony chortled, not sounding that bothered. 'I miss—'

The phone was disconnected.

'Miss you too,' Allie said to the dial tone. She knew with a grin that there was a good chance she'd sleep well that night.

10

JEREMY PEERED OUT his window. He had been awoken by the sound of a big crash somewhere out in next door's back garden. His heart was still not the better for it. What on earth had that stupid man been doing, rotavating a lawn first thing in the morning? Did he not know that people slept in beyond nine o'clock? And now the man had the two boys from next door helping him and all of them were talking at the tops of their voices. The boys were thrilled with all the noise. The fat lad, Mark, was jumping about and his little brother was copying him, and that man was letting them have a go with the rota-vator. That man would kill them yet, so he would. It all appeared to be a bit frantic with the boys racing all over the place and calling out 'Straighter!' and stuff like that. His two boys had never been as loud as that, Jeremy was sure. They'd always spoken nicely to their elders and, as far as he knew, they'd never disturbed a man when he was at work. One thing was for sure, Jeremy thought: when that chap came to work for him, those two boys were *not* coming into his garden.

Of course, he had to ask him first.

Jeremy sipped on his lukewarm tea and considered how he should ask. He didn't like asking people to do things for him, not even if he was paying them. It felt like a defeat. And, he thought, the man might not do the garden the way his wife would have liked. But at the moment, with all the weeds and dandelions, it wasn't what she liked either, so he supposed it couldn't get much worse.

Jeremy decided he should strike while the iron was hot. There was no time like the present. Nothing ventured, nothing gained. He took a deep breath, sucked his stomach in and strode out his back door. The fat boy noticed him first. In fact, Jeremy thought with a slight irritation, all he had to do was cough and the fat boy would notice. It hadn't been such a good idea to pretend to be Santa.

'Hi, Mr Lyons!' Mark said cheerfully. 'Isn't it a lovely day? We're doing the garden.'

'So I see,' Jeremy said back, managing to smile with a little effort. 'I was hoping to have a word with your gardener.'

'He's not our gardener, he's our uncle,' Mark said. 'But he will talk to you, won't you, John?'

'Huh?' John looked up from the machine and then, seeing Jeremy, switched it off. He straightened his back and wiped some sweat from his brow.

'Hello,' Jeremy said.

'It's John,' Mark said.

'Hello, John,' Jeremy tried not to sound impatient at the interruption, 'I notice that you're gardening.'

John smirked a little. 'Eh – yes,' he said.

Jeremy ignored the smirk. 'How much would you charge if you were to do mine?' he asked abruptly.

'He charges nothing,' Mark said gleefully.

'Nothing?' Jeremy found that hard to believe.

John laughed good-naturedly. 'Nothing to family, big man,' he pretended to swipe Mark's head and Mark dodged away, laughing. He looked at Jeremy. 'I'm not exactly a qualified gardener,' he admitted.

'Good, so you'll do it cheaper for me.'

John shrugged. He peered over the wall at Jeremy's wilderness. 'What do you want doing?' he asked.

Jeremy frowned. 'Well, I'll need it all cleaned up and maybe some grass and shrubs and flowers.' He paused, thinking. 'And a nice place to sit in the summer.'

'You want decking then?'

Jeremy nodded. 'Yes, that sounds right. Decking.' He rocked back on his heels. 'So, how much would it be?'

'It's a lot of work,' John said. 'You're talking about land-scaping. I reckon about four thousand euro.'

'Oh wow!' Mark was impressed.

'Too much money.' Jeremy was appalled. Four thousand euro? Was the man mad? 'I'm sure I can get someone cheaper.'

'Well then, why ask me?' John said cheerfully, turning back to the rotavator.

'Because I didn't think you'd be so expensive,' Jeremy said. 'Good morning.' He turned to leave.

'He might do it cheaper,' Mark piped up. 'Won't you, John?' He gave John a nudge. 'Think about who you're talking to.'

Jeremy winced and stiffened.

'Who I'm talking to?' John said back, puzzled. 'What do you mean?'

'He's not just any man,' Mark said, in suppressed excitement.

Jeremy felt his stomach lurch. How come one little teeny lie was haunting him like this? He turned around and glared at Mark in what he hoped was a 'You promised not to tell' way. But whatever way he looked, the younger boy saw him and started to howl in a very alarming manner, which actually wasn't too bad because they all started to give him their attention and Jeremy was able to slip away without anyone noticing.

Later that afternoon, Jeremy went on a walk. His usual stroll was through the tiny park at the top of the road, out one of the entrances and into the local shops. He wanted to see if there were any adverts for gardeners in the shop window. Four thousand euro was a ridiculous price.

He had just entered the park when, from behind one of the hedges, a teenage boy emerged, smoking a cigarette. Jeremy was startled at his sudden appearance. 'You almost gave me a heart attack,' he said, glowering at the lad, who didn't look a day over fifteen. 'And you're far too young to be smoking.'

Two or three more boys followed him out and Jeremy suddenly found himself surrounded by tall fellows with short haircuts and earrings.

'What's that you said?' the biggest boy demanded.

'I said,' Jeremy, who had taught adolescent boys for years, was not intimidated, 'that this lad is far too young to be smoking. And you,' he looked pointedly at the largest guy and the flagon of cider in his hand, 'are not allowed to drink in a local park. It's a public order offence.'

'Aw, we're shaking,' the lad chortled, pretending to quake, a big sneer on his face. 'Get lost, granddad.'

'It'd be difficult to get lost, the park is rather restricted in that way,' Jeremy said back. He always managed to sound pompous when he was correcting children.

'You are too smart,' the big lad said.

'Aw, he's just an old guy,' a girl Jeremy hadn't noticed spoke up. She looked like a prostitute, Jeremy thought, appalled. What sort of parents let their daughter go out in a short skirt and belly top and high black boots? 'Leave him alone, Philo. Come on.'

Without a word they melted away from him.

'I'd think about giving up the cigarettes,' Jeremy called after them, before resuming his walk and thanking God that his own boys had turned out a lot better than that. Then he fumbled in his pocket and pulled out a cigarette of his own.

11

Magda and Fintan agreed to mind the boys when Allie's next visit to Tony came around. They parked their car a mile from Allie's house and jogged over. When Allie opened the door Magda almost collapsed on top of her, before Fintan hauled her upright and urged her to breathe in deeply.

'Are you having a heart attack?' Mark asked hopefully. 'We did CPR in school.'

'No, I'm not.' Magda laughed a little, before adding unsurely, 'At least I don't think so.'

'You'd have to have a heart to have a heart attack,' Fintan chortled and then dodged a flap of Magda's hand.

'Come in, will yez,' Allie said. 'Mam, I'll get you a glass of water.'

Magda nodded and staggered after her into the kitchen.

'You ate an apple in the car en route,' Fintan clucked, following them, 'I told you that was a mistake.'

'Shut up, Fintan. Thanks, Allie,' Magda said, taking the glass of water from her daughter.

'I'm only trying to help,' Fintan said huffily, crossing to the sink and ducking his head under the tap for a drink too.

'You'd get a stitch from an apple, all right,' Mark agreed from the kitchen doorway.

'Is that so?' Magda said kindly, before abruptly closing the door on him and Owen and pressing her back against it so they couldn't come in.

'Mam!' Allie had to grin at the surprised expression on

Mark's face before it was unceremoniously obliterated by the door. 'What are you doing? The boys want to come in.'

'Where have you told them you're going this time?' Magda hissed in an undertone.

'Just to meet a friend,' Allie said quietly. 'Will you let the boys in? They'll wonder what's wrong.'

'What friend?' Magda didn't budge from her position.

'Someone from school. Julie, I think I said.'

'You think?' Magda didn't sound impressed.

'They don't care,' Allie said. 'As far as they're concerned I'm going out and you're bringing them to the park and McDonalds. They're happy with that.'

There was a pause. Her mother looked her straight in the eye and Allie flinched. 'Don't say it,' she said.

Her mother said it anyway. 'You should tell them the truth. It's not right lying to them like this. Getting everyone else to lie for you.'

'Magda,' Fintan said, giving her a warning look.

'You think it too,' Magda snapped.

'Oh, so you've both been talking about me, have you?'

'No!' Fintan said.

'Yes!' her mother said.

'Can we come in?' Mark knocked on the door, sounding a little apprehensive. 'We want to get bread for the ducks.'

'In a minute,' Magda called out in a high-pitched voice. 'I'm just having a grown-up chat with Mammy.'

'Are you fighting?' Mark called.

'See?' Magda raised her eyebrow and thumbed to the closed door. 'You have that child a nervous wreck. He knows something is going on, he's not stupid.'

'I was a nervous wreck,' Allie hissed back, pointing to herself. 'You and Dad always aired your dirty linen in front of me, and what good did it do? I'm not doing that to my kids.'

Magda flushed. 'That was different. Their dad is coming back to them.'

61

'Yes, and that's all they need to know.'

'And what if Mark finds out that his dad isn't on a business trip?' Magda asked. 'Do you think he'll ever trust you again?'

Allie flinched. 'He won't find out because Tony will be fine when he comes out of rehab. He's promised me and I believe him.'

'I'm sure he means it,' Magda placated, 'but what is so awful about telling the kids? At least they'd be able to visit him.'

'I don't want them setting foot in that place.' Allie's voice rose.

'What place?' Mark called out.

Allie closed her eyes and called out, 'A place Nana wants you to go with her, that's all.'

'The cinema?'

'Yes. I don't want you to go there.'

Magda sighed as if to say *More lies* and Allie looked defiantly at her. After a moment's silence, her shoulders drooped and she squeezed her eyes shut. 'I can't do it, Mam. I just can't. Mark adores Tony.'

'They'll still adore him,' Magda said gently.

'No, no they won't.' She knew they wouldn't because her image of her own father had been ruined by honesty and she wasn't prepared to do that to Tony. Whereas her dad might have deserved it, she didn't think that Tony did.

'OK, OK,' Magda placated. 'They're your kids.'

'Alleluia!' Fintan muttered and Magda glared at him.

'You are really annoying me today, Fintan,' she snapped. She turned back to Allie, her voice softer, 'I care about you all. I can't help interfering.'

'I know.' Allie smiled a little. 'And I appreciate you minding them.'

'Go,' Magda sighed and shook her head. She made whooshing motions with her hands. 'Go. I'll see you later.'

'Thanks.'

They looked at one another for a moment, before Magda

smiled and moved away from the door. Allie opened it. The two boys were in the hall, Mark's arm protectively around Owen's shoulders.

'Hey? What's up?' Allie smiled at them.

'Are we still going to the park?' Mark asked fearfully.

'Course you are. Nana is all set.' Allie bent down and kissed their soft faces, pressing them both to her. 'I'll see yez later. Be good, OK?'

'Enjoy your day with Holly,' Mark said, rubbing the kiss off and making Allie grin.

'I will. Bye now.'

'Bye, Mammy.'

The film and talk were over for the morning. The film showed the effects of drugs but it wasn't nearly as powerful as the talk given by an ex-user. Despite the lurid tattoo of a snake that curled around his neck like a repulsive necklace, he was pretty respectable looking, Allie thought. In a lot of ways he reminded her of Tony. He had the same darting anxious eyes, the quick lithe movements and the same jittery way of talking. It was only as he described his recovery, and the twelve steps he'd taken to do it, that he seemed to calm down at all. Obviously revisiting his addiction was not a comfortable journey for him to have to make.

'It's important to try to trust the addict when they get home,' he said finally as he stood up, his hands brushing down the front of his denims. 'There is nothing more humiliating for an addict than to be constantly under surveillance. If they're going to relapse, they will whether you're there to watch or not. Try to identify what will make them relapse. For some it's just being with the wrong friends; for others it's stress. There is always a trigger. Help them to recognise it. And talk to them.' He inclined his head. 'Thanks for listening.'

There was a smattering of applause and the man, whose name was Jamie, smiled shyly before exiting as quickly as he could.

'And now, folks, we just have time for a cup of tea,' the facilitator announced. 'And please take some literature, there are support groups for families living with addicts which you might like to join.'

Allie wasn't able to eat anything. She had to go meet Tony's counsellor next. She had no idea what to expect. Would he want a blow by blow into their marriage? Would Tony take offence at what she said? What had Tony told him? Though knowing Tony, he probably hadn't said anything.

'Are you OK?' Holly asked. She'd been great, introducing her to other people and sitting beside her during the talk. Holly it seemed, knew everyone.

Allie nodded. 'I'm going to see Tony's counsellor next. After last week, I'm not sure what will happen.'

Holly smiled. 'I felt sorry for you last week,' she said. 'Asking to come home, was he?'

Allie blinked, wondering how she knew. 'Yeah, actually.'

'They do that. Still, you stuck up for yourself pretty good.'

'I'm so embarrassed about that.' Allie rolled her eyes. 'Imagine calling your husband a bastard in front of a group of people you've never met before.'

Holly laughed loudly. 'Most of the people there would have agreed with you.'

Allie nodded. 'I wish I couldn't see the good man underneath,' she said softly. 'It'd make everything so much easier.'

'You go see his counsellor today,' Holly said in a no-nonsense tone, 'and you ask him everything. Don't hold back, it'll only help in the long run. Then when your meeting is over, I'll treat you to a cup of coffee and a cake.'

'Aw, you're so good.'

'I've been there,' Holly winked, taking out her compact mirror and lipstick. As she slathered it thickly on, she added, 'Trust me, a cake works wonders.'

* * *

Mark was puzzled. He found that he couldn't enjoy the playground much because two things were bothering him. The first and most important was that three big boys from his road were there and they kept hissing 'Fatso' to him whenever he walked by. He tried not to look at them but it was hard because they sometimes stood right in the middle of his path and blocked his way and they wouldn't go away until he'd glanced up. He would have liked to tell his nana and Fintan only they were way over in the baby playground with Owen. His nana was pushing Owen on a swing and he was laughing. Fintan was eating an apple and reading the paper. Mark had joined them at one stage but it had been boring because Granny Magda had sat down and asked him to push Owen as her legs were tired from standing up. So he'd done it for a bit before wandering back to the big playground. The big boys hadn't seen him at first but then they'd spotted him on the roundabout and pushed him really hard around and around and around until he knew that he was going to be sick. He probably shouldn't have eaten two packets of popcorn before the day out but he liked popcorn. He wished the big boy – Robert, that was his name – would stop the roundabout, but he didn't think Robert would. Robert's legs raced around and around and around. The other two boys were laughing and pointing and Mark's head was whirling and whirling and then he felt it. All his popcorn come up. And he puked. It was some puke. It hurled right out of his mouth like a big river all over Robert, who squealed like a big baby.

The roundabout slowed as Robert let go, yelping and yowling.

Mark tried not to laugh as Robert heaved at the smell of the sick and the other two boys with him yelped as he crossed towards them. Mark knew that if he laughed, he'd be dead. But it was funny all the same. Very funny. Just as it got slow enough to jump off, he bounded up and raced as fast as he could, his head spinning, back to his nana.

It was only later on, as he sucked on an ice pop that Fintan bought him, that the second thing that had been bothering him crept back into his head.

His mother's friend's name was not Holly. He remembered that now. She'd gone to meet Holly last week. This week it was Julie.

It was weird that she hadn't corrected his mistake.

Well, a little bit weird, he thought, as he bit into the lemon ice cream.

Some time later, Allie was ushered into the counsellor's office. Tony was already there and he smiled at her as she came to sit alongside him. He took her hand in his and squeezed it slightly, and then as the counsellor took a seat behind his desk, he dropped her hand and began to glower, like a kid in a head-master's office.

'Hello, Allie,' the counsellor said. 'Thank you for coming. This is just a preliminary session, as you know. Later on, before Tony is discharged, we'll have you into a group session with all the others. What I was hoping to do today is to tell you a little bit about what we're doing and then answer any questions you may have. As we've had Tony here now for almost two weeks, we've got a much clearer idea of the way his treatment will go.'

'OK,' Allie nodded. That all sounded fair enough.

'Well, we know that Tony has a fairly serious addiction which we hope to treat by identifying the triggers that make him use. As I explained to you already, a lot of cocaine users suffer with depression, and I have reason to believe that Tony's use is related to a former depression.'

Allie shot a look at Tony but his head was bowed. 'Were you depressed?' she asked.

He shrugged. 'I dunno.'

'He says he took hash initially to help him fit in, to chill out,' the counsellor explained. 'To get on with people. He says his whole life he felt different, didn't you, Tony?'

Tony shrugged a little but nodded too.

'He graduated to cocaine as it made him feel good, in control and confident. Isn't that right, Tony?'

'Yeah.' He still wasn't looking at either of them. 'Helped me get jobs too.'

'How long did you feel depressed for?' Allie was horrified.

'I never felt depressed,' Tony said. 'Just, just . . . I dunno.' He stared at his hands. Then he continued, 'They all say that in here. All the patients. They all say they felt different. I didn't know it wasn't normal. I thought everyone felt like that.'

There was a silence.

'So,' the counsellor broke it, 'we'll be using a treatment called Cognitive Behavourial Therapy to help Tony think in a different way. We'll also treat him for the depression. It's a slow process, it'll take time, and he'll continue to have a few more sessions when he leaves here.' He then went on to outline exactly what the aim was in these sessions. Allie barely heard him. All she could focus on was that Tony had been depressed. Oh, she knew he'd been depressed when he came down after being high, but she thought that was just the drugs. She reached out until her hand found his and, to her relief, he squeezed her hand back.

'So,' the counsellor finished up, 'have you any questions?'

'Is the outlook good?' she asked.

The counsellor flicked a glance at Tony. 'That's up to your husband, Mrs Dolan. We can only give him the tools, he has to want to use them.'

'It's just that someone told me their sister had been clean for a year and then relapsed. Can that happen?'

'Anything can happen,' the counsellor said. 'What Tony has to do is try to identify what makes him use, or what originally made him use. Because if he is going to relapse, it will be that same trigger again.'

'And you'll work that out with him?'

'Yes.'

Allie nodded. 'Well, anything I can do, I will. He knows that. Don't you, Tony?'

'Uh-huh.' His eyes met hers and he managed a small smile.

'Well, I'm glad to hear it.' The counsellor stood up to signal that the meeting was over. Tony and Allie, with some relief, rose with him. He shook Allie's hand. 'Thanks for your time, Allie. We'll talk again.'

'Thank you,' Allie said back and then, her arm linked through Tony's, she allowed him to walk her out the door towards the car park as visiting time was at an end. He rested his head on top of hers and sneaked his arm around her waist. She didn't want to spoil the moment with talk of drugs or the meeting, so she let him stay silent, just enjoying the feel of him so close.

As they reached the perimeter, he stopped. 'You'll have to go on alone,' he said softly, rubbing his thumb gently across her cheek. 'God, you look gorgeous.'

'And you look thin.' She poked him in the ribs. 'Eat.'

'I am,' he said. Then he leant his head towards her and brushed his lips against hers. Pulling away, he said, 'Tell the lads I was asking for them. I'll be able to ring this week, Wednesday night, so have them ready.'

'Oh, so you can use the telephone now, can you?'

'Yep. I had my knuckles rapped and Veronica got in trouble for giving me the money to break the rules.'

'Well, tell her thanks from me. I needed to hear your voice that night.'

'Not as much as I needed to hear yours.'

They stood for a second in silence before Tony sighed, 'I'd better get back. I'll be in trouble again.' He started to walk backwards away from her, as if he couldn't bear to take his eyes off her, and she watched him until he eventually turned and, with a wave, jogged back to the clinic.

A soft *bip* of a car horn jerked her gaze from him and she smiled to see that Holly was waiting.

* * *

68

Veronica, it turned out, was Holly's younger sister. She was twenty and had been using drugs since she was sixteen. As Allie buttered the scone Holly had insisted on buying for her, Holly talked a little about her.

'I was the eldest. Thick as a brick.' Holly tapped her head with a finger. 'Vee was the genius. She was eight years younger than me and I sort of mothered her. We were close, you know?'

Allie nodded. She would have loved a sister growing up.

'A genius,' Holly repeated. 'In her Junior Cert she got seven As and the rest Bs. That's how good she was.'

'Wow.' Allie was impressed. 'So what happened?'

'Fellas,' Holly said a little bitterly. She paused for a second before continuing crossly, 'Vee takes rejection very badly. She can't cope with relationships. A guy breaks it off with her, Vee gets high.'

Allie didn't know how to react or what to say. Holly sounded quite angry now.

'I guess,' Holly went on, 'she'd no one to learn from. Our da left us when she was eight and it must have affected her. I mean, she was fine for ages, doing well in school and all. But then she had her first break-up.' Holly shook her head. 'It just destroyed her.'

'It did?'

'Yeah. I think she thought that if she was really good at stuff, nothing bad would ever happen to her. She was determined to make everyone happy and that way, they'd all treat her well. And when that first fella broke it off with her, she learnt that even being perfect can't protect you from what other people do.'

'Poor thing.'

Holly nodded. 'Yeah, I guess.' She paused and took a sip of coffee. Allie noticed that her hands shook slightly. Talking about Veronica obviously upset her more than she let on. 'So,' Holly asked, striving for a brighter tone, 'what about you? How was your husband this week?'

'Tony,' Allie clarified, glad to change the subject, 'and he was fine. He rang to apologise after last week. Got into trouble for it too. Your sister gave him the money for the call.'

Holly grinned. 'That'd be Veronica OK.'

Allie smiled. 'She did me a favour.' She played with her knife as she said, 'Tony was the perfect kid too, his mother always says. Top of the class in everything. You'd think you had it made as a parent, wouldn't you?'

'Yeah. My mother used to be so proud of Vee. Now she won't even visit her. She threw her out of the house last month, so I took her in on condition she came back to the clinic.'

'One last chance, ey?'

Holly nodded. 'Yep.'

'Tony's on his last chance too.'

'Would you throw him out if he used again?'

Allie played with her knife. It was a question she knew she had to consider, but she'd avoided thinking about it. Maybe, she thought, if it had just been the two of them she could stick it out, but there was Mark and Owen now. Tony was good, she knew that. When he wasn't using, he was kind and funny and charming. They shared the same zany sense of humour, his quick wit never failing to make her laugh. All he had to do was wink at her and she melted inside. And she loved the unpredictability of him, the fact that he could always surprise her. But when he was on something, he scared her and the kids. Lying in bed at night, waiting for him to come back, not knowing where he was, mysterious dents appearing in his car that he said were caused by kids throwing rocks . . . And the way he snapped at her when she questioned him, the way he got defensive and rude. The way he ignored the kids one minute and shouted at them the next, so they never knew where they were with him. She was duty bound to protect her children from that.

'Yeah, I think I would.' Saying the words made her eyes water a little. She'd promised herself for better or worse on

70

her wedding day. She loved that man but not enough to live with the fear of losing everything again. 'I think I would,' she repeated.

Holly reached across the table and took her hand. 'Me too,' she said. 'And it doesn't mean that I don't love her. I do, I just . . .' Her voice trailed off.

'Hey,' Allie looked sympathetically at her before hopping from her seat and giving her a hug, 'you love Vee and I love Tony, that's just the way it is.'

'Jesus, would you look at me,' Holly attempted a little laugh as she wiped a rouge tear from her face, 'I was supposed to be cheering you up, telling you a cake would work wonders.' She rolled her eyes mock-comically. 'Jesus.'

'Well, it's true, Jesus would probably be better at working wonders than a cake.' As Holly laughed a little, Allie went on, 'But you have cheered me up. Honest. You've made me see that I'm not alone. That's the best thing.'

And it was.

12

ALLIE WAS STRAPPING a screaming Owen into his baby seat when her mobile rang. 'Mark, will you get that out of my bag and answer it?' she said, pinning Owen down and using all her strength to get the straps over him. 'Sit down, Owen, what'll happen to you if we have a car accident?' she asked crossly. 'Get into your seat.'

As usual he started to gesture to Mark's seat, his face contorted with the effort of trying to talk. For the first time Allie was glad that he hadn't yet mastered the art of speech.

'Yes, when you are bigger you can have one like that.'

'Hello?' Mark said into the phone. 'No it's just Owen screaming cause he hates his baby seat. What do you want?' He listened to the answer, with one finger plugged into his ear. 'It's Granny Magda,' he shouted over his brother as he held out the phone to Allie, who had successfully secured Owen and was now tying a belt over the straps so he wouldn't wriggle out. For such a small child he could be a brat.

Allie took the phone from Mark after telling him to strap himself in. Then she closed the car door on her screaming child so she could hear her mother. 'Mammy, hi. What's up?'

'I'd like you to come over. Now,' Magda said.

'Would you?' Allie said, half joking. 'Eh – I just happen to be in the middle of the city centre with a screaming child who thinks he's Houdini in the back seat. I've been forced to spend a small fortune on Mark's school uniform for next year and am broke. Forgive me if I just want to go home and shoot myself in the head.'

'Don't shoot yourself,' Mark said, horrified, his head stuck out the window of the car.

'Will you stop listening in on my conversations?' Allie said, exasperated.

'Don't shout at your children,' Magda said. 'I never shouted at you.'

'No, you saved it for Dad,' Allie deadpanned back.

'That is not funny, I am not laughing,' Magda said. 'It just so happens that the reason I want you over concerns your shit of a father.'

Allie's grip tightened on her phone. 'Why?' she said, her voice catching. 'What is it?'

'He has deigned to write to us, that's what.'

'What?'

'You heard. The man who probably knows every woman over the age of consent in this country has written.'

'And what does he say?'

'Are you worried, Mammy?' Mark asked. 'You look worried. Is it about Daddy?'

'No,' Allie reassured him. 'What does he say in the letter?' she asked her mother.

'You'll have to come over and find out,' Magda said. 'I really don't think we can discuss it over the telephone. Anyway, you might want to read the letter for yourself.'

'OK,' Allie said, 'I'll be there.'

Her mother hung up.

'What letter, Mammy?' Mark asked again. He was looking at her, his head cocked to one side.

'Just a letter your nana got today. She wants me to read it. Now,' she asked as she hopped back into her car, 'who wants to go to Granny Magda's?'

73

There was a deafening silence from the back seat which made Allie smile.

Even as Allie drove towards her mother's house, she thought how pathetic she was. Her dad had left fifteen years ago, written to her for a couple of months and then, after receiving no replies, he'd stopped writing. She knew she'd never have given up if it was her kids. She would never meekly vanish from Owen and Mark's lives. And now, here she was, rushing to see what he had to say for himself in the first letter to arrive in years. But not going would be akin to chopping her arm off. Pointless and painful.

'Why do we have to go to Granny Magda's?' Mark moaned as they turned into her street. 'She never has sweets in the house.'

'That's because Fintan thinks sweets are bad for you,' Allie said, knowing she really shouldn't give out about Fintan in front of the kids. But she did anyway. 'He's afraid he'll get fat again.'

'Am I fat?' Mark suddenly sounded anxious.

'No, honey, you're not. You're my beautiful cuddly boy,' Allie answered, smiling at him.

'And she has no toys for us to play with,' Mark went on. 'And she only has boring tapes and things.'

'Yes well, Granny Magda is not eight years old, is she, Mark? You can hardly expect her to have a football and goal posts in her garden.'

Mark chortled and Owen joined in. She grinned at their laughter as she turned into her mother's driveway. Opening the back door and pulling Owen from his seat, she told Mark to take him around the back and play. 'Nana just wants me to read something.'

'Does Nana have any juice first?' Mark asked. 'I'm thirsty.'

'Let's see.' She unlocked the front door and, with Mark following, walked into the hall.

'Hi,' she called, 'it's just us. Can I get the kids some juice before they go outside and play?'

'You can.' Fintan appeared from the front room. 'Hello, boys!' he boomed, making Owen flinch. 'So, what would you like – I've cranberry, freshly squeezed orange juice or apple juice?'

'Cranberry,' Mark said. 'And Owen, what do you want?'

Owen babbled something and Mark, pretending to understand, said, 'He wants cranberry too.'

Allie let Fintan take them into the kitchen.

'She's in the front room,' Fintan said to Allie over his shoulder. Then went on in an undertone, 'She's so upset, she ate four slices of bread with jam just now. She even sent me out to buy jam. We never have jam in the house.'

'I like jam,' Mark said. 'Can I have some?'

Allie suppressed a smile and entered the front room, where she found her mother plonked on the sofa, holding some pages in her hand. She looked up as Allie came in. 'The mystery of the philandering man is solved.' She waved the pages in the air.

'Is that it?'

'Yep.'

'What does it say?'

'The usual shite.' Magda never minced her words where her husband was concerned.

'How can it be the usual shite?' Allie asked in amusement. 'We haven't had a letter in years.' She squashed in beside her mother and took the letter from her. Her dad's writing hadn't changed, she thought; she would have known it anywhere. He had a tendency to swirl the letters at the beginning of words in a big flourish. Showy, like him, her mother used to say.

Hello, Magda and my little girl, Alisha,

I know it has been a long time and a lot of water, some of it extremely polluted, has flowed under the bridge. I hope that this letter finds you all

75

*well and in good health. I know from enquiries that Alisha is now married
with a little boy. I'm sure he is as lovely as his mother was. I wish I
could have been around to share your life, but as you know living normally
did not come easily to me. I was living in France for a time but have
now moved back to Ireland. I decided to take a chance to see if you could
find it in your hearts to meet me. I hope time has softened things between
us. I will be outside Clery's, under the clock, at twelve o'clock on Friday
next. I will wait for you both and if you do not come, I understand.
I'll be wearing a blue jacket with red sleeves.
Thinking of you both, always.
Love Thomas.
If Friday does not suit, you can contact me at the number at the top of
the page.*

'A blue jacket with red sleeves,' Magda scoffed. 'His dress
sense hasn't improved anyway. Who would wear a blue jacket
with red sleeves?'

Allie shrugged. Looking at the letter had affected her. Her
dad had touched that paper, had written those words . . .

'And living in France! Huh, he must have run out of Irish girls!'

Allie swallowed a lump in her throat.

Magda paused, sensing that her comments were hurting her
daughter. 'Well,' she said, trying to sound nice about it but
finding it difficult, 'at least he didn't sign himself Dad or
Husband. That would have been too much.'

Silently Allie agreed, though he had been a father and
husband at one stage. Just because he had been terrible at it
didn't deny that it had happened. 'So, what's the story?' she
asked. 'Are we going to meet him?'

'Well, I'm not.' Magda looked at Allie as if she were bonkers.
'Just because he wants us to meet him he thinks we should?
Why now, ey? He's probably looking for someone to mind him
in his old age, that's all.'

Allie shook her head, smiling a little. 'That's a bit cynical,
Mam.'

'And what other way would I be?'

'It sounds like he's trying to make amends.'

'He can't make amends,' Magda said, a poignant note creeping into her voice. 'How do you make amends for failing so spectacularly as a husband and dad?'

'He deserves a chance.'

'He had lots of chances. He messed them all up.'

Allie supposed that was true.

'I mean, how many chances do you give someone before you let go?'

'I dunno. As many as they need.'

'No!' Her mother dismissed that with a wave of her hand, her copious bracelets clinking against each other. 'You give them as many as you can cope with and Allie, by the time he left I was a mess. You know what I was like. Twenty stone for one thing. Huh, the last straw was when he went on your school tour and tried to chat up your teacher, then had the affair with Julie Leonard from the Post Office.'

'Mmm,' Allie said. That had been a bit awful, all right.

'I can't go back there,' her mother said. 'Meeting him would dredge it all up again. I have Fintan now. He's a good man.'

Allie scanned her father's letter again. It was written on the middle pages of a school copybook with a blue leaky biro. She wondered if it had taken him long to write. Did he scrap many letters before finally deciding that this was the one? Had he agonised over this new communication with his estranged family? She hoped he had.

Fintan breezed into the room at that moment, with two tall glasses of cranberry juice, one for each of them.

Magda took one but Allie shook her head. 'Thanks, Fintan, but I'm not a fan of cranberry.'

'Oh.' Fintan looked disappointed.

'It's good for your kidneys,' her mother chided. 'Put it down beside her anyway, Fintan.'

Fintan did as he was told before nodding to the letter in Allie's hand and asking, 'So, what do you think?'

'She thinks he has a nerve, don't you, Allie?'

'Eh – well, yes, I suppose he has,' she agreed.

'Thinking we'd go and meet him,' Magda snorted. 'Drink up that juice, Allie.'

'Well, actually,' Allie began, 'I wouldn't mind meeting him.'

Magda paused with her cranberry juice halfway to her lips. 'You want to meet him? Are you serious?' Before Allie could answer, she went on, 'I was tempted to ring up Clery's the day he was to turn up and tell them that the man in the blue coat with the red sleeves was planning to rob the place.'

'Mam!'

'You wouldn't!' Fintan snorted with laughter.

'I probably wouldn't,' Magda conceded with a grin, 'but it'd be tempting all the same.' She turned back to Allie. Softly she asked, 'You really want to see him, do you?'

'Well, aren't you even a bit curious?'

'No.'

'Don't feel you can't go because of me, Magda,' Fintan said suddenly. 'I don't mind.'

'Well I do,' Magda said, looking into his eyes and making Allie feel like a big gooseberry. 'Why would I want to see him? He ruined years of my life.' She turned back to Allie. 'You go if you want to, Allie, but for God's sake, be wary.'

'Do you mind, Mam? I won't go if it'll upset you.' She knew that she owed her mother a lot more than she owed Thomas.

'It's your choice,' her mother answered. There was a pause and she added softly, 'Just don't let him fool you.'

'He won't. I just, well, I suppose I . . . Well, he's my dad, isn't he?'

'Biologically, yes.' There was no mistaking the cynicism in Magda's voice.

'I think he deserves a chance to explain.'

Magda rolled her eyes and shot Fintan a look.

'What?' Allie asked.

Again the look passed between them. 'We sort of thought you'd want to see him,' Magda said. 'You're too soft, that's your problem.'

'I'm not soft,' Allie defended herself, feeling annoyed. It was not soft to want to see her father again. Her mother was too hard, *that* was the problem.

'In fact, if it was up to me,' Magda went on, ignoring Fintan's glaring look for her to shut up, 'I would have burned the letter, but Fintan said you had a right to see it.'

'She did too.' Fintan smiled a little at Allie.

'You would have burned it?' Allie said in disbelief. 'Why?'

'Because you have enough problems on your plate, that's why.'

'Tony's not a problem,' Allie said crossly, hurt at the way her mother constantly criticised him. 'He's not well, but at least he sticks around.'

'He does,' Fintan said, placating.

'Don't patronise me,' Allie said crossly.

'I was only saying—'

'I'll not have you talking to Fintan like that,' Magda interrupted.

'Well, I'll not have you giving out about Tony then.' Allie stood up abruptly, the letter still in her hand. 'I'm going now.'

'Allie!' Her mother sounded as if she couldn't quite believe this was happening. 'Allie, come back. I didn't mean—'

But she was gone, striding into the kitchen, calling to Mark and Owen and demanding that they go back to the car.

'Whatever is wrong, don't take it out on the kids,' Magda said as she followed her out.

'You're what's wrong,' Allie shot back. She hopped into the car, roughly buckled Owen in, shouted at Mark to do his own belt then slammed the door and, revving up, she left.

'Are you cross, Mammy?' Mark ventured at the top of Magda's road.

'I will be if you don't behave yourself.'

Owen started to cry.

'You've made Owen cry,' Mark said accusingly.

'And I'll make you cry if you don't stop.' Allie's voice quivered.

It was the sound of Mark patting Owen on the hand and telling him to hush that finally made her pull the car into the side of the road and put her hands to her face.

'Mammy?' Mark sounded terrified. 'Are you crying?'

'Ohh.' She unbuckled her seat belt and climbed into the back seat and hugged the two boys fiercely. 'I'm sorry,' she sobbed. 'I'm so sorry for shouting. It's not your fault, Marko, or Owen's fault. It's just me in bad humour.'

'It's OK, Mammy.' Now Mark started to hush her, making her laugh a little through her tears. 'It's OK. You'll be OK.'

'I love you two guys,' she said, pulling back slightly and then starting to cover their faces with kisses.

'Yeuch!' Mark made a face and Owen, laughing, copied him.

'Yak!'

'He spoke, Mammy, did you hear that?' Mark shrieked. 'Say it again Ownie, go on!'

'Yak!' Owen made a face again and they both laughed.

It dawned on Allie right at that moment that, despite everything, just being with her boys and laughing with them made her happy. She loved her lads and would do anything for them. Her own mother was only looking out for her. She'd thrown her dad out to help them both survive. This whole situation was bound to be freaking her out.

Allie turned her car around and drove back to her mother's, the words of an apology already in her head.

13

JEREMY'S HEART SANK as he came downstairs and saw a yellow envelope lying on his hall carpet. One letter was bad enough but, positive that it would be the only one, he hadn't thought any more about it. However, here was another. The envelope was as garish as before and this time the boy had drawn a crude figure of Santa leading a sleigh of very strange, over-weight-looking reindeer with manic grins on their faces. Jeremy doubted very much if these reindeer would be in the least bit aerodynamic. The envelope had been stuck closed with copious amounts of sellotape and bright red lettering on the front announced that it was for 'Santa'.

Shit.

Jeremy never normally thought in the 's' word, but there was always a first time. He had really landed himself in it with this boy and unfortunately there didn't seem to be a way out. How do you confess to people that you lied to a young boy about being Santa Claus, just so he wouldn't throw balls into your garden? He'd be vilified and rumours would spread about him. Jeremy swallowed hard and picked up the envelope, wondering what on earth the boy wanted now. Maybe he wanted a different present, he knew children changed their minds about that sort of thing every day. His own boys had done it a lot until he'd put his foot down and told them they had to make up their minds by September otherwise they'd forfeit a gift from him and their mother. That had stopped all their nonsense. However that tactic wouldn't be possible with

the boy. Sighing wearily, he poured himself a strong cup of
tea before getting his letter opener from the drawer and ripping
open the seal. The boy certainly knew how to sellotape things
shut.

Eventually he got the top of the envelope open and pulled
out a creased letter, with more ridiculous drawings on it.

Jeremy sat down and began to read.

Dear Santa

I am doing my bestest riting in dis letter for
you. I am riting clear so you can reed it. Dere
are three things I want to say to you in dis
letter. First off is THANK YOU.

My daddy rang on Wensday night, deh first
time in a fort night for us to hear from him.
And he was very funny and he told us all about
NY. Dats New Yourk City doh you probly no dat.
And he is staying in a hotel with lots of nice
food and a big huge bed and he says dat deh
streets are very busy and he says dat he
walked in central park and a lady came by on
roller skates and nocked him down and he looked
very funny and his story made me laugh so much
i almost got sick and he says dat he misses us
and he says dat he misses mammy and he says
dat he cant wait to come hime as he loves us.
I talked to him but Owen didnt as owen is not
talking yet well he was until daddy gave out to
him one night and now he doesnt talk much at
all. Maybe you can make Owen talk good for
Daddy coming home.

Now, also i want to say dat I hope you wont
tink dat I am a tell tale but i just want you
to no about some boys dat live on our road and

its up to you if you put dem on de bold list. Mayb you have to be reely bold to go on the bold list as one time i slapped my brudder reely hard and you still brung me stuff on Christmas. Mayb dere is a in between list where you go if you are a little bit bold but not bold enuff for deh bold list. Anyhow, dese boys live on our road and dey keep calling me Fatso and laffing at me and my brudder and it makes me cry when I am on my own. I dont like going out de front now as dey are always dere. Its james and Robert and Peter who all live in numbers 29, 34 and 50 on our road. I cheked yesterday just so i woodnt tell tales on the rong boys. Dey are bullys dats what dey are. I didnt tell my mammy as she is sad as our dad is away on busness.

I hope you are well santa and dat you have got my television for me. I have not been bold at all so far and I havent throng my ball into your garden. Your grand dauter is very nice. Does she no your secret. I haven't told anyone.
  Love mark. xxx

Jeremy frowned and reread the letter. There was no doubt that Mark was fat, but it made him cross to think that some boys were teasing the child. Jeremy remembered back to when he was a boy and he'd been fat and he'd been teased about it too. It annoyed Jeremy that Mark was afraid to go out the front and play. Besides feeling sorry for the child, and he did feel a little sorry for him, it also meant that the boy would be kicking his ball in his own back garden and Jeremy, who spent most of his time in the kitchen, would be forced to listen to the *thump, thump, thump* of the ball hitting against the dividing wall. There had to be something he could do. He couldn't just ignore it. Well, he could, but the child would only send him another letter. Jeremy knew that there would be no question of him confronting those boys, they were very disrespectful and would probably laugh. Their parents were likely the same. There was also no chance that he could inform Mark's mother as she would wonder how he knew. He supposed he could always say he'd seen it happening, but the woman was bound to wonder when. And besides Jeremy hated getting involved in other people's lives – they sucked you in then spat you out. When his wife had died, had any of the old crowd kept in contact? Only in the beginning, then he'd been discarded like an old shoe. Oh, Adam tried to make out it was because Jeremy hadn't bothered returning the invites he'd got from these people, but Jeremy knew that the invites had only been issued out of pity and he didn't like to be anyone's charity case. And besides, all the old crowd reminded him of the good times he and his wife had enjoyed and he didn't like that either. And he knew, too, that nothing was going to be fun if Nelly wasn't there by his side, so there was no point. Jeremy shook his head to clear it. He was thinking a lot of his wife these days. He guessed it was because he still hadn't got anyone to clear up his garden and he knew she'd be cross. Now four thousand seemed reasonable considering the other rates he'd been quoted.

He hastily turned back to the letter. How would his wife have handled it? In all likelihood she'd never have pretended to be Mrs Claus in the first place, but if the boys had been bullied, what would she have done? Nelly had been good at figuring things like that out.

He'd have to have a good hard think because she would have done *something*.

'The feeling I get,' Tess said, as she spooned some soup into her mouth, 'is that addicts are sort of lost people.'

'So a sat nav would sort them out?' John chortled, making Allie laugh.

Tess looked in annoyance at them. 'John, haven't you an interview to be going to?'

'Yeah,' John rolled his eyes, 'in about two hours.'

'So get ready for it. Office manager,' she said to Allie, 'that's what he's going for. Now, make sure you have all your notes about the company, that's a good tip I picked up on the internet.'

John pushed his chair in and saluted his mother. 'Sure if I don't get it, I'll offer it up for all the poor children in Africa.'

'If you don't get it, you can move out,' Tess said sternly. 'I can't be supporting you.'

'Aw, why don't you offer it up?'

'I'll offer your head up on a platter if you're not careful! Out!'

Allie smiled. Tess and John were a great double act. He knew how to drive her mad. For years, whenever Tess was confronted with any difficulty, she'd say that she was 'offering it up' for some cause or other. John loved annoying her over it.

'I'll bring my nephews to the shops and then I'll get ready. We could all do with a big chocolate bar, I reckon.' He opened the kitchen window. 'Oy! Lads! Shop break!'

Mark cheered loudly and a few minutes later John left with them, Owen perched up on his shoulders, laughing delightedly.

'They're a credit to you,' Tess said, pouring some more soup into Allie's bowl. 'The fact that they're so happy even though their dad is gone.'

Allie didn't reply. She actually wondered if they were so happy *because* their dad was gone. Mark's nightmares, which she used to put down to an overactive imagination, had stopped completely in the last week and Owen, who had been so quiet and shy, was slowly coming out of his shell. The fact that he'd gone off with John without so much as a backward glance at her was proof of that.

Tess put the saucepan back on the cooker and joined Allie at the table. 'Now, I was reading about addicts on the net,' she said, 'and one thing they all seemed to have in common was this lost feeling, as if they never quite fitted in. Does Tony have that feeling, do you think?'

Allie shrugged. 'I don't know how Tony feels, Tess.' She couldn't tell Tess that Tony had probably been on drugs as long as she'd known him. She wasn't sure she even knew the real him. 'He did say something to his counsellor about it though.'

Tess beamed. 'There you go,' she said proudly. Then added, 'He was a quiet enough boy. He did well in school and his dad was always very proud of him. And when Tony said he wanted to be an accountant just like Norman, well, that was the proudest day of Norman's life. He used to tell everyone: "My son is going to be just like me."'

Allie smiled. Tony missed his dad a lot. He'd been heart-broken when he'd died five years ago.

'I can't understand it though,' Tess said. 'Why he felt the need to use.'

Allie shrugged. She was tired of examining her husband's motivations. Stress. Upset. Not fitting in. It didn't matter, he was using stuff and it was hurting her and the kids. 'I think he has to find that out for himself, Tess.'

'But maybe if we find out what it was, we can tell him and then he'll know.'

'Yeah.' Allie didn't bother to argue. No matter what she said, Tess would do what she wanted anyway. She was more like Tony than she knew.

'What are you smiling at?' Tess asked accusingly.

'Nothing. Just thinking you and Tony are a little alike.'

'He took after his dad,' she said softly. Then she half smiled. 'Though we were only his foster parents. We always forgot that.'

Allie said nothing. Sometimes it bothered her that Tony never seemed to forget. He always called Tess and Norman by their Christian names, as if half afraid to call them Mam and Dad. At times over the years, when she'd been consumed

86

with helping Tony, she'd wondered if that had been a factor. How much did it really bother him that his biological parents had left him in a buggy alone in the city centre when he was a few weeks old and never contacted him since? And did it bother him that John was Tess and Norman's natural son? Did it make him feel left out? Tony had always denied it when she'd broached the subject. Had always insisted that he'd definitely be on harder drugs if his real parents showed up.

'We loved him as much as if he were ours,' Tess said, her eyes filling up. 'And I used to pray that his real parents would never show up. Maybe that was wrong of me.'

'Stop, would you!' Allie affected some of John's no-nonsense manner. 'You're putting me off my soup.'

'Offer it up,' Tess said back, sniffing loudly but trying to smile. 'Offer it up so that my other son will get a job.'

Allie grinned. 'I'd say I'd have a better chance of success if I offered it up for world peace.'

Tess laughed.

14

ADAM, WHOSE PARROT had just bitten his ear, was too gob-smacked to feel the pain. His dad wanted him to visit. That was a first. His heart thumped in alarm, wondering if there was a chance his father had heard any rumours, but nope, his dad sounded his usual pompous self, so there didn't seem to be a problem there. As he held a large bandage to his bleeding earlobe, he promised his father that he would be there when the filming of *Jolly Roger* wrapped up for the day.

He watched in a sort of daze as his parrot was put back in her cage, shrieking loudly. The bloody thing was a danger but she was the only animal that had been able to say 'Waz up, Jolly Roger!' in a pirate accent, and so she had a part in his show until another more docile one could be trained. As the parrot was taken away, Adam dialled his brother to impart the news that their father had actually summoned him for a visit.

Wonders would never cease.

Jeremy paced up and down his front room, his eyes scanning the road for Adam's car. It was a good day – plenty of kids were out and about, including the three named in Mark's letter. They were kicking a ball on the other side of the road and seemed to be eyeing Mark's house with particular interest. Jeremy wondered if he would have noticed this if Mark hadn't told him. Probably not, as he'd have been in the kitchen having some tea or bread around this time. A familiar roar caused him to spring to the window and there was Adam, his son, sitting in his ridiculous car, a crowd of kids being drawn magnetically to it. Adam parked, hopped out and, as usual, took ages chatting away to the kids and signing autographs for them. He'd even brought pictures of himself dressed as a pirate to distribute. Jeremy supposed it was nice of Adam to talk to the kids like that, but it was annoying too. Jeremy had asked him to come and, as far as Adam knew, Jeremy could be dying inside that house. And did it matter? No. Adam was wasting time talking to kids. Kids that bullied. Jeremy tapped loudly on the window as Adam turned towards Robert, the boy from 34. As Adam bent down to sign Robert's football, Jeremy banged louder, causing his son to glance his way in alarm. Jeremy beckoned for Adam to come quickly and he saw with satisfaction that Robert was gutted. *Ha ha*, he thought, *Serve you right, you little brat.*

He opened the door for Adam to a chorus of 'Bye, Jolly Roger!' and dragged his son inside.

'Hey Dad, what's up?' Adam looked anxiously at him.

Adam had dyed his hair a sunny blond colour. Or had it highlighted or something. It suited him, though it was a girly thing to do, Jeremy thought.

'Nothing,' Jeremy said, stalking into the kitchen and leaving Adam to follow. 'I just need a favour from you.'

His dad had never asked him for a favour in his life. Adam wondered if he was OK. 'Yeah? What is it?'

'Now,' Jeremy swallowed hard. 'It's an unusual favour and I don't want you asking why or anything, all right?'

Adam nodded slowly. The man was losing it, he thought sadly.

'I want you to knock on the house next door and ask the fat boy, Mark, if he wants a ride in your car.'

'Sorry?' Adam winced. 'You want me to what?'

'Ask the fat boy next door if he'd like a ride in your car.'

'Why?'

'You said you wouldn't ask.'

89

'Dad,' Adam looked incredulously at his father, 'I can't just go knocking on strangers' doors asking their kids to come out with me. It's weird.'

'You're Jolly Roger, kids love you. You can say that you do it every so often as a special treat and that you picked him.'

'No, I can't.'

Jeremy frowned crossly. This was not what he had anticipated. 'OK,' he said. 'I'll be straight with you. Some boys on this road are picking on him. I thought it would do him and these boys good to see you being his friend.'

Adam blinked, stunned. His dad had noticed something like *that*? His dad who rarely went out of the house? His dad being kind and thinking of another kid? He *must* be losing it. Maybe the man was dying and trying to atone for his sins. 'How do you know?'

'I have eyes. I see things.'

'Which boys are picking on him?'

'That horrible child whose football you were about to sign out there.'

'Are you sure?'

His dad didn't bother to reply. Instead he said crossly, 'Fine. Forget I asked.'

Adam sighed. 'I have to think of a way of asking the kid that doesn't make me look like some kind of weirdo. I don't even know the lad.'

'You're an actor, lies are your speciality.'

Adam gulped hard. That hurt more than it should have. 'Let me just think.'

Jeremy watched as Adam thought. And thought. And thought.

'Adam—'

'OK,' Adam said, interrupting him, 'I think I have it.' Without saying anything else, Adam strode to the front door and opened it. The kids, who had begun to wander away, raced back to the house upon seeing him. Without acknowledging them, Adam hopped over the dividing wall and into next door. Ringing the doorbell, he tried to assume a Jolly Roger-confident look.

A woman answered, short dark hair, enormous brown eyes in an attractive face. 'Hi,' he said, 'my name is Adam. I'm your next door neighbour's son.' What a ridiculous thing to say. 'I mean I'm—'

'Jolly Roger!' a voice said. 'Cool!' A boy peeked out from behind his mother.

'Yes, I'm also Jolly Roger,' Adam grinned. 'You must be Mark.'

Mark's eyes grew round. 'Yeah. How did you know?'

'My dad told me. He said you're a very good boy and that you'd like a spin in my car, is that true?'

'I never said that,' Mark breathed. 'But yeah, yeah.' He was almost hyperventilating.

'I don't . . .' The woman looked from one to the other.

'I'm a TV show actor,' Adam said. 'And I'm your next door neighbour's son, and he said that I should give Mark a lift in my car.' He shrugged, lied, 'My dad does that sometimes.' Then added, 'Of course you are invited too. I wouldn't just take Mark on his own. And anyone else you'd like to bring.' He turned his most charming grin on the woman. 'It's a Lexus,' he said finally.

'Mammy, we have to,' Mark gawped. 'Santa would hate us to refuse.'

'Santa?' his mother laughed. 'Well, there's a new one.'

'My dad would hate it too,' Adam said.

'Yeah, that's what I meant,' Mark trilled.

Allie was confused. It was all a bit strange. She'd never had anything to do with the man next door; if anything he seemed a little grumpy. But appearances could be deceptive, she knew that herself only too well. And it was nice of him to think of Mark like this. 'OK,' she agreed. 'Thank you.'

'Lock up and come on,' Adam said as he took Mark by the

hand and led him through the gaggle of kids that had gathered outside the gate. 'Make way,' he called, 'my best mate is coming through.'

From his window, Jeremy folded his arms in satisfaction. The three boys were very put out at what they were seeing. He gave himself a mental pat on the back, he'd handled that well. He watched Mark settle himself into the back seat of the car. Then the boy suddenly spotted him. His lifted his hand in a wave and Jeremy nodded in greeting, only realising as the car pulled out that he was smiling.

Some hours later, someone rang on Jeremy's door. Jeremy peered out of the kitchen. From what he could see, it looked like a woman. He hoped it wasn't one of the mothers of the bullying boys, as he had christened them. Yesterday he had confiscated the boy James' ball, then stuck a pin in it on the sly before handing it back to him. That had been fun. No one would associate him with the ruined ball at all.

The person at the door rang the bell again. She seemed to be holding some sort of a box in one hand. Or maybe it was a case. It could be that horrible nurse who had called on a few occasions, checking up on senior citizens in the neighbourhood. Jeremy had given her short shrift, told her that he didn't need checking up on, thanks very much. She had been quite upset leaving his doorstep and he'd felt a little guilty, but she hadn't come back.

'Hello?' the person called. 'I'm Allie from next door.'

Allie? He didn't know an Allie. He assumed it must be Mark's mother, the skinny one with the worried face. He wondered what she wanted. Sighing, he opened the door.

'Hello?' Allie smiled at him in the way he'd found people tended to smile at old people.

'Yes?' he barked and was satisfied to see her big smile wobble uncertainly.

'I just called in to thank you for what you did for Mark today. You've no idea how excited he was going in your son's car.'

'Oh. Well, thank you for calling in to tell me that.' He attempted what he hoped was a smile.

'Yes, and I've just brought you this to say how much we appreciated it.' Allie held the white box towards him and then, as he made no move to take it, added, 'It's a cake. With strawberries.'

Jeremy did not like eating food from other people's kitchens. One could never know the standard of hygiene they employed. 'I have no need of a cake, thank you,' he said, trying to sound both brusque and pleasant at the same time.

He noticed the boy Mark and his brother hanging around the gate. Mark was looking thrilled that his mother was talking to him.

'I bought it especially.' She smiled encouragingly at him as if he were a simpleton.

'I would never eat a whole cake. It'd be a waste.'

'Oh.' Allie hadn't thought of that. 'Well, maybe your son would eat some when he calls?'

Good God, Jeremy thought, the woman was determined to give him the bloody cake. Maybe she would think it odd if he refused. He was so out of practice in dealing with people that he'd forgotten these things. Nelly would have dealt with the neighbours and all that, though, as he never had much time for strangers. 'Yes,' he reluctantly conceded, taking it from her, 'thank you. I'll save it for him.'

'Enjoy it,' Allie smiled.

'I'm sure I will.'

'And if there's anything I can do for you, seeing as we are neighbours, don't hesitate to ask.'

Jeremy almost fell over in his eagerness to embrace her offer. 'Well actually,' he said as she turned to go, 'maybe there is something you can do.'

'Hi, Mr Lyons!' Mark called out. 'Your son has a cool car. He's Jolly Roger, do you know that?'

'Yes, yes I do,' Jeremy called back weakly.

'And does he know who *you* are?' Mark called. Then he clapped a hand over his mouth and looked at Jeremy with horrified eyes. 'Sorry,' he said.

Allie gave a laugh. 'He's mad.' She smiled fondly at her son.

He's fat, Jeremy felt like saying, do him a favour and stick him on a diet so he won't get teased. But of course he didn't. Instead, recovering from almost being unmasked by Mark, he said, 'Could you pass on a word to your gardener?'

'My gardener?' Allie smiled. 'He's just my brother-in-law.'

'Well, whatever he is. Can you tell him that if he wants, I'd like him to do my garden? Tell him I'll give him three thousand, five hundred if he does what he's done to yours.'

'I'm sure he won't charge that much,' Allie said.

'He attempted to charge me four thousand,' Jeremy said, offended. 'But an old man like me can't afford that much.'

'No, of course you can't.' Allie sounded just as offended. 'Let me have a word and see what I can do.'

'Oh, thank you,' Jeremy smiled, a genuine smile this time. 'And thanks for this.' He held up the cake box.

'No worries.' Allie grinned back and Jeremy watched as she danced down the driveway, catching her son Mark's hand in the process.

It gave him a lump in his throat for some reason.

15

'M AMMY,' MARK HAD his hands behind his back, 'can I ask you something?'

Allie jumped, as if her thoughts were written in big red ink over her head. She had just got off the phone from the clinic. She rang once a week, just to see how Tony was getting on.

'Did I scare you?' Mark asked half proudly. 'I'm practising sneaking up on people. Footballers have to be light on their feet. I read that on the internet.'

'Yes, you scared me,' Allie smiled down at him. 'If you don't make it as a footballer, you could always be a robber.'

Mark laughed. Then his expression became serious. 'I want to ask you something. It's very important.'

'What have you got behind your back?'

'Nothing.' He moved away from her.

Allie left it, he'd show her when he was ready she guessed. 'So what do you want to ask?'

'Is it possible, at all,' Mark said, 'to go on a long trip over the sea to a far away country without a passport?'

She suddenly knew what it was he had. He'd been poking around in drawers and presses and boxes again. Mark did that a lot, it was as if he was searching for something and he was never sure quite what. 'Have you been messing up all the boxes in the rooms again?' she snapped, panic making her cross.

'I was looking for my football cards,' Mark defended himself, flinching at her sharp tone. 'Well, what is the answer? Can you?'

'You have no right to go poking through things.' Allie brought her voice down a notch, not wanting to shout at Mark who, after all, had done nothing wrong except poke his nose into where it shouldn't be. It was her who was the stupid one. How could she have been so dense? 'Show me what you have behind your back.'

Mark hesitated, sensing that she was a little annoyed with him. 'I was just looking for my football cards and I found Daddy's passport,' he said, holding it out. 'And now, how will he come home if he's gone away? How did he go away in the first place?'

Allie's mind went blank. Jesus, what was she to say? 'I told you not to poke about in those boxes,' she spluttered, hoping to change the subject.

'How will he get home?' Tears began to form at the edges of Mark's eyes. 'He might never get home!'

Upstairs Owen started to cry.

'Those boxes are out of bounds, you are *not* to touch them.' Allie turned to go upstairs, glad of the excuse to get away from him.

'But Daddy has no passport,' Mark wailed.

'He has,' Allie found herself saying, an idea flashing through her mind. 'He does.' It was hard to look at Mark. How many lies was she to tell him?

'He has?'

'Yes. He thought this was lost so he got a new one.'

'Oh.' Mark nodded slowly. 'Oh, I see.'

He was so trusting that it pained her. 'So,' she forced a bright smile on her face and ruffled his hair, not feeling worthy enough to hug him, 'there is no need to worry, OK?'

Mark nodded. Then frowned. 'But, but his passport was with mine and Owen's and yours. All together.'

'He thought he lost it,' Allie said again. 'Now,' she went on, hoping to divert the subject, 'leave all those unopened boxes alone, OK? If I see you poking in any more, I'll lock *you* in a box!'

He smiled at her joke even though he didn't think it was very funny, and he also smiled because he suddenly thought of who might know about travelling around the world without a passport.

Jeremy was settling down to watch *Ready Steady Cook*. He liked that programme, though some of the chefs would give you a pain in your arse, he often thought. And some of the contestants were worse. The woman today had run ten marathons in her time – she certainly looked like she could do with a good feed. If she was an example of being fit, Jeremy thought that exercise certainly wasn't all it was cracked up to be.

He ignored the ring on his bell at first. If it was one of the boys, they'd have their own keys, not that they ever used them. But it was handy for them to have a set in case Jeremy slipped climbing out of the bath or fell down the stairs one day. They could let themselves in and help him.

The ringing continued and then Jeremy thought he heard a voice. 'Mr Lyons,' the voice was calling through the letter box, 'can I ask you something very important in private?'

Oh God, Mark from next door. Hadn't he done enough for that child? It was only three days ago that he'd arranged for the ride in Adam's car. And though he couldn't explain why, he was still peering out the window to check that Mark was OK when those bullies were out. Now here was the boy again, wanting more.

He heaved himself up from his chair and stomped out into the hallway. 'What?' he shouted. 'What do you want?'

'It's a private question.' Mark's face was barely visible through the letter box. 'I can't shout it out in the middle of the street.' His voice lowered. 'People would guess.'

Holy sweet Jesus. Jeremy raised his eyes heavenwards. Flinging open the door so that the child flew spreadeagled on to the hallway carpet, he hissed, 'What. Do. You. Want?'

Mark picked himself up and shook himself off. Then he looked at the door. 'I think you better close it,' he said.

Jeremy wasn't sure what the protocol was for having other people's kids in your house. Weren't there some warnings against it? But then again, if people heard he'd told this boy he was Santa, there'd be more than a few funny looks thrown his way. He closed the door. 'Make it quick,' he snapped, not very nicely, then sort of regretted it when Mark flinched a little. 'I'm just a bit busy,' he lied in a nicer voice.

'OK.' Mark shuffled from foot to foot. 'Well, I just wondered if you need a passport to get to all the different countries on Christmas Eve?'

'No. I don't. Now can you let yourself out?'

'Why not?'

Jeremy rolled his eyes. 'Because I'm magic, that's why.' The child was staring at him. 'I just, you know, hitch up the, the,' he winced, trying to remember, 'the animals and put all the presents in my sled and off we go.' In the front room the audience was laughing at something one of the chefs had said. 'Happy now?'

Mark shrugged. 'Can people go to different countries without passports?'

'No.'

'My daddy is in America and I found his passport today and now I'm afraid he won't be able to get home.'

Oh God, the boy was beginning to blubber.

'He probably got a new one before he went. Ask your mother.'

'I did and that's what she said, only I didn't believe her cause she looked all worried when she saw me with it and now I know she's worried too in case he can't come home.'

Oh no, now there was a tear. It plopped on to the carpet. The boy was trying his best not to cry because he rubbed his hand hastily across his eyes.

'Your daddy couldn't go to America without a passport,'

98

Jeremy said firmly, trying to sound nice but not too nice in case the child kept crying. 'So your mother is right. He would have had to get a new one.'

'Really?'

Big hopeful eyes looked up at him. He'd be a nice looking child if he lost some weight, Jeremy thought. 'Really,' Jeremy confirmed.

There was a pause. Mark nodded. 'OK. Can I ask you one more thing?'

'What?'

'If my daddy can't get home, can you bring him home in your sleigh on Christmas Eve?'

This was a bloody nightmare. 'Santa doesn't deliver people.'

'Instead of my TV?'

What were the odds? The man must have a passport if he got to America so the chances were he'd be coming home. 'Eh, well, yes,' Jeremy promised. 'If I can find him on time. America is a big country, you know.'

'You'll find him,' Mark beamed. 'I know you will. You are brilliant.' He ran across the space dividing them and hugged Jeremy. 'I love you, Santa.'

Jeremy stood quite stiffly for a second before hastily patting the boy on the head. 'Thank you,' he said, and was surprised at how his voice caught. He coughed a little. 'Thank you,' he said more firmly. 'Now you go home and be a very good boy.'

'I will. Bye.' Mark bounded towards the door. 'See you.'

Jeremy nodded weakly and, despite trying to concentrate very hard on *Ready Steady Cook*, found that he couldn't.

He wasn't sure why.

16

ALLIE SAW TESS and Tony sitting together at one of the clinic picnic tables. She was glad that Tess had finally found the courage to visit. It was about time. Tony had already spent nearly four weeks in rehab. He hadn't seemed that bothered by his mother's absence, feeling too ashamed to want her there. Tess had her hand clamped on to Tony's arm. He was doing his best to appear relaxed, though even from across the garden Allie could see the hunched set of his shoulders.

'Hey.' Allie slipped into a seat on the other side of her husband and nodded at her mother-in-law. 'How are you, Tess? I didn't see John's car in the car park. How'd you get in here?'

'Bus,' Tess answered, her voice quivering. She was obviously upset seeing Tony in this place.

'I would have given you a lift,' Allie said gently.

'No, no,' Tess shook her head, her voice still unsteady, 'John offered to bring me as well, but I needed to be alone.'

'Wow! So you hired a private bus?' Tony quirked an eyebrow, grinning.

'Oh you!' Tess playfully slapped his arm, attempting a laugh but it bordered on tears. 'No, I did not hire a private bus. I was in an ordinary bus. I just wanted to be on my own, not making conversation with anyone. John would have talked all the way in. I can't be listening to him.'

'I'm sure he would have stayed quiet if you'd wanted,' Allie said.

'John does not do quiet. He wanted to come in too, but I preferred to be on my own for the first visit.'

'I don't want to see John,' Tony said quietly. 'I told him that already when he rang me.'

Allie and Tess looked at him.

'He never said.' Tess looked puzzled.

'I don't want him to come in here,' Tony muttered, staring at his hands.

'He's not going to judge you,' Tess said. Then she rolled her eyes. 'He's the last one to judge. He can't even get a simple office job.'

'Oh no,' Allie made a face, 'was the interview hard?'

Tess shook her head. 'I have no idea what it was like. All I know is that he got a letter to say thanks but no thanks.'

'Was he upset?'

'Not at all. Nothing upsets that fella. Anyway he's got a job, he says, digging your neighbour's garden.'

Allie nodded. 'Yeah, and he'll be getting a few grand for that.'

'John is digging our neighbour's garden?' Tony looked from Allie to Tess. 'Am I missing something?'

'John dug out and replanted our garden and the old man who lives next door – you'll meet him when you come out – was so impressed that he asked John to do his.'

'John did our garden?' Tony asked. Then as Allie nodded he said, sounding hurt, 'But I was going to do that.'

Allie laughed. 'Tony, believe me, there are a lot of other things you can do in the house.'

'I was going to put up goal posts for Mark.'

'You still can.' There was no way John would get the goal posts up in the next couple of weeks. The grass needed to grow first and that would take time. 'John is just helping us out while you're in here.'

'I'll be out soon,' Tony said.

'I know,' Allie nodded.

'And he might as well help out,' Tess said, sniffing, her upset at one son being replaced by the other, 'because he has nothing else to do. It does him good to be doing something.' She stroked Tony's arm. 'So, how are you?'

'I told you, Tess, I'm fine.'

Allie felt his body tense beside her.

'So, you've just got an ice cream habit?'

'What?'

'An ice cream habit.'

'Ice cream?' Allie winced. 'Tess, it's a drug—'

'An ice cream habit is drug-speak for an occasional fix,' Tess said knowledgably.

'Oh,' Allie shrugged, suppressing a smile, 'right.'

'Well, is it?' Tess peered up at Tony.

'Sort of.' Tony fixed his gaze on the wooden table.

'So you're not going to shooting galleries and mainlining with a host of other junkies?'

'Jesus! Tess!' Tony spluttered on a laugh. 'Are you serious?'

'As serious as drug abuse,' Tess said firmly, her grip tightening on his arm. 'You don't want to be skin popping Tony. That's very bad news. Very bad for you.'

'Have you, like, visited the hood?' Tony attempted an American accent. 'Got down with a few homies?'

Allie laughed.

'I read.' Tess dismissed the joke. 'If my son is taking drugs, well, I want to know all about it.' She stared sternly at him. 'Do you remember when you'd bring friends home from school and I'd have to know all about their parents before you could be let play with them?' As Tony looked in mild exasperation at her, she added, 'Well, it's the same thing.'

'Yeah,' Tony nodded. 'And I used to tell you that I wasn't playing with their parents.'

'You always were a cheeky boy.' She smiled a little at him. 'So, tell me, did you mainline?' She turned to Allie. 'That means inject.'

Allie nodded, amused in a horrified way.

Tony shook his head.

'Well, that's something.' Tess sounded reassured. 'And how long has it being going on? Allie says she doesn't know.'

Tony shot a panicked look at Allie before he mumbled, 'Not long. Just a little while.'

Was almost ten years a little while? Allie wondered. She was chilled a little at his ability to lie to his mother. But maybe it was for the best. Tess would freak.

'So why? Why did you start? You had a lovely wife and two lovely boys and everything to live for.'

'Tess, can we just leave it?' Tony implored her. 'Please. I get enough of that in here.'

'What did you take, then? At least tell me that. I've been reading about speedballs and freebasing and honestly, Tony, it doesn't sound good.'

'I've taken a little bit of everything,' Tony admitted. 'Mostly cocaine though.'

Well, that was the truth at least, Allie thought, though obviously 'a little bit' was Tony's euphemism for 'a hell of a lot'.

'Hash?'

'Sometimes.'

'Junk? That's heroin,' Tess explained to Allie. 'They call it junk because it's mixed with a lot of stuff so it's not pure any more.'

'Oh right,' Allie nodded.

'Rat poison for one thing.'

Allie uttered an obligatory 'Ugh.'

'Talcum powder, though obviously a piece with rat poison is worse than a piece with talcum powder.'

'Piece?'

'One ounce of drugs.'

Tony was staring transfixed at his mother. 'Jesus, Tess.'

'So, have you snorted the big H?' A nod to Allie. 'Heroin. You can call it that too. Or brown sugar, if you like.'

'So brown sugar isn't the healthy alternative to white, then?' Allie asked, as Tony erupted in a guffaw beside her.

'Ha ha.' Tess looked at the two of them. 'That's your problem, right there. You both make a joke of everything.' She wagged a finger at them. 'I'm telling you now, Tony, you stay off the heroin. That's the worst. It stops you caring about things.'

'He's planning to stay off them all,' Allie said, sobering up. 'Aren't you, Tony?'

'That's the idea,' Tony nodded, smiling down at her, looking grateful for her joke.

'Good.' Tess patted his arm. 'Now, would anyone like a coffee? I know I could do with one. Allie?'

'Thanks.'

'Tony?'

'Great, yeah.'

'I hope you're drinking plenty of fluids?'

'Yeah.' He rolled his eyes.

'Don't roll your eyes. I'm your mother, I'm worried about you.' She glanced about, lowering her voice as she said, 'The other people in here don't look like a good influence at all. Have you seen that one over there?' She nodded in the direction of an older man, who wore his hair in a ponytail and had most of his teeth missing. 'He has track marks all up his arm.'

'Yeah, he's a drug addict, Tess,' Tony said, winking at her. 'That's why he's here.'

She ignored him. 'And that poor girl, look how skinny she is. Her clothes are falling off her.'

'That's Veronica,' Tony said, 'and she's sound. She's only a kid.'

'At least you look better than them.' Tess sounded as if she was trying to reassure herself more than Tony. 'You do,' she said. Then added, 'But one of the things it said in my books was not to judge. So I won't judge them.'

'God, they'll be delighted to hear that, Tess,' Tony smirked.

'Stop making fun of me,' Tess picked her bag up from the ground, 'it's true. Judge not and ye shall not be judged.'

'So Simon Cowell is basically fucked then, ey?'

Allie dissolved in laughter at Tony's comment.

Tess rolled her eyes. 'Well, at least you can laugh, I suppose. OK, I'm off to get coffees. Back in a second.'

'Thank Jaysus,' Tony whispered as she left, making Allie smile. 'She was doing my head in. I swear, if I had a terminal illness she couldn't have been as upset.'

'Well, she's had a shock, finding out you're in here.'

'I know,' Tony looked shamefaced, 'I was dreading her knowing.'

'Well, I bet it wasn't as bad as you were expecting.'

'She bawled her eyes out when she saw me,' Tony said. 'She just stood in the middle of the garden and bawled. And the worst thing was, no one looked.'

'Poor Tess.'

He said nothing.

'How are the boys?' he asked after a bit. 'Mark told me on the phone the other night that he's able to do thirty-five keepie uppies now.'

'He practises all day.'

'Good for him.'

'He found your passport the other day, too,' Allie said then. 'You know the way he roots around all the time. God, I nearly died. I had to lie and say you'd got a new one.'

He turned away from her, his smile vanishing, and mumbled, 'Sorry about that.'

She pulled on his arm. 'I didn't tell you to make you feel bad.'

'You lying to the kids makes me feel bad, Al.'

'It's for the best.'

He took a chance and wrapped his arm around her shoulder. He dropped a small kiss on the top of her head. 'I miss you.'

'Miss you too.'

'I miss holding you and kissing you and shagging your brains out.'

'Stop it!'

He laughed. Then stopped before admitting quietly, 'The cravings are terrible.'

'Are they?' She held her breath. He'd never talked about this stuff to her before.

Slowly Tony nodded. 'I could be, I dunno, brushing my teeth and it just washes over me so hard my knees buckle.'

Allie didn't know what to say. In a way it was progress, but in another it frightened her. How could she compete against something that strong? How could the kids compete? 'You have to find some way of ignoring it,' she offered up eventually.

'I'm trying. That's what they try to do in here. Show you that you've got no power over it and to get you to ask for help.' He didn't add that ignoring it was like trying to stop the rain from falling or the sun from shining. No one understood. And no one understood the massive brilliance of the highs either. Though in the last while the highs had lessened and he needed the stuff just to function, to stay normal, to keep him on an even keel. 'I love you, Al,' he said instead. 'I mean, I really do.'

She put her arms around him and he held her.

'Dis is all very cosy.' It was Veronica. 'Way to go, Tony.'

Allie looked up into the eyes of the girl. She was even skinnier close up. Her jeans hung on her hips like washing on a line. A bright pink T-shirt with the slogan *Homer loves Marge* was also too loose. Her arms, which she was making no attempt to disguise, were scarred badly. She smiled, revealing a mouthful of brown teeth. Allie reckoned she'd been nice looking at one stage.

Tony laughed. 'Hi, Veronica. This is my wife, Allie.'

Veronica nodded. 'Howya.'

'I know your sister,' Allie said. 'Is she not here today?'

'She's gone now. She only stayed for a bit. When she saw Fred, she refused to hang about.'

'Fred?' Tony said. 'Is he back on the scene?'

Veronica nodded and a shy smile crossed her lips. 'Yeah, he missed me.'

'He doesn't sound good for you though,' Tony said quietly. 'You'd want to be careful, Vee.'

'Well,' Veronica looked at him, 'if you were available, Fred wouldn't stand a chance. But yer not, so . . .' She shrugged and grinned.

Tony didn't grin back. 'Your sister might be right to get upset.'

'Aw fuck off.'

Tony didn't get offended. Instead he asked, 'You on for the film tonight?'

'Yeah,' Veronica muttered, glowering now.

'See you there, so.'

She flounced off.

'Who is Fred?' Allie asked.

'This guy who keeps messing her around. We keep telling her he's no good but she loves him so . . .'

Allie studied Tony, feeling weirdly left out of things, his arm about her no longer as reassuring as it once was. Tony knew stuff about this girl so presumably she knew stuff about him. Veronica probably understood what Tony was going through better than she did. This girl had probably heard Tony talk about his drug use, something she'd never been privy to. Maybe Veronica saw her as the cause of all Tony's upset. It didn't seem right. She wanted Tony to get better, to be happy, but not to start befriending other women. Tony had never been like that before. He knew how insecure she was over things like that.

'You OK?' Tony asked. 'You've gone all quiet.'

Allie shook her head, knowing that at some level she was being ridiculous. Tony was entitled to talk to anyone he wanted,

107

just like she was. He wasn't like her dad, liable to run off with anything that had a skirt. And, thinking of her dad, she told him about the letter.

'What?'

'Yeah, after all this time he drops a letter asking to meet us. Mum won't go but I think I will.'

'Will you be OK on your own?'

'I don't know.' Allie looked down at the table. 'I'll just have to be.'

'I'll go with you when I get out, if you like.'

'It's next week. You'll still be in here. I wrote to tell him I'd be there.'

'Wrote?'

'Yeah,' Allie nodded, 'I wasn't ready to hear his voice or talk to him. It just seemed easier.'

Tony's gaze dropped to the table, too. His heart plummeted. The one thing he should be able to do for his wife and he couldn't.

'It's OK,' Allie said, nudging him playfully, 'I'll be fine. It's only my lecherous dad whom I haven't seen in years. No big deal.'

Tony didn't smile back. 'I should be there for you. I'm sorry I'm such a bloody mess, Allie. I'm sorry I'm letting you down all over the place.'

'You're not letting me down.'

'I am.'

'Just get better,' Allie said. 'That's all I want.'

'One of the guys left last week,' Tony said, almost wistfully. 'His wife came and collected him. They had this sort of a party for him to say goodbye. He was a nice fella.'

'That'll be you in a couple of weeks.'

'Yeah.' The thought made him shiver slightly.

'So, how have things been?' she asked, ignoring the fact that his expression had darkened. 'How have the counselling sessions gone? Are you getting used to them? You seem to have got to know people, at least.'

'They're OK.'

'Tony,' she squeezed his hand harder, 'please talk to me about it, won't you?'

'It's hard.'

'I have to know what's going on with you. You have to open up. I mean, can you even tell me why you used in the first place? Have you found out yet?'

He turned his head away from her.

'Please?'

'The first time I took something,' his voice came sporadically, as if he couldn't quite get the words out, 'I dunno even what it was, was to get a job I wanted. It gave me confidence.'

'But you have confidence.'

He looked at her as if she were mad. 'Nope,' he shook his head and offered her a rueful smile, 'I've never felt confident in my whole life. The stuff filled a gap.'

Allie didn't know what to say. She had asked, she'd got an answer, and in that answer it took away the Tony she thought she knew. The drug-addicted Tony, but nevertheless the man she knew. The guy she'd always thought had supreme confidence, even though he was edgy at times.

'Why?'

'Why what?'

'Why didn't you feel confident?'

'Aw, I dunno.' He shifted away from her, took his arm from around her shoulders. 'Let's not do this,' he said, sounding slightly sulky. 'I get enough of this during the week.'

'I'm your wife. You talk to a bunch of strangers about this, why can't you talk to me?'

'You just said it!' He shook his head. '*Because* you are my wife.'

'Tony?'

'Look, Allie, I want you to think well of me.'

'I do.'

'You wouldn't if you knew what goes on in here.' He tapped his head. 'So can we not do this?'

'Fine.' She folded her arms.

'You're mad at me now.'

'I'm not.'

'You are.'

'Am not.'

'Are fucking so.' But he was smiling.

Allie knew that that smile was the reason she'd let him get away with so much over the years. Plus the fact he knew her so well. 'OK, I am,' she admitted. 'So stop smiling at me so I can stay mad, right?'

'Looking at you makes me smile.'

'Oh shut up!' She belted him one and he gave her another grin.

'We did have fun, didn't we?' he asked suddenly. 'You know, before . . .' His voice trailed off.

Before he went off the rails completely, she knew he was about to say.

'We did,' she agreed wistfully. And they had. In the early days, they'd had such a laugh. Tony's devil-may-care attitude had appealed to her. He'd got them into pop concerts by inventing elaborate ways to scale the walls surrounding the event, or by distracting the security guards so that she could dodge in unnoticed. Then later, as she'd given up hope of him joining her, he'd always appear at her side, holding aloft pints of warm beer and crisps. He always refused to say how he'd gained entry, teasing her with the mystery of it. Even now, years later, he'd never revealed to her how he'd done it. He'd constantly told her how gorgeous she was and how much he loved her, which she found endearingly at odds with the wild creature he appeared to be.

He had hooked her.

And then, one day, about five years ago, she'd found the valium in his jeans. He'd told her it was a tab, that he used it to keep him on the level.

Allie had been shocked, she hadn't known he needed to be kept on a level. She suggested that he should see a doctor.

He refused.

She persisted but it always ended in an argument. And she justified it by admitting that he never seemed that different. He got up for work, he washed, he still laughed. OK, he'd lost weight, but that in itself wasn't a symptom of anything weird going on.

Then he stayed out one night after an office Christmas party. Rang her at eight the next day to say he missed her but that he was in a friend's flat. A chill had started inside her. There was no way, she thought, that she was going to be like her mother, putting up with infidelities. And so, even though she thought it would break her heart, she demanded to know where he was. The exact address. He'd been a bit cagey, which had fuelled her suspicion and she'd freaked. In the end he had given it to her and admitted that he'd popped some E and hadn't wanted to come home. Allie remembered the relief she felt at finding out he'd done drugs with this male friend and that he wasn't seeing any other woman. Looking back now, she couldn't believe how naive she'd been. But she supposed that she'd convinced herself it was just recreational. And even though a year later he lost his job because he'd gone AWOL for two weeks with no explanation, she had agreed with him when he said his employers had to find some excuse to cut back on staff. He'd only taken some stuff to cope with the stress of maybe losing his job, he'd get another . . .

'We'll have it again,' he said. 'The fun.'

She wondered if they would. Maybe he'd been high all through their early days, it would certainly explain a lot. Though she hadn't the nerve to ask him.

'I promise,' he said.

'Just promise to get better.'

'Here you go.' Tess arrived back with the coffees. One for her and one for Allie.

'Hey?' Tony gawked in dismay as she put a cup of water in front of him.

111

'Caffeine's addictive,' Tess said knowledgeably, 'and you could transfer your addictions to it. I read that in a book I got from the policemen. We can't have you up all night now, can we?'

'Oh, I dunno,' Tony winked at Allie, 'Al never complains when I'm up all night, do you?'

'Tony!' Allie spluttered with laughter. 'Jesus!'

'That's because she's probably asleep,' Tess said, missing the joke completely.

She thought it was nice the way they both kept breaking into laughter through the rest of the visit.

17

ALLIE HADN'T KNOWN what to wear. Obviously she didn't want her dad to think that she'd made any sort of special effort for him, but on the other hand she wanted him to think she looked well. She wanted to appear as though she had thrived since he'd left. In the end, she opted for jeans and a blue T-shirt. The blue suited her, she reckoned, while the jeans looked insultingly casual.

She was standing on the opposite side of the road, so that she could see him as he arrived outside the shop. She figured she'd give it a few minutes before joining him. And then, like a beacon, she saw him across the street, the blue jacket with the red sleeves, just as he'd described. It was the most garish jacket Allie had ever seen on a man verging sixty. He stood tall and straight and Allie winced as she saw that he was also wearing jeans. Huh, she thought, he probably had a Bart Simpson T-shirt underneath the jacket and an ear piercing too. His hair was shaved close to his head and, as Allie watched, he took up position against the wall of Clery's. He peered around, before pulling a packet of fags from his pocket and lighting up.

Being critical of his dress sense was a way to distract herself from the sudden well of emotion she felt at the first view of her dad in years. A lump formed in her throat as she looked over at him and she thought she might cry, so she gulped hard to push it back. How stupid would she look? Her eyes roved over him, taking in every detail, every small movement he made. It was as if the whole world receded and there was just him, across the vast expanse of main road, wearing his big bright horrible jacket. It was too far away to see the finer details of his face, to see if he'd aged. She squared her shoulders and took a step towards the road. Then abruptly hesitated. Someone bumped into her. 'Sorry,' she said automatically.

The person barely acknowledged her apology as he strode impatiently on. What was wrong with people? Allie wondered idly. Then, forgetting the incident, she stood at the edge of the kerb, staring again at her dad. He was straightening his jacket now, maybe regretting the decision to wear it. For some reason, she couldn't quite make the move to cross the road. It hit her suddenly, despite her initial emotion on seeing him, that this was the man who had made her mother's life a complete misery. Oh, he hadn't hit them or come home drunk or anything, just humiliated them with his affairs. Allie remembered suddenly the night she'd found her mother crying softly in the living room. She was perched on the sofa, much bigger than she was now, a box of chocolates on her lap and tears flowing silently down her face, her shoulders heaving with the effort of staying quiet so as not to wake Allie. Allie had stood for a second in the doorway and then, not knowing what to do, she had turned away and crept back up to bed.

And now the man who had caused her to feel such guilt for her inaction that night was across the wide road, casually smoking a cigarette and looking as if he hadn't a care in the world. Looking as if he fully expected to be met by someone. And that someone was her. And what was more, she was on time. Why? Why was she bothering? A flash of bright anger coloured her previous emotion. Why *was* she bothering? Curiosity? Love? Allie shook her head. She didn't know. And what would she talk to him about? He hardly deserved a rundown of her life. And he didn't deserve to be told about Tony.

114

She paused. She saw him glance at his watch. She stared as, with apparent eagerness, he scanned some of the faces walking by. It had only taken him a few months to give up writing to her; a few birthday cards before they, too, had dried up. OK, she probably should have written to thank him or rung him or something, but Allie knew if it was Owen or Mark, she'd never give up. Allie wondered suddenly how long it would take him to give up waiting for her. She took another step and immediately stopped. Why should she turn up on time? She didn't owe him anything. No, she decided, she would wait right here and study him. She would see how long it took before he gave up this time. Not that she expected him to wait two months or anything, in fact she wasn't quite sure what would constitute a long wait. Maybe an hour? Yeah, she decided. If he was there, waiting in an hour's time, she would meet him. She glanced around. People were still walking by her; like a river meeting an unexpected stone, they parted then reformed as they passed her. Allie melted back into the shade of the shop window and decided she would sit down and just wait it out. She would study him and try to gauge him.

Nana and Fintan had prepared cheese sandwiches for lunch, on brown nutty bread. Fintan had squeezed some oranges to make orange juice. Mark quite liked Fintan as a person, but as a minder, he wasn't so sure. No kid would have much fun eating cheese sandwiches and drinking orange juice. In fact, Mark knew that if he went to a friend's house and all he got was a cheese sandwich he would be pretty much disappointed. But Fintan seemed to think that because he cut the sandwiches into diamonds they would taste better.

'Hey look, Mark,' Fintan said in his big booming voice. 'Look at these, aren't they cool?'

'See what Fintan has made for you,' his granny chipped in, her face all smiley.

Mark noticed that his granny wasn't eating cheese sandwiches. Oh no, she had white bread and Nutella. 'I'd like what you're having, Nana, please,' Mark said as politely as he could.

'Me too,' Owen said, making everyone laugh.

Owen was gone real good at talking. And he could do all animal noises now as well. He had been pretty hopeless up till last week – if Mark had asked him what a cow did, Owen would have made a snake noise. He did snake noises for all the animals. But now he went 'moo' and everyone clapped him. He was turning into a cool brother.

'But Fintan made you cheese,' Nana said.

'On wholegrain,' Fintan clarified. 'Brown bread makes you play football better.'

Mark studied his lunch. 'How?'

Fintan went red. 'Well,' he indicated the sandwich, 'it's a well-known fact that all the best footballers eat brown bread.'

'What ones?'

Nana sort of laughed. Mark didn't know why. He didn't think it was funny. In fact, it sounded good: eat brown bread and become a great footballer.

'Oh,' Fintan flapped his arm, 'eh, Pierce Brosnan, Jimmy Connors . . .' He frowned a little. 'Savi Balesteros.'

'I never heard of those footballers,' Mark said.

'Well, they're brilliant.'

'I never heard of them. What does David Beckham eat?'

'Er . . .'

'David Beckham. Ex-Man U?'

'Cheese,' Fintan said then, making Mark's heart plummet. 'He loves his cheese, I read it in the paper.'

'Oh.' That was disappointing. Mark hesitantly lifted the sandwich to his mouth and took a cautious bite. Then another. And chewed. It was OK, he supposed, but not nearly as nice as Nutella.

'Do you want your cheese sandwiches too?' Fintan asked Owen.

Owen glanced at Mark. 'No. Want that.' He pointed to Magda's sandwich.

'Your nana is upset, that's why she's eating that,' Fintan said.

'Want that,' Owen insisted.

Fintan sighed. 'OK. I suppose one would be all right.' He took out some bread and pasted a miniscule amount of Nutella on it for Owen.

'Once I eat this, will you take me outside and see if I've got any better at football?' Mark asked Fintan, feeling a little excited as he chewed the cheese. Maybe he would be able to curl the ball the way Beckham did.

'Of course he will, pet,' his nana said as Fintan nodded.

'You'll have to eat a lot of brown bread though,' Fintan said, 'before any major improvement happens.'

'I will,' Mark nodded. God, he thought, by the time he went back to school, he'd *definitely* get a place on the team.

After fifty minutes, Allie saw her dad look at his watch and scan the street for probably the thousandth time. He wasn't looking so cocky now and part of her began to feel a little guilty. Still, another ten minutes wouldn't kill him. Then she saw him stare at his watch again, scan the street once more and resignedly push himself off from the wall. He was leaving.

Oh God. Is this what she wanted? Did she want him to leave? But he hadn't even hung around for an hour. You'd think he could have rounded his wait off. Whenever Tony had stood her up, Allie had always waited for an hour at least. She had never left after fifty minutes or fifty-five minutes. And why? Because she wanted to meet him. She wanted to give him every chance. Her dad, looking back one final time, began to move away from the shop window.

'Stop!' Allie shouted before she realised it was her. Some people looked then swiftly turned away again. Allie strode out and tried to cross the road but the traffic was too busy.

And her voice wasn't loud enough to carry anyway. Meanwhile her dad's back was vanishing into the distance. She wished she could catch him and yet part of her felt that it served him right. It served him right if he thought he wasn't loved. That was what he fully deserved. Still she attempted to cross, but the lights seemed to be stuck on green.

And then he hopped into a taxi and disappeared from sight.

Fintan was OK at football, Mark thought. He was saving everything.

'Wow, you must have eaten tonnes of it when you were little,' Mark said as he lined up the ball again before kicking it.

Fintan dodged, the ball caught him on the leg and he winced. Jesus that kid was going to kill him.

'Eat what?' he puffed. Who would have thought that standing in goal would be so hazardous?

'Your brown bread.' Mark jogged a little with the ball, kicking it and doing cool moves he'd seen on the telly.

'No, I ate a lot of rubbish.' Fintan could barely get the words out. He'd decided to be in goal after trying and failing to tackle Mark on the pitch. For such a big guy, the kid was fit.

'OK, get yourself ready,' Mark called. He was aware out of the corner of his eye that Robert and the other lads had congregated on the other side of the green. They were watching them. Mark stood up to his full height and placed the ball a little away from Fintan. Then he walked back from it and took a run.

Fintan braced himself and winced as he saw the child thundering full-tilt towards the ball. He'd always hated soccer, being the kid who was never picked in school. Well, he supposed that wasn't surprising, he'd been totally crap at it. Who would ever have guessed that his inadequacy would come back to haunt him like this?

Mark kicked the ball straight at him. Fintan made a half-hearted attempt at a save before it walloped him in the face. His nose started to pump blood.

'Wow!' Mark gawked at him. 'Great save! Wow!'

Fintan's white T-shirt was destroyed. He tried to smile; the pain in his nose was unreal. 'Thanks,' he managed and even that hurt.

'Can I try again,' Mark asked eagerly, unperturbed by the blood.

'Eh, maybe I'll just go and get my nose sorted,' Fintan said. And that *really* hurt.

'OK,' Mark nodded, disappointed.

Mark knew that if he was to score against Fintan it'd take a lot of brown bread. The man was awesome.

When Allie eventually got back, Fintan was splayed in a kitchen chair sipping on some water. There was an ice pack across his nose.

'He was out playing with Mark,' Magda said proudly. 'And Mark had a great time, didn't you, pet?'

'Uh-huh, he's a deadly keeper,' Mark said.

Fintan managed a weary smile.

'Did you hurt your nose?' Allie asked.

'No, no, it's nothing.' Fintan waved her concern away. 'One of the hazards of goal keeping, that's all.'

'So,' Magda asked, 'how did it go?'

Allie winced and tried to feign indifference. 'I didn't bother meeting him.'

There was a small silence and she knew her mother was studying her.

'Was he not there?' Magda asked gently.

Her mother's concern brought sudden tears to her eyes. She blinked them back. 'Oh, he was there, I saw him all right.'

'Oh.' Magda didn't seem to know what to say to that.

'He was dressed a bit young, I thought.'

Magda flapped her arm. 'Oh, that was him all over. He could never accept the ageing process. He'd wear nappies if he thought he'd get away with it.' At Fintan's laughter, she added, smiling at him, 'Now give me a man who's happy growing old.'

Fintan winced, not looking as if he relished the compliment.

'So why didn't you meet him, Allie?' her mother asked.

Allie shrugged, wondering if her mother would think she'd been ridiculous. She wasn't even sure she understood herself. 'I decided that I'd be an hour late and see what happened.'

Her mother chortled with laughter.

Fintan looked vaguely perturbed. 'Why?' he asked.

'Who cares?' her mother said. 'Do him good to know that we're not all waiting for him to reappear in our lives. He thinks he—'

'Anyway,' Allie said quietly, 'he didn't wait for the hour.' Saying the words out loud made it real. He hadn't bothered waiting. Her voice caught at the end of the sentence and then, to her mortification, she began to cry. 'He didn't wait,' she blubbered, thinking that she sounded like a four-year-old but unable to help it. 'After all these years he couldn't wait for an hour.'

'Oh, honey,' Magda said soothingly, the smile dying on her face, 'he's just a fucker.' She heaved herself up from her chair and enfolded Allie in a hug. 'A complete shithead.'

Mark and Owen, who normally would have relished those words, looked on in horror as their mother cried. Then they started to cry too.

'Oh,' Magda flapped her hand, 'don't cry, boys. Your mammy is fine. Fintan, bring the boys out and play some more football, would you?'

Fintan paled. He hauled himself up from the chair and assumed his hearty voice. 'Boys, don't be upset, who's for football?'

Owen and Mark ignored him. Mark pulled on Allie. 'Mammy, what's wrong? Is Daddy not able to come home? Is that what's wrong? Don't worry cause I—'

'It's OK.' Allie pulled herself from her mother's grasp and wiped her eyes. 'I'm fine. It's just that I'm a little sad because the man I was to meet in town left before I met him.'

'Your granddad,' Magda put in for good measure, her hand rubbing Allie's back soothingly.

'Our granddad is dead and Fintan is just a blow-in,' Mark said.

'Oh shit!' Allie said, closing her eyes.

'Your other granddad is dead.' Magda ignored the comment. 'But my husband is very much alive, only he went away and has only come back now. Fintan is a blow-in but he's here to stay.'

'I sure am,' Fintan said, eyeballing Magda and smiling. Then, turning to Allie, he said softly, 'And I'm very lucky to be allowed to stay and to know you all.'

At least that's what Allie thought he said, his voice affected by his inflamed nose.

'Very lucky,' Fintan repeated.

Allie swallowed hard. It was true, Fintan was here to stay. And, she had to admit, he was more a man than her dad had ever been. He made her mother happy and he was always there for her and the kids, too. Was it any wonder her mother wanted to wipe Thomas from her life? Was it any wonder her mother had refused to meet him? The only thing that was a wonder was that Allie had always been a little luke-warm towards Fintan. She attempted a smile. 'Once you play football with the kids, you'll never be allowed to escape,' she joked quietly.

Fintan grinned back at her. 'I'd play football for ever if I had to.'

'You'd play football *for ever*?' Mark said in awe. 'Cool.'

'Well, eh—' Fintan flushed.

'There now!' Magda clapped her hands in delight. 'All sorted!'

Her mother had always been the master of the overstatement, Allie thought in amusement.

18

JEREMY LOOKED OUT his kitchen window, just to be sure that that John fellow wasn't shirking. He wasn't too sure what to make of the lad, with his cocky grin and quite frankly disrespectful attitude. He had arrived at ten that morning, which in Jeremy's opinion was the middle of the day. He'd greeted Jeremy with a 'Yo!' and some sort of a salute, before unloading a big rotavator thingy and hefting it into the back garden. Apparently the rotavator was rented and Jeremy would have to foot the bill. Well, he was not paying for it an hour more than was necessary, that was for sure, so he had to be vigilant and keep an eye on John. It was now one o'clock. Jeremy wasn't sure if the man had brought some lunch with him. He wasn't sure if he would be expected to make John's lunch. He wasn't at all sure of the protocol for employing workmen. He had been rather hoping that John would pop into his sister-in-law's house and get fed, but Allie had taken the boys out to the cinema for a treat. He knew that because Mark had helped John in with some of his lighter tools and had happily told Jeremy this information.

Jeremy watched as John switched off the rotavator and mopped some sweat from his brow. Then he turned to Jeremy and grinned. Jeremy smiled a little weakly back. John wiped his forehead with his discarded T-shirt and started to walk, bare-chested, towards the house.

Jeremy pushed open his kitchen window. 'Eh, have you got your own lunch with you?' he barked out. He thought that was the best way to phrase it. That way it wasn't an invitation to eat with him or to use up all his food. Jeremy especially didn't like eating with people he hardly knew.

'I have, Mr L,' John called out cheerily. 'But it'd be great if you could fire up the kettle and make me a cuppa.'

Jeremy nodded. He supposed he could do that. He filled up the kettle and a couple of minutes later John appeared with a bright blue lunch box. His sandwiches were wrapped rather nicely, Jeremy thought, in sort of flowery kitchen roll, and he had a rather appetising-looking bun, too.

'My mother still thinks I'm twelve years old,' John snorted as he unpacked his lunch.

'I think she has done a commendable job,' Jeremy said stoutly. Really, people these days didn't appreciate anything. Adam, for instance, had bought himself a new mobile phone and last week had tried to foist his old one off on Jeremy. 'Why would I want a broken phone?' Jeremy had asked and Adam laughed. 'This one isn't broken, Da,' he said, 'I just wanted to buy myself a more modern one.' It was a waste of money, that's what it was, Jeremy had told him. Especially when children were starving in the world. Adam had been a bit annoyed at that. He'd put the old phone on Jeremy's table and said that when he was interested in learning how to use it, he would show him and then he'd left. Just upped and left.

'So what's the story with you, Mr L?' John munched on a sandwich, still disconcertingly bare-chested. 'You've how many kids?'

'Two boys. Hardly kids.' Jeremy spoke in short sentences, not wanting to prolong a conversation about his family. He disliked talking about his family. He also disliked being called Mr L. 'One is married, the other not.' Jeremy heated the teapot by swirling hot water around it. Then he put leaves in and poured scalding water on top. He located his strainer.

'You use tea leaves?' John asked, rather obviously.

'Obviously,' Jeremy said.

124

'Cool,' John said.

What was cool about it, Jeremy failed to see.

'How much longer will it take you to rotavate my garden?' Jeremy asked.

'I'll be finished by today. Your garden is a bit uneven,' John remarked. 'I might get a couple of sleepers just to iron it out.'

'Are they expensive?'

'I'll let you know how much,' John said, as he began to munch on his other sandwich. He looked at Jeremy. 'Are you not having any lunch?'

'I might, in a bit.' Jeremy glanced out his window again. 'I see you haven't removed the fungus growing around the oak tree,' he said.

John shook his head. 'The fungus is good for the tree,' he commented. 'It protects the roots and the roots feed the fungus. They sort of depend on each other, you with me?'

'Really?' Jeremy wasn't sure whether to believe this. Was it an excuse to get out of extra work?

'It's ain't pretty to look at, but it's a beautiful relationship,' John said casually. He took a newspaper from his bag and, holding it up, asked Jeremy if he minded if he read.

Jeremy did, very much. But he muttered a grudging, 'Go ahead.' At least he wouldn't have to prolong the conversation.

John spread it across the whole table and began to read, crumbs falling from his sandwich on to the paper. It was one of those papers with naked women on every page, too, so Jeremy exited and went to sit in his front room, that way he could see out on to the street and no one could see him. Those bullies were hanging about together this morning, kicking a ball up and down the road. A few smaller children, mostly girls, were playing together with dolls and such like.

He'd stay here for another twenty minutes and if John still hadn't shifted himself by then, he'd drop a heavy hint about getting back to work. His boys were good workers, always had been. Jeremy had instilled that into them from their youngest days. When Joel was ten, he'd been working in the garden and doing odd jobs for Jeremy every Saturday. Adam had shirked a little but no pocket money had soon sorted him out. Though he'd known that Nelly slipped him money on the sly, he'd pretended not to.

Oh yes, he and Nelly had been a great team, there was no doubt about it.

Two hours later, Joel drove up in his big BMW. His sons had a thing about fancy cars, Jeremy thought. To Jeremy's dismay, Jenny hopped out from the back seat. There was no sign of Lucy or his grandson.

'Hi, Dad!' Joel said jovially as Jeremy opened the door to him. He paused. 'What's that noise?'

Jeremy felt a fleeting moment of satisfaction. 'That is the rotavator,' he pronounced. 'I have someone doing my garden for me.'

'Oh,' Joel smiled. 'Well, good for you. It's about time.'

'It's costing me three thousand euro,' Jeremy went on. 'Not cheap by any means.'

'What are you getting done?' Joel thought it was cheap actually, especially given the state of his dad's garden. It was good to see him taking an interest in something at last. After their mother died, over twenty years ago, his dad had become quite reclusive. Though, as Lucy sometimes jokingly pointed out, that was good for the rest of humankind. And to be honest, his dad hadn't exactly been a social butterfly anyway. Nelly had brought out the best in him; he would have done anything for her. The years after she'd died had been terrible ones – not just for his dad, but for them all.

'He's doing everything,' Jeremy said. 'Grass, decking, flowerbeds.'

'Wow!' Jenny piped up. 'You can have us all over for a barbecue, Granddad.'

Joel snorted back a laugh.

126

'Hmm.' Jeremy looked distinctly unimpressed. 'What are you two doing here anyway? I thought you'd be in work.' He looked accusingly at his son.

'Daddy is off work because my mammy is pregnant and very sick. She has morning sickness, that's what you get when you're pregnant.'

Jeremy coloured. How did this young girl know words like 'pregnant'?

'Lucy is expecting another baby, Dad.' Joel looked a little embarrassed to be admitting it.

'Great. Congratulations.' Jeremy tried to hide his horror behind a smile, so as not to offend Joel. Three children, all small, was not his idea of fun. Especially if they were all as vocal as Jenny.

'She's due in November,' Jenny announced proudly. 'I hope it's a girl.'

'Why?' Jeremy asked.

''Cause *I'm* a girl,' Jenny said as if it was obvious.

'I see.' Jeremy thought that was an incredibly ridiculous statement.

'So,' Joel sat down, 'what have you been up to, Dad?'

'Nothing.'

'Is that boy around from next door?' Jenny asked. 'He was fun.'

'He's gone to the cinema,' Jeremy answered.

Joel was surprised that his dad knew anything about the neighbours. That was progress. And the fact that he'd asked Adam to give the young lad a go in his car had been very thoughtful. Maybe there was hope for him yet. 'You seem to get on with your new neighbours,' Joel ventured.

Jeremy frowned. 'Get on? I hardly know them. Now, would you like tea?'

'Great, thanks.' Joel beamed.

'I'd like orange,' Jenny said. 'Do you ever have orange in the house, Granddad?'

'No, but I have milk and Marietta biscuits.'

'Bummer.'

'Jenny!' Joel admonished.

'You let me say it at home,' Jenny said.

Joel reddened.

'I'll have milk so,' Jenny said grumpily. 'But Granddad, the next time you have to have orange in. What if the boy next door comes in to play? You have to have something for guests.'

'I would never have told my grandparents what to have in their house,' Jeremy said as he strode into the kitchen.

'That's because hundreds of years ago they didn't have orange, stupid,' she chirruped.

Joel winced as Jeremy shot him a reproving look, though Jeremy had to admit he was filled with a sort of shocked admiration at his granddaughter's cheek.

'Hi, I'm Joel.' Joel stuck his hand out and John shook it.

It was one of the hottest days of the summer so far and it had been a mistake to start work on the garden in such heat, but John had to keep going or the old fella would have a fit.

'How you getting on?' Joel asked.

John shrugged. 'It's hard in the heat but I promised your dad that I'd finish the rotavating by today.'

Joel half smiled. 'Well, you better had then. In case you haven't noticed, my dad is *not* the easiest man to get on with.'

'Aw, he's all right,' John said carelessly. 'He's not bothering me anyway, except for peering out the window every ten minutes.'

Joel laughed. 'He says this is costing him three grand?'

'Yeah. It's a fair price.'

'It's more than fair.' Joel indicated the garden. 'You'd want to be on danger money.'

John grinned.

'Can you charge him one grand?' Joel blurted out suddenly. 'Just, you know, tell him you made a mistake. Me and my brother want to pay a grand each, only he won't let us if we offer. He's a stubborn man and, to be honest, he's not that well off.'

'No worries,' John nodded. 'Only thing is he'll probably think I was trying to do him.'

'He thinks everyone is trying to do him, it's not personal.'

'Was he always so . . .' John tried to frame the question tactfully and then wished he hadn't started as a sensitive word to describe Jeremy refused to materialise.

Joel, too, ignored the fact that John had stumbled to a halt. 'Well, that's that then,' he said, slapping his palms together. 'Thanks, John.'

'My nephew thinks he's great.' John tried to make up for his almost-gaff. 'Never stops talking about him.'

'Aw, he's OK, I suppose,' Joel said.

A rapping at the window made them both turn in the direction of the kitchen. 'Let the man get on with his work,' Jeremy hollered. 'I'm paying for the rotavator by the day, you know.'

'Can I take that back?' Joel joked and John laughed.

Allie insisted on feeding him. She wasn't the greatest cook in the world, but John didn't mind. She had a knack of making people feel at home when they walked into her house and the two boys were great craic. And anything was better than going home to his ma, who was still terribly upset over her visits to Tony. John felt like killing his older brother. How spectacularly could one guy mess up? And why, when he had a gorgeous wife and two great kids, would he even want to throw it away? He had adored Tony growing up; he'd followed him everywhere and tried to copy everything his older brother was doing. Tony had mostly ignored him, which only fuelled his adoration. In truth he still looked up to him. It was probably just Younger Brother Syndrome or something. It bugged John that Tony didn't want him to visit. Even though he'd messed up, John would never stop worshipping him.

'Here, I played it safe.' Allie put a plate of chips and sausages in front of him. 'Couldn't go too far wrong with those.'

'I'm starving.' John heaped about four chips on to his fork and shovelled them into his mouth. 'Maybe the office job would have been easier.'

'It would have been more long term, that's for sure.' Allie smiled a little.

'And boring. Can you see me in an office?'

'Yes.'

'Liar!'

Allie laughed. 'So what are you going to do? Tess is dead worried about you.'

'Not as worried as she is about Tony.'

'True,' Allie conceded.

There was a silence. The introduction of Tony into the conversation always caused a little bit of awkwardness. Eventually John asked, 'What will happen when he comes out, Allie?'

She shrugged. She'd been putting off thinking about it. 'The hospital says to try to be as normal as possible. He's to go to NA meetings, that's like AA only for people with drug addictions.' She idly plucked a chip from his plate and squished it between her fingers. 'When he went in first, I was dying for him to come home, but now, well, I don't know . . .'

'Why?'

'Because I honestly don't know who it is that's coming home.' She looked at John. 'He's not like the man I knew. He's much quieter for starters. When I visited him on Saturday, his counsellor told me it was wonderful that Tony had finally admitted that he has a problem.'

'But that's good, yeah?' John paused with a chip halfway to his mouth.

'You'd think so, wouldn't you?' Allie shook her head. 'But somehow, I don't know, I kept a little bit of hope alive that maybe we were overreacting. That Tony could actually control his addiction. It's scary for me that he can't.'

'We'll all help out,' John said. 'When is he due home?'

'The end of next week. I've to go to a family day and he gets out a few days later. Tess is coming with me.'

John nodded. 'And he still doesn't want me there?'

'No. I'm sorry, John.'

'No worries. I'll help when he comes out.'

Allie put her hand on his arm. 'Thanks. You've been brilliant.'

'No,' John said seriously, 'you have.'

'Hey, what was it like having lunch in Mr Lyons' house today?' Mark burst through the door and stopped dead at the sight of Allie and John looking so serious. 'What's wrong?' His eyes were wide.

John turned around and gave a quick grin. 'He made me tea,' he said to Mark.

'Wow! Was it nice?'

Allie chuckled. 'For some reason, he's obsessed with that old man!'

'The best tea I ever had,' John said, nodding.

'And you are fuelling it,' she giggled, thumping John as he patted the seat for Mark to sit up beside him. Smiling, she got up and left them to it.

19

ADAM BOUNDED UP the path, full of the joys of life. Jeremy saw him pause for a second to say hello to the granny of the boys who lived next door. As far as Jeremy could make out, she was Allie's mother. Her name was Magda, which was a perfectly awful name, reminding Jeremy of white maggots that one tied to the end of a fishing rod. Magda was a loud, jolly person who sometimes said the f word, which was perfectly awful too. She had a husband and the two of them seemed to be into sports as they always wore tracksuits. Jeremy didn't think he'd get on very well with Magda. The two boys seemed to like her though, and the husband was great at playing ball with the young lad. In fact, Jeremy had found himself smiling when Mark had kicked the ball into the man's face one day last week.

'Hi, Dad,' Adam called, 'you going to let me in?'

Jeremy wished that Adam would not draw attention to the fact that he was hiding behind his curtains peering out on to the street. Grumpily, he flung open the front door. 'What do you want?'

'Well,' Adam turned to Magda, who was looking over curiously, 'there's a nice greeting.'

Magda laughed loudly and waved at Jeremy. 'Hello, Mr Lyons.'

'Yes, hello,' Jeremy said, flustered. 'In,' he hissed at Adam.

Adam strode in. Yet again, Jeremy noticed that Adam had changed his hair colour. His dirty blond locks were tipped with a violent red now. Awful.

'What happened to your hair?' Jeremy asked.

'Nothing,' Adam was unperturbed. His glance fell to the hall table. 'I see my old mobile phone is still exactly where I put it,' he said lightly.

'Yes,' Jeremy nodded.

'If you bother to learn to use it, you'll find it useful,' Adam said. 'For instance, Dad, if you go out and you miss the bus, you can ring me or Joel and we'll pick you up.'

'I dislike public transport. Too many people.'

'If you have an accident in the house, you'll have it in your hand and you can ring.'

'I have a phone that comes off the hook.'

'If you are out painting the town red and get plastered or take too many drugs, you can ring me.'

'Hilarious.'

Adam grinned cheekily.

'Anyway,' Jeremy turned from him and stomped into the kitchen to put on the kettle – Adam always drank tea when he came, 'what do you want? You hardly just came to pawn your old rubbish off on me.'

'How right you are, Dad,' Adam cocked an eyebrow, 'I didn't just come for that. I came – hey, your garden is looking well.'

John had finished rotavating it and it was all nice and even and all the weeds were dead.

'Yes, well, it'll look better in a week or so when my gardener puts the grass in and does a decking.' He liked saying 'my gardener'. It made him sound in control, something which he suspected his children thought he wasn't.

'Decking, ey? Who's the twenty-first-century man?'

Jeremy sighed wearily. 'So, what do you want?'

'Well,' Adam sat down at the table and rubbed his hands together excitedly, 'do you know the magazine *VIP Inc*?'

Jeremy looked at him as if he were bonkers.

'Well, anyway,' Adam went hastily on, 'I'm their cover story for next month. That basically means that they're doing a

133

massive spread on me and they need old photos of me when I was a kid.'

'Oh,' Jeremy nodded.

'So, I was wondering if I can go through some pictures you might have and pull a few out?'

'Sure, fine.' Jeremy got to his feet. 'The old photograph albums are in the back room somewhere.'

Adam bounded in ahead of him, eager as a puppy. Jeremy wondered when his son would ever actually become a man. Everything he did carried the enthusiasm of a child. A sort of forced brightness, in Jeremy's opinion.

Jeremy watched as Adam began to haul books this way and that. There were a lot of books in this room. Jeremy didn't like throwing books out. Books on shelves, books on the floor, books resting on an armchair. Books in heaps across the table. Books on the windowsill, blocking out a lot of the light. Adam just hauled them out of the way, not caring that the encyclopaedias fell from the armchair with a crash.

'Careful,' Jeremy said.

'Sorry.' Adam didn't pick them up though.

Several minutes later he found the two photograph albums and sat cross-legged on the floor, examining them. 'Hey, Dad, come and have a look.'

Jeremy didn't really want to. He never looked at photographs and he hadn't looked at these ones in about twenty years. 'I'll be in the kitchen,' he said, and exited as quickly as he could.

Forty minutes later, when Jeremy should have been in bed, as it was a weekday, Adam arrived back into the kitchen with five photos. 'Is it OK if I take these, Dad?' he asked. He spread them out on the table. 'And could you tell me about them so I can tell the journalist?'

Jeremy winced. He was tired and it was late but he hadn't wanted to go to bed as Adam might think it odd that he slept with a big iron bar beside him. He wasn't going to be one of those old men that people talked about on the news who got attacked in their homes by young thugs looking for drug money. No way, he'd be the old man that had smashed some young fella's skull in if they so much as came near him.

'This one for instance.' Adam held a picture out towards him. 'Where was this taken?'

Jeremy reluctantly studied it. It was a picture of the two boys. Joel, looking all happy and skinny in a pair of denims and a stripy blue and white jumper. And Adam, looking grumpy, dressed in a matching outfit, only in a bigger size, and with his arm around his brother. Both stared fearlessly into the camera lens. 'That was taken in the back room there.' Jeremy swallowed hard. 'Your, your mother had bought you those new outfits for Christmas. She thought you both looked cute. It was Christmas Day.'

Adam smiled a little. Christmas when they were kids used to be fun. The fun had sort of melted away over the years since their mother had died.

'And this?'

Adam, alone this time. Jeremy balked. His son had appeared in a local show. He'd been a reindeer and had worn tights and sported a fluffy white tail. With his bright blond curly hair and angelic face, he looked like a girl. Jeremy had been appalled, though he had tried not to show it as Nelly had been so proud of her son. 'You. In a pantomime. I think you were about four. You must remember that.'

Adam shrugged. 'I find it hard to remember all the stuff before Mum died,' he admitted. 'I think it's because things went all weird then.'

'Things did not go weird,' Jeremy spluttered.

Adam didn't reply. Instead he studied himself at four and smiled.

'What do you mean things went weird?' Jeremy made quote signs with his fingers on the word 'weird'.

Adam shrugged. 'Nothing, Dad, forget it. Tell me about this?'

A picture of the four of them, taken by some stranger. Adam and Joel, posing in swimming trunks, big grins, gappy teeth and luminous white bodies. Jeremy stole a look at Adam. His son must definitely use a sunbed or something, he thought suspiciously. His gaze returned to the photo. He studied himself, he was much straighter and a lot more handsome than he was now. He was a fine man in his youth, he had to admit. A taller, thinner version of Joel. And Nelly. Well, she'd just . . . Jeremy swallowed a little. How had this photograph survived at all? In the months after her death he'd taken all pictures of her and put them in the attic, finding it too painful to see her in photo frames around the house or anywhere else. Nelly had been a stunner. Well, at least in Jeremy's eyes. She'd been tall too, with curly black hair and black eyes and she'd made him laugh. He was laughing in the picture at something she'd said. He'd always been a very serious man but she was a woman, he supposed, and hence not as competitive as a man, so she could afford to be light-hearted about things. Or maybe it was nothing to do with competitiveness; maybe she just loved fun. And she had made him laugh. Made him feel good. Alive. 'I don't want you to use this,' he said.

'What?' Adam looked incredulously at him.

'Your mother might not have liked to be in a magazine.'

'Dad,' Adam said gently, 'she's dead a long time now. She won't care.'

'How do you know?' Jeremy held on to the picture. 'You can't know that. Your mother was a private person.'

'She was not!'

'You just admitted that you can't remember,' Jeremy shot back.

'I can remember her,' Adam said.

'And so can I.'

Adam made an exasperated noise. 'I need pictures of my family for the magazine.'

'If you'll excuse me, I have to go to bed.'

'So I can't use any pictures of Mum?'

'Or me. I definitely don't want to be in a magazine.'

'No one would recognise you,' Adam said. 'You've changed.'

'Thank you for reminding me of my mortality,' Jeremy said back, miffed. 'Now, if you're finished you can close the door on the way out.'

'Please, Dad?'

'Sorry.'

'Great.' Adam watched his father ascend the stairs. 'Oh, by the way,' he called up, 'I've a family ticket here for the kids next door to come and see me at my Christmas show. Maybe you'd like to give it to them?'

Jeremy closed his bedroom door. Hard.

Adam sighed and picked up the remaining pictures, tucking them into his jacket. He left the ticket on the table. It'd do his dad good to talk to the neighbours.

'Bye, Dad,' he shouted up. 'See you soon.'

Jeremy heard the front door slam and sank weakly down on to his bed. He paused for a second before reverently looking at the photograph again, studying it. His finger traced the line of his wife's immortalised face, wishing he could peel back time and touch it for real. It was a physical ache. An ache he'd been avoiding for a long time. An ache he intended to avoid for a long time to come. 'Oh Nelly,' he said softly. 'My Nelly.'

And he felt the strange lump in his throat again. The one he'd got when Mark had hugged him. He wondered if he had some sort of a cancer.

Placing the picture under his pillow, he got undressed and went to bed.

20

TESS TOOK ALLIE'S hand and together they sat down in the centre of the circle. Tony was opposite them, clutching a piece of paper and swallowing nervously. Allie had told Tess what to expect, though she hardly knew what to expect herself. She'd been told that Tony had to apologise to his significant others and that they would then get a chance to explain to him how his drug-taking had affected them. It was weird to sit in the middle of a group of strangers. She spotted Veronica, lounging in a chair, her skinny arms folded, her dark hair falling across half her face. Her hair looked ridiculously healthy.

A hush descended on the room as the counsellor welcomed everyone and their families. 'OK, we'd like to say hello to Allie, Tony's wife, and Tess, Tony's mother, today.'

There was a chorus of welcomes from the group and Tess amused Allie by waving her left hand and inclining her head, like the Queen. 'Thank you,' she mouthed.

Tony flinched.

'Now,' the counsellor continued, 'over the last few weeks Tony has been part of our group, and it is almost time for him to leave. He's been sharing with us and today he has something to say to his wife and his mother, haven't you, Tony?'

Tony nodded and unfolded the page he was holding. 'This is, eh, a list of stuff I've done that I'm ashamed of. And that I want to apologise for.' He looked around at the group before fixing his eyes on Allie.

'Oh you don't have to do that,' Tess said soothingly. 'Sure

you know we love you.' She turned appealing eyes to the counsellor. 'Does he have to do that? Is it really necessary?'

'Tony?' the counsellor asked.

'It's necessary,' Tony said, without looking at his mother.

'I suppose it's sort of like going into confession, is it?' Tess said then. 'And telling the priest all your sins?'

'Yeah, a bit, I guess,' Tony shrugged. He hadn't been to mass, let alone confession, in decades.

'I always like a good confession,' Tess admitted to the group. 'It does the heart good.'

'Tess,' Tony appealed. 'Can I, like, get started now?'

'Oh, yes, right.' Tess smiled at him. 'I'm sure it won't take long, sure what sins would you have?'

Someone in the group guffawed.

Allie bit her lip. She was sure this wasn't meant to be funny.

'Well, actually,' Tony swallowed hard, 'I've quite a lot of sins.' He paused before admitting to her, 'I've been on drugs since I was about twenty.'

'Twenty?' Tess blinked, confused. 'But you told me—'

'I lied,' Tony said simply.

There was a silence as Tess took that in. 'Oh.'

Allie gave Tess's arm a gentle squeeze. Tess caught her hand and held on to it.

'Right so,' she said, trying to sound brave. 'Well, off you go then.'

Tony nodded. 'OK.' He swallowed hard and, staring intently at his list, he confessed in a low voice, 'I married you, Allie, without telling you about the drugs. I was high quite a few times when we were going out together.'

'I kind of knew that,' Allie said.

'Yeah.' Tony's leg began to jiggle. 'OK, well, eh, I frightened the kids more times than I can count. More times than I can even remember, I suppose. Once,' his eyes met Allie's, 'once, I even shouted into Owen's face when you were out and he, he . . .' Tony shook his head and squeezed his

139

eyes shut. 'He just froze. Then I yelled some more. Then Mark led him out of the room. I made Mark swear not to tell you.'

Allie flinched. 'When was that?' she whispered.

'Um, about six months ago.' His leg wouldn't stop moving. 'When I was clean for a couple of months, d'you remember?'

Allie nodded slowly. She'd left him in charge of them for the night, one of the few times she'd trusted him. He'd got wasted a week or so later. 'Was it the night I went out with the girls from work?'

'Um, yeah, I think so.'

Allie didn't know what to say to that. Why the hell had she trusted him? She suddenly felt angry at herself and even angrier at him.

'Will I go on?' Tony asked, sounding nervous.

Allie didn't reply, just continued to stare in disbelief at him. He'd yelled at Owen. Poor little Owen. She wanted to kick herself for trusting him. She wanted to kick him for burdening Mark with the secret. She should have known, though. She should have . . .

Tony went on despite her silence. His voice shook. 'I, eh, took money from our joint account and spent it. I took Mark's credit union book one day and took money out. I gave him half and kept the rest. I crashed the car and told you someone had crashed into me. I stole money from your savings jar in the kitchen, Tess.'

Tess's head shot up. 'When?'

'A couple of months ago.'

'I blamed John for taking it.'

Tony nodded. 'I figured you would.'

'Oh, Tony.' Tess blinked. 'All you had to do was ask.'

'It was easier to steal than tell lies about why I wanted it.'

'Was it?'

Tony nodded.

'OK,' Tess said in a small voice.

'Will I go on?' Tony asked the counsellor, not sounding as if he wanted to.

'Yes.'

He heaved a sigh. 'OK. I, eh, pretended I was working late when all the time I was wandering off trying to score.'

Allie had already guessed that. No one could work as much as Tony and earn so little.

There was a small silence. 'And that's it. My inventory.' He sounded relieved. 'I'm sorry, Allie. Sorry, Tess. I swear I'm going to make amends when I get out.'

'Oh, well done,' Tess said emotionally. 'Well done.'

Tony turned to Allie. 'Al?'

'I hope you mean it,' she said quietly. She was wondering if she was meant to feel all forgiving or if the anger she felt at him was normal. 'I don't think you know what you put me through.'

'What did he put you through?' the counsellor asked.

Where did she start? At the beginning, she supposed. 'He fooled me,' she said, sounding bitterer than she'd intended. 'I married a fun-loving guy and ended up with a drug-taker.'

Tony bowed his head.

'Tony?' the counsellor asked.

Tony heaved a sigh and looked hopelessly at Allie. 'All I can say, Allie, is that with the drugs,' he winced, desperate to explain, 'well, when I was fun, I was more me than I ever was without them.' He crumpled up his inventory and appealed to the group. 'I am that person, I think. I'm just stuck. I can't, I dunno, connect with the world when I'm not using.'

Tess was looking bewildered. 'Connect?' she said.

'I never meant to fool you about who I was,' Tony said. 'The rest of the stuff,' he held up his crumpled paper, 'well, yes, that was fooling you and I'm sorry for it.'

'Why can't you connect?' Tess asked. 'Connect with what?'

'With anything,' Tony said. 'I just feel as if everyone else has a script and I don't. I find it hard to live in the real world.'

'A script?' Tess glanced in frustration at the counsellor. 'Does this make sense to you?'

'He means that he never knew where he stood with people, he always felt left out of stuff,' Veronica piped up. 'You feel isolated, you don't know what people want of you and drugs let you belong. I felt like that too.' She glanced at Tony who looked gratefully back at her.

'Belong to what?' Tess asked, sounding a little distressed. 'I don't understand all this. Do you understand, Allie?'

Allie shrugged. It hurt that he said he couldn't connect. It hurt that he'd made Mark keep secrets. It hurt that she suddenly felt angry at him again when all along, whilst he was in here, she'd felt sorry for him.

'Allie?' the counsellor said softly. 'Have you anything to say?'

She bit her lip. Slowly she raised her eyes to Tony's face. Whatever he saw in them made him flinch. 'You better start bloody connecting,' she said. 'It's not my fault or Mark's or Owen's that you are like this. It's not your mother's fault that you don't connect, whatever that is. It's yours.'

'I know that,' Tony answered. He turned to the counsellor and said desperately, 'I told you she'd hate me if I confessed everything. I told you.'

'Oh get over yourself,' Allie snapped. 'You confessed! Bloody hell, you put me through hell and I still haven't got rid of you. A confession is nothing.'

'What hell did he put you through?' the counsellor asked.

Allie shook her head, regretting her outburst.

'You can tell me,' Tony said, sounding resigned. 'I'd like to know.'

'And then you can tell me how you can't connect,' Allie said. 'I mean, I thought we got along.'

'We do.'

'So why?'

'You'll think I'm blaming you.'

'Oh, believe me, I won't.' God, she thought, she sounded bitter. Was she really that angry at him? If so, she hadn't acknowledged it until now.

'OK.' Tony sat up straight in his chair. 'OK. Right, you asked me to tell you, I'm telling you.'

He sounded angry now, Allie thought, taken aback.

'Well, for one thing, you always make me feel like a complete and utter failure. You want perfection in a partner and I can't give that.'

'Pardon?' God, was he blaming her? If so he had a bloody nerve.

'You want the perfect family. Fully functioning father, doting mother and two kids.'

'Yeah? So? I certainly don't want bloody dysfunction. Do you?' It was no use. She was angry. So angry she could spit. What was he on about?

'You're getting annoyed,' Tony said. 'Please don't get annoyed, Al.'

'You're getting annoyed too,' she countered. Then when he didn't reply, she went on, 'So, what sort of a family do *you* want? Come on, tell me!'

Tony flinched, his momentary anger gone.

'Now, now,' Tess said, trying not to sound alarmed, 'calm down, Allie.'

'Explain how I'm at fault,' Allie demanded. 'You were on drugs before you met me, Tony, so you can't pin things on me!'

'I'm not pinning things on you, Al. It's just the expectation you had of me was unrealistic. I can't, you know, be perfect for you.'

'I never asked for that!'

'You did, not in words exactly but—'

'And giving up the drugs is not being perfect. It's just being normal!'

'I know that. I just . . .' He paused and gulped. 'Well, all my

143

life I've tried to live up to expectations and I just feel that it's too hard.'

'All your life?' Tess, now, sounded miffed. 'What do you mean all your life? I never made you live up to anything.'

'I know but—'

'But what?'

'They were in my head, these expectations. You know, because I wasn't really your son and—'

'You were my son.' Tess looked at the group. 'What sort of things has he been telling you?'

'I wasn't your real son!' Tony was shouting now. 'I wasn't. OK, you tried to make me feel like I was, but I wasn't. And in order to make myself feel like I was, I tried to fit in, to do the same job Dad did, to be bloody perfect, to not give you any trouble. But fuck it, I couldn't.' He stood up. 'I didn't.'

Then he walked out of the room.

Tess needed a cup of strong coffee. Loads of sugar. Allie needed to go home and cuddle her boys and feel their solid little bodies and smell the fresh scent of their hair.

They both felt trapped in the gaze of the counsellor, who was talking to them and explaining that the session hadn't been a disaster. Tony's trigger, apparently, was the expectations that he felt were being put on him. It was good that he had said it, the counsellor felt, because he'd been avoiding the issue for ages. Of course it hurt, he explained, but Tony did understand that the expectations were only in his own head.

'He equates love with being perfect,' the counsellor explained.

Allie wondered how he could when he'd failed so badly at being perfect. He hadn't even tried to be perfect. Just different. But she didn't say that. That wouldn't be productive, she felt. As the counsellor talked and Tess slurped noisily on her sweet coffee, Tony sat, head bowed, beside her.

'I have loved this man for the last ten years,' Allie eventually said. 'Now I just feel so angry at what he's done.'

'That's normal,' the counsellor said.

'I mean,' Allie went on, barely hearing him, 'he didn't confess anything I didn't already suspect. Well, except the bit about yelling into Owen's face and getting Mark to keep it a secret.'

'I knew you'd go mad at that,' Tony admitted. 'But I had to tell all the stuff I did. It wouldn't be honest otherwise. That's part of the steps.'

'Making us feel bad is part of the steps?' Tess said as she tossed another mouthful of coffee back. 'Great.'

'He's not trying to make you feel bad,' the counsellor explained. 'It's got nothing to do with you, it's all in his own mind.'

'Oh, so telling me I'm not his real mother shouldn't hurt.' Tess drained her cup and set it on the table. 'I was a real mother to him. I did everything a real mother should do.'

'I wasn't trying to hurt you,' Tony echoed the counsellor.

'Then you shouldn't have said it,' Tess snapped.

'The fact that I've never said it before is probably part of the reason I'm in here!'

'Oh.' Tess stared at Tony in horror as her eyes filled up. 'That's, that's . . .'

'I never felt I could say it,' Tony went on softly. 'You were trying so hard to believe I was yours. How could I shatter that?'

'I wasn't trying hard, I did believe it.'

Tony turned away from her in dejection.

Allie felt sick. Today was meant to build a bridge, to make things better, not pull down everything Tess and she had always believed. 'So what happens now?' she asked the counsellor.

'What do you want to happen?' he asked.

She knew what she would have said if asked yesterday. She wanted her husband home, she wanted things to be normal, and she wanted a proper family life. But was that putting expectations on Tony? 'I don't know,' she muttered.

'Do you want me to come home?' Tony asked suddenly, sounding a little apprehensive. 'If not, I'll go somewhere for a while. I can—'

'Of course I want you to come home.' Unexpected tears shone in her eyes. 'You're my husband, the kids would miss you. How can you ask that?'

'I just thought if you're mad at me then . . .' He let the sentence hang.

'I still want you to come home.'

Tony looked upwards, his eyes shining. 'Thanks,' he said without looking at her. Then he brought his gaze to hers. 'Thanks.'

'You can't help it. I know that. I swear, we'll work on it.'

'Yeah.' He swallowed hard. There was a silence while he finally seemed to get himself under control. 'Tess,' he turned to his mother, 'you really are great. It's just me, I have to sort stuff out in my head. It's going to take a while.'

She nodded briskly. 'I need another coffee,' she answered, sounding as if she might cry and not looking at him. 'I'll just be outside.'

Tony's gaze followed her from the room. 'I knew she'd take it badly,' he muttered after the door had closed behind her.

Then why had he said it? Allie wondered. Didn't people live with their feelings rather than hurt others? Wasn't that what being considerate was all about? But she bit her tongue because he *had* said it and there was no point in making him feel guilty about it. Wasn't guilt another trigger for drug-taking? It was all so bloody confusing. She thought him getting better would make everything better, but it didn't. It seemed to be making things worse. 'I'll talk to her for you,' she promised instead.

'Ta.' Tony managed a small smile. 'I will too when she forgives me.'

'Right,' the counsellor said, looking from one to the other, 'that was good work, Tony. Well done. Well done to you too, Allie. It can't have been easy.'

Understatement of the year goes to Tony's counsellor, she thought.

'So, I think we'll leave it at that for now, if it's OK with you two?' He stood up.

Tony nodded and rose to his feet, too. As Allie watched him, she suddenly experienced a longing quite unrelated to the hurt she felt. She longed for one of his big grins, his foolish jokes, and his sparkly-eyed humour. And she forlornly wondered if that was all lost with the drugs.

The counsellor came out from behind his desk and opened the door for her.

'Thanks,' she said, passing him.

Tony followed her out. He touched her briefly on the elbow. 'I will make it up to you,' he said earnestly. 'I swear.'

'OK.'

'And please tell Tess that I want to talk to her, will you?'

'Sure.'

There was a silence. Tony opened his mouth to say something but Allie, fearing what it might be, cut him off. 'I'd better go. My mother and Fintan have to go out later.'

'Yeah. Sure. OK.' He made to kiss her but somehow his lips only made contact with her cheek.

'I'll see you next week,' she said as she busied herself with her handbag.

'Sure.' Tony watched as she turned hastily and began walking rapidly away. He knew she was crying but there wasn't a single thing he felt he was able to do about it. If someone had offered him a fistful of coke right at that moment, he would have taken it. No question.

'Hey, you.'

Allie stopped abruptly and turned around. Veronica was there, standing awkwardly, her arms wrapped about her skinny frame, her legs crossed. She looked embarrassed.

Allie smiled a little and hoped her red eyes didn't give her away. 'Hi. Veronica, is it?'

Veronica nodded, her dark hair falling across her face. She pushed it back with stick-like fingers. 'He was only trying to be honest,' she blurted out. 'It's important in here. Honesty.'

147

Allie blinked.

'He means it but he doesn't,' she said. 'It's the way he thinks. It's true for him but not true, you get me?'

Allie nodded, wondering what Tony had been saying to all these people.

'He thinks you're great,' Veronica said wistfully. 'I listen to him talk and I know that. It's nice.' Then she shrugged and turned on her heel.

Allie watched her go, wishing that she could understand her husband as well as Veronica seemed able to. 'Bye,' she called out.

Veronica didn't acknowledge it.

21

T ESS SNIFFED LOUDLY and blew her nose all the way home.
Nothing Allie said to comfort her did any good, so she was
silent for the last fifteen minutes of the car journey. She knew
that Tess was in shock, her golden boy exposed as a serial
junkie, lying and stealing from her money jar. Allie had felt
like that when she'd finally confronted the truth about Tony.
Even though the evidence had been right in front of her eyes
for years, she'd refused to put all the pieces together. It hurt
too much to think that he'd rather put all their savings up his
nose than be fully with her and Mark and Owen. It was a
rejection, she guessed. As if she wasn't good enough or inter-
esting enough to keep him with her.

As Allie pulled up at Tess's, she asked, 'Is there anyone inside
for you, Tess?'

'John is there,' Tess said, dabbing at her eyes, which had
gone all red and swollen. 'I hope he's not secretly taking
anything because he thinks I put expectations on him.'

'He's unemployed and loving it,' Allie reminded her with a
smile.

'Yes,' Tess spluttered out a teary laugh, 'I suppose so.'

Allie switched off the engine and patted Tess's hand. 'Tony
is in trouble, Tess. He's trying to sort himself out. I'd overlook
a lot of what he says, you know.'

'How can I? He blames me and his dad.'

'He doesn't. He was always saying nice stuff about you when
I met him. In fact,' she remembered suddenly, 'he said that if

his real parents had stayed around, he'd probably be on a lot more drugs.'

'He actually said that?'

'Yep.'

'Oh. OK.' Tess paused, her hankie halfway to her eyes. 'Well then, I suppose I should be glad he's only on a little bit of drugs. I'll offer it up.'

Allie smiled despite herself.

'Hey!' John tapped on the passenger window of the car. They hadn't noticed him at all. 'How'd it go?' Then as his mother rolled down the window, a look of apprehension crossed his face. 'Ma? Are you OK? What happened?'

'Do I put expectations on you?' Tess asked. 'Do you feel under pressure to perform?'

'Sorry?' John looked questioningly at Allie.

'Something Tony said, I'll let your mother explain.'

'OK.' John's gaze had drifted back to his mother. 'Come on, Ma.' He opened the car door for her and gently helped her out. Putting his arm about her shoulders, he squeezed her reassuringly. 'Let's go get a few whiskeys into you.'

'You dreadful boy,' Tess half laughed.

'That's what my ex-girlfriend used to say,' he joked as he led her up to the front door. He turned back to Allie just as they went in. 'Are you coming in?'

'No, I'd better get back. My mother is going out later.'

'Will you be OK?'

'Yeah. Yeah, I'll be fine.'

'Sure?'

'Positive.'

'OK.' He smiled at her before turning his attention back to his mother.

Tess was lucky to have him, Allie thought idly, as she fired the engine. He might be a dosser, but he was a very kind dosser. Then again, he'd made huge progress on Mr Lyons' garden, so he couldn't be too lazy. Maybe he just needed the right job.

She watched as he patted Tess on the back and gently led her into the hallway. With a pang she realised suddenly that not once in their marriage had Tony ever done that for her. He'd never comforted her. Not once.

She gave her mother and Fintan the bare details of the visit, trying not to show how upset the whole thing had made her. If she cried, her mother would only start giving out about Tony and Allie didn't want that. And she didn't want Fintan getting in his tuppence-worth either. Though in fairness to Fintan, he spent most of his time trying to stop Magda from saying things. She outlined the visit as best she could but it was difficult as she had to speak in a sort of code because Mark and Owen were hovering about, looking for attention.

'So your friend upset his mother?' Magda said, shaking her head and making her curls bounce about. 'Well, well.'

'I'm sure he didn't mean to,' Fintan interjected. His voice came out sounding funny. Allie felt a twinge of guilt. His nose had gone a purply black.

'His mother?' Mark screwed up his face. 'Did you not go out with a girl, Mammy?'

'A boy and a girl,' Allie said hastily. 'Why don't you and Owen go out the front and play, Mark?'

'You never said you were going out with a boy,' Mark said. 'Did he just turn up out of the blue?'

'Yep.'

'Wow. How did he know you were meeting your other friend?'

'She told him.'

Magda sighed and looked accusingly at her. Fintan poked Magda in the arm, mouthing a 'Shut up' at her. Magda poked him back.

'Is this man nice?' Mark asked.

'Yes,' Allie squirmed, trying to ignore her mother's sighs.

'Is he nicer than Daddy?'

'No,' Allie said. 'He's not nicer than Daddy. And do you

151

know what?' She hunkered down and brought her face level with her eldest son's. 'I have a surprise for you.'

'What?'

'Daddy is coming home some time next week!'

There was a moment's silence before Mark cheered. 'Hear that, Ownie!' he said, crouching down too so he could be on his brother's level, 'Daddy is coming home. With presents for us and a kiss for Mammy!' He made a big slurpy sound on the word 'kiss'.

Owen regarded Mark for a second before taking his cue from him and beginning to cheer also.

Magda put her hands over her ears at the noise. 'Right, well, I'll ring you later,' she said loudly.

'You're going out,' Allie reminded her.

'Yes, and we'll ring you when we get back.' She lifted her coat from the back of a kitchen chair and handed Fintan his. 'Talk then.'

'I can hardly wait,' Allie said with a small grin.

'Neither can we,' Magda replied.

Later, Allie found Mark sitting on his bed. He seemed to be writing something on some yellow paper. When she came in he covered it with his hand before admitting sheepishly, 'It's just a letter to Santa.'

'Wow, you're getting in early, aren't you?' she said, amused. 'What do you want?'

'Just a television for my room. That'd be cool.'

'Oh, well, I'm sure he'll manage that.'

'Yeah, I think he will.' Mark carefully folded up the letter and put it in the envelope, which he had decorated with a picture of a sled.

'Will I post it for you?' Allie couldn't wait to read it.

'No,' Mark shook his head, 'I'll do it myself.' His grip tightened on the paper.

Allie left it. She'd have a little read when he'd gone to sleep later on. Then she'd scan it into her computer so she could keep it. She watched as Mark placed the envelope on his bedside locker and turned expectantly to her.

'Isn't it great about Daddy?' she asked.

'Yeah,' he nodded. 'And maybe he'll put some stars up on my ceiling like he promised.'

'I'd say he will,' Allie smiled. She sat in beside him and tousled his thick dark hair. 'Can I ask you something?'

'Uh-huh.'

'When I was talking to Daddy a little while ago, he told me that he'd asked you to keep a secret from me, do you remember it?'

Mark frowned. 'A secret?'

'Yeah.' Allie nodded encouragingly. 'About maybe Owen?'

'A secret about Owen?' Mark appeared genuinely puzzled.

'He said,' Allie went on carefully, 'that one night, oh, ages ago, he yelled at Owen and that you looked after Owen and that he told you not to tell me?'

'That happened loads of times,' Mark said easily. 'He always said not to tell you.'

Allie flinched. 'Loads of times?' she asked faintly.

'Yeah, he'd shout and one time he smashed a cup when I asked him why my orange was all diluted, and then he said sorry and not to tell you. He was scary but then he explained it and said he was worried about things. So I said not to worry.'

She hadn't left him in charge of the kids that many times, surely? But maybe she had. After all, she'd bought into his lies for years.

'Are you OK?' Mark asked her, cocking his head to one side. 'You look all worried, Mammy.'

'I'm fine.' She caught his pudgy face between her hands and kissed his nose. He uttered an 'Ugh' and tried to twist away from her and they both laughed.

'Daddy says,' Allie began, trying to phrase it carefully, 'that if he ever shouts at you again, or does anything like break cups, that you have to tell me. Even if he says not to, you have to. Do you understand?'

'Why?'

'Because I told Daddy that I'd like to know and he said that was OK. He just has a habit of telling people not to say things, he doesn't really mean it.'

'Oh.' Mark thought about that. It was confusing. 'Is it like a habit I have of chewing my nails?'

'Sort of.'

'And a habit Owen has of picking his nose?'

'Ugh!' Allie made a mock-horrified face.

'It's OK, Mammy, he doesn't eat it,' Mark said seriously.

For the first time that day, Allie laughed. 'Stop!' she giggled.

'He just puts it on his pyjamas.'

Mark yelped as she hugged him more fiercely than she'd ever hugged him before.

Allie couldn't find the letter Mark had written to Santa that night, though she searched all over his room. She hoped he hadn't thrown it out or torn it up. Still, she thought, there was bound to be more letters, especially coming up to Christmas.

She'd just wait until then.

22

JEREMY SIGHED AND hung up. Adam had called and asked if he could visit. It was unusual for Adam to arrive in the evening on a weekend. He normally called in on weekdays, in the afternoons, very rarely in the evening. It disrupted things for Jeremy. Saturday was the one evening he stayed up late as he always looked forward to his Saturday night movie; it was a bit of escapism. He liked thrillers the best as there was rarely any nudity in them. Not that he was a prude, but he got embarrassed with all that kissing, especially if the boys were in the room. He knew Adam would insist on talking about something or other, a vain effort to keep Jeremy's mind active in case he was planning on going senile or something, and with all that talking Jeremy reckoned that he'd probably miss the movie.

Still, the one thing that stopped him from getting too annoyed was that Mark had written him another letter telling him that he was off the hook. Jeremy wouldn't now have to get his imaginary sled out to bring Mark's dad home on Christmas Eve. It was quite a nice letter too, Jeremy thought. Very polite and friendly. In fact, Mark was a very kind little boy, Jeremy thought. And he'd done a good drawing this time. Practice made perfect, that's what Jeremy thought. Though the sled didn't look as if it was particularly aerodynamic, having, as it did, only one wheel. But it was a weight off Jeremy's mind. He had been worrying quite a lot about it, not wanting to disappoint the child or be exposed as a great big liar.

He noticed that there was very little food in his presses. Very little.

He'd have to go out and buy the fancy bread for Adam. And some cheese. Joel had brought up some biscuits the other day so he had those. Joel's wife had been with him and she'd certainly looked pregnant. She hadn't up to this point or maybe Jeremy just hadn't noticed. He congratulated her and she thanked him and that was the extent of their conversation. She really was quite a difficult person to talk to. Joel had just got a promotion at work and was beaming and then his wife muttered something about knowing what really mattered, with an extra stress on the 'really', and Joel had glared at her and they'd left soon after that.

Jeremy placed the biscuits back in the press and closed the door. He found his jacket at the bottom of the stairs and left the house.

Allie arranged to meet Holly at the top of Grafton Street. She'd asked her out as Tess had insisted that Allie should go and have a night of fun with a friend before Tony came back. Allie had to smile at the ominous way her mother-in-law had said, 'Before Tony comes back.' There was only one small snag: Allie didn't have friends any more. Not in work or outside work. There was a time she'd had loads, but as Tony's habit had escalated and her own covering up for him had become more frantic, she'd had to abandon people for fear that they would find out about her husband or, even worse, that Tony would steal from them. Looking back it all seemed so ridiculous. Why couldn't she have just been honest with herself? With them? But it was like a disease; it grew and grew so gradually that you didn't notice the symptoms until they were full-blown. She wasn't even sure she was the person she used to be. So she'd rung up Holly, who'd immediately agreed. Allie was a bit nervous about it. After all, the only thing she and Holly had in common was that people close to them were addicted to drugs – not exactly the most auspicious start.

Allie spotted Holly before the other woman saw her. She tipped her on the shoulder and Holly spun round. Well, spun as much as she could in the spiky heels she wore.

'Oh,' Holly's bright blue eyes widened in appreciation as she took in Allie's appearance, 'you look great. Cool skirt.'

'Thanks,' Allie grinned. 'I just thought that tonight I'd push the boat out. I haven't done this in ages.'

'Me neither,' Holly said. 'I haven't been out in at least a month, not since Vee came to stay.'

Allie suppressed a smile. She hadn't been out in over a year, but decided not to say that because poor Holly would probably die of disbelief.

'So, where to?' Holly asked.

'I dunno. My brother-in-law suggested a good place called Deoch. It's a cosy little pub but there's music and a dance floor too.'

'Oh yeah, I know it,' Holly nodded. 'He must be a pretty cool guy, your brother-in-law, that's the new in-place.'

'I'll pass that on,' Allie grinned. John would be delighted to be thought of as cool.

Jeremy was a bit annoyed. The tomato bread wasn't at all fresh, as it had been sitting on the shelf in the supermarket all day. Even worse, the girl behind the deli counter was refusing to cut two slices off it.

'They always do it for me,' he grumbled.

'Well,' the girl shrugged, 'I am only here in evenings, I do not know this.'

She was Polish, Jeremy guessed. 'You *do* know this,' he said crossly, 'because I am telling you.'

'That is not it,' the girl said, looking nervously about her. 'My manager, he never said to cut pieces off the bread.'

This was ridiculous, Jeremy thought, what was he going to do with a whole load of red bread?

'He—'

'Hello, Mr Lyons!'

The cheery greeting made him jump. He turned around, the bread tucked under his arm, to see Mark and his little brother being accompanied by an attractive woman with fluffy hair. Well, she was attractive in an old woman way, Jeremy thought. She was wearing a nice peach-coloured blouse and navy slacks.

'Hello, Mark,' he smiled. 'How are you this evening?'

'I'm fine,' Mark said loudly. 'This is my Nana Tess.'

'Hello,' Jeremy said to the fluffy-haired woman.

'I've heard a lot about you,' Tess said. 'It's my son John who's doing your garden.'

'Oh right,' Jeremy flushed. 'He's doing a good job,' he said, flustered.

'Our nana is minding us,' Mark piped up, 'because my mammy is gone out with her friend. And she's buying us sweets.'

'Well, isn't that nice.' Jeremy held up the loaf of bread. 'I'm buying bread for my son.' He instantly felt ridiculous.

'Well,' Tess's mouth curved upwards in an amused smile, 'that's very nice. I hope he likes it.'

'Yes, he does, it's his favourite.' Then Jeremy suddenly thought of something to say, which was surprising because normally he didn't like to prolong conversations with people. But Tess looked like a nice woman. 'I believe your son is coming home soon from his business trip.'

Tess flinched and her smile died a tiny bit. Oh God, Jeremy thought, it seemed he had upset her. His conversations skills must be very rusty indeed. 'Yes,' she nodded. 'He is.' Seeming to dismiss him she asked her grandsons, 'Now, boys, what sweets would you like?'

Jeremy watched them walk away. Mark twisted back to give

him a wave and he winked at the boy. When he turned around to argue again with the assistant she had disappeared.

The pub was heaving. Up at the front, some guy was belting out 'The Final Countdown' and not even the karaoke machine could make him sound good. Holly had just told her that Veronica, who had been discharged two days previously, had managed to secure a job in their local hotel.

'She had her first day today and she loved it. They know her history and have promised to keep an eye on her.'

'That's great.' Allie wasn't sure if she wanted Tony working at all when he came home. The idea of it made her nervous.

'Isn't it?' Holly took a slug of her pint. 'The only thing is that Fred guy, her ex-boyfriend, is back on the scene. I know he's still scoring but there's nothing I can do. I've told her he's a waster, but she won't listen to me.'

'Tony told her he's no good for her,' Allie said.

Holly nodded gratefully. 'Veronica seems to have taken a shine to Tony, maybe she'll listen to him.'

Allie didn't reply that Veronica had told Tony to fuck off when he'd said it.

'So, how are you feeling about Tony coming home?'

Allie was about to answer when she was arrested by a sudden thought. She was out to have fun tonight. Maybe the last bit of fun for a long time, who knew? 'Holly,' she said purposefully as she took a gulp of her Guinness, 'I've come to a decision about tonight.'

'You have?'

'I have decided,' Allie put her pint down and leant in towards her companion, 'that you and I haven't come out to spend all night talking about your sister or my husband. I have had it up to here,' she indicated her forehead with a small salute, 'talking about my husband.'

'You have?' Holly's lips twitched.

'I have. Even when I was madly in love with him at the start, I didn't talk about him so much.'

'No?'

'Nope. Tonight I am going to relearn the art of normal conversation with a friend.'

'OK.' Holly was grinning. 'So, what will we talk about?'

'Something happier than drug abuse for starters.'

'The death penalty?'

Allie laughed. 'Yeah, OK.'

On the way out of the shop, Jeremy had spied the latest edition of *VIP Inc.* Adam was the front page story, his cheery face, complete with pirate hat, adorning the cover. Jeremy had picked it up and put it back and picked it up again. It was a shocking price. Four euro for a magazine. Still, it was his son on the cover and if Adam was coming to visit, he wanted him to know that he was at least interested in his life. So he parted with the money and put the magazine in his recyclable bag, alongside the bread and the cheese.

When he got back, he unpacked the food and placed the magazine on the table, that way Adam would see it when he arrived. But then if he placed it on the table, it would look as if he had *deliberately* placed it there. Jeremy wanted to make it more casual, as if he'd read it. He put it beside his chair in the living room. But what if Adam didn't go in there? He'd never see that Jeremy had spent four euro on a magazine. In the end he opted for leaving it on the kitchen chair that Adam normally sat in. That way his son was bound to notice it. So, after making that decision, he went to catch some of the movie.

The karaoke had finished and a cool-looking DJ was now playing obscure dance music. He was also flipping vinyl to the whoops and cheers of the mainly early-twenties crowd.

'He's good at throwing those records about, isn't he?' Allie remarked. She was feeling pleasantly floaty.

'I wish he wasn't so good at catching them,' Holly said back.

Allie laughed. 'Yeah, I hate that type of music too. It's as if it was written by someone on a really bad drug trip.'

'Wow,' Holly widened her eyes, 'do you think they knew we were coming?'

'Yep,' Allie nodded, 'they probably wanted to make us feel at home.'

They laughed loudly at that. Two men in sober black suits standing at the bar glanced across at them. Allie gave a flirtatious wave.

'Oh, you're in there,' Holly giggled. She blew the men a Marilyn Monroe-style kiss.

The men didn't react, just continued to stare impassively.

'Are they humourless or what?' Allie scoffed.

'They have faces like,' Holly thought hard, 'buckets of concrete.'

'No,' Allie shook her head, 'they've faces like Leonard Cohen fans at a Westlife concert.'

Holly, who had just taken a gulp of her pint, coughed it out all over the table.

'Feel free to chat them up if you like,' Allie said generously.

Holly laughed harder. 'Nope,' she pronounced, standing up, 'forget about men. I think we should dance.'

'Good idea.' Allie stood up too. 'When I was in my twenties I could do a mean moonwalk. D'you want to learn?'

Holly grinned. 'Eh, I don't think a moonwalk is—'

'Come on!' Allie shouted, causing people to look over. 'We're grown women, we can dance how we want to, we can leave our friends behind . . .'

Allie was plastered, Holly realised suddenly. Totally drunk. She wasn't too sober herself but she was better than Allie. She followed her from the table, grinning as Allie shoved and pushed her way to the centre of the dance floor. There she came to a halt and stared down at her feet, swaying slightly, her forehead creased up in a frown. 'It'd be easier to remember if I hadn't had so much to drink,' she chortled suddenly.

'If you hadn't had so much to drink you wouldn't be up here,' Holly joked.

'True,' Allie nodded. 'Now, let me see.' Her foot moved a little. 'Oh, now I remember. OK, Holly, follow me, slide your left heel back.'

Holly rolled her eyes and made a half-hearted attempt.

'Come on,' Allie cajoled.

Holly did it again.

'Yeeaahh!' Allie cheered. 'Now do this.' She pivoted on both her heels and changed direction.

'Wow.' Holly now looked impressed as she tried to do it.

'Now this.' Allie deftly turned her right heel forty-five degrees.

Holly flapped her hand. 'I can't do that.'

'You can.' Allie did it again, and again, her moonwalk becoming more impressive despite her inability to steady herself. 'Just take off your shoes.'

'I can't leave my shoes in the middle of the dance floor, they'd be stolen.'

'No one else would be able to wear them,' Allie snorted as she did a backwards slide.

'You're really good at that,' Holly remarked. There was no way she was taking off her shoes.

Allie grinned. 'Tony taught me. He doesn't like to admit it but he knows the whole dance sequence from Thriller. We were real saddos.'

'No wonder he went on drugs.'

'It's a wonder I didn't join him.'

They laughed.

'D'you know what me and my friends used to do?' Holly said, gaining courage from Allie's display of contempt for the acid house music. 'We used to wear a Walkman and dance to the rhythm of the music we played ourselves so it looked like we were really bad dancers.'

'Oh,' Allie stopped her moonwalk, 'that's good! Will we do that? Let's pretend its Abba's "Dancing Queen" playing.'

Holly figured it was better than moonwalking all over the dance floor.

And it was, until Allie started to sing it at the top of her voice, making Holly laugh and cringe both at the same time.

Adam arrived at nine-thirty, just as the Saturday film was starting. Jeremy heard him and went into the hall to greet him. Adam looked a little pale, Jeremy thought.

'Hi, Dad,' he said, attempting a grin, 'how's tricks?'

'Good.' Jeremy led him into the kitchen where he flicked on the kettle. 'And you?'

Adam made to sit down and then found the magazine on the chair. 'Oh, hey,' he said, not sounding as cheerful as Jeremy thought he might have. 'I see you got *VIP Inc.*'

'Yes,' Jeremy nodded. 'Well, you did say you were in it and I saw you on the cover and I bought it.'

Adam was confused. 'Eh,' he said as he placed the magazine on the table and sat down, 'did you read it?'

There was always something, Jeremy thought in exasperation. It wasn't good enough to just buy it, his son expected him to read it as well. And why on earth would he read it? Sure he knew all about Adam already. And besides, he didn't want to read what Adam had said about Nelly. He wasn't ready to read about his wife.

'I, eh, started to but then someone rang,' he lied.

'Who rang?' Adam looked surprised. His dad never got phone calls.

'Oh, just one of those telemarketing people,' Jeremy said airily. 'Anyway, I put down the magazine and meant to pick it up but then I didn't.' He made a rueful face. He was a little appalled at the ease at which he lied to his son but, he thought uneasily, if you could tell an innocent child you were Santa, you could pretty much do anything.

'Right,' Adam nodded. 'Well, I'm glad about that, Dad, because you see—'

'Joel bought some biscuits.' Jeremy hopped up and placed them on the table, then began to make the tea. 'Would you like some of that tomato bread?' he asked.

'Eh, no.'

'I bought a whole loaf,' Jeremy said. 'It'll go to waste.'

'OK.' Adam heaved a sigh. This was not how he'd planned it. He hadn't meant to break his news while munching on stale tomato bread.

He watched his dad hack an enormous slice off. In order to speed things up, Adam made the tea and brought the cheese and butter to the table. Jeremy handed him a plate.

'Dad, could you sit down for a second?' Adam asked.

There was something in his voice that arrested Jeremy's movements. It was the sort of 'Sit down' that Nelly had uttered when she'd had to tell him that she had inoperable cancer. At that time, he'd been so stunned he hadn't even made a move to hold her or comfort her, and instead he'd declared it nonsense. But of course it hadn't been and she'd died two months later. If Adam was going to tell him the same thing, he didn't know how he'd cope. But he would attempt to hug him, of that he was sure.

'Yes?' Jeremy slid into a seat opposite his son and regarded him nervously.

'Well, Dad, I'm glad you haven't read the article because there is something in it that I'd like to tell you myself.'

He paused. Jeremy waited, his heart thumping.

'I probably should have told you a long time ago but I thought you might guess.'

Jeremy frowned. What was he on about?

'I'm gay, Dad.'

Jeremy, who had been expecting some sort of medical confession, blinked. 'What?'

'Here,' Adam thumbed through the magazine to the centre pages. There, on the right, were some of the photos Jeremy had allowed him to take from home and then, on the other side, there was a picture of his son with his arm around another man. A weedy-looking man with a receding hairline.

'That's Peter, my partner,' Adam went on, licking his lips. 'I've known him for the last two years.'

'Your partner?' Jeremy could barely get the words out.

'My, eh, lover, I suppose,' Adam said.

Jeremy swallowed hard, coughed and then abruptly stood up. 'I don't understand,' he shook his head to clear it. 'You're a man.'

'Yes,' Adam nodded. 'A gay man.'

'No,' Jeremy shook his head. 'You're my son. You can't be gay. That's just a fad.'

'It's not a fad.' Adam almost laughed at the ridiculous statement. He stood up too. 'It's who I am, Dad, and I wanted you to know.'

Jeremy shook his head. Stared at Adam. At his blond red-tipped hair, his tanned face, his nice clothes. He didn't look gay. He didn't go around with his hand on his hip or talk in a girly voice. 'If this is a joke, it's not funny.'

'It's not a joke, Dad.' Adam attempted to come around the table towards him.

Jeremy backed away. 'I suppose Joel put you up to it.'

'He's been on at me to tell you, yes.'

Jeremy just wanted to go and watch the end of his film now. He had not anticipated this. An illness, maybe. Gayness, definitely not. Adam was a handsome man, he could have had any woman he wanted. 'You just haven't been lucky with girls,' he offered weakly.

'I'm gay, Dad.'

Adam sounded pretty sure of it, Jeremy thought.

'I'm gay. I wanted you to know. I'd like you to accept it.'

How could he accept that? Jeremy rubbed his forehead.

'And you announced it in a magazine?' he said, feebly thinking of the whole country reading it.

'It wasn't an announcement. Everyone knows.'

That was worse. Jeremy had to take deep breaths.

'Do you want me to go?' Adam said.

He didn't want him to go but he wasn't sure what to say to him either. So he nodded. 'Yes, I think it might be best,' he said back faintly.

There was a pause. 'I'm sorry, Dad.'

Jeremy could only nod.

'Will you be OK?'

'Of course I will,' Jeremy snapped back, suddenly making Adam flinch. 'Just – just go, would you?'

Adam seemed unsure but eventually he turned and walked out of the kitchen. Jeremy heard the front door close after him.

Jeremy sank down onto a kitchen chair and wondered if it was just a very bad dream.

'They're coming over, those two guys from the bar,' Holly hissed in Allie's ear.

'Let them.' Allie was dancing with abandon. She had now started the Macarena to a banging, jarring soundtrack. It looked so weird. People on the dance floor were looking at them and giving them a wide berth.

'They don't seem happy,' Holly warned.

'Yeah, well, who cares?' Allie jumped to the left and began the movement again. 'They won't be any happier when we get a drink out of them and then leave.'

Holly had to laugh at that. Still, her drunkenness seemed to be wearing off in direct proportion to the proximity of the two men. She tended to steer clear of guys, not wanting to complicate her life any further.

The two men, big and burly and looking like clones of each other, arrived up beside them. 'Ladies,' the bigger of the two said, his arms folded, 'how you doing tonight?'

'A pint of Guinness and I'll be doing great,' Allie said over her shoulder, flicking a semi-seductive smile at them.

'And I'll have one too.' Holly followed Allie's lead. She tried to join in the Macarena so she wouldn't have to stand looking at the two men, but copious amounts of alcohol had spoiled her rhythm so she stopped.

The men glanced at her, then at Allie, and finally at each other.

'I think it might be better for us if you both left,' the big guy said ponderously.

'Sorry,' Allie said in a sing-song voice. She held up her left hand and wiggled her fingers, showing off her rings. 'I'm married. We can't leave with you but we'll take the drink, won't we, Hol?'

Holly didn't reply. It was a long time since she'd allowed herself to be chatted up, but she vaguely remembered that most guys smiled and attempted to grope you when they did it. These guys had their arms folded and didn't even affect any interest in the two of them. Things in the chat-up stakes couldn't have deteriorated so much, could they?

'I think you've got the wrong idea, Miss Macarena,' the smaller clone said to Allie's back. 'We, that is my friend here and I, would like you both to leave the premises now, together, unaccompanied.'

'If we're together we won't be unaccompanied,' Allie, ever the English teacher, said. Then she stopped, arrested by what the man had proposed and turned around to face him. 'Are you asking the two of us to leave?'

A few people nearby were watching the exchange with interest.

The two men looked at each other. The big one said, 'We're the security here. We don't allow drugs in this club.'

'Drugs?' Allie and Holly said together. Then again, 'Drugs?!' and they both started to laugh. Allie continued to do so while Holly stopped, her mouth wide open.

'Is there something funny?' The bouncers looked confused.

'Sorry?' Allie stopped her giggling and asked, 'What was that you were saying about drugs?'

'We don't allow it. Now, we're not going to search you both but we'd appreciate it if you left.'

'Hang on a second,' Allie was facing them both now, her hands on her hips, 'you think my friend and I are on drugs?'

'Yes,' they both said impassively.

Allie clamped a hand over her mouth so she wouldn't start laughing again while, beside her, Holly looked outraged.

'We're not on drugs,' Holly spluttered.

'We've been watching you both,' the big bouncer said.

'Yes,' the smaller one added, 'we've seen you in action.'

'We are having fun,' Allie snorted, still trying to keep the giggles in.

The two men looked at each other again, then one of them thumbed towards the entrance. 'Out.'

'We wouldn't touch drugs with a barge pole,' Holly said, still appalled. 'We've seen what it can do, haven't we, Allie?'

'Obviously the bouncers here think it just ruins your dance moves.' Allie couldn't help it, she started to laugh and grabbed on to Holly for support. 'Oh God, Holly, the irony.'

'We won't be back,' Holly said indignantly, nudging Allie to shut up.

'Good,' the bouncer said, 'it might bring the average age of the punters back down again.'

'Now that,' Allie said, 'is an insult.'

'I'm only twenty-nine,' Holly said.

The men didn't reply. They merely escorted the two of them towards the door and out into the street.

'I'll get on to the radio about this,' Holly threatened.

'You do that, love,' one of them called after her.

'Yeah,' Allie shouted, 'it's a lack of freedom of expression on the dance floor!'

'Bye now,' the bouncer sneered, walking back inside.

'Bastard!' Holly gasped. 'Jesus, thinking I was on drugs.'

'Well, you did attempt to ballroom dance with yourself.'

A small smile lifted the corners of Holly's lips. 'Yeah, I guess.'

'Like this.' Allie gave her a demonstration.

'You make a lovely couple,' Holly chortled.

'Thanks.' Allie kept dancing, humming loudly to herself as she did so and enjoying the fact that Holly was smiling.

'I had a great time tonight, Allie,' Holly said suddenly. 'Even if we did get thrown out of a pub.'

'Yeah, me too.' Allie stopped dancing, her arms embracing empty air. 'I had a fabulous time.'

'Will we do it again?'

'You bet we will,' Allie nodded. 'In fact,' she cocked her head to one side, 'the worse things get for us, the more we'll do this, deal?'

Holly caught her hand and shook it. 'Deal.'

'So let's hope we never have to go out again.'

They grinned at each other.

'And let's hope your brother-in-law doesn't recommend anywhere the next time.'

'Oh, so you've gone off him, have you?'

'Totally. But what I could use would be a packet of chips.'

'Lead on so, if you can in those mad heels.' Allie linked her arm through Holly's and thought that at least one good thing had come out of Tony being in the clinic.

23

'HE'S COMING, HE'S coming!' Mark yelled. He was standing on top of the low wall that ran around the front of his house.

'Stop jumping about, you'll fall,' Magda said crossly as she hurried over to steady him. 'And what state will you be in then?'

'He's coming now!' Mark insisted. 'See, that's the car.'

Magda, holding Owen by one hand and balancing Mark with the other, saw the car as it crawled down the road towards them. Allie, who was at the wheel, was driving carefully as there were always smaller kids darting on to the road. And, as it was the second last week of holidays before school, the majority of children in the neighbourhood were outside, making the most of the weak summer sunshine.

Mark waved furiously as the car drew up outside the house. He expected his daddy to wave back but instead he seemed preoccupied trying to unbuckle his seatbelt. His mammy had warned him that his dad might be tired when he came home and to go easy on him, but Mark failed to see how a flight would make anyone sleepy.

He hopped down off the wall, Magda protesting in his wake, and wrenched the car door open. 'Hiya, Dad!'

Tony, having unbuckled the seatbelt, turned to him. 'Hey, big fella,' he grinned. 'Just gimme a second to get out of this car.'

Mark stepped back and watched as his dad unfolded himself slowly out of the passenger seat.

'Do they have nice food in America, Dad?'

Tony blinked. 'Huh?' He felt slightly overwhelmed to be on the outside again. He'd found it hard to travel down this unfamiliar street and know that it was now home. He steadied himself against the car.

'You got fatter,' Mark said. 'You look nicer.'

'That child misses nothing,' Tony said to Allie with a small grin.

She came around the car and wrapped her arm about her husband's waist. 'That's because he's a clever chap, aren't you, Mark?'

'I can do forty-seven keepie uppies,' Mark boasted.

'Later,' Allie warned.

'Yeah, show me later.' Tony tousled his son's hair and turned to Owen. He flinched as he saw his mother-in-law protectively cradling his two-year-old. And what was worse, Owen was peering at him with suspicious eyes.

'Hiya, Owen,' he said, not attempting to move nearer.

Owen buried his head in Magda's chest.

Tony gulped hard.

'Six weeks is a long time for a two-year-old,' Allie explained quietly. She crossed to her mother and took Owen from her arms. Cuddling her son, she coaxed, 'Say hi to Daddy.'

'He can talk now, Daddy,' Mark said excitedly. 'We didn't tell you on the phone cause it was meant to be a surprise for you.' He tugged at Owen's sleeve. 'Go on, Ownie, show Daddy how you can say hello.'

There was no one like a child for sizing you up, Tony thought, wincing under Owen's penetrating stare. He knew he'd shouted at the little boy and probably scared him, but if it was the last thing he ever did, he was going to make it up to him. To them all.

'It's OK,' he said gently to Owen, 'you don't have to talk to me if you don't want to. I know I was very cross sometimes but I'm sorry about that. You talk when you are ready.'

171

'Owen!' Mark was not happy about that. 'Come on. Show Daddy how you can talk.'

'It's fine.' Tony crouched down to Mark's level. 'D'you know what, can you come out the back and show me those keepie uppies?'

'OK,' Mark beamed, 'come on then.' He grabbed Tony's hand and dragged him through the house and out the back.

Magda and Allie stared after them.

'He looks well,' Magda said, and Allie wasn't sure if there was a hint of bitterness in her voice. 'The place obviously suited him.'

'He looks well because they looked after him in there,' Allie replied. She locked her car; she'd get Tony to take his suitcase out later on. 'Here is where real life begins.'

'Are you worried?'

'Terrified.' Allie heaved a sigh. 'Like it's almost too good to be true to see him like this. He seems happier, he looks good, but I'm almost scared to hope it will last, you know?'

'Oh, I know,' Magda nodded. 'It was like that with your dad all the time. He'd promise me the sun, moon and stars and then take them right back.'

'Tony's not like that,' Allie said with a hint of annoyance.

'I didn't say that,' Magda corrected, 'I said I know how you feel, getting your hopes up, that's all.'

'Oh, sorry, Mum.' Allie shook her head. 'It's just me; I'm a bit on edge.'

'I know.' Magda gave her a brief hug and together, with Owen in Allie's arms, they walked into the kitchen.

'I put a stew in the oven for you,' Magda said, 'so you can have that for your dinner. And Mark helped me to clean the living room, so make sure you notice it.'

Allie smiled. 'Thanks, Mum, I don't know what I'd have done without you. '

'You'd have Tess. One thing about your husband, he does have a lovely mother.'

'Yeah, and a great brother.'

There was a silence as Allie flicked on the kettle for a cuppa. She was dying for one – the whole day had been quite stressful, checking Tony out, talking to his counsellor, she hadn't slept a wink the night before worrying about it. It wasn't that she didn't want Tony home, she wanted it more than anything, but the place had been so relaxed without him there, so predictable, and she was afraid that now everything might get stirred back up again and she hoped she'd be able for it. And that the kids would cope.

'So,' Magda asked softly, her eyes darting to the door in case Tony and Mark arrived back in. 'What happens now?'

Allie glanced towards Owen to make sure he wasn't listening. He seemed happy enough banging a spoon off the top of a saucepan. Even though he was making a racket, Allie answered in an undertone.

'Well, whatever we want to happen basically.' She pulled some cups from a press and heated up the teapot. 'It's recommended that he go to NA meetings.'

'NA?'

'Narcotics Anonymous. Sort of like AA only for drug abusers.'

'Oh,' Magda nodded, 'right. And what will that do for him?'

'Well,' Allie shrugged, 'apparently they follow a twelve-step programme to get better, the same thing he was doing in the clinic. He meets other people like him and they talk about how they're coping day to day. And he gets a sponsor who helps him. The sponsor is usually an ex-user.'

'Oh,' Magda rolled her eyes, 'the last thing you both need in your lives is another druggie.'

'Mum, it's not like that,' Allie half laughed. 'The sponsor is well off the stuff. It'll be his or her job to help Tony.'

'Hmmm.' Magda didn't seem impressed. 'And that's it, is it?'

Allie shrugged. 'It's up to Tony; there really isn't anything anyone can do. He just has to want to get better.'

At the sound of a shriek, both women turned to look out the kitchen window. Tony was doing tricks with the soccer ball, much to Mark's delight. He was kicking it from foot to foot then from knee to knee, and then he flicked it upwards and caught it at the back of his neck, where he balanced it while doing push ups.

'Mammy!' Mark shrieked, 'Send Owen out so he can see!'

Allie lifted Owen up so he could look out the window. Tony turned towards him and began again. Flipping, kicking, balancing the ball with unnerving accuracy.

'Well,' Magda shook her head, 'that'll win Mark over.'

Allie said nothing, just watched as her husband thrilled Mark with a series of tricks. Tony had always been good with his feet, Tess used to say. And Tony always used to reply that it was just as well as it helped when he was chasing Allie. Remembering, Allie felt a mixture of sadness and joy as she watched her husband entertain his son out the back garden. They both looked so free and the sound of Tony's laughter warmed her. At one point he glanced up and paused, then he winked at her and she winked back.

Maybe, she thought with a flutter of hope, it would be OK.

Jeremy watched from his bedroom window as the strange man in the garden next door flipped the red soccer ball from the front of his feet to the top of his head. He watched as Mark danced around the man, laughing and shrieking and clapping He was surprised to recognise a sort of jealousy inside him. For the last six weeks he had fancied that the little boy liked him, and now this man had arrived home and was able to do things with a soccer ball that Jeremy wasn't able to do. In fact, if Jeremy had been asked, he would have said that prancing about with a soccer ball on your head was a bit of a waste of time, but Mark didn't seem to think so. Still, this man didn't have a magic sled or a magic workshop or whatever it was Santa had. *And neither do you*, a voice whispered in the back of his head. Jeremy dismissed it. He didn't like things that forced themselves on him. He liked his life. He really didn't need a little boy in it. Or, he thought, a gay son. He hadn't contacted Adam since. Well, he never contacted Adam, it was usually the other way around; Adam always rang him.

But Adam hadn't rung him this week at all. Maybe he was busy or something. Jeremy had not read the article in the magazine though he hadn't thrown it out, just put it away out of sight. At least Joel was married and had a load of kids. Thank God for—

He was jerked out of his thoughts by a pretty spectacular display of footballing skill from Mark's dad. The man ran with the ball and flipped it up behind him. Mark declared that his dad should be on a talent show. His dad laughed and handed the ball to Mark and started to show him how to do it.

Jeremy watched how patiently he showed Mark things. Jeremy had been patient with his boys too, showing them how to add and subtract and explaining the finer points of chemistry to them. But they'd never smiled at him like the way Mark was smiling at his dad.

Jeremy pulled away from the window. For some reason it hurt him to look.

24

THE PHONE RANG around noon the following day.

'Tony, will you get that?' Allie called. She was in the kitchen preparing lunch. Tess had taken the boys out for the day to give them time on their own. Conversation between Tess and Tony had been painfully stilted as Tess was still very upset about that day at the hospital. Allie resolved to ask her to dinner that evening to try to break the ice.

The phone continued to ring.

'Tony!' she yelled.

'It's probably for you!'

'I'm making lunch!' She gritted her teeth. The least he could do was help her. Or answer the phone. Since coming home yesterday, aside from entertaining Mark, he'd just watched the telly. She'd asked him tentatively about going to an NA meeting but he'd evaded her query by going to bed early and getting up late.

The phone stopped ringing, unanswered.

Allie put down the knife and walked into the television room. 'Why didn't you get that?'

'I thought you would.' He looked guiltily at her.

'You just didn't want to answer it, did you?'

He looked down at his hands. Then back up at her.

'Why not?'

He shrugged.

'Tony, I'm struggling here. You're back but all you're doing is talking to Mark.'

'That's ridiculous, I'm only back a day.'

Now he sounded annoyed. Well, Allie amended, not annoyed. Defensive.

'It's not ridiculous,' she said firmly.

Again he bowed his head.

'Tony?' she ventured.

'I talk to you,' he said. His tone suggested that the subject was closed.

'That phone rings again, you answer it,' Allie snapped, walking out.

Once in the kitchen she placed her hands on the kitchen table and closed her eyes, willing herself not to cry. She didn't know what she'd expected when he came back, but it had been a more enthusiastic person certainly. One who was hell-bent on kicking his habit. Not someone who was just sitting around doing nothing, afraid to answer the phone.

The word hit her.

Afraid.

He was afraid.

Or at least that's what she thought it was.

She didn't hear him creep up behind her, she only felt his arms as they encircled her waist and the feathery kiss that he placed on the nape of her neck. 'Sorry,' he murmured.

She turned within the circle his arms and faced him. 'Are you scared of talking on the phone?'

He froze.

'Please, Tony.' She placed the palm of her hand on his face and stroked his cheek with her thumb. He leant towards her touch, his eyes closing briefly. 'Let me in.'

'You'll despise me,' he said simply.

'Never.'

'You'll think who is this complete weird mess?'

'I thought that the day I met you.'

He cracked a small smile.

'You are so bloody strong, Allie. I'm not.'

177

Allie hugged him. 'I'm not strong,' she said into his worn blue T-shirt, 'I'm only doing this because of you. Because, Tony Dolan, I love you. I really do.'

He held her for a long few seconds before saying slowly, 'Imagine it's winter and you go outside in a T-shirt.'

'You'd only do that if you were on drugs,' she joked.

He didn't smile back. 'For a lot of my life I've been going out in winter with a hat and scarf and jumper and boots and jeans on.'

Allie wondered where this was going. 'And?'

'And now, I'm in a T-shirt.'

'What?'

'It's like, without the drugs, I'm missing a layer of protection. I feel like I'm standing in the middle of a battleground and there are snipers all over the place. I have to adjust, you know?'

'That's what you think life is, winter in a T-shirt?'

'Pretty much.'

'Oh Tony.' She felt desperately sorry for him. 'It's so much more than that.'

He didn't answer.

'You need to go to an NA meeting,' Allie said urgently. 'You need to meet people who live in their T-shirts and survive. I can't help you. I can listen but I don't know what you feel.'

'I can't walk into a meeting on my own.'

'You won't have to.' She entwined her fingers with his. 'I'll go with you.'

'You can't. It's only for addicts.'

'We'll go to an open meeting where anyone can go.'

He bit his lip. 'I don't want you in that sort of situation. You and Mark and Owen are separate from all that shit. You're like,' he sought out the words, 'like the top of a mountain I have to climb.'

'You'll freeze climbing a mountain in a T-shirt,' Allie half smiled. 'So the people on the mountain are going to come down and wrap you up in a nice warm blanket.'

Tony bit his lower lip as he smiled. 'That is the corniest piece of shit I ever heard.' Then his smile faded and his eyes grew serious. 'Thanks.' He brought his forehead down to meet hers and was about to kiss her when the shrill ringing of the phone broke the moment.

Allie gave him a gentle shove. 'Now answer it. Go on.'

He didn't refuse this time. With Allie following him, he crossed into the hall and picked up the receiver. 'Hello?'

'Oh, hello, Tony,' Fintan said, 'how are you? I believe you came home yesterday?'

'Eh – yeah. I'm, eh, fine thanks.' Tony coughed. He hated the way his voice shook slightly. When he was on something, he wasn't so bloody pathetic. 'Do you want Allie?'

'Yes please.'

Tony handed the phone to his wife. 'Fintan,' he said.

She was surprised. 'Fintan, hi.' Then, '*What?*' Then, 'Is she all right?' Then, 'I'll be over in a minute.' She slammed down the phone and hissed 'Bastard' under her breath.

'What's the matter?' Tony asked. He tried to keep his mind from freefalling. It was stressful times that made his resolve to give up drugs weaken, and if anything was wrong with Allie then he didn't know how he'd cope. 'Al?' he asked, 'you OK?'

Her eyes had filled with tears and she gulped. 'Of all the times he chooses,' she said.

'What?'

'My dad,' she said. 'He called into my mother this morning. Just out of the blue. Like when we didn't meet him, he didn't get the hint. Poor Mum is really upset.'

'You should go over,' Tony said.

'What about you?'

'I'll be fine.'

'You could come with me.'

'Naw, thanks. I'll stay here and organise dinner or something.'

'Tess will be back with the boys around six, OK?'

'Yeah, sure. I'm not going anywhere.'

179

'Be nice to her.'

'I am nice to her.'

Allie didn't reply. Instead she said, 'I'll just get my coat.' She raced upstairs, pulled on her jacket and, stopping only to kiss Tony briefly, she left.

Out of sight of her house, Allie pulled in. She took out her mobile, her hand shaking slightly. She knew Tony would be incredibly hurt by what she was about to do, but at the same time she just couldn't afford to take a chance. She dialled her mother-in-law's number and when Tess answered she explained the situation.

'So you want me to stay with Tony and the boys until you come back,' Tess said, assessing the situation before Allie had to ask.

'Yeah, Owen is a bit wary of him and to be honest, Tess, I'd feel better if you were with them.'

'I know.' Tess sounded sad as she said it. Then she asked, 'Do you want me to go back now, so Tony isn't on his own?'

'No, I think he'll cope,' Allie said. 'He's not going back on the drugs today. He'll probably watch the telly or something.'

'OK.' Tess didn't sound so sure. 'Well, good luck with your mother, Allie, give her my best.'

'I will. Thanks, Tess.' Allie paused before adding, 'And when you talk to Tony, don't be too hard on him. He's finding it very difficult.'

'When have I ever been hard on that boy?' Tess scoffed.

'I suppose.' Allie smiled into the phone. 'Say hi to my boys for me.'

'I will. Bye now.' Tess clicked her phone off.

Fintan let Allie in when she arrived. He looked as shocked as Allie felt.

'He just knocked on the door,' he explained in a shaken voice. 'Asked your mother if he could come in, and she was so taken aback that she pulled the door open for him. Next thing I knew, I was making him tea and feeding him organic biscuits and your mother was just staring at him. I don't think she heard a word he said. She's in there.' He pushed open the kitchen door and Allie saw her mother, flicking through the pages of her wedding album.

'Mum?'

Magda raised her eyes to her daughter's face. 'As bold as brass,' she half whispered. 'He just came in as if he owned the place.'

'When did he leave?'

'He left when your mother started to cry,' Fintan said grimly. 'I told him to get out.'

'Seeing him again,' Magda shook her head, a fat tear leaking from the corner of her eye and dripping on to the page of the album, 'I thought I was over all that pain. But he just brought it back with him.'

Allie sat down, not knowing what to say. She caught her mother's hand and squeezed it. The only time she'd ever seen her mother so upset had been when she'd finally decided that enough was enough all those years ago. She'd been convinced that her mother would have punched her dad if she'd seen him, not break down in a mess.

'I'm sorry,' Magda sniffed. 'This shouldn't be happening to you, not with what you're going through with Tony and everything.'

'Here,' Fintan pressed a piece of bright blue kitchen paper into her hand, 'wipe your eyes with this, love.'

'He even had the nerve to ask who Fintan was,' Magda sniffed, wiping her eyes vigorously. 'As if he thought I'd still be on my own.'

'And I told him I was the man your mother should have married,' Fintan said, sounding cross.

'Yes,' Magda smiled a little. 'That threw him. Huh, that threw him.'

'I just wish I hadn't been wearing the flowery kitchen apron

181

at the time,' Fintan muttered. 'I think he found it hard to take me seriously.'

'Who cares what he thinks,' Magda hiccupped.

'So,' Allie rubbed her mother's arm, 'what did he want?'

Fintan and Magda exchanged glances. 'To see you, mainly,' Magda answered. 'He wanted to know if something had happened to you because you didn't turn up that day. He's been worried, apparently.'

'Bit late to worry now, I told him,' Fintan cut in. His arm was protectively on Magda's shoulders.

'And he told Fintan to butt out.' Magda sounded indignant now.

'Butt out, apron boy,' Fintan elaborated huffily.

'And I said to him that it was he who should butt out, after all he'd butted out of your life a long time ago. I told him that as far as your kids were concerned, they looked upon Fintan as their granddad.'

There was an awkward silence where Allie felt she was expected to say something. Preferably in the affirmative. Instead she muttered, 'I see.'

'And I told him that you had gone to meet him but had decided against it at the last minute,' Magda said.

But, Allie wanted to say, unlike last time, her dad had come back. He'd tried again.

'So,' Fintan finally finished, 'he left you his address in case you wanted to meet. Apparently he's now living in Kildare, a mere thirty-minute drive away.' Slowly he unfolded a piece of paper from his pocket and passed it to Allie. 'Just in case.'

Allie studied it. Address, phone number, mobile phone. Everything she would need to resume contact. If she wanted.

'Look,' her mother said then, 'see how beautiful I was.' She shoved the album towards Allie. 'See how hopeful.'

'I'll make us a smoothie,' Fintan said. He began taking out copious amounts of fruit from the presses and a massive tub of natural yoghurt.

'That would be lovely.' Magda gave him a wobbly smile.

'And I'll even put some chocolate sprinkles on yours,' he said, tapping her nose affectionately, 'as a little treat.'

'Thank you.'

Allie studied the album. She hadn't seen it in years. Ever since her dad's first fling, her mother had wrapped it up and hidden it away.

'I got it down to remind me what a fool I was,' Magda said, sounding a little bit like herself. 'And to see if there was any trace of the cheating lying horrible man in your father's features.'

There wasn't, as far as Allie could tell. Her dad looked as proud as punch as he stood with his best man outside the church. He hadn't been exactly a handsome man but there was a wicked look in his eye that made her smile. His mouth was turned up in a crooked grin, showing his crooked teeth. His hands were sunk into the pockets of his wedding suit and he looked like a man totally at ease with himself and the world.

Allie turned over the page and blinked. That surely wasn't her mother. That curvy glamorous woman with the glorious mane of dark hair. 'Wow, Mum, you were gorgeous,' she breathed.

Magda laughed ruefully. 'I like the use of the word "were",' she teased. She took the album from Allie and studied it. 'I used to be so much thinner,' she said. 'It wasn't until your father started his ride through the neighbourhood that I began to pile on the weight. I'd sit inside and plough my way through boxes of chocolates and packets of biscuits. It's all his fault I got so overweight.'

Fintan placed a smoothie in front of her. 'Emotional distress,' he said. 'But you got over it. I have to say, you looked great today when you opened the door to him. That pink tracksuit is stunning on you. Now drink that up, that's a good girl.' He turned to Allie. 'Which one would you like? I can do a mean Banana Blast.'

'I'll have a coffee, thanks,' Allie said.

'You sure I can't tempt you with a Strawberry Bomb?'

'No, thanks. A coffee is fine, Fintan.' Allie turned another page. 'Mum, who are all these people?'

Magda began to explain the relationships between various people in the photograph. Then her finger pointed to a frumpy woman in an oversized hat. 'That was your father's first conquest after we married. You were about eight months. That was my best friend in work.' Magda got up and went to a kitchen drawer. She pulled out a black pen and wrote 'Bitch' over the woman's head.

Allie laughed.

'Ah, I feel a little better now.' Then, turning suddenly serious, she patted Allie's hand. 'If you still want to see him, go ahead. He's still your father, but just be careful, he's really not a man you can trust.'

Allie fingered the paper in her pocket. She didn't know what to do.

When she got back, it was seven. Tony had made chips, his one and only dish, for dinner. Tess was sitting in front of a half-finished plate and Tony was opposite her, attempting to make conversation. The boys were out the back.

The minute Allie arrived in, Tess jumped up. 'Hi, listen Allie, sorry to leave so suddenly, but John is expecting me back, he's bringing me to Bingo. I just hung on to say hello to you.' With that she knocked on the window and blew kisses to the boys, awkwardly told Tony to take care, hugged Allie and was gone.

Allie dumped her coat on the chair. 'Was it terrible?'

Tony shrugged. 'Yep.' He plucked a chip from his mother's plate and ate it. 'We didn't know what to say to each other. I tried to talk normally but I think I hurt her a lot. I even apologised for taking her money and saying all that stuff I did on the family day but she said that there was no need to apologise, if that's the way I felt then that's the way I felt.'

Allie said nothing.

'I don't know what I can do now to make it up to her.'

'You've just got to keep trying,' Allie said. 'Would you make me a coffee, Tony? I could use one.'

He glanced at her but didn't ask any questions. Instead he hopped up and expertly made her a beautifully frothy cappuccino.

'Thanks.' She took a sip and marvelled once again at his ability to make coffee taste so nice. Then she pulled the piece of paper with her dad's contact details from her pocket. Pushing it across the table to Tony, she said, 'I think my dad is trying to make it up to me.'

Tony glanced down at the paper and then regarded her solemnly. 'Well, not ever having known him, but speaking as a guy who needs to make a hell of a lot of amends to a hell of a lot of people, I think that maybe you should let him?'

Allie's eyes unexpectedly filled with tears. 'You think so?'

He caught her hand and kissed it. 'But, speaking as a guy who fucked up, you take care of yourself first, OK?'

And Allie realised that he wasn't just talking about her dad, he meant himself. He was saying he knew it would take time to trust him.

'Love you,' she said.

'Love you even more.'

'Ugh!' Mark made a face as he stomped in the door with his brother. 'Soppy stuff!'

They laughed. All four of them, even Owen.

Despite everything, Allie didn't think she'd felt as content in ages.

25

JEREMY HAD PULLED out all his photograph albums. Nelly had been meticulous in filing the pictures. Each album was dated and the ages of the boys put on the front. Underneath the pictures, Nelly had written a little description of where the picture was taken and for what occasion. Jeremy was startled to realise that there were only a handful of them as a family – it was usually Jeremy behind the camera and Nelly with her two boys in front of it.

It hurt him to see Nel. Last week was the first time he'd looked at a picture of her since she'd died, and back then he'd only done it so he could choose a photo for her memorial cards. He remembered the one he'd picked. Nelly at thirty-five, holding a wide-brimmed hat and laughing as the breeze from the seaside town they were staying in had attempted to lift it from her head. Thirty-five. Five years before the cancer had taken her away from him. Jeremy didn't think he'd fully appreciated his wife. He guessed it was because he'd been ten years older than her. He'd considered himself far more mature than his bride. But looking back, he probably hadn't been. She'd been the one who'd done all the running. Flirting with him over her test tubes, asking him questions about various chemical formulas. Once she'd even asked him, in the middle of the lecture theatre, if there was such a thing as a love potion. Nelly had been a very forward girl and Jeremy had loved it. So they'd got married, a fledgling professor and his student. It was the most reckless thing Jeremy had done in his whole life and he had never regretted it. Well, once or twice when they'd rowed about how to bring the boys up he'd wished that he'd married someone a lot less romantic, but in the end they'd been happy. Jeremy shook his head, clearing it. That wasn't the reason he was looking through the pictures. No, he'd come up to have a look to check if there was any way he could have foreseen that his younger son was gay. So far, he'd come up with nothing to suggest that his son was anything other than a normal boy. In one, taken when he was around five, Adam, wearing a cowboy outfit, was pointing a pistol at the camera. Jeremy remembered taking the gun away from him. There had been a lot of tears on Adam's side, though Jeremy remembered explaining to him that he wasn't comfortable with him pretending to shoot other children. It was not healthy. There was another picture of Adam showing off his muscles with Nelly, dark hair thrown back over her creamy white shoulders, pretending to feel his biceps. There was one of Adam blowing out candles on a birthday cake in the shape of a car. All very boyish poses. Jeremy turned the page and paused. Adam dressed up as a Christmas tree. Now he definitely looked a bit odd in that, Jeremy thought. For one thing, he was wearing women's green tights and he had a pink bow on one of his branches. But how else was a Christmas tree supposed to look? It was very confusing. Jeremy looked through more photos, his heart twisting up every time Nelly smiled out at him. The boys had loved her, Jeremy knew. It had been hard on them when she died. Adam had only been twelve and Joel had been nine. Jeremy hadn't really known what to do with them, what to say. He'd tried his best to explain death to them, but it was hard. Hard because he didn't understand himself. Adam had wanted to leave his window open for her every night as someone in his class had said that spirits enter and leave that way, and Jeremy had flatly refused to allow it. Adam just had to accept that Nelly was gone. There was no point in him fantasising that his mother was visiting them. Maybe that was the problem?

Maybe Adam was afraid to love women as his mother's death had left him scarred, and so he turned to men instead? Jeremy bit his lip. It certainly could be a possibility. Maybe he would mention it to Adam when he rang. Tell him that it was a phase. That loving women was rewarding and he shouldn't be afraid of it. Yes, Jeremy thought, that was certainly intuitive of him. He felt quite proud. He'd say it to Adam. He would. Whenever Adam rang again.

'Oy! Mr L! Mr L!'

Jeremy flinched. John had a very loud voice and every time he called him, it made Jeremy jump. 'Yes?' he replied irritably.

'Looks like I'm all done here,' John called back. 'D'you want to come and take a look?'

'You bet I do,' Jeremy mumbled, hauling himself upright. Though in fairness John had been a hard worker and he hadn't bothered him too much. He left the spare bedroom and joined John in the back garden. His wilderness had been transformed over the last few weeks and it amazed Jeremy every time he looked out his kitchen window. The soil was turned and grass had been planted. September was a good time for grass, John had told him, so they'd seeded at just the right moment. But there wasn't too much grass to worry about. John had put in a lot of decking and built a little wall around the garden, filling it with soil, and planted lots of easy care plants in it. They'd cost a bit of money but John said they were included in the price. The oak tree had been cleaned and the fungus around it had died off, though John had told him sternly to leave it to flourish when it came back next year.

'Well?' John asked expectantly.

Jeremy looked around and nodded. 'It's a good job,' he conceded. Then he asked the dreaded question, 'So, I suppose you want paying?'

'It didn't work out quite as expensive as I'd thought,' John lied easily. 'And, as you already paid me a three hundred euro deposit, it'll only be another seven hundred euro.'

Jeremy's eyes narrowed. 'I thought you quoted me three thousand.'

'Yeah, well, I made a mistake. I'm not used to pricing things.'

Obviously, Jeremy thought dryly. Out loud he said, 'Well, thanks for your honesty anyway. I suppose it's good news for me.'

'Eh, yeah,' John said slowly, making a face.

'I'll go to the bank today and have your money tomorrow, how's that?' Jeremy said, not liking John's expression at all.

'You can drop it in next door for me to pick up,' John said. 'I'm not around for the next few days.'

'Oh?'

'Yep.' John shoved his hands into his pockets and nodded. 'Good doing business with you, Mr L. Recommend me to all your friends.'

'Indeed,' Jeremy said. 'Well, thank you for your hard work.' As there seemed nothing else to say, he thumbed in the direction of the house. 'I'm, eh, just going back into the house now.'

John watched him go. He wondered in amusement if Jeremy really believed that doing a garden this size only cost a thousand euro. The man was barking if he did. Joel and Adam had paid him weeks ago, they were decent guys. Having cleared the garden of his tools, he hopped over the back wall to say hi to his older brother, whom he hadn't seen in weeks.

'Hey!' he called as he let himself into the kitchen, 'anyone home?'

Mark and Owen raced out to greet him, both boys throwing themselves at his legs. 'Whoa,' John scooped Owen up in his arms, 'you nearly knocked me over, big guy. Where's your dad?'

Owen buried his head in John's shirt.

'He's inside watching the telly,' Mark answered, catching John by the hand and dragging him into the house. 'And Mammy is upstairs on the computer getting ready for school on Monday.'

John allowed Mark to pull him along. He was a tiny bit

apprehensive about seeing Tony. It had hurt him that Tony hadn't wanted to see him while he was in the clinic, but Tess had explained that Tony probably didn't want John to see him as an invalid.

Mark pushed the door open to reveal Tony sprawled across the sofa, munching a bag of crisps. He looked good anyway.

John grinned. 'Hey, how's it going? You're looking well.' He set a wriggling Owen down. Owen grabbed on to John's jeans and stood there, hugging his leg.

Tony straightened up and held out the six pack of crisps. 'D'you want a packet?'

'Yep,' Mark said, darting forward.

'Not you,' Tony said affectionately, 'you've had one. I was talking to John.'

'Naw, thanks,' John shook his head. 'I'm on a flying visit. I paid for an ad in a local newspaper and now I've a couple of gardening jobs to price.' He would have sat down only Owen still hadn't let go of his leg. In fact he was sucking his thumb, which was unlike him.

'Oh, so you've found your calling, have you?' There was a hint of a smile in Tony's voice.

'Aw now, steady on, I wouldn't go so far as to say that.' John grinned at him.

'Will you bring us to the shop?' Mark interrupted.

'You know I will,' John laughed.

Both of the boys cheered.

'Lads,' Tony said, 'calm down, will yez?' He sounded suddenly annoyed, John thought, but hadn't time to ponder it as Allie joined them.

'Hi,' she smiled, 'you're finished next door then?'

'Yep. Mr L is going to drop the money in here if that's OK.'

'That's fine. Hey boys, come on and let your uncle John talk to Daddy, he hasn't seen him in ages.' Allie caught her two sons by the hand.

'Don't forget the shops!' Mark called out as Allie rolled her eyes.

After they left, the two brothers regarded each other.

Tony broke the silence as he blurted out, 'I'm sure Tess told you about me taking the money from the jar? I'm really sorry I let her blame you.'

'Aw, I guess it was payback time,' John said easily, sliding into a chair opposite him.

'Huh?'

'D'you remember when we were kids and you got the blame for smashing the kitchen window with the football?' At Tony's nod John laughed and, pointing to himself, said, 'Well, ta da, guess what?'

'You fecker,' Tony grinned. 'I thought you hated football.'

'Only because I couldn't do all those fancy tricks you could. That day I was trying to practise catching it on my head, the way you did, and I hit the window instead.'

Tony laughed.

After a beat, John said quietly, 'I'm glad you're OK now.'

Tony's face darkened slightly, and his smile faltered. 'Thanks. Though OK might be pushing it a bit . . .'

'You should have told us. We would have helped you.'

'Told you what?'

'About the drugs.'

Tony said nothing. He hadn't thought he had a problem, not until the heavies from his supplier had turned up at the door. Allie had really gone off on one that day. Threatened to leave him and everything. He felt sick just thinking about it. Losing her would kill him.

'I mean—'

'Look, John,' Tony interrupted suddenly, trying to get the images of that awful evening from his head. 'Thanks a million for what you did for Allie and the kids when I was in,' he gulped, stumbling over the next words, 'in the clinic. I appreciate it.'

191

'No worries. What else is a chronically dissatisfied worker meant to do with his time?'

Tony smiled briefly and ploughed on, determined to say what he'd been longing to say ever since he'd first heard that John was doing their garden for them. 'Like don't get me wrong, I really appreciate it, but, well, I'm back now, aren't I?'

John nodded, wondering where this was going.

'And I'd like if you'd let me, you know, do all the rest of the odd jobs now. You know, putting up the goal posts in the garden for Mark, stuff like that.'

John looked confused. 'Sure. Yeah. No worries. I was only helping out.'

'Thanks.'

'Sure.'

There was more silence. John shifted uneasily and rubbed his hands on his jeans, which were dirty from the garden. He probably shouldn't have sat down, he thought. Tony looked good, but he seemed different. Quieter, more inside himself. For the first time ever, John didn't know what to say to Tony.

'Well,' he stood up, 'I guess I'll go. I'll just bring Mark and Owen to the shops and be on my way. D'you want to come?'

His question made Tony flinch. 'Eh, no, no thanks,' he answered.

'Fine so. I'll see you next week when I come to collect my money.'

'Sure. Good luck with the jobs.'

'Thanks.'

As John left and Tony heard the excited squeals of his sons as they scampered up the road with him, Tony put his head in his hands. He hoped he hadn't hurt John's feelings about the goal posts but it had killed him to see Owen happily greeting his brother when he still cowered away every time Tony spoke to him. He needed to have his son to himself to make him see how much he loved him. He wanted to do things for them both, to prove that he was going to be there for them . . .

192

He left the television room, only realising that he was searching for Allie when he saw her, bent over her laptop. He embraced her from behind and that made him feel right again. As long as he had her, he thought, he might just hang in there.

26

JOEL ARRIVED FOR his Saturday visit alone. It niggled Jeremy a little as Joel had a tendency to broach delicate subjects when it was just the two of them. Past topics had included invitations to dinner at his son's house, flyers tentatively offered outlining the activities available at the local senior citizens' club, forms to be filled out in case Jeremy took it into his head to go with a load of old people to pray at Knock Shrine. He'd produced papers extolling the craic to be had in the bingo hall. All his efforts were aimed at getting Jeremy out and about. Jeremy had refused each one and Joel, always unable to take a hint, still kept trying to force him out into the world. Now, as he watched Joel press the car alarm, Jeremy wondered what on earth he could want him to do now. The trick was to divert his attention.

'Hello,' he called.

Joel looked up in surprise at the cheery greeting. 'Hi, Dad. How are you?'

'Good,' Jeremy nodded. 'How's your new job going?'

Joel liked talking about his work, Jeremy knew.

'Not too bad, still finding my way.'

'And the family, how are they? Little Jennifer not with you?'

Joel looked a bit taken aback and Jeremy flushed. Maybe he'd been a bit too obvious.

'All fine. Jenny wanted to come to play with that boy next door but there was something I wanted to discuss with you first.'

'The boy next door, his name is Mark. A very nice lad. He could do with a friend or two. The boys on the road are not nice to him at all.' Jeremy shuffled into his kitchen. He was hoping that Joel would notice the back garden. This thing he had to discuss sounded ominous. Jeremy hoped they weren't going to invite him on a holiday. They had tried that before. Lanzarote of all places. Lands are grotty, that's what Jeremy called it in his head whenever someone mentioned it. He had explained to Joel and his wife that he was very grateful, which he sort of was, but that he wasn't a holiday person. He wasn't a bingo person or a senior citizens' club person or most definitely not a Knock pilgrimage person. He was very firmly a stay-at-home, walk-in-the-tiny-park-up-the-road person.

'Yes, he seems like a nice boy.' Joel sat down.

'Did you see my garden?' Jeremy asked.

'Dad,' Joel said abruptly, 'I'm here to talk about Adam.'

Jeremy stiffened. He should have guessed. He said nothing though, just remained where he was by the window, intent on studying the newly planted shrubs as they swayed in the slight breeze.

'I believe he told you he was gay?'

Gay. What an ironic word. Just hearing it plunged Jeremy into despair. 'Hmm.'

'He said that he thought you were shocked. He was worried about you. He sent me over because he didn't think you'd like to see him.'

Jeremy turned to Joel. Haltingly he said, 'I have a theory about him actually.'

'A theory?' Joel's eyes narrowed.

'Yes,' Jeremy nodded, 'I have a theory that he's not really gay.'

'He's really gay, Dad,' Joel said firmly.

'No,' Jeremy shook his head, 'he doesn't even look gay. He wasn't always gay.'

'Dad, he's been gay for ever. I'm here to tell you that it really isn't a big deal.'

Jeremy resented the pragmatic, almost condescending tone in Joel's voice. 'Not a big deal?' He crossed towards Joel, making him pull back slightly. 'Well, it is to me.' He jabbed at his chest to emphasise his point. 'It's a very big deal to me. Everyone knowing and reading about him in a magazine. He's living with a man, for God's sake.'

'I know it's a shock to you, Dad,' Joel affected a soothing tone, 'but Peter is a very nice man.'

Jeremy gawked at Joel in disbelief. 'You've met him?'

'We all have. The kids and everyone.'

Jeremy pursed his lips. 'You let your children meet this person?'

'Yes.' Joel heaved a sigh. 'Dad, Adam was terrified of telling you. He knew you'd go off the deep end.'

As far as Jeremy was concerned it wasn't he who had gone off the deep end. It was everyone else. 'My theory is,' he said, his words tumbling over themselves, 'is that Adam misses his mother. That's the whole root of his problem. I figured it out yesterday when I was looking at some photographs.'

'We all miss Mam,' Joel said, 'but I hardly think—'

'He was devastated when she, when she . . .' Jeremy couldn't get by the word, so he didn't say it. 'He was devastated and hurt,' he went on, 'and so it made him afraid to love women in case he'd have that hurt again. So he turned to men instead. Adam just needs therapy.'

To Jeremy's indignation, Joel spluttered in a sort of laughing way.

'Excuse me?' Jeremy said loftily. 'I would rather you didn't make fun of it.'

'Well, Dad, I'm sorry but that's just about the most ridiculous thing I've ever heard.' Joel looked incredulously at him. 'You have lived in a bubble for so long now that you really aren't in touch at all, are you?'

'In touch?' Jeremy's voice shook just a little. Joel had never laughed at him or told him he was ridiculous before. Joel was the son who had got a normal job. Joel never insulted him. 'You cannot come in here and say that I live in a bubble.'

'Sorry,' Joel said. 'But Dad, I'm not trying to be cruel.'

'Well you were.' Jeremy folded his arms.

'Have you ever considered that it's not Adam who misses Ma, it's you?'

The words were like tiny little missiles that made him twitch. Jeremy drew himself up. 'We all miss her,' he answered, choking up in a funny sort of way, 'you said so yourself.'

'She died over twenty years ago, Dad, and yes, it's terrible, but Adam and me, we have gone on and made lives for ourselves.' Joel paused and added softly, 'You haven't.'

Jeremy was unable to move. He couldn't open his mouth to retaliate, nor lift his arm to gesture for Joel to leave. He just stood still as an ice statue as Joel's words sank into his bones and froze him.

'Ever since she died, you've shut yourself up in this house, refusing to get involved in anything,' Joel went on gently. 'You never went to parent teacher meetings, you never brought us on holidays because you missed her being there, you went through the motions of bringing us up but you weren't there, not really. You cut yourself off from anyone who might have cared or helped.'

'How dare you,' Jeremy croaked out the words. 'I did my best.'

'I know you did,' Joel nodded. 'But these days, Dad, your big adventure is going to the local shops and arguing with them over tomato bread. Or sparring with teenagers in the park. It's not a life.'

'You stop it now!' Jeremy's voice rose a little.

'You need to get out, mix with people. Accept Adam's life, accept mine and get one of your own.'

'Accept a son who married early and is determined to have a pile of children? Accept another son who lives with a man and who prances about on TV in a pirate costume? I don't think so.' The words spewed out of him, sounding horrible and hateful and angry. He didn't know where they came from and he regretted them, but how dare Joel think he had the right to criticise him and analyse him when he was going about with a grumpy wife and having masses of kids year after year?

Joel's mouth dropped open. His face went red, his jowls shook and his body trembled. He was, Jeremy realised, furious. 'Did you ever wonder why I chose to marry early and have kids or why Adam became a children's entertainer? Did you?' Without waiting for his father to answer, Joel stood up in a very confrontational manner and wagged a finger at him. 'It's because we never had a childhood of our own!'

'What are you on about?' Jeremy spluttered as Joel wrenched open the kitchen door.

Joel whirled towards him. 'When I was five you told us Santa was invented by people who hadn't grown up properly. You and Mam had a huge row over that. When she died, it was like you decided all the fun in the world had gone. We never got any more parties or celebrated anything ever again. We excelled in school to make you bloody happy, to put a smile on your face, but nothing worked. You were miserable all the time. If anything, Dad, I'm surprised Adam is with a man. You'd imagine he'd want to stay well away!' With that Joel strode through the hall, yanked open the front door and slammed it closed.

Jeremy didn't move for a long time.

After a bit he became aware of the ticking of the clock on the wall. It was almost dinner time. He didn't feel hungry though. He decided on a nice ham sandwich with some cheese.

He'd forget about what Joel had said. That was the best thing. Put it out of his mind and he was sure Joel would do the same.

That was the best thing.

27

ALLIE WASN'T SURE who was more nervous, her or Tony. His nerves were for himself – he'd confessed that he had problems with new situations and new people. Allie's nerves were for him, too. She desperately wanted him to get something from this NA meeting, some little shred of hope that might make him want to go again. She needed him to want this, she realised. It was their only hope. Despite the fact that he was still seeing his counsellor at the clinic, he still had to go to NA. Holly had recommended this meeting as it was where Veronica went. She thought that if Veronica saw Tony going, she'd keep it up too. 'He seemed to be a great influence on her,' Holly said.

As they climbed out of the car opposite the meeting hall, Allie caught Tony's hand. 'There are worse things in the world than being drug-free and having to go to a meeting.' she said.

'I know,' he said back. He didn't sound as if he quite believed it.

There was a crowd of about ten people outside the hall; most of them seemed to be in their twenties. Some of them obviously knew each other as they chatted away comfortably, swapping cigarettes and laughing. A few glanced in their direction. Tony shifted his gaze away as Allie grinned and got a few smiles of welcome in return. There was no sign of Veronica. Holly had said that she might be working that night.

'Out of the way!' A woman's voice cut through the chat. She was brandishing a set of keys and as she came towards the crowd they moved to let her pass. Shouts of 'Hiya Imelda' cut through the air.

'Hi yez, hi yez,' Imelda shouted cheerily as she inserted the key into the lock. She glanced at her watch. 'Now, who's going to fill the kettle?'

A hand went up.

'And I've got the biscuits.' Imelda unveiled two packets of chocolate digestives, to the cheers of some girls in the front.

'Given up the diet have ya, Imelda?'

Imelda smirked. 'Nope. I didn't say I was going to eat them.'

'I gave up the smack,' the girl who had volunteered to fill the kettle said. 'But giving up the biscuits, now that's a step too far.'

A few people laughed and one by one they filed into the room.

It was a small but cosy space. Chairs were lined up along the walls in a circle and a few extra had been stacked up in front in case anyone needed them. The chairs filled rapidly, the attendance higher than Allie had expected. Tony made his way to a corner and sat down, glancing hard at his trainers. Allie sat in beside him.

'Eh,' a young man wearing a T-shirt approached, 'would either of ya like a cup of coffee or tea?'

'That'd be great, thanks,' Allie nodded, smiling. 'Tony?' She nudged him.

'Eh, yeah, coffee would be good, thanks.'

'We'll have two coffees,' she said.

'You sit there, I'll get it.' The man left.

'Wasn't that nice?' Allie remarked.

'Uh-huh.'

There was a lot of good-natured banter in the room. There were some, however, like Tony, who sat staring at their hands. One girl, around sixteen, was pulling hard on a huge hoop earring. She seemed oblivious to any pain she might be feeling. Allie winced every time she did it.

'Here yez go.' The man held out a coffee for each of them.

'Thanks.' As Allie took hers she noticed that his arms were covered in vicious looking track marks. She quickly turned away, not wanting to be caught staring.

'It's the first time I've had the nerve to wear a T-shirt,' the man explained, in a remarkably upbeat way.

'Fair play.' Allie felt weirdly emotional at his admission. 'Well done.'

'Mind that coffee now, it's hot,' he said.

After about ten minutes, the woman who had unlocked the door took a seat at the top of the room. 'Hi, everyone, and for those that don't know me, I'm Imelda.'

'Hi, Imelda,' everyone chorused.

Tony jumped, startled, then caught Allie's eye and grinned.

'I'm the Chair for tonight. Now, to start, Billy will read out "What is an addict?"'

'Hi,' Billy said.

'Hi, Billy,' everyone said back.

Once again Tony jumped, and once again he and Allie almost laughed.

Billy, haltingly and in rushed embarrassment, read out from a page in front of him.

Imelda then asked another person to read out why they were all there.

After a series of pieces had been read describing the work and the steps of NA, Imelda then went through the rules governing the night. She asked that a cup be passed around for donations.

'Shit,' Allie whispered, 'I don't have any money.'

'Were you not listening?' Tony teased. 'Anyone who is not a member isn't meant to contribute. Only the addicts.' Tony dug into his jeans and pulled out a few coins. 'I kinda thought we'd need it,' he said.

When the collection had been taken, Imelda turned to a

man across from her. 'This is Graham,' she said loudly over the hubbub of chat.

'Hi, Graham.' Allie joined in with the rest of them. It was the man who had made them coffee.

'Graham is our speaker tonight,' Imelda went on. She nodded encouragingly at Graham. 'It's all yours.' She indicated the room.

Graham smiled a little shyly. There was a small silence as he shifted about in his chair. He coughed slightly and began, sounding a little self-conscious. 'I've never done speaker at a meeting before. And to be honest, I'm only doing it cause Imelda asked me and I fancy her like hell.'

There was laughter.

'Join the queue,' Imelda shot back.

'Yeah, when she's finished her diet the queue'll be bigger,' a girl piped up.

More laughs.

Graham grinned. 'Anyway, like I said, I've never done speaker. And since I agreed to do it, I've been going around worrying about what to say. And as you all know, no one does worry quite like an addict.'

A few people clapped in appreciation of the joke as others laughed.

'Like I was dreaming about it . . . I was up at the top of the room and instead of saying what I meant to say, my voice turned into Chinese. Or another time I was naked.'

'That'd put Imelda off,' someone slagged.

Graham laughed. 'And anyway, all week I'm going about thinking, What am I going to say? What the fuck am I going to say? And then it hit me, just this morning, that I was actually worrying about the fact I had to do just that.'

There was a silence as Graham's gaze swept the room.

'It dawned on me that I was actually going to say some- thing. That no matter what, I had agreed to get up in front of a room full of people and talk and it dawned on me that that's the whole point. The fact I've agreed to speak at all is the whole point.' He paused. 'A couple of years ago, I came in this door and I sat in that corner there.' He pointed to where Tony sat.

Tony swiftly looked down.

'I sat in that corner and I shook. It wasn't the DTs, it was terror. I was in this room with a load of strangers, they were all talking and I was petrified that I might have to say something. If the person beside me spoke, I just wanted to get up and leave. I just wanted to disappear. I hadn't the courage even to say my own name. And the weeks went on and for some reason, I kept coming back. I suppose I could relate to people here in a way I never related to anyone before. I finally found a place where I fit in. My worries were their worries. My life might as well have been theirs. And every week I thought maybe this week I'll introduce myself and every week I chickened out. And then,' he coughed a little and said on a gulp, 'then my younger brother died of an overdose.'

There was a murmur of sympathy from the room but Graham overrode it. 'And instead of getting high, like I'd done before when bad stuff happened, I realised that I needed my meeting. I needed it to stay clean. If I hadn't come that night, I'd be back on the stuff no question. I went that night and it didn't seem so scary to speak because the alternative was scarier. I told everyone that my brother had died that day and that I needed major help to stay clean. I got a sponsor and we started doing the steps and it hasn't been easy, but I'm still here.' He paused as a ripple of approval went around the room. 'Giving up a drug,' Graham went on, 'means giving up your life as you know it. It means stepping out into a world that scares you stupid. And the reason it scared me was because I always wanted to be in control. I spent my life trying to second guess people, trying to fit in. So I used. And for a while it did give me confidence, until I eventually lost control of my life. I realise now the only control I have is choosing not to use. The only control I have is in choosing to accept myself as I am. It's a paradox. The whole giving up the drugs thing is a paradox.' He turned to Imelda. 'Is that the right word?'

Imelda shrugged. 'I dunno, depends on what you're going to say.'

Graham grinned. 'Yeah. I guess. OK, well, basically what I mean is that by doing step one of the programme and admitting that you have no control over your addiction means that finally you have some control.'

'That is a paradox,' Allie piped up.

Beside her Tony stiffened, as everyone looked in their direction.

'Thanks,' Graham nodded, grinning. 'So, what I want to say is that a year on, I am here talking in front of a crowd. My recovery has let me do that. And while I can't control the world, I have finally found that I can control myself.' He paused. 'And that's it.' He suddenly seemed a little embarrassed. 'And look,' he displayed his ravaged arms, 'this is part of me accepting myself. I'm not covering them up any more. I think of it as a badge of honour. I am now happier than I have ever been in my life.'

There was applause. Graham did a mock bow which made them laugh. Allie found herself smiling and glanced at Tony. He was clapping but he still looked as if he couldn't wait for it all to be over. Her heart sank slightly.

'Thanks,' Imelda grinned. 'That was great, Graham, and if you do take me out, I'm delighted to know that you can control yourself.'

More laughs.

'So,' Imelda went on, 'the meeting is now open.'

'Hi, I'm Julie,' a girl said.

'Hi, Julie,' everyone said.

'Thanks, Graham, that was brilliant.' She stared at her hands as she spoke and her face flushed a deep red. 'I'm off two weeks now.'

People murmured, 'Well done.'

'This is the first time I've had the nerve to talk. It's good to know you were worse than me. Anyway, today was the hardest day I had so far. It's awful when you look out your window and you can see dealers queuing up to sell. It just makes your head spin. But I got through it and it gives me hope.' She stopped.

Someone else spoke about their day.

It was followed by an older man telling them about his child being banned from school and of how he was so tempted to use. 'It was the reality I needed to escape from,' he said. 'The knowledge that through my drug use I've fucked up my kid. But then I thought, What use is that to my kid?'

One by one people spoke of their hopes and fears and bad times and fun times. Allie was stunned to hear the laughter and the banter. Beside her Tony remained silent.

Once the meeting had officially closed, badges were awarded to people for their clean time. As far as Allie could make out, different badges were given out for different lengths of time. Finally, the girl in charge of the badges asked, 'Any new members here tonight?'

Tony said nothing. Allie put up her hand, not sure if it was the right thing to do. 'We're new,' she said. 'I'm Allie and this is my husband, Tony.'

A chorus of welcomes. Tony rubbed his hand over his forehead and swallowed hard.

'It's Tony who's the member,' Allie said then.

Tony attempted to smile around at the group. 'Guess who is in control of my life?' he joked feebly.

It was met with laughter and Allie beamed at him, inordinately proud of his ability to joke. Since he'd come home she'd been surprised at how sensitive he was. He didn't seem to have the ability to understand the way things worked, that it was OK to go outside and chat to the neighbours. Tony agonised over what to say, how to end a conversation, how not to sound stupid. So he stayed in instead. The drugs had propelled him along for years. Now he really did only have a T-shirt. Allie was finally beginning to understand that the man she had married, while the same with her, was a stranger to the world at large.

The NA member handed Tony a badge which he immediately shoved into his pocket.

Finally Imelda called the meeting to a close. Everyone stood up, held hands and said the serenity prayer, and then Allie found herself being embraced by a tall man on the left. Tony was being hugged too, much to his horror. Around the room, people were embracing and laughing.

'Let's head,' Tony said, not waiting for Allie to answer.

She followed him out the door and to the car.

'Jesus,' he said when he was behind the wheel, 'I can't go back there.'

'What?' Allie stared at him, aghast. 'But it was great. They were all so friendly.'

'It was all so false,' Tony said. 'All that "Hi, Graham, Hi, Billy". Jesus.'

'They didn't judge, that was nice.' Allie felt her heart sinking. 'I thought it was great.'

'It was just everyone talking about their day, how will that cure me?'

'Because you'll see, Tony, that you are exactly like these people. I could recognise you in their descriptions.'

Tony didn't reply, he just fired the engine and started to drive. Allie sat beside him, swamped by a feeling of hopelessness. 'They told you to go to NA in the clinic,' she muttered.

Tony's only answer was to speed up.

'So how exactly are you planning to stay off the drugs?' she demanded.

'I'm doing OK,' Tony said back.

'You can't stay in for ever watching TV and eating crisps,' Allie said through gritted teeth.

206

'I won't,' Tony said. 'I'll start job hunting. I'm going to ring up a few contacts and see if they have any work for me. The last place I was in only let me go as they were downsizing. They'll give me a reference for definite.'

Allie's heart twisted and she felt sick.

'It's not as if I ever let them down,' Tony went on.

Allie bit her lip. 'A job will solve nothing.' She hoped her voice didn't betray her anxiety. 'I would rather you go to meetings.'

'I can do the steps on my own.'

'No, Tony.'

'It's bullshit.'

'You are scared,' Allie snapped. 'Just like you were scared of answering the phone. Just like you're scared of going out of the house. Well, Tony, I'm bloody scared too. I'm scared you'll start using again, I'm scared of waking up on my own at night and hearing you bang your way into the house. I'm scared that you'll frighten the kids and shout at them. I'm scared you'll take away this lovely happiness we finally seem to be having.'

Tony's grip on the steering wheel tightened. 'It won't happen.'

'Why? Why won't it happen? You've been clean before. What's so different now?'

He didn't reply.

'The only thing that's different is that you went to a meeting. That you found people who are like you.'

'They were like me. They're not now. I'll never go on like they did, hugging and stuff.'

'You judgemental bastard,' Allie snapped. 'You sat there mocking them and they never once passed a comment on you. Let me out.' She banged the door of the car.

'No.' Tony looked alarmed.

'You stop this car now or I'll jump.'

'Aw, Allie—'

'Let me out!'

He stopped the car abruptly, earning a horn blast from the man behind. Allie hopped out, slammed the door and walked off.

'Allie,' Tony called, jumping out of the car after her. 'Allie!'

'Piss off!' Even as Allie said it, she was aware that people were looking.

'You're right,' Tony yelled then. 'I am scared.' His voice dipped. 'Please don't go.'

The man behind, the one who had beeped, stopped, rolled down his window and stuck his head out, watching avidly.

Allie turned around. Tony stood at the driver's side of the car, looking mortified, his eyes imploring her to get back in.

'I wouldn't throw you out of bed for eating crisps,' a girl remarked as she walked by.

'Do you mind?' Allie said. 'That's my husband.'

The girl chortled.

'And actually all he does is eat crisps,' Allie yelled after her. 'And watch TV!'

'Jesus, Al!' Tony sounded horrified to see his wife yelling in the street.

'Don't "Jesus, Al" me!' Allie said crossly.

'Hello? Late for a meeting here,' the man in the car behind called irritably. 'So if you'd hurry up, I'd appreciate it.'

'Allie, get in,' Tony said urgently.

Allie folded her arms.

'I'll go to the meeting.'

'There's no point in going for me, you have to want to go for yourself.'

'Hello?' the man in the car said again, 'Did you not hear me? I'm running late for my meeting!'

'Yeah, well, it's better than not going to a meeting at all, isn't it?' Allie said to him.

'Pardon?'

Tony spluttered out a laugh.

'Oh, laugh away,' Allie said. 'You've let me down too many times, Tony.'

'I know I want to get better,' Tony said, his smile fading. 'So yeah, I promise to give it a go. OK?'

'A year minimum.'

'It'll take me a year to get to my meeting if yez don't wind it up.' The man behind harrumphed.

Both of them ignored him.

'A year,' Tony nodded. 'Deal.' He walked around to the passenger door and opened it for her. 'Now will you get in?'

'OK.' Without looking at him she stalked by him and into the car. She allowed him to close the door.

He got back in his side and, indicating, he pulled off.

Allie was unable to look at him. She was shaking, afraid she might cry.

'Sorry,' Tony muttered.

'Don't do that to me,' Allie gulped. 'Don't, Tony. I need to believe that you want to recover. I need to believe that you will do anything. If I thought for one minute that you didn't mean it . . .'

'I do mean it. I promise.'

'Well, good.'

More silence.

'I love you when you're angry,' Tony said softly, the hint of a laugh in his voice. 'You really showed the man in the car behind.'

Allie considered not answering, she was still a little annoyed, but when Tony smiled at her, her resolve slipped. 'I did, didn't I?'

'Yep.' He winked. 'Come here.' He held out his arm and Allie rested her head on his shoulder. 'You can do gears for me,' he said, kissing the top of her head, 'I can't reach now.'

Without saying any more, they drove back home.

28

JEREMY WAS BORED. It was a strange sensation as he'd never actually felt bored before. He supposed that was because his boys would be ringing him and annoying him and he'd spend his days thinking up lies to combat their probing questions about his social life and his eating habits. But now, it seemed as if they were not going to bother ringing him at all. A whole week had gone by and he hadn't heard from either of them. And he wouldn't mind, but in order to have one up on Joel when he rang, Jeremy had taken to walking every day, even when he didn't need to go to the shops. The whole perambulation took about thirty minutes, but along the way he encountered the same faces. Young mothers chatting away as they sat on park benches, while their children guzzled all sorts of unhealthy foods. These women sometimes smiled at him and one or two had taken to saying hello. Even the children smiled at him and, because he was used to Mark chatting away to him, Jeremy felt a lot easier with these children than he might have. He also met men his own age walking dogs that looked older than themselves. He nodded to these men and they nodded back. He also, unfortunately, met those awful teenagers who drank and smoked in the hedges bordering the park. They seemed never to go to school. They'd taken to calling out greetings to him as well. Asking him for fags and drink and laughing at his pompous way of talking.

The girl who hung about with them seemed the only one with a hope of redemption, Jeremy thought, so he'd taken to telling her at every opportunity that she should give up the smoking and go to school.

'Well,' she countered, 'if giving up the smoking and going to school makes me end up like you, I'd rather take me chances and die.'

Jeremy had looked her up and down and said in a voice that intimidated his boys, 'My dear girl, you look like me already. I cringe to see what another sixty years will do to you.'

That had created a lot of laughter and now he found himself quite popular with this horrible bunch of teens.

However on days when it rained, Jeremy didn't venture out. Instead he grew bored. He tended to drink a lot of tea and watch television. Today he had made himself a cup of strong tea and a few ham sandwiches and was idly flicking through the stations. Suddenly he caught a glimpse of a familiar face and he flicked the station back. Adam. Dressed in his pirate uniform and singing loudly about sailing the waves on his pirate ship.

His son looked quite manly as he hopped from one side of the pirate ship to the other, barking out orders to his crew, who carried them out with sunny smiles and a 'Heave ho, off we go.' Adam was a good singer, Jeremy thought, astonished. He never remembered hearing Adam sing before. Suddenly, on the TV, a shot rang out. The singing stopped. A member of Adam's pirate crew pointed towards the stern.

Jeremy found himself leaning forward in his chair as a full scale battle between the two pirate ships broke out. He learned that Jolly Roger was a good pirate who robbed from bad pirates to give to the poor. A Robin Hood of the high seas, Jolly Roger devised cunning plans to see off his enemies. Jeremy's eyes drank in his son as his handsome face dominated the TV screen. He found himself relaxing in Adam's company in a way he could never do when his son was physically in the room with him. Just when it looked as if Jolly Roger's ship was about to be captured, the credits began to roll and the presenter announced that they'd be back on Friday to see what happened.

Jeremy groaned. Imagine leaving the episode at that. Ridiculous. He had a good mind to ring up Adam and tell him that it was ridiculous. Yes, he thought, that's what he would do. And it would let Adam know, in a roundabout way, that he had watched his show. So before he could change his mind, he set his mug of tea down on the floor and went into the hall to the phone. He picked it up and pressed the button for Adam's number.

'Dad?' Adam answered on the first ring. 'Hey, how you doing?'

Jeremy cleared his throat. 'I'm actually ringing to complain,' he said.

There was no response.

'Adam, are you there?'

'Dad,' Adam said wearily, 'I have to go. Ring me back when you want to talk, OK?' And he hung up.

Jeremy stared at the phone. That wasn't meant to happen. OK, maybe he shouldn't have used the word complain. Maybe his tone was wrong. But did his son have to hang up? What if Jeremy wanted to complain about a bad pain in his chest? What if he wanted to complain that his house was being flooded? What then? Some sons he had. All he wanted to do was to say that he'd enjoyed Adam's show a lot and why couldn't they just have finished the episode? But saying it out like that wasn't his style. That kind of thing embarrassed him.

It wasn't manly.

Which was probably why Adam had hung up.

Some son he was.

Allie felt physically ill as she pressed the final digit of her father's phone number and listened to the sound of ringing at the other end. She willed herself not to hang up. To stay on the line. To—

'Hello!'

She jumped.

'Hello?' he said again.

She knew it was him as his voice hadn't changed. It still had that confident tone, that unfailing cheeriness. 'Hello,' she croaked back.

There was a light hesitation. Then, 'Yes? Who is this?'

'It's me,' she said. She coughed to clear her throat. 'Allie.' Outside, Tony was playing with the boys. Owen was mellowing slightly, Allie could hear him laughing and it made her smile despite the sick feeling invading her.

'Alisha?' Some of his liveliness seemed to have ebbed away. 'Is it you, Alisha?'

He was the only one who had ever used her full name. 'Yes.'

Allie heard a long sigh, as if her dad had been holding his breath for years until this minute. When he spoke next, his voice shook. 'Thank you,' he said. 'Thanks for ringing.'

Allie didn't know what to say to that.

Her dad didn't seem to know what to say either.

When they eventually spoke, it was together.

'Would you—'

'What do—'

'You first,' her dad said.

Allie pulled at the phone cord, twisting it around her finger. 'What do you want?' she asked. It sounded abrupt. She wasn't sure if she meant it that way.

There was no hesitation. 'Just to meet you. To see you.' His voice was quiet. Intense.

'Why?'

The question seemed to wrong-foot him. He swallowed hard. 'You're my daughter,' he said simply. 'I've wanted to see you every single day. I wrote to you, you never replied. Then I wondered if your mother was giving you my letters.'

'She gave them to me.'

'Oh.'

213

'I never replied because,' Allie took a deep breath, determined not to let her voice shake, determined to say what she wanted to say without chickening out, 'because I didn't know what to say to you.'

'Oh,' he said again.

'What does a kid say to a dad who humiliates her and her mother?' Sudden anger sparked. 'And then writes about his new life in France?'

Silence. Then, 'I also wrote that I missed you.'

God he was such a charmer. 'In between writing about the winery you were intending to open and the gorgeous sunny weather.'

'Yeah, well, that didn't quite work out,' he mumbled. 'Fecking vines all rotted on me.'

Allie said nothing, kind of glad it hadn't worked out for him.

'I had to leave it.' He stopped abruptly, perhaps aware that Allie mightn't want to hear about his disastrous years in France. 'Would you like to meet me?' he asked instead.

Allie hesitated. Would she like to meet him? Yes, she would. But did she want to meet him? She wasn't so sure. It would open up a whole dimension to her life that she hadn't bargained on. How much of a part would he want to play in it? What would her mother think? Tony had told her that it was up to her how much she saw him. She asked him if he ever thought about his own parents, his real ones. He'd shrugged and said that, yeah, he sometimes did but that if they showed up to meet him he'd refuse. 'I've enough trouble managing my life without making it more complicated,' he'd grinned. 'You on the other hand,' he said, winking, 'are good at this whole life thing.'

'Well?' her dad pressed, 'Would you?'

Cautiously Allie replied, 'I'd like to meet you, but it might be only the once, I don't know.'

'That's fine,' her dad said, and for some odd reason she felt let down by him.

'I'm back at school on Monday,' she went on.

'You're a teacher?'

My God, they had a lot of catching up to do. 'Yes. English and History. I'll meet you next weekend, in Dublin city under Clery's clock. I won't back out this time.' She was proud of how efficient she sounded.

'OK. Does one o'clock suit you?'

'Perfect.'

More silence.

'Well, eh, goodbye.' Allie didn't wait for him to say it back. Instead she put the phone into the cradle and walked out the back garden to her boys. To give all three of them a massive hug.

Jeremy counted out his money before putting it into a brown envelope. He hadn't managed to drop it in yet so he'd included a twenty euro tip which he hoped would be sufficient to cover the delay in paying. Besides, John had been honest about the cost and that deserved some recognition in Jeremy's opinion. He also brought the family ticket to Adam's show that his son had given for the neighbours. Then he left the house.

Those horrible boys were sitting on the ground, outside one of their own homes, sucking on ice pops.

'Hi, Germy,' one of them called to an explosion of laughter from his pals.

Jeremy paused, thought about saying something and then decided that he would. To the horror of the six boys on the path, he began to walk towards them. Cries of 'Leg it!' accompanied a scrambling to their feet and away they ran, across the green at the top of the road. Oh, Jeremy thought, if only he was twenty years younger. Or forty.

Muttering to himself, he retraced his steps. Pushing open the wooden gate he entered next door's driveway. Allie really did keep the place looking well, Jeremy thought in approval. Her bell was shining. He pressed it and heard it emit a satisfying 'ding dong' inside the house, and then a tall silhouette obscured the mottled view of the hallway.

The silhouette was probably the husband. Jeremy hadn't met him yet. He looked like the sort of man who would be good to chat to, not that Jeremy chatted to too many people.

The door opened and sure enough, it was the husband. He didn't look like John at all, was Jeremy's first thought. John was tanned and smiley and had blue eyes that crinkled up at the edges. This man was the opposite. Up close he was pale, unhealthily so, as if he hadn't been outside in a while, though Jeremy knew that he had been in the garden a lot with Mark. He wasn't smiling and his eyes were a curious black-brown.

'Hello?' he said. It was a question which meant, What do you want?

'Hello,' Jeremy said. 'I'm Jeremy from next door.'

There was no reciprocal greeting so Jeremy continued, a bit miffed, 'I've some money to drop by for John. He said to leave it here.' He fumbled at the envelope, which was refusing to come out of his pocket.

The man watched silently as he struggled with it, tearing paper in the process.

'Who is it?' Allie called.

'Next door neighbour with money for John.'

To Jeremy's relief, Allie joined her strange husband at the door. 'Hi, Mr Lyons,' she said cheerily, 'come on in.'

'Oh no no, I couldn't possibly—'

'Of course you can.' She pulled the door open wider and Jeremy stepped into the hall. It was the first time in his life he had been in one of his neighbour's houses. 'I see you've met my husband.'

'Eh, yes,' Jeremy mumbled.

'Jeremy is the man who arranged for Mark to have a lift with Jolly Roger,' Allie explained to Tony. 'He's his son.'

'Oh right.' Tony stuck out his hand and smiled in a strangely awkward manner. 'Pleased to meet you.'

'And, eh, you too.' At last, the money came free from Jeremy's pocket, though the envelope ripped. Some of the twenties fluttered to the ground. Tony picked them up and handed them back to him. 'There now,' Jeremy passed over the money. 'Can you give this to John?'

'Will do,' Allie said, taking it from him. 'Would you like a cuppa?'

Jeremy ignored the question. 'And my son Adam thought you might like this,' he said as he handed her the family ticket.

'Oh wow!'

To his horror, Allie hugged him. Jeremy froze and over her shoulder his eyes met the amused gaze of her husband. 'Eh, it's only a ticket,' he spluttered out, detangling himself.

'But it's so nice, thank you.' Allie beamed at him. 'Now, come on in and have a cuppa.'

'No, no.' And then suddenly, Jeremy changed his mind. Having tea with the neighbours would show Joel that he did have a life. The next time Joel called he'd tell him all about it. 'Well, actually, yes, that would be nice,' Jeremy said. He followed Allie into the kitchen and sat down at the table. The walls were nice and bright, he thought. His own kitchen was very brown. It never looked like this. Knowing that some conversation was expected of him, he turned to the husband, who was hovering about near the door as if anxious to leave. 'Did you enjoy your trip?' he asked.

Tony jerked. 'Trip?'

'Mark mentioned that you were on a business trip.'

'Oh that,' Tony stared into middle distance, 'yes, that was good.'

'Were you in the States?'

'He was.' Allie deftly laid a plate in front of Jeremy. 'Would you like a sandwich, Mr Lyons? We were just about to have our tea.'

'It's Jeremy,' Jeremy said.

'Would you like a sandwich, Jeremy?'

Joel would never believe this, Jeremy thought in triumph. 'Yes, that would be lovely, thank you.' Then he wondered at the wisdom of it. But Mark would never let it slip that Jeremy was Santa, would he? No.

'Tony, will you put on the kettle and call the boys?' Allie said.

Tony gave her a look of something akin to relief, Jeremy thought, before hopping outside to call his sons.

Jeremy watched as the boys hurtled inside, stopped dead at the sight of him, then Mark whooped and said, 'Hey, class! Are you having tea with us, Mr Lyons?'

'Your mother has kindly asked me to stay,' Jeremy smiled.

'Do you eat meat?' Mark pushed his body into the space between Jeremy's leg and the table.

'Yes.' Jeremy felt flattered that the boy wanted to be near him. He liked the way the child smiled at him.

Mark slipped a warm hand into Jeremy's cold one. 'Not reindeer meat though?'

Allie gave a guffaw at the question. 'What made you ask that?'

'Nothing,' Mark said. 'I just don't think Mr Lyons would eat reindeers.'

A light sweat broke out on Jeremy's forehead. 'Eh, no, no I don't. Just regular meat.'

'No one really eats reindeer meat,' Tony said, sounding amused. 'Now go wash your hands, both of you.' As they left, Tony grinned at him. 'Kids, ey?' he said.

'Yes, yes indeed.' Jeremy swallowed, his mouth felt like sandpaper. He'd really have to tell Mark that he wasn't allowed to say anything at all relating to Santa when they next met.

'So, you eat ham?' Allie asked.

'Yes.'

'And cheese?'

'Just the orange one, nothing else.' These people probably

218

ate all sorts of stuff he wasn't used to. He stole a surreptitious glance at the bread. But it was white and ordinary looking.

Allie was buttering what looked like a mountain of food. Tony had disappeared and Jeremy could hear him instructing the boys to dry their hands. He seemed like a fairly hands-on dad. A lot of giggling came from the bathroom as they washed.

'They seem to have fun together,' Jeremy remarked.

'Yeah,' Allie said. She smiled at him and Jeremy thought she looked quite beautiful, not the stressed looking woman he had perceived. 'I'd say you were good with your own boys,' she said. 'Mark adores you.'

Jeremy coughed uncomfortably. 'Well,' he reddened, 'we all make mistakes. But I did my best.'

'We all do that.' Allie passed him a sandwich and patted him on the shoulder. 'Just hang on a minute until I get those lads, they'll have the bathroom destroyed.'

As Jeremy bit into his sandwich, he wondered if there were any moments like that when his boys were growing up. Was there squealing and laughter? He was sure there must have been. He tried to think and couldn't. He found himself smiling as Mark emerged, soaked to the skin after his dad had thrown a wet towel over his head.

29

'WHAT DOES JUNKIE mean?' Mark asked.

Allie, trying to overtake a car that was doing about ten miles an hour, felt her heart flip and she inhaled sharply. 'What?'

'Junkie,' Mark asked again. 'What's it mean?'

Jesus, Allie thought, she didn't need this. The first day back at work had been a tough one. It had started badly because she and Tony had argued. Tony had offered to take care of Owen while she was out, but Allie had insisted on sending Owen back to creche. She tried to soften the rejection by telling Tony that she wanted him to have a stress-free environment so he could get better. The truth was that she still didn't quite trust him on his own with the kids, and he knew that and she knew he knew and was hurt over it. Allie had worried that it might just send him back over the edge. But on the other hand, Owen had come out of his shell so well this summer that she wasn't prepared to jeopardise it for the sake of making Tony feel better. Then, much to her horror, Tony had announced that he would job hunt and she'd told him that no, that wouldn't be a good idea. 'But Veronica has a job,' he'd said. She'd told him firmly not to and he'd flipped. He'd said he felt useless and she'd said better to feel useless than high. But he couldn't look for a job, not yet. She needed time to screw up the courage to tell him what she'd done . . .

'Junkie, Mammy, what does it mean?'

Then, after dropping Mark to his school, she'd spent the day getting to know her new classes, most of which had no appreciation of English. At three, when Mark finished school, she picked him up, brought him to her school where the receptionist was kind enough to keep an eye on him until four, when her own classes ended. On the way home, they had to swing by and collect Owen from creche. Allie was exhausted from all the juggling and now this . . .

'Mam!' Mark pressed. 'What is a junkie? Robert from up the road said to me in the yard today that everyone knew that Dad was a junkie.'

'What?' Allie nearly crashed the car. 'What did you say?'

'Everyone says that Daddy is a junkie but you said he was an accountant,' Mark went on.

'He is an accountant,' Allie affirmed. 'Don't listen to Robert.'

'He came up to me, I didn't go near him.' Then Mark said, 'He's not nice. He calls me Fatso.'

'He what?!'

'He calls me that all the time.' Mark picked at a scab on his knee. 'I try to ignore him but he still does it.'

Allie blinked back sudden tears. How dare that little brat call her son Fatso! Mark wasn't fat, he was just . . . a good eater. 'If he does it again,' she said firmly, 'tell him that I will call up to his house and tell his mammy.'

Mark winced. His mammy go up to Robert's mammy's house? That would be awful. Everyone would know what a rat he was. 'I could call him ugly butt,' Mark said instead, 'cause he is sort of ugly.'

'I will deal with this,' Allie said firmly. 'You just let me know if he bothers you again.' Then she muttered to herself, 'Little bastard.'

'Oh, you said a bad word.' Mark clapped his hands gleefully. 'Bastard! Bastard! Bastard!'

For once, Allie let him get away with it.

Mark got his dictionary out. He wasn't quite sure how to spell the word 'junkie' but he guessed it began with a 'j'. He found 'junk' and then a 'junkie'. That looked right. He ran his finger over the explanation. 'A drug addict.' What was that? He knew what a drug was of course. You got them when you were sick. He didn't know what an addict was. Maybe it was someone who added things which would make sense as his dad was an accountant. He decided to look up 'addict' all the same. He thumbed through his dictionary again and found the word. It was explained as 'a person who is addicted to something'. But what was addicted? That was the next word in line. 'Doing something as a habit.' So it meant that his dad did drugs as a habit. Mark frowned. That didn't make sense at all. Maybe it just meant that when his dad was sick, he took drugs as a habit, which was something everyone did. Mark closed his dictionary, puzzled. Maybe Robert wasn't insulting him when he said it.

He wondered if he should ask his dad if he did drugs as a habit, but his mammy had said not to. She had said not to tell his dad anything at all about Robert as it would make his dad cross. But this wouldn't be about Robert, this would be just something he would ask. He wouldn't say Robert said it. The trick was, Mark thought, to get his dad on his own.

Eight o'clock. Mark squealed as his dad hoisted him over his shoulder and began to tramp up the stairs. His mammy was laughing, telling them not to wake Owen. It seemed like his mammy and daddy were friends again, which was good cause they'd had a big row that morning and Mark had worried all day in school about it.

Mark brushed his teeth and let his daddy wipe his hands and face, then he climbed into bed. His daddy took out a book that they were reading. It was a boring book but his daddy was good at putting on the voices and making it sound really funny. Mark snuggled up beside him and grinned at the story. After a bit, his dad closed the book and kissed Mark on the forehead. 'I've got to head out, buster, see you in the morning.'

'Can I ask you one thing?' Mark said.

'No, you cannot leave the light on,' Tony smirked.

'It's not that.' Mark looked up at his dad. 'I just want to know if you use drugs as a habit.'

For some reason his dad jerked a little backwards. There was a silence that Mark thought went on for a long time. Then his dad came closer to the bed and sat down. 'Why do you want to know that?' he asked quietly.

Mark bit his lip. He couldn't say about Robert because that would mean his mammy would get mad. 'It's just a question,' he evaded.

'Did someone say something to you?' his dad asked. He didn't sound mad, just a bit, well, sad, Mark thought, baffled.

'I don't know.' Mark began to panic, his mammy would kill him. 'Mammy said not to say. I just want to know what it is.'

Tony swallowed a little. 'Well,' he began, 'sometimes a person who uses drugs can sometimes use too much of them and like them too much, and then I guess it becomes a habit.'

'Oh.' Mark nodded. 'And is that not good? Don't drugs cure you when you're sick?'

'They do,' his dad said, and he seemed to be choosing his words very carefully, like the way Mark chose the biggest biscuits in the box. 'But taking too much of them can make you sick. Like eating too many sweets makes you sick.'

'Are you sick?'

For some reason his dad hugged him hard before saying, 'Well, I was, but I'm a lot better now.' His voice cracked a bit. 'And I hope to stay better.'

'So you're not a junkie?'

Against him, Mark felt his dad flinch. 'Not now, buster. Not any more.' He pulled away, but held Mark by his shoulders. 'Not any more,' he repeated. 'I go to meetings to help me stay away from drugs.'

'Like Dietwatchers for Granny Magda and Fintan to help them stay away from food.'

His dad grinned. 'Yeah. Just like that.'

As he left, Mark snuggled up under his Man United duvet. He knew Robert was wrong all along.

Tony squeezed his eyes shut when he closed Mark's bedroom door. Then, taking deep breaths, he opened them again and went downstairs in search of Allie.

'Hey,' she smiled at him from the sofa, 'all settled?'

He nodded, not able to speak.

'What time is your meeting on?'

'He asked me if I was a junkie,' Tony said quietly.

Allie groaned. 'I told him not to.' She sounded annoyed. Then at Tony's lack of response she asked, 'What did you say to him?'

'I told him I was but that I was getting better.'

'Aw, Tony!' Allie rubbed her hands over her face.

'Well what else could I say? Do you want me to lie to him? Is that it?'

Allie laughed a little bitterly. 'Well, I lied to him all summer and you didn't have a problem with that!'

'I did,' he snapped. 'Of course I did. I hated that you had to do it, but I figured you knew best.'

'Well, you tell me what I should have said? How about,' Allie stood up to face him, saying airily, *'Oh Mark, your dad is in a clinic getting clean because he snorts coke and gets off his head and forgets to come home and steals money off his mother. Is that it? Would you have liked me to tell him that?'*

Tony stared at her, hurt. Then looked down at his trainers.

'Oh God, Tony.' Allie was instantly ashamed. She risked touching his sleeve. 'I'm sorry. Jesus, I'm sorry.'

'Don't be,' he gave a rueful smile, 'it's the truth.'

'Still . . .' her voice trailed off.

There was a silence, until Tony said tentatively, 'Maybe you could have said that I was in a clinic as I had a problem giving up drugs, just like some people eat too many sweets and they have to go on a diet.'

Allie shook her head. 'He'd worry,' she answered. 'Mark worries, or haven't you noticed?'

'Yeah, but he's not stupid.'

'He's a kid.'

Tony sank down on to the sofa and put his head in his hands. After a second he mumbled, 'I am sick of lying to people, Allie. It doesn't help. Even that old fella the other day asking me about America.'

'Well, would you prefer if everyone knew?' Allie stared down at him. Was the man living in reality at all?

Tony uncovered his face and looked up. 'Yeah,' he said simply, 'I think I would.'

'Oh for God's sake,' Allie looked at him despairingly, 'what will people think?'

'They'll think I'm a junkie.'

'Jesus!'

'That's what you're worried about, isn't it?' Tony said, realisation dawning slowly. 'You're worried about yourself and your image.'

'I'm worried about the kids, too. How will people treat them?'

'I never had you down for someone who worried about the neighbours, Allie. I always thought you didn't give a damn.'

Allie rolled her eyes. 'My father made my mother and me the hot topic of conversation in our street so yes, I do worry, and I do not want to go back there.' Her voice shook.

'Your father was the main topic, not you.' Tony stood up and caught her hand in his. 'No one judged you. It wasn't your fault. And if they talk here, it'll be about me.' He paused and swallowed. 'Look, Allie, my whole life has been a lie. Tess and John were not my real family, I never wanted to be an accountant, and I never wanted to be who I was.' He paused before continuing, 'My drug taking was a lie to myself, to you. I don't want my recovery to be a lie.'

As Allie absorbed his words, her anger dissolved. He was right, she admitted reluctantly. Right about it all. She had lied to protect her kids but also to protect herself, and maybe it had been unfair on Tony, making him out, yet again, to be something he wasn't. 'You really want this?'

He nodded. 'Yeah, I think I do. It's the only true thing about me.'

'No, it's not,' she said. 'There are lots of true things about you. You're a laugh when you want to be, you're good with the kids—'

'Just don't lie any more, OK?'

She had no choice, though it made her feel sick to agree. 'OK,' she said slowly, 'if the subject comes up, we'll be honest.'

'Thank you.' Tony kissed her briefly on the forehead. 'And for the record, Mark seemed happy enough with the explanation.'

'You'd better go to your meeting then,' Allie pushed him away, 'Holly said Veronica is going tonight.'

'Good,' Tony said, not moving. Then added, 'Veronica and me both said that we'd screw up our courage and speak out tonight.'

'God love them,' Allie half joked, 'they'll never shut you up now.'

She was rewarded with one of his cute grins.

30

ALLIE STOOD WATCHING Clery's clock as it ticked towards one. She was standing exactly where she'd been the first time she'd come to meet her father. Ten minutes to go. She took out her mobile and texted home.

Hows tings?

The answer came back immediately:

Worry bout yurslf. All gr8

She had decided to trust Tony alone with the kids for a couple of hours. He really seemed to be getting so much better. The meetings were helping, Allie was convinced. He'd even managed to get himself a sponsor, a person he could call on when he found things were getting tough. She was ridiculously proud of him at the moment and she smiled thinking about it.

Her reverie was smashed by the sight of a gaudy blue and red jacket. Its wearer had taken up a space underneath Clery's clock. It was him. Her father. Allie's knees turned to water and she suddenly felt sick. She'd know that horrendous jacket anywhere. She watched, fighting to get herself under control, as he set down a bag and leant against the wall. He rummaged a bit in the pockets of his jacket and pulled out a packet of smokes. Lighting up, he rested his head against the brickwork of the shop.

Allie took a deep, calming breath and started towards the pavement. It was surreal, meeting a dad she hadn't seen in years. She wondered suddenly what they'd talk about, realising that at least it wouldn't be a problem for the moment as they had so much catching up to do.

The lights changed, the traffic stopped and Allie joined the crowd crossing the road. She made sure she was submerged in the middle of a group as she didn't want her dad to spot her too early. So far he hadn't noticed her, though his gaze was darting left and right as people marched on past him.

When she reached the far side Allie took another breath, smoothed down her long denim skirt and adjusted her coat. Like the last time, she had attempted to go well-dressed without looking as if she'd put in too much of an effort. Tony had ruined it by whistling when she came into the kitchen, but he'd assured her it was just because he always thought she was gorgeous.

She began to walk towards her father and the nearer she got, the more faint and sweaty and breathless she felt. She began to doubt that she'd even be able to get so much as a 'hello' out when she reached him. Step by step, his features grew clearer. When she was about five feet from her dad, his gaze suddenly met hers. And stopped. And his black brows came tighter and he opened his mouth in an 'Oh' of surprise.

Allie forced herself to continue walking until she was near enough to get out a shaky, 'Hi.' She wasn't able to add 'Dad'. Besides the fact that he hadn't been around, he didn't look like anyone's dad. His blue and red jacket was teamed with a faded pair of denims and a sparkling-white pair of trainers. His head was shaved and his face was sort of paunchy. He hadn't aged particularly well, Allie thought. He looked like some reject skinhead from the seventies.

'Hi,' her dad said back. He sounded just as nervous. He looked her up and down, his eyes crinkling up at the edges.

Allie wasn't sure if it was a smile or confusion. 'You're all grown up.' His voice was husky from too many cigarettes.

'Yes,' was all Allie could think to say to that. She swallowed and coughed apprehensively.

There was an uncomfortable silence.

'You look great.' Now he was definitely attempting a smile.

'Thanks.'

'So, eh,' her dad made a sort of gesture, 'I suppose we could go for a coffee, yeah?'

'That'd be nice.'

'In here?' He indicated the shop behind him.

'Sure.'

He discarded his half-smoked cigarette and picked up his bag, before opening the door for her. 'After you.'

'Thanks.'

She felt quite self-conscious as she walked ahead of him to the coffee shop, aware that he was probably gazing at the back of her neck, but once there, he took charge by grabbing a tray and asking her what she wanted. 'You get a seat and I'll follow you down,' he said.

Allie took a seat by the window and took off her coat. She wished she'd worn something lighter as she was now sweating profusely. This was worse than a first date with a guy she hardly knew. With a guy, if it failed it failed, but if it failed with her dad it would be horrible. If asked, she couldn't have described the mix of emotions she was feeling. Anger had turned to hope which cycled back to anger again. She watched as he reached the top of the queue and paid for a coffee and a cake for both of them from a battered brown wallet.

He carried the tray over and set it down in front of her. 'Always loved a cream cake at lunch time,' he said, handing her hers.

'I just love them anytime.'

He laughed a little too heartily at the joke, which embarrassed them both.

'So,' his laughter died out abruptly and he nodded a little before venturing, 'it's good to see you, Alisha.'

'Everyone calls me Allie.'

'Allie,' he amended. Then he asked, half shyly, 'What have you been up to? Or do you not want to tell me?'

It was the only thing to talk about and at least it was a neutral subject. Still, it was hard to know where to start, so she told him about her job and her family. She omitted the fact that Tony was an addict and it wasn't because she cared what her dad thought, it was just none of his business, at least not yet. Finally, she told him about Mark and Owen.

'So, I'm a granddad,' her dad said, seeming to relish the words. 'Well, isn't that something?' He chewed his lip for a second, pondering the implications of being a grandfather, before asking, 'Do they know about me?'

'A little,' Allie said. 'They know that Fintan is not my dad and that my dad is . . . gone.'

He winced at the word. 'OK. Right. Fair enough.' He chewed his lip some more. 'Have you any pictures of them?'

Allie took out her mobile phone, secretly pleased he'd asked. 'I have a few here,' she said, scrolling through her picture files. 'Here,' she thrust her phone towards him, 'this is one of Mark in his new school uniform this year. If you press on, you can see Owen.' She watched as he examined the pictures, bringing his face really close to the screen so he could see. He obviously needed glasses and was too vain to get a pair.

'Mark's a big lad,' he remarked. 'And the little fella has a look of you.'

'Mark's not that big.' Allie looked at Mark's picture. She supposed the uniform did look a bit tight on him, which probably made him look bigger than he was. 'It's not a great picture of him. He actually looks like his dad.'

'Have you a photo of him?'

'No,' Allie smiled a little, 'isn't it awful? I've loads of the kids and none of Tony.'

Her dad smiled back. 'You look so good, Allie,' he said sincerely, 'you turned out so well.'

The words embarrassed her. 'Yeah, well, Mam was great.'

There was an awkward pause. A gap as big as China appeared in the conversation. Her dad sipped his coffee.

Allie took a bite from her cake. It was hard to eat a cream cake in front of someone she hardly knew. Bits of flaky pastry seemed to explode everywhere.

'She was great,' her dad eventually agreed.

'Still is great,' Allie muttered.

Silence.

'I, eh, think I gave her a fright the other day calling in like that,' Thomas muttered as he stared down at his nicotine-stained hands.

'She was fine,' Allie lied loyally. 'Not a bother on her.'

He looked at her in disbelief. 'She was crying when I was there,' he said.

'Dad, no offence,' Allie said back, 'but she always seemed to be crying when you were there.'

'Ouch.'

'You gave her an awful life.' She hadn't planned on going into all this but couldn't help herself. If she was to start over with this man there could be no pretence that what he had done was acceptable. 'And me too,' she tacked on.

'I know. I was terrible. Nothing went well for me after-wards.'

'Good.'

He looked a little startled at that before smiling contritely. 'I guess I got what I deserved,' he admitted.

'So what did go wrong?' Allie asked.

'Well,' her dad made a comical face, 'it'd be easier and quicker to tell you what went right.'

'What went right?' She couldn't help smiling at him. The man had charm. Even the horrendous red hairy jumper he wore only served to add to it.

'Nothing,' he answered without rancour. 'Absolutely nothing went right.'

'Wow, that's impressive.'

He laughed. 'I guess you could say that. When I moved to France there was the worst weather for vines ever and I lost fields of the bloody things. The following year was the same. It was like the potato famine in Ireland. Only no one was starving. And no one died.'

'So, it wasn't like the famine then.'

'It was,' he smirked. 'Nothing was growing. In the end, I had to sell up. So I moved house and job and ended up with a share in a restaurant where the management were robbing us blind. They eventually ran off with most of the money.'

'Were they caught?'

'Nope. And of course I hadn't paid any insurance on being robbed blind. I mean you don't, do you? So, with very little money, I decided to go into the chip van business.' He took a slug of his coffee. 'Well, don't ever go into that. I got shut down for poor hygiene. No one died. No one got sick.'

'So what did you do?'

'Well, I opened up again without telling them and I got prosecuted and thrown in jail for a bit. So, don't ever do that.'

Allie couldn't ever see herself running an illegal chip van business.

'Then some little feckers got my van from outside my flat and rolled it into the sea. That was the end of that.'

'God.' What an amazing run of bad luck, Allie thought.

'So, I got myself out of France and came home and here I am.'

'Are you working?'

'Well, yes, in a local restaurant. It's quite fancy. Only I have to put on a French accent because they think I'm French. I call myself Desmonde.'

'Jesus.' Allie bit her lip.

'One night a gang of French people came in and talked French to me so I had to pretend to the boss that I had a sore throat. I mean, I can talk French but any native would know I'm not a native. That was pretty hairy, I can tell you.'

A bit like his jumper, Allie thought but didn't say.

'And that's my life,' her dad said, spreading his hands wide. 'I guess you could argue that, unlike you, I didn't turn out so well.' He gave a self-deprecating grin. 'But I'm glad we've met.'

Allie guessed that she was as well. 'Me too,' she said.

They sipped their drinks in companionable silence. After a bit Thomas asked carefully, 'Do you think you'd like to do this again?'

'I might.' Allie shrugged and added, 'I just don't want to go upsetting Mam.'

'Hmm.' He made a face as he considered that. 'Yes, I think she still hates me.'

'She does.'

There was a pause. 'And you?'

Allie didn't answer immediately. Truth was she wasn't sure how she felt. 'I don't hate you,' she answered slowly. 'I suppose I'm angry and I know when you left that I was dreadfully hurt—'

'I didn't leave,' he interrupted indignantly, 'your mother threw me out. Well, technically, she didn't throw me out; she just wouldn't let me in. Then she dumped all my bags out the window.'

'You were lucky she didn't dump you out the window,' Allie spluttered. 'You had an affair with two of our neighbours, for crying out loud.'

A few people glanced over at Allie's raised voice.

'Yes,' her dad conceded. He leant across the table and spoke in a low voice so that the earwiggers couldn't hear him. 'I did. That was wrong. But one of those bags hit me on the head and I had to be hospitalised.'

233

Allie ignored that. Yes, he'd had concussion, but then again her mother had been aiming for him. 'You were a shit father,' she said. She didn't care who heard.

He bowed his head. 'I know.'

'But . . .' Allie hesitated. She didn't want him to think she'd welcome him back with open arms and yet, she realised, that was exactly what she wanted to do. 'But I'm glad you contacted me.'

His intense brown eyes met hers, the only thing that remained of the attractive man her dad had once been. Cautiously he reached across the space between them and took her hand. 'Thank you,' he said, 'I'll do my best to see that you won't regret it.'

Allie blinked back sudden tears and swallowed hard. That would be good, she thought. That would be really good.

31

ALLIE WAS JUST about to call the boys for bed when the phone rang.

'Hello?'

There was a silence from the other end. Well, there was the tentative sound of breathing, as if someone was trying hard to find their voice.

'Hello?' Allie said again.

'Allie?' It was Holly. She sounded a little upset. 'Is, eh, Tony back from his meeting?'

'Yeah, he's back ages. He went to a five o'clock.'

Holly inhaled sharply. 'That's the one Veronica was to go to, too.' She paused and added, whispering, 'She's not home yet.'

Allie froze. Her grip on the phone tightened until she felt her fingers grow a little numb. Tony had mentioned to her, casually, that Veronica hadn't been at the meeting, but neither of them had given it a second thought.

'Allie?' Holly asked warily, 'Are you there?'

'Yeah, yes.'

'Did Tony see her at the meeting?'

Oh God. Allie swallowed. 'He, eh, said that she wasn't there. I didn't think anything of it. I just thought—'

'She hasn't been into work today either.' Holly's voice spiralled upward. 'She left the house this morning, I dropped her off outside the hotel but—'

'Calm down,' Allie said, trying to sound calm herself. 'Think. Have you called her mobile?'

'Yes. No answer. Oh God, Allie, I'm so worried. She hasn't been too great these last few days. Did Tony say anything?'

'Nothing. No.'

'She went out to work yesterday morning, you know the way she got fixed up with the hotel job?' Without waiting for Allie to answer Holly went on, 'She came home awful upset, she wouldn't say why, though I know she had an argument with that bastard that calls himself her fella, and I was worried. And then today,' Holly gulped, 'well, she didn't show up for work. I've only found that out now. I've been just praying that she'll call or do something, but she hasn't. And if she wasn't at that meeting . . .' Her voice trailed off.

'Did you call her sponsor?'

'Yeah. Nothing. Oh God, Allie, do you think she's using again?'

There was no think about it. When an addict didn't keep appointments, you just knew the worst. 'Oh, Holly.' She wished Holly was in front of her so she could hug her. It was her own worst fear that Tony would somehow snap too and be off.

There was a pause. Then Holly said quietly, 'I think I might go look for her.'

Allie hesitated before asking, 'Are you sure that's wise? You know—'

'I know they say to do the tough love bit, but Allie, she's my only sister.' The words tore out of Holly. 'My mother won't have anything to do with her, she's alone on the streets and I can't,' her voice broke, 'I just can't—'

'OK,' Allie said softly, knowing that if the roles were reversed she'd probably do the same. 'Well, if you're going, then I'll go with you.'

'Oh, no, you don't have—'

'I do. You're my friend and you can't go out alone looking for her. I'll just tell Tony and he can stay with the boys. Hang on a second.' Allie put the phone down and went in search of her husband. He was in the garden, taking some newly bought goal posts out of their box. Owen was hanging back shyly and Mark was nowhere to be seen.

In an undertone Allie explained to Tony where she was going.

'Aw Jesus,' he groaned, 'I should have known. She was in shit form at the last meeting. I joked with her and she told me to fuck off. I should have known. I can't believe . . .' His voice trailed off. 'I never thought . . .'

'Well, let's hope she's in a mate's house somewhere,' Allie said, though she knew neither of them believed that.

'I think I know where she might be,' Tony said suddenly. 'I know the areas she goes to score.'

'Where? How?'

Tony set the side of the goal post down carefully, not taking his eyes from it. 'We talked,' he said warily. 'In the beginning, it's all you talk about. The highs.' He laid another piece of the goal post beside it. 'And, well, I think I know where she might be.'

'Where?'

'I'll get her.'

Allie looked at him as if he were bonkers. 'Are you bonkers?' she said to the back of his head. 'You can't go into that environment.'

He turned and his eyes met hers. 'Neither can you,' he said, 'it's not a place for you.'

'Tony, I looked for you everywhere when you were using.'

He winced, recoiling at the words. 'I know,' he said, 'and I let you because I was so flipping out of it. But I'm not now and I won't let you go.' He paused. 'And besides, the kids need you more than they need me, Allie. If anything happened to you, I'd be less than useless.'

'That's ridiculous.'

'No. It's the truth,' he said firmly. 'Tell Holly I'll look for Veronica. Jesus, she's only a kid.' He rubbed his hands over his face. 'If Holly likes, she can come with me.'

Allie felt sick. All her instincts told her not to let him go.

237

'But what if someone offers you something? You know you're meant to stay out of it, Tony.'

'Today is a good day for me,' he said simply. 'I feel I can do it.'

'Tony, you can't jeopardise yourself over this. You're only four weeks out of hospital.'

'Veronica was a good mate to me. I know she's young, but she helped me get sponsored. Got me talking in the meetings. I'll give her sponsor a call, too.'

'Holly already has. You can't go, Tony!'

'I don't think I'd be here without her, Allie.'

It hurt a little, him saying that. Allie wanted to be the one to have helped him. 'Oh,' was her only response.

Tony seemed to sense how his words had made her feel. He tried to explain it more clearly. 'She made me see that if I didn't at least talk, I'd lose everything.'

Allie stared at him.

'I need to feel useful,' he said suddenly. 'As if my existence is worth something.'

'It's worth something to us that you stay clean,' she said.

'I will.'

'You said that so many times before,' she answered.

Owen began to whimper at the sharp tone. He wrapped his arms about Allie's legs and she hoisted him up in her arms.

'I know. I know I did. I mean it this time.'

'You meant it those times, too.'

He groaned. 'Trust me, Al, please.'

It was those words that made her realise she had no choice. If they were to make it at all, she had to trust him. She couldn't keep second-guessing him every time he went out the door, on tenterhooks until he came back. She had to let go. Her being worried would do neither of them any good.

'Promise me you won't be tempted,' she said, wanting to grab him and never let him out of the house.

'I can't promise that.'

Ironically, that simple statement convinced her. At least he was being honest with himself. With her. Before, he would have sworn on all their lives that he wasn't tempted by drugs. He only took them for a laugh. Allie gave him a tiny smile. 'OK, go then. But for God's sake, be careful.'

His sudden grin made her catch her breath. It was a glimpse of the old Tony. 'Is Holly still on the phone?'

'Yeah.'

He tilted her chin upwards and kissed her on the tip of her nose before walking into the house. Allie resigned herself to the fact that all the weeks of work he'd put in might just shatter into nothing.

The teenagers were behind the hedge again. Four of them today. Jeremy nodded as he went past.

'Hey,' one of them yelled after him, 'is that the only coat you have?'

Jeremy stiffened. It was, as it happened. 'No,' he said, 'I have a range of different coats.'

They snorted with laughter. 'A range?' one of them said. 'Is that not something you keep horses and cows on in America?'

Jeremy shook his head. 'You youngsters should spend more time in school learning the English language and less behind hedges.'

'A lot can happen behind a hedge,' the girl boasted, to guffaws of laughter from the three lads. 'A biology lesson, maybe.'

Jeremy flushed. 'Well, when you're minding your child in a dingy council flat with infested toilets and smelly wallpaper, I hope you'll remember these days fondly.'

'Contraception,' she said loudly.

'Saying no is the only foolproof method,' Jeremy shot back, surprised at himself. Still, he'd always liked a good debate, though normally his sparring partners were a lot more intelligent. He hadn't had a good verbal joust with anyone in a long time.

239

'Aw, you're great,' the girl said then, in a vaguely patronising manner. 'Go on and enjoy your walk.'

'I shall,' Jeremy nodded. 'Good day to you all.'

Shouts of 'Bye now' followed him down the path.

He was glad his boys hadn't turned out like that. At the thought of them, he felt quite sad.

The kids were in bed. Allie sat in the kitchen nursing a cold coffee, her hands wrapped around the mug. She'd been that way for a while now, unable to move, her thoughts paralysed by worry. Where were they? What were they doing? She'd tried texting Tony and then Holly. Tony had eventually replied that they were out searching for Veronica in her usual haunts but that it wasn't proving too easy. He told her he'd text her again when they had any news. That had been two hours ago. It was now nine.

Jeremy picked up the envelope. A big X was marked across it. He wondered what that could mean. Tearing open the flap, which had been stuck down by a copious amount of saliva, Jeremy took out the copybook page.

Dear Santa.

How are you? We learned in skool to put ? after a qusten. I am riting to tell you dat i don't need a tv right this year. I hav somting else to ask you four so i hope you can get it. My daddy used to be a junkie in case you dont no it means dat he used drugs as a habit. He says he is getting bettr now and i wud like it if you could make him fully bettr so dat him and my mammy wud stop fiteing. And so dat mammy wont worry about him. And so dat me and owen wont worry either. So can you make him bettr please. And mayb you could get rid of all deh bad drugs or somting. Also

can you put Robert on the reely bold list as he
keeps calling me Fatso even though i told him dat
he is a butt head he didnt stop. It is not me
starting it. And in skool he picks me for teams
and then says he made a misteake and everyone
laffs xcept my friend. And even my friend wont
come to our house anymore.

If getting my daddy bettr is not too hard
den mayb you can bring deh TV but i dont mind.
Owen wants a football.

Tanks. Love mark.

Jeremy reread the letter. A junkie. Mark's dad was a drug
addict. He, Jeremy, was living next door to a drug addict.
People could be selling drugs right outside his house and he
wouldn't know. He folded up the letter, his heart hammering.
Maybe noisy students were better after all, he thought shakily.
But no, they'd been rude and disrespectful. Mark's family had
been nothing but welcoming and courteous. Mark had hugged
him, for God's sake. Mark always smiled at him and said hello.
He'd forgotten what it was like to walk outside and have neighbours greet you. It had been so long now since it had happened.
And Allie had brought him a cake. She'd made him a ham
sandwich and John had done his garden for a very reasonable
sum. They were a nice family and the dad seemed all right, if
a bit odd. A bit withdrawn. But maybe the poor man was
struggling. It couldn't be easy – not that Jeremy knew much
about drugs or anything like that. Jeremy kept a strict reign
on mood-altering substances. He only drank nine mugs of tea
a day, that was the extent of his drug-taking. Apart from the
cigarettes, which he didn't think really counted. He scanned
the letter again, feeling a little queasy. There was no way that
he could help the man stay off drugs. He just couldn't promise
this to the boy. He'd have to tell him. Not confess to lying
about being Santa, of course – it was a bit late for that and

241

besides, loath as he was to admit it, he liked Mark liking him. He could maybe tell the boy that Santa didn't grant presents like getting people off drugs.

And as he read the letter again, he wondered idly what he could do about Robert.

The ring of the house phone around nine-thirty caused Allie to jump. Grabbing up the receiver she said breathlessly, 'Yes?'

'Hiya, it's me.' Tony's voice sounded oddly flat and her heart constricted.

'What's the story?'

'We're in Vincent's Hospital. We found her an hour ago.' He gulped as he added, 'She'd OD'd.'

'Is she OK? Is Holly OK?'

'Well, I think Holly could use a mate.' He paused and said with difficulty, 'Vee was dead when we got to her.'

'Oh, Tony.' Tears sprang to Allie's eyes.

'Yeah.' He gulped and continued, 'Anyway, I'm on my way home now, you can drive over here when I get back.'

'And you,' Allie asked. 'Are you OK?'

'Talk to you when I get back, yeah?'

And he hung up the phone.

Jeremy pondered long and hard about Robert. If he couldn't solve one problem for Mark, he was damn well going to solve at least another. He'd always been good at fixing things, he'd spent his life fixing things for his family. It just needed a little thought.

Tony arrived back forty minutes later. He looked shattered, his eyes had a haunted look and he didn't say anything to Allie as she held him. Instead he just hugged her tightly before kissing her on the top of her head. 'Go on,' he pulled himself from her embrace, 'Holly is on her own in there.'

'Are you OK?' Allie called after him as he ascended the stairs.

'Go on,' he said by way of reply.

Allie had grabbed her coat and purse and raced through the almost deserted streets. She parked in the hospital car park and, pulling her coat around her as it was drizzling, she went into the emergency department. They directed her to the mortuary.

Allie paused for a few seconds outside the door. Through the small square window she could see Holly, shoulders heaving as she sobbed over the lifeless body of her little sister. Holly's appearance didn't fit with her grief, was Allie's first thought. Even though she was dressed casually in jeans and a coat, she still had an air of someone who had just come in from a night out clubbing. Her jeans were tight, her coat electric-pink. Holly deserved to be on the arm of a handsome guy, she deserved to eat chips on a park bench and laugh at his stupid jokes as he licked vinegar from her fingers. She should be partying with her mates and getting drunk and going on holidays. She certainly should not be standing alone in the middle of a cold room alongside a bed where her little sister lay. Allie felt a painful lump wedge itself in her throat as she saw Holly use the sleeve of her hot-pink jacket to wipe away her tears. She stood, incapable of movement, as Holly smoothed her sister's hair and kissed her face and held her hand between her own. Oh God, Allie thought, what the hell am I supposed to say? Her heart began to beat faster in a panic. How could she find words to comfort Holly? There were no bloody words. There was nothing she could do. Then Holly turned and Allie met her heartbroken gaze with one of her own. Reaching for the handle, Allie pushed open the door and Holly fell into her arms.

'Oh God, oh God, I'm so sorry, I'm so sorry,' Allie sobbed over and over as she clasped Holly to her.

'I know, I know,' Holly sniffed, hugging her hard. 'I know you are.'

They hugged for a long time, before Holly eventually disentangled herself from Allie's embrace and gently led her towards the bed. Allie stood in tearful silence and watched as Holly gently stroked Veronica's face.

'She looks peaceful though, doesn't she?' Holly asked. She sounded as if she desperately needed to believe it.

'Yeah, she does,' Allie agreed. 'She really does.' And she did, kind of. It was the peace of stillness. The spiky edginess of addiction was gone.

'We found her in a horrible squat, a derelict flat,' Holly whispered, her gaze not leaving Veronica. She shook her head, as if finding it impossible to comprehend. 'She didn't deserve to die there.'

'No.' Allie squeezed Holly gently on the arm.

'The police came then. They quizzed me and Tony. Poor Tony, he's devastated.'

'He is.' Allie swallowed hard.

'Tony knew everyone,' she said. 'Everyone.'

He was bound to, Allie thought, all those years using.

'He was so good,' Holly sniffed.

'He liked Veronica,' Allie answered softly.

Holly didn't appear to have heard. She went on smoothing Veronica's hair. 'So good,' she repeated. 'We went into squats and pubs and we walked down alleyways. Tony knew everywhere anyone went to score.'

Allie flinched. She hated to think of her lovely Tony in that world.

'Eventually,' Holly stood a little back from Veronica and studied her, then, seeming satisfied, she turned her gaze back to Allie, 'eventually, after Tony gave a lad a tenner, he said that he remembered seeing her go into a squat. And we found her.' Holly's voice caught and, sounding incredibly hurt, she said, 'All on her own.'

'Oh, Holly.' Allie felt the other woman's pain wrap around her heart. 'I'm so sorry.'

Big bright tears shimmered in Holly's eyes and Allie felt her own grow moist again in response. 'Everyone had left her and she was just lying there, Allie.' A big tear streaked its way down Holly's face, a track of mascara in its wake. Holly used her fist to rub her eyes, reminding Allie of Mark.

'Oh Holly, don't.' She wrapped her arm about Holly's shoulder.

'She was all on her own, Allie. And she was still warm and I thought she was still alive and I was shaking her and shaking her and Tony just let me. I told him to ring an ambulance and he just stood there. I think he was in shock. He just stood over us and just let me scream. He knew, I think. Then he did call an ambulance and they came and they just, they just . . .' She couldn't finish. 'Poor Veronica,' she sobbed, her shoulders heaving.

Allie held her and rubbed her back and couldn't think of anything to say.

After a while Holly stopped crying and Allie found a chair for her, pulling it up to the bed. Holly sat down and held Veronica's hand. Allie stood behind her, rubbing her shoulders and hugging her when she felt Holly needed it. The only sounds were the coming and going of other people outside the room. The room grew a little lighter as midnight turned to dawn.

'I don't know what to say to my mam,' Holly eventually said, startling Allie.

'You'll think of something when she comes.'

'She'll think it's my fault.'

'No, no, she won't,' Allie rushed to reassure her. 'You did a good thing, Holly, you did. You know you did.'

Holly didn't reply, she just turned away again.

After a bit Allie left to buy coffee, which neither of them drank, and finally, after four o'clock, Holly's mother did arrive and embraced Holly and told her that no, she didn't blame her at all, that Veronica had got lost a long time ago and just hadn't found her way back. Allie didn't wait to hear any more, she stole away. She didn't go straight home, instead she drove

245

out to Dun Laoghaire and parked her car, closed her eyes and listened to the waves as they slapped against the harbour wall. Finally she got out and walked along the pier, and she could just see the waves as they rolled in, some big, some small, all with one aim. To smash themselves off the rocks and die back into the sea.

It was oddly comforting.

32

T HE CHURCH WAS packed. Allie, with Tony beside her, slid into a seat at the back. Two girls moved up to accommodate them and Allie murmured a quick thanks. She was glad for Holly that so many people had turned out to say goodbye to Veronica, and she wondered idly if as many people would have attended had it been Tony. In the last few years, as Tony's problems escalated, she'd cut herself off from friends. She remembered with a pang Clare and Duncan from their old estate with whom they'd been such good mates. She was sure they were totally bewildered at how she'd treated them but it had seemed so important at the time to keep Tony's addiction a secret. She knew now, beyond doubt, that it had been the wrong thing to do. She needed her friends, just like Holly needed hers now. As she stood, waiting for the mass to begin, she flirted with the idea of ringing Clare and explaining, fantasised that they could go back to the way things used to be. But then a quiet murmur made her aware that Holly and her family had entered and Allie knew that it was way too late to do that. So much had happened.

As the singers that Holly had booked for the service started to sing 'Human' by The Killers, Allie turned briefly in her seat and saw Holly, who looked shell-shocked, escort her mother gently up the aisle. Her mother was bent over, as if someone had hit her hard in the solar plexus. Holly's arm was protectively about her. As Holly went by Allie touched her briefly, and Holly acknowledged her with a small smile. Beside Allie,

Tony coughed and shuffled his feet uneasily. He'd been in a weird mood since that night – it had only been four days ago but it felt longer. He hadn't spoken about the search or about finding Veronica; instead he'd deflected Allie's questions with shrugs or by turning away and changing the subject. Allie reckoned he was having a hard time coming to terms with the fact that his ally was gone. His one support at the NA meetings.

When Holly reached the top and the song had ended the priest welcomed them all and the mass began. Allie had to admire the priest as he didn't try to airbrush Veronica's death. Holly had told him to be honest and he was. And, instead of painting a portrait of horror, what he managed to do was show that Veronica had been human. Her flaws and weaknesses could be anyone's. Allie turned to say how brilliant he was to Tony, but he'd started to climb over people to get out. She was about to call him back but realised she couldn't; the church was so quiet as the priest talked that Allie was reluctant to deflect attention away from him. As it was, people were looking at Tony's hasty exit with raised eyebrows.

Allie had to wait for at least half an hour, until people began to file up for communion, to go in search of him.

She was slightly panicked when she couldn't see him immediately. Fighting hard against rising fear, she steadied herself against the door of the church. She knew she had to trust him. Just like she'd trusted him that night. But it was so bloody hard. If she could keep him with her every hour of the day she would. The worry when he was out of sight consumed her more than she'd expected. Taking calming breaths, telling herself not to panic, she left the shelter of the church and, to her relief, spied him leaning against the bonnet of their car, staring down at his black shoes that he'd polished especially.

'Hey,' she called out.

He raised his head in greeting.

Allie sat in beside him, aware that the dust from the car would wreck her black suit, but he looked such a forlorn figure that being alongside him suddenly seemed the most important thing in the world. She entwined her hand with his and squeezed it. 'You OK?'

He closed his eyes and Allie wanted to reach out and touch his long curly eyelashes. She used to tease him about them, telling him they made him look like a girl. She was startled to see a tear slide down his cheek.

'Aw Tony, come here.' She wrapped and arm about him and kissed his face.

He pulled her close and kissed the top of her head. 'I'll be fine,' he said.

'You haven't been really fine since that night.'

There was a long pause. When he spoke, his voice had the tone of a bewildered kid. 'I've just never seen a dead body before, Al. Well,' he clarified, 'not a dead body like that.'

'I know,' she gave his hand an extra squeeze, 'it must have been awful.'

'Holly kept trying to wake her up, shaking her and pulling at her. It was not right, Al.' More tears sparked in his eyes and he looked upwards to stop them from falling.

'I know, she told me.'

He continued, speaking almost in a whisper, 'What scared me, though, was that I knew it could just as easily have been me. That Holly could have been you.'

Allie said nothing.

'It's like that time, d'you remember, when we were going out together and the car in front of us stalled on the motorway and I had to sew our car to the ground to avoid smashing into him.'

She remembered. 'Yeah.'

'That's how I feel,' he looked at her, 'like I just narrowly avoided a car crash.'

'So keep avoiding it.'

'I don't know if I can. If she gave in, what hope have I?'

'You ring your sponsor. You go to meetings. You keep talking to me. That's your hope.'

'I was this close,' he made a tiny space between his finger and thumb, 'this close to scoring on the way home from the hospital that night. I even drove up to my old dealer's house and parked outside.'

The words hit Allie like physical blows.

'And I was going to get out, I had the seatbelt off, the door open and I stopped. I dunno how.'

Allie couldn't speak.

'That's why I went up to bed when I got back; I was shaking so much I could barely drive the car. It's so fucking hard, Allie.'

Allie felt sick. There it was again, the uncertainty. The fragile thread that kept him with her. She turned to look at him, he was close to tears. 'Come here.' She enfolded him in a sudden hug. 'I am so proud of you. I am.'

'And you've no idea how proud I am of you,' he said back fiercely. 'I just hope I can live up to you.'

She didn't answer that. She had never hoped for anything more in her life.

33

A LLIE WAS CLEARING up their bedroom, which had got into an awful mess, when she found a job application form that Tony had filled out. He'd mentioned to her in passing that he was going to look for work and, though she had tried to dissuade him, telling him he didn't need the stress, he obviously hadn't listened. Attached to the application form was Tony's CV. Scanning it, Allie had to admit that if she were recruiting, Tony would be top of her interview list. He'd worked in a lot of prestigious firms and his exam results were excellent. He'd put his boss from his last place of work down as a reference. Allie winced. There was no way she could let him apply for jobs, not whilst she knew what she knew. She looked at the deadline for the application and saw that it was in two weeks' time. Maybe if she threw it out, he wouldn't be able to get another application in on time. Or he'd forget about it. So, only feeling a little guilty, she tore it up and shoved it in the bin bag.

'Phone, Mammy!' Mark yelled from downstairs.

She hadn't even heard it ring. It was surprising that the kids had, they were having such fun in the back garden with John. All she could hear were screeches and yells. She told John that if the gardening didn't work out, he could always get a job as a children's entertainer.

'Yeah,' he'd said, 'cool.'

Allie grinned. John reminded her an awful lot of what Tony was like in the early days. She made her way down to the phone and picked it up. 'Hello?'

'Hi, Allie, it's me.'

'Holly, how are you? I was going to call over to you later.'

'Aw, I'm not great,' Holly admitted, 'I'm still off work.' She gave an audible gulp and admitted on a sniff, 'I keep having dreams about finding her.'

'Aw, Holly.' Allie knew she shouldn't sound as if she was going to cry, but she couldn't help it. 'It'll take time.'

'I know.' She paused. 'I'm just ringing to see if you'll come out tomorrow night with me. I plan on getting really drunk.'

Allie said nothing.

'D'you remember we made a pact that the worse things got, the more we'd party?'

'Yeah,' Allie said cautiously, 'I remember. Are you sure?'

'I need to do this. Don't worry,' Holly gave a little laugh, 'I'm not going to get hooked, but just for one night, I need to forget.' She paused. 'My friends are great, you know, but they're not you.'

Her friends would never understand, she was trying to say.

'You'll never forget,' Allie said softly. 'You know you won't.'

'Being drunk will ease the pain for a bit. I keep thinking about her, I keep wondering what if I'd just not let her go to work that day, what if I'd told that boyfriend of hers to get lost, like I was so tempted to do?' There was a brief pause before she added, 'It's driving me mad, Allie.'

'You took her in when she had no one,' Allie said. 'You did your best.'

'It wasn't good enough.'

'It was. You gave her a chance, that's all you could give her, you know.'

'That's why I need to go out with you,' Holly said, and Allie could tell she was trying to smile. 'You say the best things.'

Allie smiled back. 'Tomorrow night so.' She unconsciously picked up the photo beside the phone. It had been taken on her and Tony's honeymoon and it was her favourite one of Tony. He had his arm wrapped around her and was grinning so happily into the camera lens that every time Allie looked at it, she had such a longing to go back there it was a physical ache. What would she do if anything happened to him?

'Thanks,' Holly said. Then she asked, her tone brighter, 'Is that your boys I can hear laughing?'

Allie felt guilty. 'Yeah, they're playing with John, my brother-in-law, out the back.'

'John of the terrible taste in pubs?'

'The very one.'

Holly managed a gentle laugh. 'You should join them, they seem to be having a great time.'

'They are.'

Holly gulped. 'Tomorrow so.'

'Tomorrow. I'll pick you up.'

'Thanks.' The phone went dead.

Allie put down the rubbish bag and went into the garden. John was holding Owen upside down and pretending to kick him into the goal. He and the kids had obviously erected the posts in the last hour. Tony hadn't got around to it, having forgotten about it since Veronica had died. Allie had warned the boys not to bother Tony too much right now.

Mark was in goal, laughing himself sick as he tried to save Owen.

'And John has the ball,' John was yelling as Owen shouted out between laughter that he was a boy, not a ball.

'That's what I said,' John yelled back, 'the ball.' He lifted Owen up in the air. 'And now, he's going to kick the ball so hard that the goalkeeper Mark Dolan will not be able to save it.'

'I will save it!' Mark shouted.

'And a one,' John lifted Owen into the air, 'two,' Owen was lifted higher, 'and a three!' John ran full-tilt towards the goal as Mark shrieked.

'And he's in!' John dumped Owen inside the goal and ran around the garden cheering.

Allie laughed and was only aware that Tony had come back

from his meeting and was standing beside her when he said sharply, 'I told you not to put up those goal posts.'

All four looked at him.

'You did?' John made a face. 'Sorry, I don't remember. Anyway, the lads were begging me—'

'Do you ever listen to anything I say?' Tony snapped.

'Yeah,' John looked suddenly bewildered, 'course I do, but—'

'You don't. I said not to put up the goal posts. And you put them up.'

'Aw, Jaysus, Tony, come on,' John laughed in disbelief.

'Yeah,' Allie asked, 'what's the problem, Tony?' She kept her voice calm for the sake of the boys, who were looking warily from one to the other.

'The problem is that my brother,' Tony said aggressively, 'who only came over to visit, has put up the goal posts. Not only has he done our garden, which I was meant to do, he has also put up these.' Tony went and pushed one of the posts.

'Daddy, don't,' Mark said. 'Don't knock them down.'

'You go inside,' Tony barked. 'Go on.'

'You don't knock them down,' Mark said with spirit.

'You don't order me around!' Tony shouted back.

Mark's eyes filled with tears and Owen whimpered from his position in the goalmouth.

'Tony!' Allie snapped. 'Stop it!'

'Listen,' John said, his hands up in the air in a placating gesture, 'I'm sorry. We thought it'd be a surprise.'

'No you didn't,' Tony glared at him. 'You just wanted to undermine me. Just get this into your head, John. This is my house, and these,' he pointed at his two boys, who Allie was desperately trying to comfort, 'are my sons.'

'I like John,' Owen wailed. It was the clearest thing he'd ever said.

There was a beat of silence.

'I like John!' Owen said again.

Tony's sudden anger vanished. It was as if he'd abruptly become aware that he was scaring his kids. He gazed down at Owen, who had his head pressed into Allie's chest. 'Shit,' he said, appalled.

'I'll go,' John muttered. He sidled out behind Allie. 'Sorry, OK? It wasn't meant like that.'

'No!' Owen wailed.

'I know that, John,' Allie said firmly. 'Thanks for minding them.'

'Yeah, sure.'

John left the garden. Allie turned her attention back to Owen, patting him on the back and telling him it was OK.

Mark stood beside his mother, his body rigid and his eyes brimming with unshed tears.

'Shit,' Tony said again.

'That's what you can be OK.' Allie stood up, pulling Owen to her. She took Mark's hand in hers and marched back into the house.

'Al!'

She held up her hand. 'Don't.' For once she didn't care how her mood affected him.

Jeremy heard the tapping on the door and knew it was Mark. He was the only person who called not tall enough to reach the bell. Not that anyone called any more. His sons seemed to have abandoned him. In the past few days he had lifted up the phone to call them but been overcome by not knowing what to say. So he hadn't bothered. What was the point in having visitors if he didn't know how to talk to them? But still, at the moment he would have even welcomed a visit from that annoying health nurse.

Jeremy wondered what Mark wanted. He hoped it wasn't more impossible Christmas presents. He had quite a good story made up as to why he wasn't able to grant him a drug-free daddy for Christmas and if he got the chance now he would tell him, but the whole thing was getting out of hand. He was a little freaked by it, if he were honest. But Mark was a nice little boy and Jeremy had come to like conversing with him, even if it was under false pretences.

'Hello, Mark,' he said as he pulled open the front door.

Mark looked at him with something approaching amazement. 'You're smiling,' he remarked, then, without waiting for an invitation, stepped into the hallway. 'Is it because it's coming up to Christmas and you have the elves working hard?'

Jeremy winced. 'Eh, yes,' he agreed.

'Wow,' Mark marched ahead of him into the kitchen, 'I sure do know a lot about Santa, don't I?'

Jeremy didn't answer. He watched as Mark sat down at the kitchen table.

'I don't have any orange,' Jeremy said regretfully. 'Would you like milk? I have some nice biscuits though.'

'I'm not feeling very hungry.' Mark's face was suddenly serious. He looked sad, Jeremy thought. Then, to Jeremy's horror, the boy's lip wobbled and a big tear dripped down his cheek. 'My daddy is gone,' he said, hiccupping a little. 'He had a fight with my uncle John today and then with me and Owen and then with my mammy and then she took me and my brother to the cinema and switched off her mobile phone so she wouldn't have to talk to Daddy who kept ringing her and now when we came back, he's gone. And she is worried cause she couldn't eat her tea so I ate hers for her.'

Jeremy's mind tumbled in panic. What was he to do? How do you comfort a little boy who's crying? He didn't think his own boys cried much, or if they did he used to tell them to pull themselves together, which had obviously been the wrong thing to do according to Joel. He crossed to the table and slid into a seat beside Mark. 'Everyone fights,' he said conversationally. He took the risk of patting Mark's tiny pudgy hand. 'My boys fight with me and I fight with them.'

'Santa fights?' Mark gawked at him in amazement, sniffing hard and rubbing his nose on his sleeve.

'Eh yes.' Damn, he kept forgetting that bit.

'Did you get my letter?' Mark looked at him hopefully.

'Eh, yes, I've been meaning to talk to you about that,' Jeremy began haltingly.

'Will you be able to help my daddy not be a junkie?' Mark asked. 'Have you got magic for it or something?'

'Well, eh,' Jeremy coughed hard, 'eh, no, actually. I only have magic enough to fly a sled.'

'You can make time stop.'

'Yes, that too,' Jeremy stuttered. Then added, 'But I can't change people. They um, are out of my control.'

To Jeremy's dismay, Mark looked devastated. 'How?' He sounded as if he might cry again.

'Well,' Jeremy said hastily, not wanting the boy to cry, 'well, eh, if your daddy wants to change, he has to work the magic himself, see. The magic is in here.' Jeremy tapped his chest.

'In your bones? You have magic in your bones?'

'In your heart,' Jeremy said. 'Some people, like your daddy, might find it hard to find but it's in there.'

'Can you help him find it?'

'He has to find it himself,' Jeremy said. 'Only when you find it yourself can it work.'

'So, like, if I found it for him, it wouldn't work?'

'No.' A light sweat broke out on Jeremy's forehead. He hoped the boy would leave it at that. He wished he could do more but he couldn't. If he could have, he would have, he knew that without any doubt.

'What does it look like?'

'What does what look like?'

'The magic,' Mark said, as if Jeremy were stupid. 'Does it shine? Is it glittery? Will my daddy be able to see it easy?'

Good Christ. Jeremy bit his lip. 'If your daddy really wants

257

to give up drugs,' he replied slowly, 'he'll find the magic. Sometimes you don't even have to look for it, it just comes.'

Mark didn't look convinced. 'But—'

'When people want to change badly enough, Mark, they find the magic.' He patted Mark's hand again and said softly, 'That's all I know.'

Mark was silent.

Jeremy got up from the table and pulled out some chocolate digestives from the press. 'I bought these especially for you,' he coaxed gently. To his relief, Mark took one. He even said 'Thank you' which showed what a well brought-up boy he was. 'Now,' Jeremy sat down again, 'I've been having a think about Robert.'

'Is he on your bold list?'

'Well,' Jeremy shrugged, 'the thing about Santa, eh, about me, is that he— I,' he hastily corrected, 'I like to believe that everyone can change and that maybe if Robert was nice to you before Christmas, then maybe he could be on the good list again. We all deserve a second chance, don't we?'

Mark made a face.

'I know he's been mean to you,' Jeremy went on, 'little hooligan that he is. But just saying he was nice, would you let him be on the good list?'

'He'd have to be very nice,' Mark said a little grumpily.

'Oh,' Jeremy smiled a little, 'I think he'll be very nice to you from now on. My dwarves told me that—'

'Dwarves?'

Jeremy flushed. 'Elves,' he quickly said, 'my elves told me that he might find his magic in the next few days. That they think he might be off the bold list and on to the good one.'

'Really?' Mark looked amazed.

Jeremy nodded. 'Really,' he said, sitting back in his chair, feeling satisfied that Robert was one problem he might be able to sort out for Mark. He had come up with quite a good plan, he thought.

'MARK!' Allie's voice, loud and slightly panicked, filtered in from outside. 'MARK!'

Mark hopped up from the kitchen chair. 'My mammy,' he said unnecessarily. 'I better go.'

Jeremy went with him to the front door. 'Mrs Dolan,' he called as Mark hopped out. 'He's here. He just called in to say hello.'

'Mark,' Allie said in exasperation, relief making her cross, 'you should have told me where you were.'

'Sorry.' Mark looked shamefaced.

'Go on up and wash your hands and face and get into your pyjamas. Go on,' Allie said. She smiled apologetically at Jeremy. 'I hope he wasn't bothering you.'

'Not at all,' Jeremy smiled at her, 'he's a great little lad.'

Allie returned the smile in a sort of distracted way. 'OK, thanks. He thinks you're brilliant, you know.'

Jeremy nodded, guilt worming its way right through him. He could think of nothing to say to that, so he just said, 'If you ever need anything, you know where I am.'

Then he went back inside and shut the door firmly.

What a curious thing to say, Allie thought. Then she wondered if Mark had told Jeremy anything about earlier, but nah, Mark wouldn't. But it was puzzling, her boy going to see that old man. She'd have to ask him what the attraction was. As far as she could see, Jeremy didn't give him sweets or anything. Maybe it was just because his son was Jolly Roger. Still, it was worth keeping an eye on. She was about to follow her son into the house when she saw Tony at the top of the road. She was pretty sure it was him; she knew his slouching walk, the way he kept his head down as if afraid to look the world in the eye. She stood frozen as he got nearer, looking for tell-tale signs of mania or dopiness. He was not coming into the house if he was in a state. She knew this suddenly. She knew that there was no way she was letting him come near their kids in any sort of a state ever again.

He stopped when he was about six feet away, as if suddenly spying her too.

'Where were you?' she asked softly, not wanting anyone in the vicinity to hear.

'I went to a couple of meetings,' he said, drawing closer.

He hadn't used. He'd gone to meetings. Tears pricked her eyes. But she said, 'You could have left a note.'

'I rang you. I left a message on your phone.'

She still had her phone off. 'Oh.'

'I'm so sorry about today, Al.'

'You scared the kids, Tony, and you were making such progress.'

'I didn't mean to, I just . . .' He looked upwards, then brought his gaze to meet hers. 'I just was so,' he winced at the admission, 'jealous of John. He's so much better at all this than I am. Owen loves him.'

'He'd love you too if you were just yourself.'

He was now only a foot from her. 'I don't know who that is. All I know is that you and the kids mean everything to me.'

He could always get her. Every time. She touched his arm, squeezed it gently. 'Come on, let's say good night to them so.'

Bodies touching, hip to hip, they entered the house.

He made love to her that night. Oh, they'd had sex since he'd come out of the hospital but there was something different about it that night, Allie thought afterwards as she lay awake in the dark, Tony asleep, his gorgeous eyelashes brushing his cheek and making her heart ache with how childish they looked. What was different about the way he kissed her and held her, she couldn't pinpoint. But, as she finally closed her eyes, she decided that it was a good difference. Positive. And she smiled.

34

THE INSISTENT RINGING of the doorbell woke Allie. Heart pounding, she sat up abruptly, making her head spin. Oh God, she felt sick. She'd matched Holly pint for pint the previous night and had the headache to prove it. Holly had drunk methodically, determined to blot out the pain, and Allie wondered how she was this morning. She'd ring her later.

The bell buzzed again.

Suddenly she wondered if something had happened to Tony. Was it the police? It was a fear that she had lived with for the last ten years, the unexpected police caller in the middle of the night. Blindly she began to pull the duvet cover from her legs.

'I'll get it,' Tony said groggily as he wiped sleep from his eyes. 'You look like death.'

It took Allie a second to realise that he was here, beside her. That he'd been there all night. She smiled in sudden relief, pausing in her frantic efforts to disentangle herself from the bedclothes.

'What's that smile for?' Tony grinned, winking at her as he pulled on a pair of jeans.

'Nothing.' Allie was unable to stop smiling. Another long peal of the doorbell and her smile faded.

'You stay there.' Yanking on a black T-shirt, Tony padded barefoot downstairs.

Allie heard him open the front door.

'I'd like a word.' Tess. And she didn't sound happy.

'Is everything OK, Tess?' Allie called down. The words made her head pound. Oh God, she thought she might be sick.

Mark poked his head into Allie's room. 'Is there something wrong?' he asked fearfully.

'I just want a chat with my son, Allie,' Tess called back up.

'It's only Nana, she wants to talk to Daddy,' Allie said to Mark. 'You go back to sleep, honey, or play your computer games. I'll just go down and make her a cup of tea.'

'She sounds cross,' Mark whispered.

'She doesn't,' Allie rolled her eyes. 'Your Nana Tess is never cross.'

'You really have done it this time!' Tess barked from downstairs.

Mark looked at Allie, who mentally kicked herself. Why was she continually lying to her son? Yes, she wanted to protect him, but damn it, he wasn't stupid. 'Well, she does sound a little cross,' she conceded, 'so let me see what I can do.'

'If you want me to come down just yell,' Mark said seriously. 'I'll mind you.'

'I know you will, honey.' Allie hugged him hard. 'But it'll be fine, you'll see.'

She wished she believed it as she descended the stairs and headed into the kitchen. Tony was standing sulkily beside the sink and Tess was glowering at him in a very un-Tess-like way.

'Hi,' Allie attempted to lighten things. 'Tea, Tess?'

'You look sick,' Tess said instead.

'Hangover,' Allie explained apologetically.

'From living with him, no doubt,' she snapped, glaring again at Tony.

'What's this about?' Allie asked, though she thought she knew.

'It's about the way he treated his brother the other day,' Tess snapped. 'John was very upset when he got back, he didn't know what he'd done wrong. And then, not even a phone call to apologise.'

'I'd nothing to apologise for,' Tony said. 'He'd put up the goal posts I said I wanted to put up.'

'He was trying to help out. He thought it'd be a surprise.'

'Yeah, it was, the way a kick in the teeth is a surprise.' Tony ignored her snort of disbelief. 'Anyway, what sort of a guy is he, running to you with tales. What is he? Ten or something?'

'He did not run to me with tales,' Tess said, her chest heaving. 'I noticed there was something wrong, he is my son, for God's sake.'

'Oh right,' Tony nodded, as if she'd just said something enlightening. 'Funny how you never noticed there was anything wrong with me, isn't it? Maybe it's because I'm not your son.'

'Tony!' Allie said, horrified.

Tess looked bewildered, as if Tony had just landed an unexpected punch.

'Well, she didn't,' Tony said, sounding about ten years old himself.

Tess blinked and swallowed. 'Maybe,' she rallied, her hurt turning to anger, 'it's because you just weren't as emotionally honest as your brother. You never admitted to yourself there was something wrong, did you? How would I know?'

'I think we all should calm down.' Allie laid a hand on Tony's arm. 'Tell Tess what you admitted to me, Tony.'

'What did I admit?'

'That you were jealous of John? That—'

'Jealous of John?' Tess spluttered incredulously. 'What would you be jealous of him for?'

Tony paled. He glanced at Allie. 'I told you that,' he said, stressing the 'you'.

'Yeah, well maybe it's time you told your mother,' Allie prompted.

'Are you jealous of John?' Tess asked.

'No,' Tony answered a little hastily.

'He is,' Allie said.

Tony rubbed his hands over his face. He knew something

was expected of him. He knew he was sick of pretending. He knew Allie was sick of him pretending. Problem was, pretending was emotionally a lot easier. At least in the beginning. You didn't upset anyone, you didn't hurt feelings. But he'd done well since he'd come out of the clinic, better than he thought he would do. He took a deep breath and, not looking at Allie or his mother, he admitted reluctantly, 'He put up the goal posts, OK? The lads were thrilled. I wanted to make them smile like that. I've made their lives so bloody miserable that I just wanted to do something to make them smile and I had planned that I would do it. Then he came in and did it instead. I just, well, it was the only thing I had to offer, you know?'

'He was just trying to be nice,' Tess said, not sounding as cross now.

'He has you.' Tony paused before adding softly, 'All I have, that's really mine, is the boys.'

'You have me too,' Tess said. 'You know you have.'

Tony didn't answer.

'What you said in the clinic really hurt,' Tess said. 'And I know we haven't been the same since. But maybe we were never as close as I thought in the first place. But I loved you just as much as I loved John,' she said with conviction. 'More, maybe, because you'd been abandoned.'

'You felt sorry for me,' Tony stated flatly.

'No!'

'How do you think I felt when John came along?' Without waiting for an answer, Tony ploughed on, 'Like an outsider, that's how.'

'Well, I never made you feel like an outsider,' Tess retorted, stung. 'That was all you. You obviously felt like that and if you did, there was nothing I could have said or done to make you feel otherwise. I know I never once did anything to make you feel out of place.'

'Tess, calm down,' Allie said.

But Tess was on a roll. 'And do you know what,' she pointed

a finger at Tony, 'the only one who feels sorry for you is you. I loved you and there was a time you used to call me Mammy. Then you stopped. Maybe it was after John came along, I don't know. I thought it was a phase. But if you wanted to feel out of place then that was the way to go.'

'I—' Tony began.

'You have no idea how much you hurt me and your father by doing that,' Tess went on. 'But we accepted it, just like we accepted you.' Her voice wobbled and her chest heaved. 'We accepted you,' she went on, 'but you obviously never accepted us.'

'Tess,' Allie was horrified to see her mother-in-law begin to cry, 'don't.' She put her arm about her and led her to a chair. 'Don't be upset.'

'How can I not be?' Tess pulled out a hankie from her sleeve and dabbed her eyes. 'How can I not be? This is the same stuff he spouted at the clinic. How do you convince someone that you love them?'

'You can't,' Allie said, glancing at Tony. 'I think they have to love themselves a bit first.'

Tony's jaw tightened and he turned away.

'You've been a brilliant mother to him, John has been a brilliant brother, and you're right, it is Tony's problem.' She hugged Tess again.

Tony rubbed his hands through his short dark hair and shuffled from foot to foot. He wasn't sure what he was expected to say, though it shocked him to see Tess upset. He guessed she ought to be because of what he'd said, but still, he wouldn't have wanted to hurt her, which was a bit mad as obviously his words would have hurt anyone. 'I'm sorry,' he murmured from his position at the sink. 'You're right, it was all me.'

Tess looked up at him from the shelter of Allie's arms, but said nothing.

Tony knew more was expected of him. 'I so wanted to be John,' he admitted haltingly. 'To know where I belonged.

I'm not saying that's why I did drugs, I probably would have done them anyway, but they did help take the edge off the bitterness of him being yours and not me.'

'You were mine,' Tess said softly. 'I'm going to say it now and that's the last time I will. I can't make you believe me.' She pulled herself out of Allie's arms and rose to her feet. 'Now, I've said what I came to say, I'll go now.' She pulled her purple coat around her, almost as protection. 'Bye.'

Allie didn't ask her to stay, there was no point. Tony had to be the one to do it, but he didn't. Instead he said, 'Bye, Tess.'

Both of them knew they wouldn't see her in the house again unless Tony initiated it.

Allie knew there was no point in talking it over with him, it was laid out and all he had to do was make his choices. 'I'll go talk to Mark,' she said, 'you stick on the kettle.'

His response was to nod.

'Hey, how you doing this morning?' Allie asked.

Holly groaned. 'Well, I was dead to the world until you rang, now I've a headache and feel sick.'

'Welcome to my hangover,' Allie chuckled a little. 'Sorry for waking you. Tony got an earbashing from his mother this morning so we were all up early.'

'No!' Holly sounded a teeny bit more alert. 'Why was that?'

'Oh, you know the row he had with his brother? Well his mam came to say that he'd been unfair to John and it ended with poor Tess marching out of the house all upset. I swear, I could kill that man sometimes.'

Holly was silent for a second.

'What?' Allie asked.

'Just keep an eye on him,' Holly said. 'I know from,' she gulped, 'well, from Vee, that emotional rows and stuff freak them out. Just, you know, be nice to him.'

Allie felt chilled. 'Yeah. OK. Thanks.'

'Though Tony is great,' Holly said hastily. 'I wouldn't be too concerned, you know.'

'Sure,' Allie nodded, already wondering where Tony had got to. It suddenly seemed urgent to find him. 'OK. Well, I'll let you get back to bed, right. Talk soon.'

As she hung up, she heard him upstairs, making Mark giggle at something he was saying. She felt so relieved, she had to sit down on the floor and blink back tears.

Dear Santa

I no Im riting to you a awful lot but i keep changing my mind about my Christmas present. It is good you live next stoor as i wouldnt be able to do dis otherwise. My wish list for Christmas is in order

Number one make daddy happy so dat he does not fite with nana tess. He had a big row dis morning and he had a row with his brodder too but i think nana is more upset.

Number too make daddy be friends with uncle john dat is who he fighted with also and me and owen miss uncle john.

Number tree make daddy not be a junkie and not shout and if your elves tell you about my daddy finding his magic can you tell me.

Make Daddy love himself the way we love him as mammy said this morning dat he doesnt love himself.

Number five is make Robert stop calling me junkie son and Fatso dat would be good. He still hasnt found his magic at all. I fink your elves were wrong.

Number six is can i have a television for my room. Mammy says only one Christmas present is allowed but i no lodas of kids who have a list so dat is why i am making one.

Number seven is to bring owen his present too. I think he still wants a football.

I no dis is a long letter but other kids probably havent ritten to you yet so you have loads of time to read it. i did call in de udder day but you must have been out on a walk. I suppose you have to keep fit coming up to cristmas and all. say hello to Rudolph and mrs claus.

From mark who lives next stoor to you in your pretend house.

XXXXXXXXXXXXXXXXXXX

Jeremy folded up the letter and smiled a little ruefully. Guilt was eating at him. Wish number five had been sorted. He supposed it was better than nothing.

He felt quite angry at Tony, wishing he could somehow tell the man to cop on. He'd spent his life arguing with people. Arguing over little things like parking spaces and the fact that the boys' uniforms were not good quality and the lack of homework given by certain teachers. He'd prided himself on keeping the world in order, on showing people the right way to live. Maybe because when his own world had fallen apart he'd needed to feel in control somehow. He wondered now how his sons had felt about it all. He'd never really considered them.

For the first time, Jeremy wondered how he could have done better.

For the first time Jeremy wished he could turn back time, like Santa apparently was able to do.

For the first time Jeremy realised that he had quite a big wish list of his own.

35

M ARK, ALONG WITH some of his classmates, stood waiting to be picked for the school-break football team. He hated this part because he always got picked last. And then, no matter what position he was in, no one passed him the ball. Still, it was cool to be involved, and he pretended that he was playing for United. As he jogged along, hoping that someone on his team would kick the ball in his direction, he commented on the match in his head. That was his favourite part. The only downside today was that Robert was picking teams. Robert always said stuff like, 'Oh, I pick Mark' and then as Mark walked towards him he'd say something like, 'Sorry, I thought we'd to pick the fattest player first.' Most of the boys would laugh but some didn't, which was good.

Mark didn't let that put him off though. He knew he had to be picked at some stage. As Robert glared sullenly at the line of boys, Mark braced himself for his sarcasm.

'Mark,' Robert called first. It came out sounding like a spit.

Mark didn't move. He wasn't going to be fooled again.

Some of Robert's friends groaned and asked, 'Why him, he's useless!'

Mark flushed.

'Mark,' Alan, his friend, nudged him excitedly, 'you've been called.'

All the boys were looking at him.

'I'm not stupid,' Mark said, his voice only shaking a little bit. 'I know you're just going to laugh at me.'

Robert glowered at him. 'Do you want to play on my team or not?' he demanded.

Mark shrugged.

'It's your last chance,' Robert said. 'I pick you.'

Mark felt a bit sick. It would be great to be on Robert's team cause his team always won. But if he walked over to Robert maybe Robert would laugh at him. But Robert didn't have that nasty look on his face, Mark thought. He looked grumpy and serious. He decided to risk joining Robert. If he was messing, Mark decided that he would hit him.

Slowly, trying not to look excited, he slouched across to Robert.

Unbelievably, Robert said nothing. Mark stood there, wanting to smile but not daring to. He was the first picked. The very first. For the first time ever.

It was worth waiting for.

Santa had been right after all.

'Hello, stranger.' Magda opened the door wider to let Allie in. 'We haven't seen you in the last couple of weeks.'

'You could have called over to me.' Allie set her bag on the table and tried not to flush. If she were honest, she deliberately hadn't called on her mother and Fintan, knowing that they'd ask about Thomas. And she hadn't been quite sure what to tell them.

Her mother peered out the door. 'Where are the boys?'

'Tony has them.'

Magda raised her eyebrows.

'He's really trying hard at the moment,' Allie said. 'He plucked up the courage to bring the lads to the cinema this evening.' She didn't tell her mother that Tony had also started talking about working again. He'd spent the last few days hunting for the application form that she'd thrown out. Allie thought that minding the boys would be a diversion for him. He might forget about the form altogether. Or forget that it was due in in two days' time.

'I see.' Magda broke into her thoughts. Her lips were pressed together in a straight line and her tone suggested that she didn't actually see at all. It killed her to recognise that hopeful look on Allie's face, that fragile longing for everything to be normal. She'd worn it herself once upon a time. She only hoped that Tony turned out to be a more worthy recipient than her own husband did. Which reminded her. 'How is Thomas?' she asked, arching an eyebrow. 'Or do you not want to say?'

'Hello!' Fintan shoved the back door open so hard that its frame hit the kitchen wall. The noise effectively cut off any answer Allie was going to give. 'Just doing a bit of gardening,' he said cheerily, as he sat on the doorstep and peeled off an enormous pair of wellies. 'We haven't seen you around in a while, Allie.' He stepped into the kitchen in his sock-clad feet.

'I was just saying that,' Magda nodded. 'I think she's been deliberately keeping her distance.'

'Oh now, not at all.' Fintan winked at Allie. 'I'm sure now what with Tony and the boys she's been very busy.'

'And Thomas,' Magda interjected. 'He'd keep anyone on their toes.'

'Ballet dancer, was he?' Fintan snorted at his feeble joke. He pulled some fruit from the fruit bowl and, holding up a bag of apples, asked Allie if she'd like a fruit juice.

'I'll have a tea,' Allie said.

'Caffeine, not good.' Fintan wagged a finger at them both as he filled the kettle, after which he busied himself getting the juicer from the press.

Allie wondered in amusement if all Fintan did was make juice.

'So, let's cut to the chase,' Magda said. 'How is the scumbag, Allie?'

'He seems fine,' Allie answered carefully. 'I've met him a few times now. He has a job in a restaurant, pretending to be French.'

Magda clapped her hands. 'My God, he hasn't changed,'

271

she chortled. 'When I met him, he pretended to be French too. He can do a mean accent. He's not bad at the language either. Eventually I found out he was lying but I'd fallen for him by that stage. He spun me some line about it being the only way he felt he could compete with all the other guys.'

'Maybe it was,' Allie said.

Magda gave her a disbelieving look. 'There wasn't exactly a queue for me,' she said.

'How did you find out he was lying?' Fintan shouted over the noise of the juicer.

'We bumped into his mother in the city one day. Remember your grandmother, Allie?'

Allie laughed. 'Yep. She was the biggest Dub you ever met. Born and bred in the inner city.'

Magda nodded. 'Aw, at that stage, I should have known what I was getting into.'

'You should have,' Fintan nodded.

The kettle clicked off and he abandoned the juicer and made Allie a pot of tea.

Magda pulled out a packet of chocolate digestives from a press. Fintan looked at her accusingly.

'I need food whenever I think of him,' she defended herself.

Allie swallowed. She knew the next bit would be harder. Her mother might freak totally. In fact, she'd probably eat the whole packet of biscuits in one sitting. 'Anyway,' she went on brightly, pretending that it was good news, 'the good news is . . .' She paused before continuing in a rush, 'He'd like to meet the boys.'

There was silence. From behind Magda Fintan made an anguished face. Magda unconsciously reached out and took another biscuit from the packet.

'And I've said yes.' Allie spoke over her mother's crunching.

There was a small beat of silence before Fintan, attempting to match Allie's chirpiness, said, 'Well, he is their grandfather, I suppose.'

272

Fintan's smile was a little overstretched, Allie thought. She felt suddenly bad for hurting him. 'Biological grandfather,' she said. 'You have been brilliant, Fintan.'

'Yes, he has,' Magda nodded vigorously, 'so I don't know why you would want to replace him!'

'Oh Mum, I'm not doing that. The boys would never stand for that.'

'They do have a right to get to know their real granddad,' Fintan said generously.

'Their real granddad!' Magda chewed her biscuit vigorously, before saying, '*You* are their real granddad!' Bits of digestive sprayed from her mouth. 'You! You have done everything for those two boys. For God's sake, Mark even broke your nose.'

'He broke your nose?' Allie winced. 'Was that the time when he kicked the football into your face?'

Fintan waved it away. 'It was nothing. I quite like it. It gives me a rather battle-hardened look, don't you think?' He gave Allie a view of his profile and his crooked nose looked very odd from that angle.

'I am sorry,' she gulped out. 'I'll have to tell Mark to be more careful.'

'It was my fault. I was never a sportsman. I got in the way of the ball.'

'That's what goalies are meant to do,' Magda said. She looked Allie up and down. 'I hope you won't build their expectations up,' she added.

Allie shook her head. 'No, I won't. Tony has said the same.'

Magda nodded. 'Well, at least I agree with him on one thing.'

There was more silence. 'He hasn't aged well,' Allie offered. 'He looks old.' She was about to add that life had been hard to him since he'd left, in the hope that her mother might be more sympathetic.

Instead Magda laughed delightedly and nodded, 'I thought that too. Did you see the ridiculous black he has dyed his

eyebrows? It's as if two overweight caterpillars died on his face.'
She shook her head. 'Pathetic.'

Allie's lips twitched. She didn't want to laugh, though, and encourage her mother. Fintan seemed to sense it and he placed a reassuring hand on Magda's shoulder. 'The most pathetic thing about him,'_ he said as he dropped a kiss on Magda's hair, 'is that he lost you. I'm grateful to the man for that.'

Magda's expression softened. 'Aww,' she cooed, nuzzling against him.

Allie smiled as Fintan winked at her over Magda's head.

She was grateful to Fintan for making things easier than they had a right to be.

Owen hadn't said a word all day, Tony thought despondently, as he sat on the bus with his two sons on the way home from the cinema. The child had barely smiled and had shaken his head when Tony had offered him an ice cream. You'd think after six weeks at home, the kid would at least talk to him. As if to make up for it, Mark had been in great form. He'd told him all about getting picked first for soccer in school and of how Robert had passed him the ball and of how Mark had scored a goal.

'Isn't that great,' Tony said to Owen, 'isn't Mark a good footballer?'

Owen had regarded him solemnly from great brown eyes, then he'd shoved his thumb in his mouth and turned away, his small hand grasping for Mark.

'It's OK,' Mark said loudly to Tony, 'he's just a bit scared of you since you shouted the other day.'

It might have been nice if Mark hadn't spoken so loudly himself, Tony thought, as a number of heads turned discreetly in their direction.

'And he heard you shouting at Nana Tess too,' Mark went on, oblivious to the interest of the surrounding passengers.

274

Tony desperately tried to change the subject. 'Who's for chips? Mammy said to get some on our way home.'

'Me!' Mark cheered, and then gently he asked Owen, 'Would you like some?'

Owen gave a small nod.

'He'd like some, Daddy.'

'Well, if Owen wants some, he shall have some.' Tony smiled down at his younger son.

Owen turned away.

'It'll take more than a bag of chips,' Mark said, sounding uncannily like Allie.

'I know,' Tony agreed quietly. He wrapped an arm about Mark's shoulders and whispered in his ear, 'But will you tell him that I love both of you very much?'

'I will.' Mark grinned up into his dad's face. 'And you just wait, Dad, you'll find your magic.'

'What?'

'To get better.' Mark nodded wisely. 'You just have to find the magic.'

Tony wondered where he'd heard that from. Probably Allie or her mother.

'Well, I can promise you that I am looking very hard for it,' Tony said, his voice catching. 'Very hard.'

'Then you'll find it,' Mark said happily. Suddenly he frowned. 'You didn't by any chance leave it behind in America?' he asked.

Tony was confused. 'America?'

'The magic? Say you left it behind you in America.'

Tony wasn't going to start talking about America again. It made him uncomfortable that the kids still thought he'd been away on business. They'd be asking why he wasn't working soon. 'If I left it there,' he said firmly, 'I'll get it back.'

Mark looked doubtful.

'I promise,' Tony added.

Mark looked even more doubtful.

275

'I promise on your Granny Magda's life,' Tony said, grinning. Mark nodded reassured.

Tony suppressed a laugh. He jokingly thought that he couldn't lose either way!

36

A LLIE KNEW THERE was something up the minute she pulled the car into the driveway. She knew because Tony, upon hearing them arrive back, normally came out to the door to greet them. He'd hoist Mark on to his shoulders and they'd all tramp into the kitchen, where he'd make a cup of coffee for her. Today, Tony didn't come to the door. It was only a small thing, but it made her heart beat a tiny bit faster.

'Where's Daddy?' Mark peered out the window.

'Inside, I suppose,' Allie said cheerfully as she unstrapped Owen from his seat. 'Let's go find him.' She kept her voice normal for Mark's sake, knowing that he'd immediately sense any upset.

She unlocked the door and, to her relief, Tony was sitting at the kitchen table, his head buried in the paper. He barely looked up as they entered, smiled briefly at the lads before glaring down at the newspaper again.

He wasn't high, as far as she could tell. He just seemed really annoyed over something. Dread crawled up Allie's spine like an ice-cold snake. Oh Jesus, no . . . he couldn't know, could he? It felt hard to breathe suddenly. Something had rattled him, she knew. And she also knew that whatever it was, he seemed to be blaming her as there was unmistakeable hostility in his refusal to acknowledge her. He appeared absorbed in reading the business section of the paper, but he never normally read those pages so something was definitely eating him. The trick, she hoped, was to pretend that everything was normal.

But even the kids could sense he was annoyed as they'd stopped at the kitchen door, obviously not wanting to come in any further. Allie's heart went out to them, they were so sensitive at this stage to any change in atmosphere.

'Hi,' she said as lightly as she could. She walked by and ruffled Tony's hair, hoping to elicit a smile.

He pulled out from under her hand.

'So how did your day go?' Still striving for brightness, she pulled some frozen meals from the freezer.

The pause before he answered seemed to fill the kitchen with menace. 'Not great.'

'Oh?' Allie arched her eyebrows, her heart hammering furiously, praying that he hadn't found out yet knowing somehow that he had. 'Did you get to a meeting?'

'I phoned my old employers looking for a reference. I mean they only let me go as they were scaling down, didn't they?' Tony swivelled on the chair to glare at her.

In the doorway, Owen whimpered. Mark instinctively wrapped an arm around him.

Allie froze. Carefully she laid the Tupperware carton down on the table. 'I was going to tell you,' she said quietly, shooting a glance at Mark and Owen.

'Really?' Tony stood up and faced her. He was taller than her. His voice was quietly furious. 'When?'

'Soon.' Allie gulped hard, wanting to cry. This couldn't be happening. She knew when he found out he'd hate her for it.

'You know I wanted to go back to work and you never told me what you'd done?' Tony spoke slowly, his face inching nearer Allie's. 'Do you know how stupid I felt when I rang them? Do you?'

'They shouldn't have told you,' Allie said. She tried to touch him but he pulled roughly away. 'I only did it for the best.'

Tony barked out a kind of laugh, then threw his eyes to heaven and walked around in a circle. When he spoke again his voice was a lot louder. 'You tell me that I'm a liar, that I'm a cheat, and you'd be right. But you,' he jabbed his finger at her, 'you beat them all. You lie to the kids, you make me lie to the kids, you then tell me 'Oh, we won't lie any more' and then you don't tell me *this*!'

'Mark, take Owen upstairs,' Allie said, without looking at them.

'No!' Tony shouted, making them all jump. He crossed towards the boys. 'From this moment on, there are going to be no more lies in this house.'

'Tony!'

'I wasn't in America, Mark,' Tony said. He brought his voice down but the two boys took a step back just the same. It disconcerted Tony. 'I wasn't in America,' he began again. 'I was in a—'

'Tony, you just stop it!' Allie shouted, making Mark jump.

Tony flinched. Then he closed his mouth and, turning to her, said in a dangerously low voice, 'I am not going to keep lying to them about New York.'

'I'll tell them when they're ready,' Allie said.

'Oh, and when did you think you'd tell me about my job?' Tony's voice rose again. Allie had never heard him sound quite so furious. She knew she'd messed up big time by not telling him. It was like watching a train heading towards her and not being able to stop herself being run over. 'You're the one who didn't want me to lie any more, and what do you do?'

'I never lied,' she said. 'Please—'

'You just didn't tell me the truth, did you? You're the reason I lost my last job. You!'

'Yes!' Allie nodded. 'Yes, I am.' She paused. 'And do you know what, I'd do it again. I would.' Her voice rose, remembering the day the man had come calling. Remembering how she knew she had to stop this terrible destructive path Tony had them all on. 'I would do it again!' she screamed into his face. She was crying too, she realised. 'Yes, I rang them up, told them to fire you. I did! I did!'

'Thanks!' Tony spat back.

'I didn't want you having money.' Allie wanted to hit him now, to shake sense into him, to make him understand. 'I wanted you to have nothing so you couldn't spend it and make our lives miserable.'

'Well, you could have told me. Instead I just made a gigantic fool out of myself.'

'That's not exactly a first!'

It was as if she'd hit him. Tony swayed a little, then paused, and the kitchen seemed to grow very quiet and still. Then he turned abruptly, pushing past the boys, and wrenched open the front door.

'Tony! Tony? Where are you going?'

'I don't know!'

The door slammed shut and Allie burst into tears.

Mark tried to make her feel better but she didn't seem able to. She just gathered him and Owen into her arms and tried to tell them that everything would be all right.

'Is that why Daddy had no passport?' Mark asked out of the blue.

'What?' Allie lifted her head from his shiny hair.

'Daddy had no passport and yet I thought he was in America.'

She hugged him tighter. 'I'm sorry I told lies, Mark. But I didn't want you to worry.'

'Where was he, if he wasn't in America?'

Allie closed her eyes and said wearily, 'He was in a hospital, Mark, trying to get better. Trying to get off the drugs.'

'Oh.' Mark looked shocked. 'Did you ever visit him?'

'Uh-huh.'

'When?' he asked in a small voice.

'On a Saturday and sometimes a Wednesday.'

Mark absorbed this. 'Those were the days you told us you were with your friends.'

'I was with Daddy.'

Mark shook her off quite suddenly and walked out of the room.

'Mark!' Allie called, but he told her to go away.

Tony wasn't answering his phone. He hadn't come back at all. They'd made a pact that he'd keep in touch whenever he thought she might worry about him and he hadn't rung to say he was fine. Allie was in such a panic that she was totally unable to decide what she should do. Her thoughts tumbled like leaves in the wind, circling and whirling and not resting anywhere. Should she look for him? Was he OK? Was he maybe at a load of meetings? Was she overreacting? Was what she had done so bad?

She'd call his sponsor, that's what she'd do first, she decided. She stopped her pacing and pounded her way up to the bedroom and, taking a load of papers from Tony's side, she searched frantically through them until she found what she was looking for. Ciaran's number, written on a blue sheet of writing paper. Her hands fumbling and sweaty, she dialled his mobile. The call was answered on the first ring by a cheery voice.

'Hello,' Allie said breathlessly, 'this is Allie. I'm Tony Dolan's wife. You're his sponsor in NA. Has he contacted you at all?' She raked her hand through her hair, letting it tumble over her face as it fell back.

'Tony?' The caller sounded puzzled. 'No, he hasn't. Why?'

Allie explained about the row. She tried to do it calmly but instead she ended up weeping into the phone. 'And now he's gone and I don't know where,' she sobbed. 'And it's all my fault and if anything happens—'

'Hey, hang on,' Ciaran said gently. 'First, if Tony uses, that's his choice. You had a row with him, that's all. You made a mistake. You didn't force him to take anything. The way I see it, he's in charge of his own life.'

'But he was so hurt—'

'Yeah. He has to learn to deal with that,' Ciaran said matter-of-factly. 'We all get hurt along the way. You have nothing to blame yourself for. Now, he hasn't been in touch with me at all but I'm at home, so I'll sit tight here in case he shows up. I've told him to come here if he's in trouble, OK? I'll let you know. Have you got a mobile number I can contact you on?'

Allie gave him her number. 'Thanks,' she sniffed. 'You're very good.'

'I've put people through what you're going through,' Ciaran said gently. 'I have to make it up to them somehow, ey?'

'Mmm.' She couldn't answer, she felt so emotional.

'You take care.'

Ciaran hung up and Allie sat on the bed, biting her nails, wondering what she should do. Even though Tony had only been clean for a just over two months, she had half forgotten the dread she'd experienced so many times before. It was back now with a vengeance, washing right through her thoughts, blinding her with panic. All those nights he'd come in high and hyper-talkative, all the time and energy she'd spent in trying to gauge his mood, trying to keep him from flying off the handle, all those mysterious phone calls that had worried her sick even though she had tried to normalise them, all the lying, the living on a knife edge of denial. Should she look for him? She thought of Veronica lying on her own in a horrible squat, dying, and she knew that there was no way she could let that happen to Tony. She had to go out. She had to find him. Even if it was the last time she'd ever do it, she had to find him.

And soon.

Half an hour later, she knocked on Mark's bedroom door. He hadn't come downstairs since Tony had left.

'What?' Mark snapped and Allie knew he was cross with her.

'Mark, honey,' she peeped around the door at him, 'I've called into Jeremy next door and he's going to come in and mind you for a bit.' She was gratified to see that this bit of news interested him.

He lifted himself up on his elbow. 'Why?'

Allie swallowed.

'Why?' Mark asked again.

'Well,' she tried to say it in such a way that it wouldn't frighten him, 'your daddy isn't answering his phone. I'm worried about him. Me and Holly are going to look for him.'

'But you haven't gone looking for Daddy in a long time. Not since . . .' His voice trailed off.

Not since that horrible day when he and Owen had come in from the garden, Owen's nose all bleeding, and found her crying on the floor, Allie thought. And she hadn't found him then either. Allie sat down beside her son on the bed and wrapped an arm about his shoulders. 'Will you look after Owen and make sure that he's no trouble to Jeremy?'

'Is Daddy sick again?' he asked.

'I don't know.' Allie shook her head. 'I honestly don't know. I think he's hurt by me not confessing to what I did.'

Mark nodded. 'You told lies,' he said flatly. 'You told them to me. And Daddy told them.'

'Sorry,' Allie hugged him tighter, 'we just didn't want you to worry.'

'I thought Daddy was a really cross man, I never knew he was sick.'

'Would it have been easier for you if you'd known?'

Mark nodded. 'It wouldn't have been as scary,' he said.

Allie felt her heart break a tiny bit at his admission. 'I'm so sorry, Mark.'

He pondered this and then said, 'I'll mind Owen.'

'Thanks.'

He allowed a little smile. 'If Daddy goes into hospital again, can I visit him?'

'I hope he won't.'

Mark said nothing.

Eventually Allie nodded. 'Yes, you can visit.'

'I missed him a lot when he was away. I would have liked to see him.'

Allie hugged him fiercely. 'I know you would. I should never have kept you away from him.' And, she thought regretfully, she should never have kept Tony away from them. It hadn't been fair on him. No wonder Owen was so cautious. Maybe if it had been explained to him that his daddy was getting better, he might have accepted the new Tony instead of being frightened his daddy was going to flip any moment. In that second Allie knew that while the drug problem had been Tony's, it was also hers. She had never faced up to it, no matter how she told herself she had. She'd never gone to the family meetings with Holly, reluctant to share her life with yet more strangers. Yet she'd insisted that Tony go to his meetings. If he came out of this OK, Allie swore that the next time a meeting was on, she'd be there.

'You better go and find him,' Mark said solemnly.

'OK.' Allie released him and kissed his head. 'I'll talk to you later.'

Mark watched his mammy leave. Downstairs he heard her giving hurried instructions to Mr Lyons.

He smiled a tiny bit. It might be fun to have Santa in charge. Maybe he might even know where his daddy was. Then they could ring his mammy and let her know.

Jeremy was panicking. It had been a long time since he had been responsible for two young boys. OK, he conceded, he had never been responsible for two young boys; his wife had done most of that stuff until she passed away. But at least his boys did what they were told and rarely argued. This Owen kid was like a statue. It was quite disconcerting the way he stood quite still, thumb shoved very firmly in his mouth, while he gawked at Jeremy with these enormous brown eyes as if he could see into Jeremy's very soul. Jeremy shivered at the thought.

He would be very uncomfortable having his soul scrutinised. Mark, on the other hand, was a very pleasant chap. He had offered Jeremy some jellies and the two of them were sitting side by side on the sofa, chewing away. Jeremy never bought jelly sweets for himself, seeing them as a waste of money and quite unhealthy. But they were nice.

'Owen will come over soon,' Mark whispered to Jeremy, 'he loves the orange jellies.'

Half an hour later, around nine, Owen was still standing, staring at the two of them. Jeremy sighed. It was nine o'clock, well past the boys' bedtime he was sure. He stood up. 'I think I'll put the two of you to bed,' he said. 'It's getting late.'

'Can we just stay up until Mammy comes home?' Mark asked. 'I just want to see how Daddy is.' Jeremy frowned. Allie had been quite vague on the details, just telling him that she needed a big favour. She told him Tony was out and she had to go and there was no one to take the boys. Would he mind? He had been tempted to say no out of pure fear, but he didn't have it in him when he saw the look of desperation on her face.

Jeremy didn't want to pry, but he felt that he had to. 'Is your daddy sick?'

'Mammy doesn't know. She thinks he might be being a junkie again.' Mark's voice wobbled.

Good God. Jeremy had a sudden vision of himself and Tony going at it, hand to hand as he fought to keep a drugged-up Tony away from his children. Maybe the man would have a needle and he, Jeremy, would contract AIDS or something equally horrific. There was no way a man his age could fight off a man like Tony. He'd need help. He'd also need help with Owen, who was backing away from him, his face all puckered up ready to scream if Jeremy so much as touched him. 'I'm just going to make a quick call,' Jeremy said, exiting the room. 'Mark, will you keep an eye on your brother?'

'Yep, Santa,' Mark said. Then as Jeremy flinched he added,

'There's no one here, only Owen, and he won't tell.'

Out in the hallway, Jeremy tried to remember Adam's home phone number. If anyone could soothe a little boy and also fight off a drug-crazed dad, it would be Adam. Though he wouldn't want Adam to be hurt of course . . .

'Hello?' someone said on the other end of the line, startling Jeremy out of his panicked reverie.

It didn't sound like Adam.

'Adam?' Jeremy asked.

'I'll just get him, who's calling please?'

Jeremy winced. This was probably Adam's . . . he tried to think of what this man was . . . Adam's . . . partner, he supposed. He sounded a little girlie. It was a slight relief to know that at least Adam was manlier than that. 'His dad,' Jeremy said loftily.

'Oh hello, Mr Lyons,' the man said. 'I'm Peter.'

'Hmm. Hello, Peter. Can you get Adam, please?'

Adam must have been standing by the phone because a second later he too said 'Hello.' He sounded wary.

'Adam,' Jeremy said brusquely, 'sorry to bother you this time of night, but I need your help. Urgently,' he tacked on.

'What is it? What's happened?'

Jeremy was gratified to hear the worry in his son's tone. At least he still cared, despite not having rung in the past few weeks.

'Well, I'm looking after my next door neighbour's boys—'

'You're what?'

Jeremy prickled at the astonishment in Adam's voice. 'You heard me,' he said. 'And one of the boys is scared of me.'

'No!'

Now it was mock-astonishment. Jeremy frowned. 'I did not ring you up to have you laugh at me, Adam,' he barked. 'But if that's all—'

'Sorry, Dad, go on.'

At least he sounded contrite. 'Well, one of the little boys is afraid of me and I'm afraid of the boys' father. He's a,' he lowered his voice so Mark wouldn't hear, 'he's a drug addict and I'm afraid he'll come back and I won't be able to deal with him.'

'You're joking!'

'Does this sound like a joke?' Jeremy said impatiently. 'So, Adam, I'd like you to come and help me with these boys and also to hang on until the mother gets back. I don't want anything to happen to them.'

'OK, Dad, I'll be there. Which house is it? The one attached to you?'

'Yes.'

The line went dead.

Jeremy smiled at little to himself. It would be good to see Adam again. He'd missed him.

37

ALLIE DROVE THROUGH the city centre as Holly peered out the window. 'I'm so sorry I had to ask you to come,' Allie said. 'But you were the only person I could think of.'

Holly looked at her in surprise. 'Sorry?' she said. 'Why would you be sorry? Down here.' She suddenly indicated a derelict road in a derelict area of Dublin. Turning to Allie she added, 'I'm glad to come. Jesus, Tony was so brilliant that night, you know when . . .' She didn't finish, her eyes misted over and she turned to look out the window again.

Allie nodded and patted her arm briefly, knowing that she wasn't expected to say anything. The street she was driving down now was unnaturally dark, due to the number of broken street lights. The one or two that remained shed watery yellow light upon uneven cobbles and discarded takeaway cartons.

'I swore I wouldn't look for him,' Allie said after a bit, 'but the row was my fault too.'

Now it was Holly's turn to stay silent.

'I don't know what I'll do if I find him,' Allie went on. 'I mean, if he's taken something, I can hardly bring him home, can I?'

'Well you could, but do you want to?'

Allie didn't answer. Saying no would mean that she thought she and Tony were over, and she wasn't ready to face that yet.

'Could he go to his mother's?'

'I don't know, his brother would probably kill him.'

More silence.

'He only gave it up in the first place cause I told him I'd leave him. I had all the stuff packed and I told him we were going. He begged me to give him a chance. He cried, I'd never seen him cry before.' Allie's voice trailed off, remembering. The hope she'd had. It just wasn't fair. That's why she hadn't asked her mother or Tess to mind the boys tonight. The *Told-you-so* in her mother's eyes would have crushed her, and the heartbreak she'd cause Tess by having to tell her that Tony was gone AWOL . . . It wasn't fair; she shouldn't have to do that.

'He's done well, you know,' Holly said, surprising her. 'Veronica barely lasted three days the first time she came out. Jesus, she was so stoned she could have rebuilt the Berlin wall.'

Allie gave a splutter of laughter at the analogy.

Holly smiled a little. 'The second time she lasted the year. But my mother had warned her that she was out if she used again. Most of them lapse the first time, Allie. They're not sure how to handle certain things and situations, you see. They have to learn.'

'I refuse to let him experiment with me and my boys,' Allie said, a flash of anger igniting inside her.

'He's a good fella,' Holly said quietly. 'Vee was mad about him. I reckon she stayed clean so long because of him.'

And now she was dead, Allie thought desolately. He hadn't managed to save her. He hadn't managed to save himself.

'He's a good fella,' Holly said again.

Jeremy heard Adam roar up the road in his fancy car. He debated whether or not to answer the door before Adam rang the bell. He didn't want his son to get the impression he was waiting for him or anything . . . but then again, he *was* waiting for him. He was looking forward to seeing him actually. So he got up from the chair and, with Mark dancing behind him, he opened the front door.

Adam was trotting up the drive with a bag of sweets in his hand.

'Hey, Mark.' Adam grinned delightedly as if Mark was his best friend. 'How are you?'

'I'm good.' A massive smile lit up Mark's face. 'Did your daddy ask you to come?'

Adam, ignoring Jeremy, leapt into the hallway. 'He did. He said,' Adam's eyes found Owen, who was standing in the doorway of the dining room, 'he said that there were two boys who needed to be put to bed and told a bedtime story and that I was the person to do it!'

Owen hugged the door frame tighter.

'Hey,' Adam crouched down in front of Owen, 'do you remember me?'

There was a silence as Owen regarded him suspiciously.

'Do you remember, Owen?' Mark coaxed.

Slowly Owen nodded. 'Jolly Roger,' he whispered.

'He can say Jolly Roger!' Mark laughed. 'Well done, Owen!'

Owen smiled shyly under his elder brother's approval.

'That's me,' Adam grinned. 'Will you let me put you to bed?'

'I'd like to wait up until Daddy comes home,' Mark said.

'When your daddy comes home, we'll get him to call right up to you. If you're asleep, we'll make him wake you up, how's that for a deal?'

Mark looked unsure.

'And just to help you sleep, I got a few sweets.' Adam shook the bag he'd come in with.

'Sweets won't help them sleep.' Jeremy spoke for the first time, but withered under the look Adam shot at him.

'They're special sleeping sweets,' Adam said cheerily, as he ushered the two boys up the stairs.

There was no sign of Tony along the street. No sign of him in the grimy bar that Allie knew he had frequented before he'd got clean. She had even screwed up her courage and asked the barman if he'd seen him. He'd regarded her as if she were something out of the gutter and said he hadn't seen Tony in months. 'And I don't want to neither,' he shot after her.

Holly squeezed her hand as they left. 'We'll find him,' she said.

After about forty minutes, Adam crept downstairs. He hesitated before entering the kitchen.

'Tea?' Jeremy held up a pot.

Adam nodded and slid into a chair opposite his dad.

Jeremy poured him a cup and pushed it across the table. 'Thanks for coming,' he said gruffly.

'No problem.'

'You're good with kids,' Jeremy admitted. 'You must have got that from your mother.'

Adam allowed himself a wry smile. 'Well, no offence, Dad, but I didn't get it from you.'

Jeremy flushed, hurt, but tried not to appear as if he cared. 'Are they asleep?' he asked instead.

'Nah. Owen will be soon though. Mark is hyper. He's worried about his dad and thrilled that you're minding him.' Adam shot his dad a keen look. 'Have you drugged the boy or something?'

Again Jeremy flushed. 'I resent the implication that just because I did not do well with the two of you, all children should by default hate me.'

Adam looked ashamed of himself for a second. 'Sorry.'

'I did my best with you both,' Jeremy said, staring into his cold tea, unable to look his son in the eye. Emotional things embarrassed him. 'I did my best. I know I was probably hard but it was all I had to offer, my help with your homework and such. I wasn't a playful man.'

'Dad—'

Jeremy held up his hand. 'Just let me finish,' he said. Then when Adam remained silent he went on, 'I've thought a lot in the past few weeks. I need to say it.' He coughed and rubbed a hand over his beard. He tugged on it from time to time as he continued to speak. 'When your mother died a part of me died. I wanted to lock myself away and never talk to anyone again, but I had you two boys and I had to be strong. And I know,' Jeremy's voice wobbled a little, 'I know that if I'd broken down once, I'd never have got up again. So,' he coughed some more, 'I focused on you both. It stopped me from thinking about myself.' In the silence that followed, he slowly raised his eyes and looked at his son.

'We know that, Dad,' Adam said softly.

'You do?'

'Yeah,' Adam nodded, as if it was obvious. 'But you don't have us any more so you have to get a life for yourself.' He glanced around the kitchen. 'Still, you seem to have made friends here. I can never remember you having friends in the neighbourhood before.'

Jeremy gulped. Seeing as Adam seemed ready to forgive and forget, he wondered if he should confess . . .

'So is the dad really bad on the drugs or what?'

Jeremy shrugged. 'I think he was off them but his wife is afraid that he's using again.' Jeremy swallowed. This was his chance. He knew if he didn't tell someone soon, the whole thing was going to get way out of his control. 'The little boy Mark, he, eh, asked me to help his dad give them up.'

'You?' Adam gawked at him. 'Why? Did you do a counselling course or what?'

This was it. Jeremy braced himself, the way a motorist might before a car crash. 'He thinks I'm Santa.'

Adam laughed loudly. 'Kids are gas,' he said, grinning.

Jeremy didn't smile back. Instead he looked down at his hands before taking a deep breath and, his voice faltering slightly, he said as firmly as he could, 'No, Adam. He *really* thinks I'm Santa.' He stressed the 'really'.

'Yeah, but you told him you weren't, right?' Adam asked.

He waited for Jeremy to state that yes, of course he'd told him, but instead his dad looked away.

'Right, Dad?'

'Eh, it got sort of complicated,' Jeremy muttered.

'Complicated?' Adam looked in bewilderment at his dad. 'How can it be complicated? You just say, "No, I'm not Santa.".'

'Well, I didn't just say "no",' Jeremy winced. 'I eh, just said "yes".'

'Jesus Christ!' Adam sounded incredulous.

'Don't take the Lord's name,' Jeremy snapped.

'Well, don't go around pretending to kids that you're Santa! That could get you locked up, you know.' Adam stood up, running his hands through his hair. Finally he turned to Jeremy. 'You're gonna have to tell him. I mean why—'

'It was more a threat to keep him in order.' Jeremy realised how horrible that sounded, realised that it *was* horrible. 'I know,' he bit his lip as Adam looked on in disbelief, 'but I didn't think he'd really believe it. Then he starts writing me letters, telling me things. And it was nice, you know. No child has ever liked me before. We became sort of friends, I suppose. But now, now he wants me to sort out his life for him.'

'Well, congratulations, Da, you've really fucked up this time.' Adam started to clap mockingly.

'Stop!' Jeremy said. 'The boy likes me. I like him.'

'Well he won't like you for much longer,' Adam said. 'You've got to tell him.'

'I was actually hoping I'd die, then he'd think Santa was someone else.'

'Oh yeah, I can see him believing that all his life,' Adam nodded vigorously. 'He won't think for a minute that a nasty old man ever lied to him. Of course not.'

Jeremy sank his head into the palms of his hands in despair at Adam's tone. 'How do I tell him? I mean, I know I have to but—'

'No time like the present,' Adam said.

'No!' Jeremy was horrified at the prospect. 'I can't just go up and tell him now.'

'Why?'

'Well, he's worried about his dad for one thing.'

That was true. Adam nodded. 'I guess. But what if he asks you to cure his dad if his dad comes home?'

'I already told him I couldn't. I said his dad had to cure himself.'

'Did he ask you to turn water into wine yet?'

'Don't be facetious. Anyway, that's Our Lord, not Santa.'

'Dad, you have to go up and tell him. I cannot believe you've done this.'

'I was hoping you'd have some fun way I could break the news.'

'Eh, sorry, but there is no fun way to tell a kid that you're not Santa.'

'You're not Santa?' Mark's voice from the doorway shocked them both. His brown eyes searched Jeremy's face. 'You're not Santa?' he repeated. He'd heard Santa and Jolly Roger talking as he lay in bed trying to sleep. Their voices hadn't sounded too friendly, so rather than worry about what was happening he'd decided to go and see for himself. At least when he knew the situation he could think about it and try and understand. So he'd snuck down, quiet as a cat like his mammy always said, and caught the last sentence. 'You're not Santa?' It came out as a devastated whisper.

For the first time since his wife had died all those years ago, Jeremy felt as if his whole world was being sucked out from under his feet. 'No, Mark,' he gulped. 'I'm not.' He didn't attempt to move towards the boy. Behind him, Adam muttered a 'Shit.'

'But you said—' The words tore from Mark. 'You *said*. You told me you were.'

'I was wrong to do that.' Jeremy blinked back sudden tears. 'I was so wrong, Mark. I should never have done that.'

294

'No, no you shouldn't.' Mark began to back away. 'I wrote you letters. I liked that you lived beside me. I wrote you letters and you told me about your reindeers.'

'Mark—' Jeremy took a step towards him.

'You go away!' Mark sobbed. 'Go away!' He began to back towards the stairs.

'I kept it up because I wanted you to keep liking me, Mark. You're such a nice chap. I'm sorry.'

'My mammy lies, my daddy lies and now you!' Big tears leaked down Mark's face. 'You're not Santa. You can't help me. You can't help Daddy.'

'Hey Mark—' Adam tried to intervene.

'And you're probably not even a real pirate,' Mark said tearfully.

Adam winced.

'Is Robert being nice to you?' Jeremy asked suddenly. 'Is he treating you well?'

Mark sniffed in a hiccupping way and scrubbed his eyes with his fist. 'What?'

'I bet you Robert is being nice,' Jeremy said quietly. 'I bet you he won't be on the bold list at Christmas.'

There was a silence, broken only by Mark's heaving. 'He's being nice enough,' he sniffed.

'He's not teasing you any more, is he?'

Mark shook his head.

'See, I can help a little.'

'You made Robert be nice to me?' Mark's eyes narrowed suspiciously.

'Yes, in a way.'

'Dad, no lies,' Adam hissed into his ear.

'How?' Mark challenged.

'Well,' Jeremy was unsure how to answer that question, 'let's just say he doesn't want to be on a bold list and leave it at that.'

'You're still a big fat liar,' Mark said tearfully. 'And I don't

295

ever want to talk to you again. You'll be on the bold list, so you will!' He turned on his heel and pounded his way upstairs.

Jeremy made to go after him but Adam's hand on his shoulder arrested the movement. 'Leave him, Dad.'

'I'm going to have to tell his mother now, aren't I?'

''Fraid so.'

Both of them sat back down at the table and pondered what to do next.

Allie and Holly had grabbed a takeaway coffee in an all-night shop and were sitting in the car, thinking about where to go next, when Allie's mobile rang. She sloshed the hot liquid all over her jeans in an attempt to wrangle it from her pocket.

It was Ciaran. 'Hi, hello?' she said breathlessly.

'Is that Allie, Tony's wife?'

'Yes? Hi, Ciaran.' Her voice came out in a rush. 'Have you news of him? Where is he?'

'He's here.' Ciaran sounded curiously flat. 'He arrived about thirty minutes ago, said he couldn't go home. I'll let him stay the night and you can see him in the morning.'

Allie's mouth went dry. Her heart started to hammer. 'Has he –' She couldn't get the words out. 'Did he—'

'Yes,' Ciaran said. 'I'm sorry, Allie. We'll talk tomorrow.'

With a moan the phone fell to the floor of the car, and next thing she knew Holly's arms were about her.

38

JEREMY COULDN'T STAND the silence any more. Adam was twirling a spoon on his finger, weaving it in and out between his digits, and for a while Jeremy had watched, quite enamoured by the trick. Then Adam started tapping the spoon on the table and beating out a rhythm. That was annoying. Jeremy wished he'd talk instead. They'd spent the last hour going over and over what Jeremy should say to Allie, but nothing had sounded right. Jeremy knew he was going to be in for it, he was dreading it and the only way he could possibly keep his mind off it was to talk.

Mark's letters to him lay in the centre of the table, like an uncrossable fortress between them. At Adam's behest he had gone and fetched them from his house. He'd kept the later ones. Adam had read them and Jeremy was appalled to see his son swallow hard as he did so. 'The kid really believed it,' he said softly, with a lot of emotion.

'Yes, I know.' Jeremy was irritated. 'Don't make me feel worse.'

'You didn't let us believe in Santa when we were eight.' Adam sounded like a child now. 'I think I was five when you told me.'

'I thought the world was hard enough without believing in fairy tales,' Jeremy said gruffly.

'Well it's certainly hard when your dad makes it so,' Adam replied.

'Sorry.'

There had been silence since. Jeremy wished this awful night would end. 'What happens in *Jolly Roger*?' he blurted out suddenly.

'Huh?' Adam looked surprised.

'Your programme,' Jeremy said, 'I was wondering what happens next. I hate the way they always leave it on a cliffhanger. I like when things are solved within an episode.'

'You watch it?' Adam looked amused.

'Well, lately it's been the only way I can see you.'

Adam grinned. 'And do you like it?'

'You're, eh, very good in it.'

It was the first time his dad had ever praised him for his acting, Adam realised. 'Thanks,' he smiled, touched. 'I'm glad you like it, Dad.'

'It's funny and I suppose children would find it exciting.'

'They do.'

'So what happens?'

'Sorry, can't tell you that. No leaks allowed.'

'Oh.' Jeremy nodded. 'I suppose that's understandable. *Coronation Street* is the same.'

More silence.

They looked at each other.

'I think I believe that you are gay now,' Jeremy said haltingly, his face flushing deep red. 'I didn't before, you see, but I've been reading about it. I got a book from the library, which was embarrassing because I think the lady thought I wanted it for myself, which I did, in a way, but anyway, I read it and, you see, and well, I mean, I don't understand it. I really don't but,' he swallowed, 'I've only ever wanted you and Joel to be happy at the end of the day. So if you want to, you know, go about with,' he found the words difficult, like a large piece of food had got wedged in his mouth, 'well, with a man, I suppose you could say, well then all I can say is, you know, good luck and all of that.'

'Aw, Da.' Adam blinked furiously. 'Aw, Jesus, you don't know what that means, you don't.' He hopped up and hugged him.

Jeremy wasn't sure if he liked it. But having Adam back meant a hell of a lot.

Allie dropped Holly off at her apartment and *bip*ed a goodbye. Holly had offered to stay the night with her but Allie had insisted that she'd be all right. All she wanted was to crawl under the covers and sleep. She didn't want to think about Tony any more. Tomorrow she'd ditch work and go and see him first thing. See for herself what sort of a state he'd gotten into. She pulled her car into a lay-by just as she reached the outskirts of her estate, she wasn't quite ready to go home and face the boys – though she supposed they'd be asleep by now. Tomorrow was going to be a tough day; she'd have to talk to Tess and her own mother. But worse than that, she was going to have to talk to her sons. Their faces flashed before her and she let the tears fall unchecked as she started up the car again.

'You should go see Joel,' Adam advised.

'I said some terrible things to him,' Jeremy muttered. 'He's really angry at me. He hasn't rung in weeks.'

'Lucy is due soon; it might be nice to make your peace before then.'

Jeremy nodded. Right this minute, he wanted to make amends with everyone he'd hurt. He was going to start a new sort of life. He'd make it up to Mark, he would. Somehow.

Just then the front door opened and both men looked nervously at each other.

'Hi,' Allie called softly from the hall. 'Are they asleep?'

'Yes,' Jeremy nodded as she came in, 'I, eh, got Adam over to put them to bed, he's good with children.'

'Hello.' Allie smiled a bit distractedly, her hands shielding her face, hoping they wouldn't spot her red eyes. 'Thank you both. I appreciate it.'

'Is Tony not with you?' Jeremy felt he had to ask. It would appear rude not to.

'No, he's, eh, at a friend's house.' Allie's gaze swivelled to a pile of yellow paper lying on the table top. 'What are these?' She picked one up and grinned, her mood lightening momentarily. 'Was Mark showing you his Santa letters? I was wondering where he put them.'

'Eh, in a way, yes.' Jeremy swallowed.

Allie's eyes scanned the letter, a slight frown appearing between her brows. 'What the—' She turned the page and read the next one. And the next. Then she reread them. What with Tony being back on drugs, she wasn't sure she was reading them correctly. Her mind was skittering about like water drops on a hotplate. *He keeps calling me Fatso . . . Make Daddy love himself . . . Make him fully bettr so dat him and my mammy wud stop fiteing . . .* Her eyes jumped from phrase to phrase. 'Oh God,' she whispered, looking at Jeremy anxiously, 'it says here he's being picked on. I never knew it was that bad. I didn't know he was being picked on like that.' She flipped through the small pile. 'It's odd he wrote them so early.' She looked questioningly at Jeremy. 'Was he going to post them? Is that why he showed you?'

'He, eh, did post them.' Jeremy shot a look at Adam, who nodded encouragingly. Jeremy was sure this was not the right time. The woman looked on the verge of hysteria. But Mark would tell her anyway. 'He, eh, posted them to me.' He attempted a smile, but it didn't quite come off.

'To you?' Allie was confused. Why would Mark post his letters to a neighbour? She sat down on a chair and swallowed hard. 'To you?' she repeated.

'Yes,' Jeremy said, his voice a little louder. 'He thought, well, no, that's not strictly true . . .' His voice trailed off.

'Thought what?' Allie asked.

Jeremy gathered his courage. 'I, eh, told him I was Santa Claus,' he announced.

Allie blinked. Was she in some surreal parallel universe? 'Sorry?'

'I told your son that I was Santa Claus. I told him I had a sled and reindeer and a toy shop.'

Allie did a double take. She lifted her gaze from the letter, opened her mouth to say something and then closed it. Then opened it again but nothing came out. The puzzled frown remained between her brows.

'You heard him,' Adam said apologetically. 'My father told your son that he was Santa Claus and your son started to write to him. Dad is sorry, aren't you, Dad?'

'I am.' Jeremy wished he could evaporate. He wished he was like Santa right now. 'It sort of became complicated . . .' he finished weakly.

Allie's mind reeled. First Tony, then these letters and now . . . this. 'Sorry?' She attempted to understand – it was late, she was tired, but she thought that she'd heard . . . 'Are you telling me that my son believes that—'

'Not any more,' Jeremy said. 'He knows I'm not now.'

'He was upset about it,' Adam said softly. 'As anyone would be. My dad is very sorry.'

'You told Mark that you were Santa?' Allie gulped out. 'You told him—'

'Yes. I'm sorry. I don't know why I did it. It was a spur of the moment thing, I wanted to keep him out of my garden and next thing he's writing me letters and I like him calling into me and I find then that I can't get out of it.'

'You could have got out of it. You could have told him!' Allie said incredulously, anger seeping into her voice. 'How, how *dare* you! How dare you do that to my son!' As she said it, she realised how hypocritical she sounded. She'd lied to him, too. But that was different. Or was it? She shook her head to clear it. She was angry, at Jeremy or Tony, it didn't matter. 'Get out, go on. Get out of my house.'

Jeremy nodded. 'Of course. I'm sorry. But Robert isn't bothering him any more, just in case you're worried—'

'GET OUT!'

*   *   *

301

'Well, that didn't go too well,' Adam murmured as Jeremy let himself into his house. 'But you did the right thing, Dad. It's over now.'

If it was the right thing, Jeremy wondered why he felt so empty inside.

'Can you stay the night, Adam? In your old bedroom?' He made no attempt to stop the pleading tone in his voice. 'Please?'

Adam smiled a little and patted his dad's arm. 'Of course I can. You're my dad. Aren't you?'

And it made things a little better.

Allie held Mark's letters in her hands and cried. All she'd ever wanted for her kids was the kind of security she never had. And instead she'd blown it. She'd married a drug addict who had, just like her father, promised her the moon and stars but had never given her the sun. And without the sun, there was no moon to see. If she'd any doubts about what to do, she had none left now.

Mark listened to his mother cry and crept out of his room and into hers. He climbed into bed beside her and wrapped his arms about her tummy.

'Hey.' She brushed her tears away, turned over and kissed the top of his head.

'Daddy is a junkie again, isn't he?' he whispered.

'Yes, honey.' Allie kissed his forehead.

'You gave out to Mr Lyons, didn't you?'

'Yes.' Allie held him tighter. 'I cannot believe that a man would go about pretending to be Santa—'

'I don't want to talk about it,' Mark said.

'OK,' Allie said gently. 'Whatever you want.'

She lay awake until he fell asleep. It was the longest night of her life.

39

ALLIE GOT MARK to school and Owen to creche the next morning. Disturbingly Owen hadn't mentioned Tony at all, but Mark had asked her what was going to happen to Daddy now and she'd been forced to tell him that Daddy might not be coming home. He'd asked why and she had told him honestly that she thought it would be for the best. Then she'd posed some delicate questions of her own, trying to ascertain if Mr Lyons had in any way interfered with Mark. Not that she believed the man would have, but you never knew. Mark had been reluctant to talk about it, but the only complaint he seemed to have about the man was that he'd never had orange juice in his house, only milk and water. It made Allie smile.

Ciaran, Tony's sponsor, had told her where he lived and Allie followed his directions until she found the house. It was a small terraced house in a street not far from the city centre. No wonder Tony had gone there, she thought, as she pulled up outside. She wondered if nine o'clock was a little early to be calling on someone and then decided that she didn't care. The sooner she said her piece the better. She hopped out of the car and marched as determinedly as she could up the small driveway to the front door. She pushed all her emotions to the back of her mind and instead focused on what she was going to say and how she was going to say it, and what she was going to do afterwards. The door opened just as she was about to ring the bell. Tony stood in front of her, his dark hair dishevelled and his face chalk-white. Part of her melted at his look of remorse, but she quashed it. Her presence in his life was not doing either of them any good.

'Hi,' he said. He attempted a smile.

'You are not to come home.' Allie stared right at him as she said it. She tried to keep her voice firm and hard. 'You walked out last night, you didn't give a shit for me or the kids and you got wasted. I'm not putting up with it any more.'

His eyes registered the shock. 'It was just a slip.'

'You still left. I still went looking for you. Remember you said you never wanted me to do that again? Well I did, and you never gave it a thought.'

'You let me make a fool of myself. You could have told me what you did, Al. No more lies, remember?'

His shortened use of her name made her eyes water a little but she took a breath and said as steadily as she could, 'Do not put the blame for this on me. A man came to our house demanding fifty grand, which *you* owed him. Do you not agree it was the sensible thing to take away your income, before you got us into more debt? The minute he left the door that day, I rang your job before I even went near the bank. And I don't regret it. Not for a second. And, until you are cured, I don't want you having money.'

'I will never be fucking cured, I'm an addict!' His loud voice made her flinch. He seemed just as startled at what he'd said as she was. It was a second before he spoke again. 'You agreed, no more lies. You should have told me.'

'Yes, maybe I should have and I'm sorry about that, but people *argue*, Tony. They argue and they sort it out. They don't go and buy drugs and not come home.'

Tony was silent for a second before admitting softly, 'It wasn't just the row with you, though I hate falling out with you. It all just got on top of me.' He shoved his hands into the pockets of his tattered jeans and dipped his head, his gaze resting on his grey socks. 'Veronica, me ma, John, you. The way Owen is with me.' He looked hopelessly at her. 'I needed to feel good again.'

304

'So fucking work at it!' It came out sounding harsher than she'd thought and she knew she'd startled him with the bad language. She so rarely lost it. 'Work at it like a man. The outside is no good unless you work on the inside. Are you a fucking moron that you still don't know that?'

She was vaguely aware that a neighbour had come out of the house next door and was staring curiously in their direction. What was it about her and Tony that they had to argue in public?

'Do you know Mark wrote a letter to Santa? Well, Mr Lyons actually, and one thing he wanted,' she tried not to cry, 'one thing he wanted was for you to be happy. That's what he wanted for Christmas.'

Tony blinked. 'Mr Lyons?'

'Yeah,' Allie nodded, sniffing back her tears. 'You and me were so wrapped up in your bloody problems that we failed to notice that our eight-year-old son thought the old man was Santa.'

'What?'

'And that he was being bullied and being called Fatso and that he was sick with worry over you. That is not going to happen any more. I am going to take care of my kids and you can take care of yourself!'

Tony's mind reeled. He could barely take in what she was saying. 'I only took a small line,' he eventually said.

'So?'

'I stopped. I stopped myself. It was just a slip, Al.'

'So?'

'So, please give me a chance. Please.'

'I gave you chances,' she said. 'We have two boys, Tony, who need me more than you do. I'm not having it. Do you hear me? I. Am. Not. Having. It.'

'I love you, Allie, I swear I do. I love the kids. Don't do this to me, please.'

She couldn't bear it. He looked so hurt, so devastated, but

she knew that look. She'd seen it before. 'And I love you,' she said, her calm wobbling, 'but Tony, you're wrecking our lives. And I am sorry about yesterday, I really am, I should have told you but I was terrified of you going out into the world again. Out of my control. I wanted you to stay at home and I know that was wrong, but this,' she indicated his scruffy state, 'this is not how normal people deal with stuff like that.'

He blinked and his shoulders slumped. 'I know,' he agreed fervently, 'I fucking know. And if I could turn back time, I swear I would. I'd do it all different.'

'You can't turn back time, Tony.'

Then she turned away and walked back to her car.

He didn't run after her and she didn't look back.

Ciaran listened to him, told him that what Allie said was right; he couldn't turn back time, but he could make the most of the time ahead. It was his only hope. Ciaran stressed the 'only'. 'And also,' he added, 'your wife is not depriving you of anything. You did it to yourself. You knew the rules.'

'It was only a slip,' Tony said.

'When people fall down the stairs and get brain damage, it's just a slip too,' Ciaran said.

'That's different,' Tony said sulkily.

'Nope, it's not.' Ciaran had handed him a bag of crisps. 'Your drug of choice for now.' He grinned slightly then added, 'Tony, we all make mistakes, we all fuck up. That's how we learn, yeah?' Then he'd generously offered Tony a place to stay on condition he remain clean, before leaving for work.

Tony had showered, dressed, and finally he'd plucked up the courage to go outside. It was like the first time he'd ventured out alone without drugs, big, scary and noisy. Only now, he didn't even have Allie beside him. The knowledge hit him suddenly, so much so that he gasped. The longing for something to obliterate the pain came over him in such a wave that his knees buckled and he had to sit on a wall for support. One line. That's all he wanted.

'Hey, mister, are you all right?' A teenager was peering curiously at him. 'Only if you need an ambulance, I can call you one up.' He held out what was obviously a brand new mobile phone. 'I have a speed dial for the hospital,' he said proudly.

Tony shook his head. 'No, thanks, I'm grand.' He sounded normal. Maybe that's how it was, he thought. Normal on the outside and a total screw-up on the inside.

The young boy looked a little disappointed. 'OK. If you're sure.'

'I'm sure. Thanks.'

He watched as the boy slouched off. He wondered why on earth a teenager would have a speed dial for a hospital on his phone. He'd never find out now. Slowly he stood up. He was on his own now. The knowledge hurt but damn it, he was going to have to survive. He thought of Veronica and knew that he didn't want it to be him. He thought of his boys and knew that he did want to be a proper dad, the way his own foster dad had been. His foster parents had been what he had hoped to be for Mark and Owen. He'd been doing well too, but that was shot to hell now. He'd taught Mark so much, the kid was a neat little soccer player, could do keepie uppies like a pro. And then, like a flash on his mind's eye, he saw Mark doing his keepie uppies, messing up, running after the ball and starting over. Over and over again until he grew better and better. He saw himself telling Mark that it all was down to practice. Doing it right was different for everyone, he'd told Mark, some footballers just needed more practice than others.

Tony guessed he'd just have to take his own advice.

Starting from that minute.

40

TESS OPENED THE door and didn't know whether to be relieved or angry when she saw that her visitor was her eldest son. Since Allie rang a week ago telling her what had happened, Tess had been worried sick – but had followed Allie's advice and not gone running after him.

'Hello.' She decided on a slight touch of anger. 'This is a surprise.'

Tony met her gaze. 'Were you talking to Allie?'

'Yes.' Tess turned on her heel and marched ahead of him into the kitchen. 'And before you ask, you cannot stay here. I'm not going to be your crutch.'

'I wasn't going to ask,' Tony said bleakly, following her. 'I know that isn't good for either of us.'

'Well. Well good.' Tess knew that she didn't sound convincing but damn it, he was her son. And, she thought as she observed him, he looked wretched – all she wanted to do was hug him, but she wasn't sure if he'd allow it. Or if she should. Tough love, that's what she and Allie had agreed on. 'So what is it you want?'

Tony hesitated before saying, 'Two things, neither of which I probably have a right to.'

Well, he didn't sound as if he was high, which was positive. 'Go on.' Her voice softened.

Tony sat down at the kitchen table and Tess's heart twisted as she saw him shove his shaking hands into the pockets of his jacket. He looked like a scared little boy. It was the way he'd been on his first day of school and she remembered how she'd left him in the yard and come home and cried her eyes out.

'The first thing is,' Tony's voice intruded on her reverie, 'is that, well, that I'm sorry.' He paused. Tess was appalled to see his eyes water. 'I'm really sorry.' He looked upwards. Blinked rapidly. 'I've been such a, such a –' He brought his gaze back down to meet hers before flicking it away again, not wanting her to see his tears. 'I'm sorry.' He paused. 'Mam,' he added brokenly.

'Oh.' Tess's resolve to do the tough love bit dissolved as her own eyes welled up at the sadness in his. There was a moment as she tried to compose herself before she said 'Oh' again. She took a step towards him. And then another. 'Ohh,' she flapped her hand, 'come here, pet!' In two more strides she was beside him and she enfolded him in a huge hug, pressing him as hard to her body as she could. To her gratification, there was no resistance. She caressed his head, loving the feel of his hair under her fingers. 'What you had a right to was a mother and a father who would have kept you,' she hugged him harder, kissed his hair, 'but we don't all get what we have a right to.'

Tony wrapped an arm around his mother's waist and buried his head in the fabric of her blouse. 'I just felt so left out,' he gulped. 'I wanted to punish you for not being mine. I—'

'Now, now.' Tess kissed the top of his head again, something she hadn't done since he was five years old. 'It's all right.'

Tony pulled away slightly. His voice shook but he was holding it together, he'd promised himself he would. 'I know that you and Dad were better parents to me that I've ever been to Mark and Owen. Sometimes the real thing isn't so great, you know.'

'You *are* great.' Tess pressed his face between the palms of

309

her hands. 'Those boys are lucky to have you.' She smiled at him through watery eyes and went on with feeling, 'You are great when you are clean, Tony. Mark adores you. And you,' she shook her head, her voice dipping as she added passionately, 'you were so loved, Tony.'

'I know.' He tried to turn away in case she saw how unbearably moved he was. That was the thing about being clean, you felt everything so much harder, good and bad stuff. For years he hadn't felt anything. The emotion he felt now was so strong it scared him. Tess wouldn't let him turn away though, she held his face firm and stared at him, trying to convey with her eyes just how valued he was.

Tenderly, though with passion, she said, 'It's OK to cry, you know. It's OK to be angry at the parents who left you. It's OK to wish that they were here. It's OK to *feel*, Tony.'

And for a moment, as he looked at her, he felt nothing. All the emotion he'd experienced earlier vanished. And then, from somewhere in the centre of his chest, he felt a loosening. It made him feel a little sick. And he realised that feeling nothing seconds earlier was the calm in the centre of the storm. He swallowed hard, determined to get rid of the sick feeling invading him, rubbing his hands over his face furiously, but it was as fruitless as trying to stop a swollen river from bursting its banks. He tried to turn away, to twist his head, but once the tears came he realised that he couldn't stop them. He felt as if he was being torn inside out. And they kept on coming and with them the feelings he had spent his life trying to avoid. The rejection, the hurt, the insecurity, the terrible feeling of never being quite good enough. Of marrying Allie and of wanting to be her hero, knowing she wanted it, and at the same time knowing that he could never be that, knowing that he was flawed. With his mother stroking the top of his head and his arm still about her waist, he cried for the child he'd once been. The scared kid who had spent his life just trying to fit in and who found out that

310

the problem with trying to fit into everyone else's life was that he'd never learned to fit into his own. It seemed that everything he'd ever felt, every slight, every hurt, every emotional scar he'd ever carried came tumbling out before finally easing up, slowing down and trickling to stop. There was nothing else left to cry for. And in the quietness that followed, he realised in a slow amazement that for the first time in for ever he felt . . . he tried to think what he felt, sought for the word. He felt . . . calm. Still. Whatever it was, whatever emptiness had been inside him had gone. Or had been tamed. At least for now. It was as if for the first time, his head was clear. Like all his life a storm had been raging inside him and now it was gone.

He let the silence descend, then he pulled slowly away from Tess and in a half-embarrassed way he scrubbed his face. 'Shit,' he gulped.

Tess released him. She bent down to peer into his face. 'You OK now?'

'Eh, yeah. Yeah. Sorry about that.'

'Don't be.' She ruffled his hair. Squeezed his shoulder. 'Don't be.'

Tony couldn't look at her. Instead, he studied his hands.

There was more silence. Tess broke it. 'So, the second thing?'

'Sorry?'

His head jerked up to look at her and, seeing his bewildered eyes, Tess wanted to embrace him all over again. But she knew he'd hate it now. What they had shared would never be repeated, but that was good. Instead she made her voice gentle. 'You said you came for two things?'

'Oh, yeah.' Tony took some more time to compose himself. To get his head back together. He gulped, hesitating, hoping that she wouldn't believe he'd apologised just so he could ask for this. 'You can say no,' he said slowly, 'but I need money.'

Tess flinched.

311

'For my rent,' Tony clarified hastily. 'I'm staying with Ciaran, my sponsor, and I'd like to give him a few bob towards my keep, but I'm not interested in cash for nothing.' He paused. 'And I know I have no right to ask but I was hoping that maybe John might, you know, let me work alongside him for a bit, that way I could earn it.' He winced a little. 'I'm not finding it easy to get a job as an accountant, not right now.' A rueful smile. 'Would you trust *me* with your money?'

'As it happens,' John strode into the kitchen, a grin on his face, 'I'm looking for a partner in my ever-expanding gardening business.' He stopped and, looking at Tony, said steadily, 'Only family need apply.'

'Were you listening outside?' Tess asked crossly.

'Yeah.' John didn't take his eyes from Tony. 'So what do you say?'

Tony swallowed, touched. Jesus, he hoped he wouldn't blubber again. As it was he didn't want John to see his red eyes. 'I'd be honoured.'

'The money could be shite.'

'I'd still be honoured.' Tony forced himself to look at John. It was the least he could do.

'Honoured, my arse.' John rolled his eyes.

They regarded each other. Tony tried to form the words to say how sorry he was, how grateful he was, but nothing came out. John broke the silence by saying softly, 'You know I think your boys are bleeding brilliant, don't you?'

'John,' Tess tutted. 'I hate that word.'

He ignored her. 'They're two great guys,' he said.

'I know.' Tony bit his lip.

'I was only trying to help.'

'I know. I always knew that.' Tony stared hopelessly at John. 'And I also know that while I was making them miserable, you've kept them sane. I should have got down on my knees and thanked you instead of shouting and stuff.'

'There's still time,' John grinned. 'Loads of space on the floor.'

'He's not doing any such thing!' Tess snapped. 'He's been very upset, haven't you, Tony?'

'I'm fine. I—'

She overrode his embarrassment. 'Now, Tony love, would you like a cup of tea? I've got nice chocolate biscuits in.'

'I could do with a packet of Cheese and Onion instead,' Tony said.

John rummaged about in the press and tossed Tony some crisps. Then he plonked down beside his brother and stretched his legs out under the table. 'I vote, as the boss, that this company takes a day off today.'

Tess hit John with a tea towel and called him a lazy gobshite.

'Ma, wouldn't it be worse if I couldn't work?'

'I have to say, I wouldn't notice much difference,' Tess grumbled.

Tony laughed. It occurred to him suddenly that while things were the same on the outside, while his mother and John had always gone on like this, inside him something had changed. Which made the outside look a whole lot different.

Allie put down the phone. Tess had rung to say that Tony had called and that he had cried a lot but that it seemed to do him good. Allie had worried when she'd heard that. Tony crying? She wanted to pick up his mobile and call him and make sure he was all right, but she didn't. He had to stand on his own now. Only then could he ever be what they needed. Still, she missed him badly. She hadn't heard from him since that awful morning. She had texted him to pick up his stuff when she was in work and he had come and collected some bits and pieces. He'd left her a note with a landline number for him. Allie gathered that he must be staying in Ciaran's house. At least that was good; he wasn't bunking down with his old friends which she had been afraid of. He'd also asked if he could have the boys one Saturday. She had texted him a 'Yes'. But, she had specified, only for a couple of hours, and not until he was clean for at least three weeks.

He hadn't objected.

It was the first time out in days for Jeremy. He was surprised that he'd missed his walk so much, he normally preferred looking at the television, but he supposed that was because he'd always taken the fact that he could leave his house and go outside for granted. Now, however, he felt compelled to scout the road for any sign of Allie or Mark before venturing out. Or Tony, though he didn't think Tony lived with them any more, which was good if he was still a junkie but not so good if he wasn't. Jeremy didn't think he'd ever find out.

He took a deep breath, inhaling the crisp autumn air and then sighed. It'd be a lovely afternoon to be out if what he was about to do didn't go against every little bit of conscience he had. But then again he'd told a child he was Santa, so really his conscience shouldn't bother him too much, should it? He had taken the trouble to highlight the health warning on the boxes to salvage his principles but that was all he could do, a promise was a promise and seeing as they had carried out their end of the bargain, he could hardly shirk his, now could he?

He eventually arrived at their usual meeting place.

'Hey, it's grandpa!' the tallest lad shouted. 'How you doing?'

There were the usual six, sitting on a patch of grass and swilling cider from a can.

'I'm very well,' Jeremy answered. He pulled out the cigarettes from his shopping bag and handed them out. 'Though I'm afraid after smoking all these you lot won't be.'

'Let us worry about that,' the tall guy said as he tore open the packet and pulled out a cigarette, which he then lit with a fancy-looking lighter. After he'd taken the first drag, he fixed Jeremy with a stare and asked, 'So, Robert is behaving himself, yeah?'

'Apparently so,' Jeremy nodded. 'I don't know what you said to him.'

'Oh, we told told him we'd cut—'

Jeremy held up his hands. 'Please, don't. I feel bad enough about this whole thing already. But, thank you, boys. And girl.' He bowed to the one female.

'Aw, you're lovely,' she said. Turning to her friends she went on, in the manner of one talking about a cute puppy, 'Isn't he lovely? Dere's no manners like that about now. You speak real English and everything.'

'Anytime you need a hand with Robert, let us know.' The tall guy had obviously become the mouthpiece of the gathering. 'The next time we'll do it for free.'

This statement was met with cheers and promises of solidarity.

Well, they had some good in them then, Jeremy thought. 'Thank you,' he said, 'and if you lot would like to avail of some extra tuition in the more mathematical of the school subjects, then I will do it for free also.'

'Fuck off!' they said, almost in unison.

Jeremy walked away with a much dignity as he could muster.

41

MAGDA AND FINTAN arrived five minutes after Tony had left with the boys.

'Owen in bed?' Magda asked.

'No,' Allie smiled a little, 'Owen is gone with Tony this week.'

'Wow,' Magda shed her coat, hanging it at the end of the stairs, 'that's a turn up for the books.'

On the first week Tony had called, Owen had screamed at the thought of going anywhere with his daddy.

'Tony told him that John was going too.' Allie followed her visitors into the kitchen. Her heart pinged a little as she recalled Tony hunkering down to Owen's level and saying in a voice that melted her heart, 'Hey, John is in the car outside, he'd like you to come.'

Owen had looked past his dad and, upon spotting John's car, raced down the driveway. Allie had felt sorry for Tony then. 'You'll win him over,' she said softly as she handed him Owen's coat.

'Yeah.' He'd given her a glum smile.

'And you're talking to John now, are you?' she'd asked, pretending that Tess hadn't filled her in.

He had nodded and looked at her from under dark lashes. 'I was an asshole.'

'You were hurt.' She couldn't help it; Tony seemed to bring out the mother in her.

He had offered her a small grin. 'I was a hurt asshole.'

They'd laughed a little and then he'd said, 'I'm sorry about it all, Al. I really did try.' Without waiting for her response, he had turned on his heel and gone to join the others in the car.

'Bribery.'

'Sorry?' Allie hadn't been listening.

'I said, it was bribery.' Magda pulled a book from her bag. 'Here, read this, I'll help you.'

Allie took the book. *Breaking the Addiction to the Wrong Men*, she read. Then she giggled girlishly, 'Mum, where did you get that?'

'She's reading self-help books,' Fintan answered in her stead. 'She thinks it'll help her keep to her ideal weight if she understands how her own brain is programmed. Personally I think a brisk walk followed by a visit to the gym is better.'

'Apparently I was addicted to your father,' Magda ignored Fintan's barb, 'I wanted to prove I could tame him. You're the same with Tony. You probably, subconsciously, think that by holding on to him you're making up for the father who abandoned you.'

'Eh, Tony isn't actually living here any more,' Allie pointed out.

'Yes, well, he was here for ten years. You probably married him because you saw your father in him.'

'I did not!' Allie snorted. 'Despite his faults, Tony was mad about me. I knew he'd never go off with anyone else.'

'He still had a mistress,' Magda said with authority. 'Drugs.'

And in a way it was true, Allie realised: Tony addicted was Tony dependent. He'd never stray on her, not while he needed her so much. On the other hand, she was in constant competition with his addiction. She pursed her lips, stung by her own insight. 'He's a good man,' she defended him, knowing she believed it.

'And he still adores you,' Fintan nodded soothingly, shooting warning glances at Magda. 'Anyone can see that.'

'Well, wouldn't you adore someone who put up with your every bad behaviour?' Magda asked archly.

'I adore you,' Fintan answered dryly. 'And you, my gorgeous, refuse to put up with anything.'

'I've been damaged,' Magda gave a nod in the direction of the book, 'so I have to relearn all my behaviour.'

'Aw,' Fintan made a face, 'poor damaged woman. Let me make it all better for you. Here, I'll hit you over the head with this tome of a book and maybe you'll see sense.'

Magda laughed. 'Now, isn't that nice, Allie?'

'It'd be nicer if *I* could hit you over the head with it instead,' Allie smiled.

Magda smirked. 'Fintan, pour me a glass of water, would you, I'm gasping.' As Fintan made a move to do so, she said, 'And may I ask, has that horrendous excuse for a human being I previously married been sniffing around since?'

'I met him a couple of weeks ago.'

'Has he met the boys yet?'

Allie steeled herself. 'No. What with all the hassle over Tony, I put it off for a bit. In another couple of weeks' time, I think I'll meet him.'

Magda looked a little pained but didn't say anything.

'He's really looking forward to it,' Allie went on, encouraged by her silence.

'And is he still poncing about pretending to be French?'

'Yes.' She didn't add that Thomas had told her he was seeing a woman who believed he was French. Allie thought it was a bit much and she knew her mother would have plenty to say about it. There was no point.

Jeremy stopped mid-step, like a cartoon character. It was too late to scurry back inside, too late to disappear from sight. He was caught, good and proper. All he'd wanted to do was to go out and visit his eldest son, something he'd been trying to pluck up the courage to do for weeks now. Oh, he'd taken the bus to the top of Joel's road, but he'd always turned back. He wasn't sure he could face both Joel and his haughty wife on their own turf. But as Adam had said to him on the phone just an hour ago, he had to seize the day. Go for it. What did he want? Adam had asked. Jeremy had replied that he wanted to talk to Joel. So do it, Adam had said. And he was all fired up, and now, just as he'd taken two steps out his front door, he had to bump into his neighbour and her mother and that big tall man that was her husband. It was after four and they were obviously leaving Allie's house.

'Oh, there he is,' the mother called loudly, leaving Jeremy in no doubt that she was referring to him, 'the Easter Bunny!'

'Mammy!' he heard Allie caution.

'Sorry, got it wrong. The Tooth Fairy, isn't it?'

The man with the mother started to laugh and tried to cover it up by making coughing sounds.

Jeremy decided that the only course of action was to acknowledge the comments. He straightened himself up and turned around. The three of them were looking curiously at him, though it would be fair to say that Allie's mother was glaring balefully.

'It was Santa actually,' he corrected her. 'And as I've already told your daughter, I am extremely sorry and embarrassed over the whole incident.'

'I should hope so,' Magda sniffed. 'Telling an innocent little child a lie like that.'

'Mammy, leave it.' Allie put a hand on her mother's arm.

Jeremy swallowed. If he wanted to redeem himself, he should do it now. Allie hadn't talked to him since. And whenever Tony called to collect the kids, he glared in the direction of his house, which made Jeremy feel quite intimidated. Plus Allie was keeping the kids away from him, which he could understand, but now she was here in front of him and he could say what he'd wanted to say for the last month, even though Adam had told him he was nuts to want to say it – but then Adam

319

had also told him to seize the day. 'Well, actually,' he began, trying to sound confident, 'if I may say so, Allie . . .' He suddenly found he had to cough, then swallow hard. 'If I may say so,' he began again. Then he stopped and sighed heavily. It was no use. He'd sound mental. So he just nodded and muttered contritely, 'I'm just very sorry.'

Nodding to the three of them, he walked away, his head bent.

'Well!' Magda snorted, 'What a strange man. You should get a mental health professional out to him, Allie.'

Allie shrugged. 'He's a bit odd, all right,' she conceded, 'and I was so mad at him at first, but you know, I learnt a lot from those notes Mark wrote to him.' She gulped as she remembered all her son's hopes and fears exposed on those yellow pages. 'And, well, they helped me see what I had to do to make him happy. It made it easier for me to let Tony go, so in a way it was a good thing.'

'I don't know.' Magda rolled her eyes. 'What next? Do you want Fintan to lie to him and say he was the first man in space?'

'That's not a lie,' Fintan wrapped his arms around Magda, 'sure, I haven't come back down to earth since I met you.'

Madga laughed loudly. 'You charmer. That's a fatal flaw for women like me.'

'Sounds promising.'

'Oh God,' Allie pushed them away, 'too much information. Go home.'

Magda linked her arm through Fintan's. 'Come on, Fintan, let's go. Let's leave Allie to her wonderful sons and faithful husband.'

'And her bonkers neighbour,' Fintan added.

'Precisely.'

Well, they thought he was bonkers, Jeremy knew, after that display. But if any fessing up had to be done today, it was far better that he do it to his youngest son and his wife. And probably Jenny and Len, too, as their parents seemed to treat them like mini adults – something which was quite irritating in Jeremy's view, but then he supposed every parent did what they thought was best for their children.

As he had done. In his own way.

42

WHILST OWEN WAS playing with John, Mark sat with Tony on the grass. He liked to sit with his dad when his dad was in a happy mood. And he wanted to sit with him now because he wasn't around at night-time any more.

'You OK?' his daddy shot him a look out of the corner of his eye.

'Yeah.' Mark settled himself more comfortably on the grass, inching nearer.

Tony, sensing it, reached out and slung an arm about Mark's shoulders. They sat in silence for a bit before Tony asked carefully, 'Have you seen that old guy who lives next door since?'

Mark flinched. 'No.'

'He was a bit mean, huh, telling you he was Santa?'

Mark shifted uncomfortably. He didn't like talking about it. His mammy wanted him to talk about it, but he couldn't. He guessed it was his daddy's turn now.

'It's OK if you don't want to talk about it.' His daddy wasn't looking at him now. 'I mean, I reckon if I'd been your age, I would have thought he was Santa too. He sure looks likes Santa.'

'He acted like Santa too,' Mark said before he could stop himself.

'Yeah?'

'He told me all about the reindeers and Mrs Claus and he promised to pick you up in his sleigh if you got stuck in America and couldn't make it home for Christmas Eve.'

'He did?' Tony wanted to throttle the man but at the same time he wanted to laugh.

'Yeah. Only he couldn't have, could he?' Mark pulled up some grass. 'But I guess everyone lies to kids.'

'Everyone?' Tony was taken aback.

'Parents and stuff.'

'Mark, people lie to kids because they want to protect them. Your mammy and I thought you'd be frightened if you knew about me. We're sorry about it.'

'So why did Mr Lyons lie?' Mark asked, sounding tearful.

Tony shrugged, tried to choose his words carefully, 'Well, I don't know about him. I'm more interested in why you believed him.'

Mark looked puzzled. 'He looked like Santa. He had a beard and he was fat and—'

'I bet you he made you feel safe too, didn't he?'

Mark said nothing.

'You were probably a little scared moving house and scared of me a little.' It hurt Tony to say that but it had to be done. 'And having Santa living beside you could only be a good thing? Yeah?'

Mark gulped and didn't look up.

'It's easy to believe stuff when we need it to be true,' Tony went on. When Mark still made no reply, he said quietly, 'I have been a terrible dad, Mark. I'm sorry.'

Mark felt a little tear drip down his face but he brushed it away quickly. His dad ruffled his hair.

'I want you to know,' his daddy said then, 'and I'm not a hundred per cent sure just yet, but I think I've found my magic.'

Mark forgot that he didn't want his dad to see his tears and looked up. 'You have?' Then doubt clouded his features. 'But finding the magic isn't true. It's just something Mr Lyons said when I told him about you. There's no such thing.'

'There is,' Tony nodded. 'He didn't make it up.'

'He didn't?'

'He mightn't be Santa, Mark, but that doesn't stop him from being right. The magic is in here. You just have to want to look for it. I found mine, I think.'

Mark was amazed. His dad had found his magic and Robert was being nice. He wondered how that was possible. Did Mr Lyons know stuff after all?

'Sometimes,' his dad went on, 'you don't need Santa beside you to be safe. All you need is someone who cares.'

'Did Mr Lyons care about me?'

'Even though he did a very stupid thing, I think he did. Very much. Just like me and Mammy.'

'I wrote him lots of letters,' Mark whispered. 'I told him everything.'

'I know.' Tony squeezed his son. 'But you can tell me and Mammy, you know. No matter how hard it is, you can tell us.' He paused. 'I have let you down. All I can say is, I will try never to do it again. I can't promise, but I am going to hold on to the magic as hard as I can.'

Mark felt the inside of his chest sort of swell. He felt all warm and cosy and . . . he tried to pinpoint the feeling. Safe. He felt safe with his daddy. 'Good,' he said. 'I love you, Daddy.'

Tony couldn't answer.

Jeremy dabbed at his forehead with a handkerchief as he stood outside the enormous white door of Joel's large house. Joel's car was there, as it was Saturday. Jeremy took a deep breath and, his finger damp with sweat and shaking badly, hit the bell. His finger slipped so that the bell made a *blip* sound.

He rang a second time. This time properly.

He stood up as straight as he could, taking deep breaths. He'd read somewhere that deep breathing slowed the heart-rate, but quite frankly it left him feeling slightly light-headed so he stopped.

The door was opened by Jenny, who made no attempt to

disguise her surprise. 'Wow, Granddad,' she said loudly, 'what are you doing here? You never come here.'

'Who is it?' Lucy called, and then stopped as she caught sight of her father-in-law. 'Well,' she sounded flustered, 'this is a surprise. Hello, Jeremy, won't you come in?'

There was a friendliness in her voice that he'd never heard before. 'OK, thank you.' Jeremy stood awkwardly in the hall, a massive, bright space that was about the width of his front room at home. Joel had done well for himself, Jeremy thought, feeling a momentary surge of pride. He became aware that a silence had developed and what was more, his daughter-in-law and granddaughter were looking at him as if they expected him to say something.

'I've actually come to talk to Joel,' Jeremy said. 'Is he in?'

'He's out on a walk with Len but he'll be back soon,' Lucy said. 'Would you like a cup of tea while you're waiting?'

He could go, he realised. She would be sure to tell Joel that he called and then the ball would be in his son's court, but he knew that would be unfair. And besides, he owed the whole family an apology. Jeremy fumbled in his pocket for his hand-kerchief and mopped his brow again. 'That would be lovely, thank you,' he said.

Lucy led the way into the kitchen, Jenny dancing ahead. 'How come you're here?' Jenny asked. 'We haven't visited you in ages, I thought you were dead.'

'Jenny!' Lucy admonished.

'Well, I'm not dead, as you can see,' Jeremy answered as he sat at a huge table, far too big for a family of four, soon to be five. 'I'm very much alive and I just thought that I would like to see your daddy and you all so here I am.'

'And we're very pleased to see you,' Lucy smiled as she placed a cup before him. 'How have you been?'

'Oh, fine.'

'Does that boy still visit you?' Jenny asked.

'Jenny!' Lucy admonished again and her tone let Jeremy

know that Adam had probably filled her in on the whole sorry Santa saga.

'Sorry.' Lucy had gone red.

'It's OK.' Jeremy managed a small smile. 'No, Jenny, he doesn't. I hope he will soon though. But I was hoping you and your brother will start to visit again. I've even bought orange.'

Jenny looked doubtful. 'It wasn't much fun in your house. It was boring until that boy came along.'

'Would you like to run next door and call for Louise?' Lucy asked her brightly.

'You said I was grounded.'

'Not any more.'

'OK.' Jenny was off in a flash of blue denim skirt, the front door slamming behind her.

'Sorry about that,' Lucy rolled her eyes fondly, 'she says what she thinks.'

'It's OK,' Jeremy nodded. 'She's probably right.'

Lucy flashed him a smile and didn't contradict him, which was a little bit awful. He watched her bustling about the kitchen making him tea. She was enormously pregnant and looked a lot kinder than when she wasn't.

'Eh . . .' Jeremy wasn't good with the whole female reproductive thing, but her stomach was so enormous he decided that something had to be said. 'When is the baby due, exactly?'

'Another few weeks,' Lucy said cheerily. 'Now, what sort of biscuits do you like?' She pulled a tin from the press and had a look. 'Chocolate, plain, wafer?'

'Oh, just tea is fine.' Jeremy knew he wouldn't be able to eat anything until he'd seen Joel. 'How is Joel?' he ventured. 'I, eh, haven't seen him in a while.'

Lucy hesitated before answering, then she laid the biscuit tin down on the table. 'He's a bit miserable, to be honest,' she said, eyeballing Jeremy so he squirmed in his seat. 'You hurt him a lot. He idolises you, you know.'

Jeremy took out his handkerchief again. 'It was said in the heat of the moment. I didn't mean it. I—'

He was saved from saying any more by the front door opening with a bang. 'Home!' Joel shouted. 'Len is outside playing with Mick.'

Jeremy's stomach rolled nervously.

'We have a visitor.' Lucy ran to the kitchen door and Jeremy guessed she was doing something with her eyes to warn her husband that his father was in situ.

It obviously didn't work as Joel said, 'Who?'

'Your dad,' Lucy announced in a falsely bright voice.

'Oh,' was Joel's only response.

Jeremy composed himself. He stood up, pulling his coat around him as Joel entered. The two men faced each other across the room. Joel looked very red, Jeremy thought. Stressed.

There was a silence.

'I'll leave you to it,' Lucy said, rubbing Joel's arm lightly and giving it a squeeze. He caught her hand momentarily in his and then let it go.

Lucy closed the door behind her.

Jeremy coughed. 'Well,' he began.

'Yes?' Joel asked.

'I, eh, came to apologise for my unforgiveable remarks,' Jeremy said, forcing himself to meet his son's gaze, even though he was far more tempted to look at his twenty-year-old shoes. 'I came to say that I actually think it's wonderful that you married early and had kids.'

'No, you don't think it's wonderful,' Joel spluttered incredulously.

Jeremy winced. 'OK, I don't,' he admitted swiftly. Then stopped. 'But . . .' He sought to explain, to tell his son of the gaping fear that he had for him, the fear he'd had since Joel had looked with such love at his bride all those years ago. 'Well, Joel, it's only because it's what I did and I ended up alone.

327

Loving someone can hurt. A lot. I found it hard, very hard, to cope with two boys whom I didn't understand. I didn't want that for you. Children need a mother.'

'They need a dad, too,' Joel said quietly.

Jeremy bowed his head.

'You didn't have to understand us.'

'I didn't know that at the time,' Jeremy answered, his voice growing quieter but more intense. He shook his head hopelessly and spread his arms wide. 'There was no guide book.'

'Everything I did,' Joel said emotionally, sounding on the verge of tears, 'I did to impress you, Dad. *Everything*. It took me years to realise that nothing impressed you. You were so caught up in your own grief you couldn't see beyond it to notice anyone else.'

'That's not true,' Jeremy stressed, horrified that Joel would ever think that. 'Of course I was impressed. You had a normal job, you got a good wage. I was very impressed. It was Adam's job I had the problem with, not yours.'

'Adam has a good job.'

'Yes, yes he has, but you know me.' Jeremy paused, considering that remark, then backtracked. 'Well maybe you *don't* know me, but I like traditional things.' He paused. 'I swear that when your mother died, I did my best. I'm not a man who talks about feelings and, and, wheels babies up and down the street and changes nappies and cries at the drop of a hat, but I did my very best.' Jeremy rubbed his hand over his face. This talk was stressing him out. He pulled at the collar of his shirt, hoping to loosen the top button, but his hands wouldn't do what he wanted at all. 'My best,' he repeated. 'The best that I knew how and it must have been pretty good because you and Adam found your lives and did well and are just,' Jeremy swallowed, 'just great, really.'

Joel blinked. Once. Twice. His eyes widened, as if in sudden understanding. 'Dad,' he said, sounding shocked, 'are you dying or something?'

'I most certainly am not!' Jeremy spluttered.

'Oh.' Joel seemed taken aback. 'Well,' he eventually said, nodding, 'thanks for that. That was nice to say.'

'I mean it.'

'Thanks.'

'And, eh,' Jeremy attempted a small smile, 'I would very much like if you would resume visiting me. At least I can watch Adam on TV but I can't get to see you at all.'

Joel swallowed, seeming to have some difficulty finding his voice. 'OK.'

'And of course your wife and children would be welcome and I'll get in some nice biscuits and cakes and such. I have a lovely decking now.'

'OK.'

'And John has planted flowers. Your mother would have approved, I think.'

'Yes,' Joel said quietly, 'I'd say so.'

'Well,' Jeremy smiled again and heaved a sigh of pure relief, 'I'll be on my way. Tell Lucy there is no need for the tea now, I said what I came to say and I look forward to your visits.'

'OK.' Joel, stunned, watched as his dad walked by him, then just as Jeremy reached the door he said softly, 'Dad?'

Jeremy turned.

Joel looked at him for the longest time. Then uttered a 'Thanks.'

Jeremy smiled a little, swallowed a huge lump and nodded. 'I should have said it a long time ago.'

'It was worth the wait,' Joel said quietly.

Jeremy wished that Joel was Adam, that he would hug him or touch him or something. Instead, the two looked at one another across the expanse of the kitchen and, in the silence,

329

an understanding descended – at least Jeremy thought so. He nodded once to Joel, pulled his coat around him and nodded again. 'Good,' he said.

Joel smiled.

Jeremy smiled back.

He had really missed that boy.

43

E VERY WEEK TONY seemed to improve, Allie thought, as she opened the door to him. It had been six weeks since he'd moved out and already he'd put on some weight and there was colour in his face. Digging gardens with his brother obviously suited him. But it was his smile that made her catch her breath. He looked happy, relaxed, at ease. Not the same Tony who had come home from the clinic over four months earlier.

'Hi,' he grinned at her, 'are the lads ready?'

'Yeah, stand in, I'll call them.'

'You look well.' His dark eyes appraised her.

'Thanks. So do you.'

He grinned. 'You going out somewhere?'

'I was supposed to go into town with Holly but her friends booked a surprise weekend away for her. She only found out an hour ago.'

'How is she?'

Allie shrugged. 'As good as can be expected, I guess.'

Tony nodded. 'Tell her I said hi.'

'Yeah, I will.'

'Why don't you come out with us?'

The invitation caught her off guard. 'What?'

'You're all dressed up, be a shame to waste it.' He winked at her.

'But Saturday is your day with the boys.'

Her remark stung, she could see it in his eyes.

'I didn't mean it like that—'

'Owen will be much happier if you're there,' he said, cutting her off. Then added, half in admiration, 'He's an unforgiving little guy.'

Allie smiled. 'He's mellowing. The trip to the indoor playground last week went a little towards it.'

Tony grinned, then, tipping his head towards the car he'd borrowed from John, said, 'Come on, we'll have fun. We're going bowling.'

Allie considered it. She really wasn't sure it'd be a good idea. 'Are you sure? You don't want to be on your own with the lads?'

'I would like you to come,' Tony answered seriously. 'Please?'

Yes, Tony looked better, Allie had to concede. Yes, he seemed to be coping. And yes, the idea of the four of them out together as a family was appealing. However she did not want to be his crutch ever again. But that was up to her, she did have a choice.

'OK,' she said.

She was rewarded with another wink that, despite her resolution, made her knees go weak.

There was a ring on the door. Jeremy had just come in from his walk and was removing his scarf.

'In a minute,' he called. Placing his scarf on top of his coat, he shuffled towards the door and opened it to find Adam and an older man standing on the doorstep.

Jeremy looked from one to the other.

'Hey, Dad,' Adam said in his usual cheery manner, though his voice shook a little. 'I'd like you to meet Peter.'

Jeremy had not been expecting this. He blinked, then as Adam made to enter he stood aside and both men stepped into the hall. Peter was dressed normally, Jeremy thought. No flowing blouses or billowing trousers. He looked OK in his jeans and jumper.

'Peter is my—'

'Yes,' Jeremy interrupted, not wanting to hear Adam say the words. 'Yes, I'm aware of who Peter is.' He nodded to the balding, pasty-faced man. 'Hello, Peter. I'm Jeremy.'

'Hi,' Peter smiled.

He sounded a little nervous too, which made Jeremy feel a tad more at ease. Though Peter was quite gay-sounding, which made him uneasy again. So Jeremy wasn't quite sure how he felt. He decided to pretend that Peter was a girl, that way he'd know how to handle things. 'Well, come in,' he said. 'I've some biscuits and tea and things in the kitchen. I've no tomato bread though.'

'Thank God for that,' Adam grinned.

Jeremy shot him an uncomprehending glance and turned back to Peter. 'It's, eh, nice to meet a friend of Adam's.'

'And it's nice to meet Adam's dad,' Peter said. 'You live in a lovely street, I was just saying to Adam as we drove over here how nice and peaceful it seems. We live in the city centre, as you know, and it is so noisy there.'

'Yes, I'm always telling Adam to move,' Jeremy answered. 'Lots of stabbings and everything in the city these days.'

Adam spluttered out a laugh but Peter seemed to take Jeremy's comment very seriously. 'It's true,' he nodded, 'times have changed so much. Knife crime is on the increase.'

'Too many knives available,' Jeremy said. 'It's ridiculous.'

'Yes, I'm currently filming a documentary on crime in the city,' Peter sat down on a kitchen chair, 'and you would not believe the stories we've been told.'

'Oh, I'd say I would,' Jeremy nodded vigorously, 'the world has changed.'

Adam, looking at his dad chatting to his gay lover, smiled and silently agreed.

Tony was showing her how to throw the bowling ball. No wonder he'd brought them bowling, Allie thought in amusement.

He was just looking for a chance to show off. He kept getting strikes all the time. She'd forgotten that about him.

'Now.' Tony stood behind her, his body moulding hers. He took the hand which held the bowling ball and pulled it back. 'Look at the arrows on the court.' She could feel his breath on the back of her neck and it sent shivers down her body. 'And let go.'

He released her arm and she let the ball go flying off into the air, where it landed with a *thunk* on to the lane before falling into the gully at the last minute.

Tony cracked up laughing, making people in the other lanes stare in their direction.

Mark chortled and clapped his hands and Owen said haltingly, 'No good, Mammy, no good.'

Tony gestured despairingly. 'You just can't teach some people,' he teased.

Allie punched Tony on the arm. He caught her hand, then didn't seem to know what to do with it so he let it go and grinned at her instead.

They were still smiling at each other when Mark shouted out. 'Hi! Hi, Clare! Hi, Duncan!'

'Oh shit!' Allie gulped in panic.

Mark was waving at a couple from their old estate, oblivious to the fact that Allie had distanced herself from them once Tony's habit had started to escalate.

Clare and Duncan waved back at Mark.

'It's us!' Mark shouted. 'Hi!'

To Allie's horror, Duncan and Clare began to make their way over. Allie froze, her first reaction was to run. Tony, however, waved back easily.

'Hi,' Clare smiled as she reached them, 'how are you all? Hi, guys.' Her eyes fell on Owen. 'No way! Is that you, Owen? You've got so big.'

Owen smiled shyly and hid behind Allie's legs.

'Hey, Clare,' Mark said loudly. 'Have I got big, too?'

'You have,' Clare grinned. 'Hasn't he got big, Duncan?'

'I didn't recognise you,' Duncan said. 'I thought for a minute you were your daddy.'

'No way!' Mark said delightedly.

There was an awkward pause. Allie felt saddened, she knew that Clare and Duncan had doted on the boys, having no kids of their own. She had dumped them without so much as an explanation.

'It's nice to see you both,' she ventured.

Clare smiled. 'Nice to see you lot, too.'

More silence.

'Sorry I never rang you,' Allie said then. 'We, eh—'

'I wasn't well,' Tony interrupted, his hand on Allie's arm, halting her from any more apologies. 'I put Allie under a lot of stress.'

'Oh,' Clare's eyes widened. 'Really? Well we heard something but I can't believe —'

'He was a junkie,' Mark volunteered.

Allie let out a yelp as Tony flinched slightly. Then he grinned, 'That about sums it up OK, buster.'

'Ouch,' Duncan said feebly, 'that's a real conversation stopper.'

Tony laughed slightly. 'I was in rehab,' he admitted, 'it hasn't been easy. I lost us a lot of money.'

'We heard that,' Duncan said. 'But we found it hard to believe.'

'Well, start believing. Allie has been a trooper.' He smiled down at Allie and she smiled back up at him. Without thinking she caught his hand in hers and held it.

'Well, whatever they did in rehab, you look great,' Clare nodded.

'They gave him counselling,' Mark said, 'and they told him how to stop.'

'Really?' Clare arched her eyebrows. 'Cool. Bet you're glad your daddy is better, hey?'

'Yeah.' Mark caught Tony's free hand.

'Me too,' Owen piped up, not wanting to be left out.

Allie laughed. 'We're all glad,' she said.

And Allie wondered why on earth she'd tried to keep it a secret, what was the point? He'd been sick, and now he was trying his damnedest to get better. That's all that mattered.

'Well, it's been wonderful to meet you.' Peter shook Jeremy's hand very vigorously. 'Wonderful,' he said again.

'See you, Pops,' Adam grinned on his way out. 'You'll have to come over next weekend and let us cook for you. Peter does the most incredible shepherd's pie.'

'I do,' Peter said. 'You'd be very welcome.'

Jeremy wasn't sure if he was prepared to go that far. It would all be very weird, he was sure.

'I'll come and pick you up,' Adam said before Jeremy could answer. 'And do you know what we can do then?' He flicked a glance at Peter, who nodded a little. 'We'll visit Mum's grave, it's her birthday next week. Joel and the kids are coming over too, we're making a day of it.'

Jeremy swallowed. This was like a set-up. 'Oh, I don't know . . .'

There was a pause. 'What don't you know, Dad?' Adam asked gently.

'The grave,' Jeremy gestured weakly, 'all that, I don't know.'

'We'll all be there with you,' Adam nodded. 'All the family.'

Jeremy blinked. 'I don't like visiting graves.'

'No, you don't like visiting *her* grave,' Adam clarified.

Jeremy didn't respond.

'Come to visit on Saturday anyway and see how you feel, no one will force you.'

He eventually agreed to a visit. He supposed after all these years he owed Adam that much.

They went to McDonalds after the bowling. The place was packed as there seemed to be a concert on and people, mainly teenagers, were filling up on food before going along.

'D'you remember when we were going out together,' Allie said as she bit into a massive burger, 'and me and you used to dodge the security guards to sneak in to those concerts?'

Tony grinned.

'Jesus, you had me climbing walls in my tight jeans and everything.'

'Yeah,' he laughed, 'nice view.'

Allie belted him. 'I don't know what you mean,' she said mock-primly.

'Nice view from the top of the wall,' Mark said, as if it was obvious, making them laugh.

'Another time he arranged a pretend fight to distract the guard so that I could dodge in, and he joined me twenty minutes later. And you would never let on how you did it!'

'Al, I don't think you should tell the kids this stuff.'

'No, I guess not.' She grinned at him. 'You were such a chancer.'

'Aw, I wasn't really.' Tony set his burger down and grinned across the table at her. Then, his glance flicking between her and his hands, he admitted shyly, 'In those days, when I was still thinking straight, I never would have taken a chance with you.'

'What do you mean?'

'Well,' he half shrugged, smiling a little uncertainly, 'I didn't want you getting into trouble, did I?' Without waiting for an answer, he added, 'So I paid for the tickets anyway.'

'What?' Allie laughed in disbelief.

'I had the tickets already bought.'

'What? You what?'

'I had the tickets bought,' he repeated. He smiled, enjoying her surprise. 'I just, well, normally I would have bunked in but I didn't want you getting into trouble, so I bought the tickets, just in case.'

'So why make me climb over walls and dodge security guards?'

'It was fun. I thought you'd like it.'

Allie's smile died and yet she wanted to hug him so hard and never let him go. '*You* were fun, Tony,' she said. 'All I needed was you, nothing else.'

'That's a nice thing to say,' Mark remarked. He had been following the conversation avidly.

'Yeah, it is,' Tony nodded, looking a little sad.

Allie wished she'd said it ten years earlier.

She watched then as he turned abruptly from her and started to tickle Mark's face with one of the chips. Owen was cautiously smiling at them.

Allie realised that to outsiders they were a normal family having fun on a Saturday afternoon, and it dawned on her that her wish was here. In this tiny space, her wish had come true. And even if it never happened again, it was every bit as good as she thought it would be.

44

T HE BOYS LOOKED cool, Allie thought, as she let them out to play in the back garden, with strict instructions to stay clean. Both of them were dressed in denims and soccer jerseys. They'd had cool spiky haircuts and had been scrubbed to within an inch of their lives in the bath that morning. They were a little hyper as she'd told them all about their granddad and of how he was calling in to meet them today. Owen, of course, hadn't really got a clue, but once Mark told him something was going to be great, he believed him.

She'd also warned her dad about the questions that Mark would probably ask him. Though she'd tried to answer everything the child wanted to know, she knew what Mark was like. Her dad had paled a little and asked her how on earth he could discuss serial marital infidelity with an eight-year-old. Allie had laughed, actually laughed, which was something she thought she'd never do, and told him to use his brilliant imagination to come up with a nice way of couching it. He hadn't seemed convinced.

Tony was the one thing she hadn't told her dad about. She'd probably end up doing it today. The kids were bound to tell him anyway. Allie took a final glance at the boys to make sure that they weren't indulging in any games that might result in large amounts of muck being deposited on their clothes, before beginning to make a start on the kitchen, giving it another clean before her dad came. She had flirted with the idea of the kids meeting him somewhere else, in town,

maybe, or over a meal in a burger joint, but with the explan-
ations and questions, home just seemed the better solution.
She began to wipe down the counter tops, humming a little
to the song on the radio. She jumped when the doorbell rang.

It was an hour too early. It couldn't be him.

Allie made her way to the door and smiled when she opened
it to find John holding a big bunch of flowers. She hadn't
seen him in ages. 'Hey,' she greeted him, opening it wider to
let him in. 'What are you doing here?'

'From Tony, me and the ma, to wish you luck today.' He
bowed as he presented her with the blossoms.

'Aw,' Allie laughed delightedly and buried her face in the
blooms, 'they're gorgeous. Thanks.'

'Glad you like them,' he grinned. 'Tony couldn't come with
them as he got stuck on a job. He said he'd call you later
instead.'

'Oh right.' Allie flushed. She hadn't seen Tony since the week
before when they'd all gone bowling. It had been such a lovely
day that at the end, when he'd been leaving, she'd attempted to
kiss him. Not a big smooch, just a peck on the lips, but he'd
deftly avoided her and pretended not to notice that she had been
left with her lips puckered into mid-air. Allie had been taken by
surprise at the level of disappointment and embarrassment she'd
felt. Instead, Tony had nodded to her and said his goodbyes
after first kissing the lads. He probably wasn't stuck on a job at
all, he was probably trying to avoid her.

'How is he?' Allie asked as she made her way into the
kitchen to find a vase for the flowers.

'You've seen him,' John said, 'he's doing great.'

Allie smiled and, placing the flowers on the sink, she opened
a few presses to try to locate a vase. Or a bottle. Or anything.
The one vase she knew she had was already sporting loads
of carnations, her mother's offering of luck for the occasion,
which had touched Allie something rotten.

John sat astride a chair, his elbows resting on the back.

'Yeah, him and Ma had this big emotional scene. Jaysus, it was like something from a horror movie. I was stuck in the front room, afraid to come out.'

Allie giggled a little.

'When I did come out, I thought I was in an episode of *The Waltons*.'

'Stop!' She located a half-used bottle of 7UP. Emptying it down the sink, she cut the top off with scissors and filled it with water. 'You haven't a sensitive bone in your body.'

'I'll have you know, I loved *The Waltons*.'

The doorbell rang again. Allie jumped.

'I'll get it.' John stood up. Squeezing her shoulder lightly, he added, 'If it's your auld fella, I'll split.'

'Thanks.' Allie smiled gratefully at him. 'And tell Tess and Tony thanks.' She began to cut the flower stems, pulling off the lower leaves, thankful to be doing something when her dad came in.

Out in the hall, John opened the door and Allie heard Holly's voice ask if this was Allie Dolan's house.

'Yep. Come in. All donations welcome.'

Allie heard Holly laugh, then she entered the kitchen with John following. Behind her back, John was feigning lust and mouthing, 'Wow!'

Allie tried to ignore him as he put his hand on his heart and rolled his eyes as if he was in love. 'Holly, hi!' she said brightly.

'I just thought a few good-luck flowers would help you today.' Holly held out a massive bunch of lilies. Then her eyes fell on the ones Allie was arranging. 'Oh,' she winced, 'have you loads already?'

'You can never have too many flowers,' Allie proclaimed. 'Hey, John, have a look in the fridge and see if you can find me another soft drink bottle that I can decapitate.' Taking the bunch of flowers from Holly, she hugged her. 'Thanks. That's so nice of you.'

'Oh, it's nothing. I just thought—'

'Coke?' John interrupted, waving a bottle around.

'Perfect.' Allie took it from him. 'Oh, by the way, Holly, this is John, my brother-in-law.'

'Hey,' John said, holding out his hand and assuming a cool, relaxed stance. 'Nice to meet you.'

'You too.' Holly shook his hand. 'Has Allie told you that your taste in pubs is crap?'

John looked momentarily startled. 'Eh, no.' He glanced at Allie in confusion.

'Well it is,' Holly raised her eyebrows, 'and will I tell you why?'

'You can tell me over a cup of coffee in the deli down the road if you like,' John grinned, attempting to regain his composure.

'Oh God,' Allie groaned, 'you're as bad with the lines as your brother.'

'He's as bad with the lines as he is in picking pubs,' Holly smirked.

'You wound me,' John grinned.

'I can't believe you haven't told him,' Holly said to Allie.

'You tell him, I'll make the coffee.' Allie turned to put the kettle on.

One cup of coffee later, John was laughing hard as Holly retold the story of the disastrous night in Deoch. 'I know one of the bouncers there,' he said eventually. 'You come with me one night, I'll get him to apologise to you.'

'I might just do that.' Holly flicked him a quick smile that seemed to transfix him, much to Allie's amusement. Then she slowly stood up, giving John the benefit of her long lean legs encased in black tight jeans. She picked up her bag from the table and turned to Allie. 'Best of luck today, I'll be thinking of you.'

'Thanks.' Allie hugged her again.

John immediately hopped up. 'I've to be heading as well, Al,' he said. 'Good luck, favourite sister-in-law.'

'Thanks, extra favourite brother-in-law. Come on, I'll see you both off.'

She let them out, smiling to herself as John attempted to be gallant by offering Holly a lift. Holly waved her own keys at him and told him she was fine.

'You are,' he said, 'you are so fine.'

Allie closed the door on Holly's peal of laughter. It was good to see her friend laugh again, and John was definitely the right guy to do it.

Ninety minutes later, Allie was feeling sick as she nursed a cold tea at her kitchen table. Maybe, she thought, she'd got the time wrong. Maybe he was only leaving his house now. Maybe there was a traffic jam. Maybe he'd been in an accident. Thomas was almost forty minutes late, he'd never been late before. Always early. She'd give him another ten minutes before ringing him, she decided.

'Mammy, I'm sorry but I fell.' Mark peered fearfully around the kitchen door. 'I got a bit dirty.'

A bit was an understatement. His clothes were destroyed. Allie glared at him in exasperation.

'Oh, for God's sake! Can you not stay clean for a few minutes?'

Mark flinched. 'It's been longer than a few minutes. It's been—'

'Just, just go upstairs and change.'

'Into what?'

'I don't care.'

Mark came into the kitchen. He stood just inside the door, his head cocked to one side. 'Are you sad?' he asked.

Allie swallowed hard. What was she like, taking her frustration and anxiety out on her child? 'I'm sorry for getting mad.' She pulled her gaze from the table to look at her very mucky son. 'It's just Granddad hasn't come and I'm a little worried.'

'Oh,' Mark nodded. He crossed towards her. 'Well, maybe he forgot.'

If he forgot, she'd never forgive him, she knew that much. But just say he'd been in an accident. He'd never get to meet his grandchildren. She should have let him meet them sooner.

'Or maybe he went to the zoo.'

'The zoo?' Allie suppressed a smile.

'Or the movies. Or maybe he met someone who he just wanted to talk to. Or got killed.' Mark seemed to relish that. 'He could have been in a bank that got robbed, like the one on the news and the robbers could have shot him.'

'You go upstairs, Mark, and change. I'm just going outside to see if I can spot him.'

'OK,' he nodded. 'But he could be dead, you shouldn't get mad.'

Allie followed him to the hallway and watched him go upstairs, a faint smile on her lips. She was about to open the front door to look up and down the road, in case Thomas was having difficulty finding her house, when her mobile rang. She darted back into the kitchen and, locating it on the counter top, she saw her dad's number.

'Dad?' she said breathlessly into the phone, 'Where are you?'

There was the briefest of pauses. 'I'm sick, Allie. I'm sorry, love, I can't make it today.'

It was as if for a few seconds the world stopped and her father's voice telling her he was sick echoed down the line. Then the hum and clatter of the house reasserted itself as Allie absorbed his words. He had to be joking. He had to be. She and her two lovely children were all ready and waiting to meet him, her boys looked adorable – well, Mark *had* looked adorable – and her friends had bought her flowers and she had had her hair blow-dried just yesterday. And now he was sick?

344

'I'm waiting for you here,' she spoke slowly, telling herself not to cry. Not to shout. To stay as calm as she could. 'You were meant to meet us today.'

'I know, love. I'm so disappointed.'

'So why not ring earlier? We've waited forty minutes for you.'

'I was too sick to ring earlier, I fell asleep.'

It was like an echo from a previous life. The slightly defensive note in her dad's voice. She'd forgotten that whenever he let her mother down, he'd sound exactly like the way he did now. Self-pitying, charming, stubborn. She knew instinctively that he was lying. 'Dad,' she said as calmly as she could, 'I don't believe you.'

There was a silence from the other end. 'Well, it's true. I don't know why you wouldn't.'

She said nothing.

'OK,' he finally admitted, 'I got a bit, you know, drunk last night. The pressure of this visit was all a bit much, you know, and I went home with the girlfriend and one thing led to another and I slept it out.' He paused. 'If you give me an hour I'll be there.'

He hadn't given her an hour once. 'I gave you over twenty years, Dad,' Allie said.

'Wha'?'

In that second Allie turned to look at Mark, who had stumbled back into the kitchen in a jersey that was too small for him and a pair of jeans that had a massive hole in the knee. And in the garden, Owen was shoving a fistful of soil into his mouth. He was even filthier than his brother had been. Her two boys. Two little lads who deserved to be cherished and loved by everyone they met. 'I think, Dad,' Allie said slowly, 'that telling a woman you're French in order to sleep with her is horrible, but telling your daughter that you've chosen this woman over your own grandkids is even worse.'

345

'Aw, Allie, come on, give me a chance—'

She hung up and turned her phone off.

They were looking expectantly at him. All of them. Despite the excellence of the shepherd's pie, Jeremy hadn't been able to eat much of it. The impending visit to his wife's grave weighed heavily on him. Adam's flat was very nice, he had to admit. 'Flat' probably wasn't the right word for it, though. It was a massive affair with a huge kitchen. Weird artwork adorned the walls and even weirder sculptures were positioned in various nooks and crannies. It was a bright and airy place and very Adam.

'So Dad,' Joel asked, 'are you coming? We're just going to put some flowers on the grave and say a silent prayer or whatever?'

'You should go,' Jenny admonished, 'wasn't she your wife? I thought everyone loved their wives.'

'It makes Granddad sad to think that his wife is dead,' Lucy explained gently. 'Just because he doesn't want to go doesn't mean he didn't love her.'

'Exactly,' Jeremy nodded, relieved. 'That's it exactly.'

'Oh, OK.' Jenny smiled at Jeremy. 'I'm sorry you're sad, Granddad. I'll tell Granny hello from you, will I?'

To Jeremy's horror, he felt the beginnings of tears at his granddaughter's offer. What a lovely thing to say. He coughed and said abruptly, 'Yes, that would be very nice if you could do that.'

'So will you stay here then, Dad?' Adam asked. 'Will you be OK? I'll drive you back when I get home, it should only take about an hour.'

'Fine,' Jeremy turned away from them. 'I'll be fine.'

He felt a sense of relief as they left.

Allie brought the two boys to McDonalds. She was standing at the counter, her hand in Mark's, Owen kicking furiously from his buggy. She hadn't cried, she hadn't got upset, instead she'd told the boys that she was going to treat them. Anything to escape the house. She called out her order to the woman behind the counter.

'I'd like a large chips and Coke and cheeseburger, please.'

'And you?' the woman smiled down at Mark.

'I'll have the same,' Mark said.

The same? The words echoed in Allie's head. Her eight-year-old was having the same as her. He was eight. She was an adult. 'Would you not have a small meal?' Allie suggested to him.

'I always have the large,' Mark answered.

'Do you?' Allie blinked. She'd never noticed that before. And in that instant, when she was doing everything not to think of her father and his betrayal, she suddenly realised that every time she got upset, she fed herself and her kids complete rubbish. They'd moved house and she had let Mark chomp his way through every packet of sweets in the place. Tony had fought with John, so she'd brought them to the cinema and bought popcorn and fizzy drinks and sweets. Their dad got high and she ordered pizza. It was as if by feeding them what she thought they liked, she was making up for all the distress she felt responsible for putting them through. It was her way of trying to be a good mother. Feeding them was the only way she could comfort them, she realised. It was the only way she could comfort herself. It was how she'd comforted her mother when her dad had been unfaithful. Buying her chocolates and hugging her. And it wasn't right. She looked at Mark as if seeing him from an outsider's perspective. Her dad had said that he was 'a big lad' and she'd completely denied it. She had never ever thought that he was fat, but actually, looking at him now, at the way his jersey rode up on him, she had to concede that Mark was a little overweight. How could she have never seen it before? He was such a good-looking child with his black hair and dark eyes that she'd never noticed how his clothes never seemed to sit on him right. Mark had been bullied about his weight, he'd written it down and she'd somehow not acknowledged it even then. OK, the bullying seemed to have stopped, but there were other bullies out there. And she was setting him up for it. And how had she never copped on? But then again, she was used to living in denial – hadn't she done it with Tony? With her dad? It seemed she'd chosen that way of living. Bam! Bam! Bam! As one thought flowed into the next, her head spun.

'Mammy,' Mark was tugging on her hand, looking anxiously at her, 'the lady is asking what Owen wants.'

Allie blinked, her sudden insight making her confused. 'What?'

'Your other little boy, what does he want?' the woman asked patiently.

'Sorry,' Allie gasped out, 'we've got to go.'

'Mammy!' Mark said. 'You can't do that!'

'I can.' She said. 'I can.' She turned the buggy around. 'Sorry,' she said to the girl, who was looking at her as if she was bonkers.

'But I'm hungry!' Mark wailed.

'I'll make your dinner for you.'

'I want chips!' Owen screamed, startling not just Allie but the whole shop.

'Well, tough,' Allie said. And she knew that it wasn't only Tony that needed tough love, it was her kids too.

There were pictures of Adam and Peter all over the place, Jeremy thought. Smiling into the camera, smiling into one another's eyes. Doing coupley things like standing on top of the Eiffel Tower together, wearing matching T-shirts, on the beach together, holding hands. Two men doing these things was all still a little strange to him, but Jeremy could recognise love when he saw it. Nelly and him had pictures like that.

Only he'd buried the photos away when she'd died. Would he like it if Peter did that to Adam's memory if anything happened to his son? No, he would not. His boys must have felt terrible when he'd wiped all pictures of their mother away. He wondered why he'd done it now. Had he thought that it'd make the pain go away? It hadn't. Would steering clear of Nelly's grave make the pain go away? Probably not. Would it help him feel better if he went? He doubted it. Would it help his boys feel better? Would it? He had to concede that maybe it would. And perhaps, instead of thinking about himself, he should do this for them.

He walked uncertainly back into the kitchen and found the phone. Dialling Adam's number, he haltingly asked if his son would come back and collect him.

'Sure,' Adam said, and Jeremy knew that in this at least, he'd make his children happy. 'Give me ten minutes.'

Jeremy would have waited for ever.

When they arrived home, Allie handed the boys a ham sandwich and told them to go watch TV. Both of them grumpily went inside without looking at her and Allie had to fight the urge to hand them a bag of crisps each to cheer them up.

Alone in the kitchen, Allie knew she had to get to grips with what had happened. She had to accept the fact that her dad didn't care that much at all. However when she was confronted with the three bunches of flowers displayed so hopefully on the table and the windowsills, she had to blink back her tears. She was not going to cry over him. He was not worth it. She was going to . . . going to . . . Her gaze fell on the plant in the garden that John had said was choked with ivy. She decided to tackle that – John had never got around to it. She would bloody well save that plant, she thought. If her father was a lying cheating scumbag, well, at least something would benefit from him not turning up.

Allie got her gloves and some gardening tools from the

349

little wooden shed out the back garden and attacked the plant with a vengeance. She was going to spend the afternoon working hard, not thinking about anything, just focusing on work. She'd push the pain away until she had time to deal with it. There was no way she could cry in front of her boys. They'd seen enough upset already. If she kept going, she'd be all right.

The grave was very well tended, Jeremy had to admit. The lads had planted a little shrub which seemed to be thriving. At first they all stood around saying silent prayers, even Jenny was quiet, her eyes closed and her hands joined in a very reverent way. Then one by one they drifted off until only Jeremy was standing there. He waited to feel the pain he thought he'd feel, braced himself for its impact. Instead, a sort of peace crept up on him. It was a strange calm, as if for the last twenty years he'd been running and running and getting nowhere and now, he felt as if he'd suddenly come to a halt. Instead of the crushing ache he had run from he experienced a sort of mellowing, a thawing, deep inside. As if finally now he could catch his breath. His eyes filled up and he brushed away a tear that had stolen out.

'Nelly,' he whispered.

The woman he'd loved so much was buried in that small patch of lovingly tended soil. This patch of soil told anyone passing that Nelly Lyons had existed. That she'd lived and breathed and been married and had two sons and a husband who missed her. It was comforting that people wandering through the graveyard would see her name, read her head-stone and calculate how old she was and maybe mutter about what a tragedy it was that she should have died so young. And it was a tragedy, that much was true, Jeremy thought. But that was all that was tragic. Her life certainly hadn't been tragic, it had been wonderful and happy and she'd given him two amazing sons. She'd made him laugh, she'd loved him and he'd never loved anyone as much as he'd loved her. She'd killed him too, by dying, but was it worth it? Was the love he'd had for her worth the numbness afterwards? He had to concede that it was. He wouldn't have swapped it for anything.

'I wish I'd come sooner, Nell,' he whispered. He wiped another tear away.

He didn't notice Adam and Joel come up and stand on either side of him. He only noticed when his two sons embraced him. He had never felt sadder or more blessed in his life.

And he thanked her for waiting for him.

Inside the phone rang and Allie froze in the act of hacking off tendrils of stubborn ivy. She hoped the caller wasn't her dad as she didn't feel ready to talk to him, but then she realised that she'd never given him her home number. Maybe in a way she'd subconsciously recognised that he'd let her down eventually. At least she could change her mobile number and never have to hear from him again. Or is that what she wanted? She didn't know. But how could he neglect her in favour of some strange woman? How could he throw it all away for a night with a woman he was lying to? Had he ever changed? Or was he just the same as always?

Allie blinked rapidly and shoved her trowel into the soil as hard as she could. She was *not* going to think about it. Not now. She dug all around the shrub, hoping to get to the ivy at the root and eradicate it for ever. It was intricate work.

Mark must have answered the phone because he was saying 'Goodbye' to someone. Allie wanted to ask him who it was but then he'd come out into the garden and maybe she wouldn't be able to hold it together and he'd get upset and she didn't want that. And anyway, if it had been important he would have told her.

She heard Mark tell Owen to go back to the television and Owen begging Mark for a story and Mark agreeing.

She smiled. How could anyone not want to meet those two little boys? How could they? She gulped hard and concentrated on her gardening, she was nearly there. Bloody ivy was really hard to remove, she thought. It seemed to have tangled its way right down to the root system of the shrub.

Ten minutes later the front doorbell rang.

'Shit,' Allie cursed softly. She did not want to talk to anyone. She hauled herself up and it was then she realised that she was in her best jeans and that two huge muddy patches now adorned the knees. 'Bloody great.' She was so busy figuring out how on earth she'd ever wear them again that, when she glanced up and saw Tony and Mark looking at her from the kitchen doorway, she jumped, startled. What the hell was Tony doing here? It wasn't his day for the kids. Did he forget that they were meeting her dad today or something? But it was five o'clock and only now she realised how dark it was, so he couldn't have forgotten.

'What are you doing here?' she asked, pushing her hair behind her ears and streaking her face with muck.

'He rang to see how we got on today and I told him that Granddad didn't come,' Mark said, appearing behind him.

'Oh,' Allie said as nonchalantly as she could. 'Right.'

'I came to see how you were,' Tony said. 'What with him—'

'I'm fine, yeah.' Allie turned away from him, the concern in his eyes making her own water a little. 'I'm grand.' She flapped her arm in the direction of the house. 'You might as well play with the lads seeing as you're here.'

'Al?' Tony asked again.

'What?' Oh no, her voice shook and she knew if he kept asking, she'd cry. She walked further away from him and dashed a hand over her face, hoping he wouldn't notice.

'We went to McDonalds,' Mark offered. 'Only Mammy walked out before we could order.'

'Cool,' Tony said, sounding a little distracted. Allie heard

352

him unzipping his jacket before he said, 'Now, Mark, I'm going to have a chat with Mammy and you and Owen are going to watch this. I bought this for you both. *Crazy Dogz 2*.'

'Hey —' Allie turned around to protest but Mark had grabbed the DVD from Tony, shouting, 'Cool! Hey, Owen, look at this! Come on.' He grabbed Owen by the hand and led him into the front room.

'I told them they were too young for that,' Allie said weakly.

'They'll survive,' Tony said.

She still couldn't look at him, so she turned on her heel again and walked back down the garden.

He followed her. Then she heard him laugh a little before he asked, 'Hey, what did you do?' He was eyeing the carnage of broken ivy on the grass.

'Saving the plant.' Allie was glad of a chance to sound indignant. It stopped her thinking of her dad. 'The ivy was all wrapped around it. See,' she indicated the brown leaves, 'it's going to kill it.'

'If you don't kill it first.'

'Ha ha.'

'Here,' Tony winked at her and, bending down, he took the trowel from the grass. 'Let me.'

Allie said nothing as he went to work. She wondered why he was bothering, he had never liked the garden before, though maybe working with John had changed that.

Ten minutes later he sat back on his heels. 'Plant is fucked,' he said. 'I think we killed it.'

'Really?' She felt stupidly sad for the plant.

'Really.' He put down the trowel. 'I probably should have left it alone. I'm a shite gardener, John just lets me do the digging.'

'But you sounded so confident when you took the trowel from me,' Allie said a little huffily.

'Well, I was confident until I hacked off the main root of the bloody thing.'

'You eejet.' But he had her smiling. 'I sort of equated that plant with me, you know. I wanted to feel I was discarding all the crap in my life by taking its ivy away.'

'Oh shit. You should have equated yourself with the ivy, you'd still be alive right now.'

'Eejet,' Allie smiled again. Then bit her lip because she thought she might cry for some weird reason.

Tony's eyes softened. He stood up and wiped his mucky hands along his jeans. 'That was a lousy thing your dad did,' he offered.

She flinched. 'Yeah, I know.'

'I'm sorry, Al. I know you were—'

She held up her hand. 'Don't. I'm fine about it, honest.'

'You don't have to pretend,' Tony took a step closer, 'I'd be upset if I were you.'

'You don't know how you'd feel if you were me,' Allie snapped, turning away. She didn't need his pity.

'I know what it feels like to think your folks don't want you,' Tony said quietly. 'I know what that feels like.'

And of course he did. He who had never known his parents. His parents who had never claimed him so that he could never be adopted by anyone. It wasn't easy coping with rejection. Allie closed her eyes, wondering how she could have been so insensitive. Slowly she turned back around to face him.

'I'm sorry,' she said, gulping. 'I didn't mean that.'

'Hey,' he spoke gently, offering her a small smile, 'I'm only saying I understand.'

And for the first time she understood him too. A tear slipped out and ran down her face.

'Aw, Al . . .'

She scrubbed it away. That wasn't meant to happen. 'I'm fine.'

He came closer, looking at her in concern, unsure of what to do. When the next tear slipped out, he slowly extended his hand and wiped it away with his thumb, smearing dirt all over her face. And still more came and suddenly she was in his arms as he pulled her towards him. 'Hey,' he said as he pressed her to his chest and she inhaled the familiar scent of him, 'I'm so sorry, Allie.'

'I thought he'd changed,' she sniffed, 'I really did.'

'Maybe he has, change takes time. People fuck up sometimes when they try to change, Al.'

Perhaps he was right, but she didn't answer. Instead she let him lead her into the kitchen. His arm was slung about her shoulders and he was hugging her close to him, kissing the top of her head. He sat her down on the kitchen chair and, after washing his hands, he dug out the coffee percolator from the depths of the press and began the complicated process of making her a cappuccino.

Her comfort drink, she'd always called it.

He loved messing around with that machine, she thought affectionately. It hadn't seen daylight since he left. Every so often he'd turn around and wink at her, and Allie was suddenly reminded of John leading his mother up the driveway the day her and Tess had gone to see Tony in the clinic. And now, Tony was looking after her. Maybe for the first time in their marriage. But then again, when had she ever let him before? She had been independent, made so by years of neglect from her dad and her heartbroken mother. She was not giving control over to anyone else and maybe by choosing Tony, she'd ensured things stayed that way. That she was the one in control. In charge. Her being there for him had only enabled him to continue taking drugs. But in the end, his addiction had ended up controlling both of them. It was weird but so comforting to have him take charge for once.

Tony cursed under his breath as the machine made a funny noise.

'I'll have instant,' Allie said. 'There's no need—'

'You'll have this,' Tony pressed a button and the machine

started to bubble away happily. He gave her a quick smile and patted the coffee maker. 'I love this bloody thing. No matter how much I fucked up, this was the one thing that always turned out perfect.'

She smiled a little. 'OK so.'

'OK so,' he mimicked her affectionately.

'Thanks, Tony,' Allie said then. 'It's nice you're here.'

He didn't answer, just concentrated on making her the perfect cup of coffee.

45

'W ELL,' HOLLY SAID, 'did you ask him?'

Allie hopped into the passenger seat of Holly's car, waving goodbye to the boys and her mother as Holly pulled off. Slamming the door shut, she clipped her seatbelt on and turned to smile at Holly's expectant look. 'I did. Last Saturday, after he dropped the lads back.'

'Well good for you.' Holly gave a little cheer, which made Allie laugh.

'I don't know why you're cheering, what makes you so sure he said yes?'

Holly rolled her eyes. 'Of course he said yes,' she snorted. 'John said that Tony looks forward to Saturdays so much. So I would imagine—'

'Stop!' Allie held up her hand. 'Rewind. What did you just say?'

'I said that Tony looks forward to Saturdays and—'

'No, no, no,' Allie raised her eyebrows and jabbed a finger in Holly's direction, 'you said that John said that he looks forward to Saturdays.' She stressed her brother-in-law's name.

'Oh right, yeah,' Holly said nonchalantly, tossing her hair back over her shoulder and grinning. 'Maybe I did.'

'You and John?' Allie poked her arm teasingly. 'Since when?'

'Since he asked me out for a drink and his car broke down on the way and he had to call the AA and he gave them the wrong location and we were sitting in his car waiting for them to turn up for over an hour, sans radio and sans heater.'

'Oh no,' Allie winced, feeling sorry for John, 'was it a disaster?'

'No,' Holly shrugged, 'after about forty minutes we were so bloody cold we were forced to snuggle up together to keep each other warm, so it worked out well.'

Allie laughed.

'He's a nice guy,' Holly admitted candidly, 'I like him.'

'Well, I'm delighted,' Allie nodded. 'Two nicer people you could not meet.'

Holly blushed. 'Thanks.' Then suddenly her smile dipped and she added in a small voice, 'I never would have met him if it wasn't for Vee. Isn't that,' she tried to think of the right word, 'kind of, I dunno, sad?'

'No,' Allie shook her head adamantly, 'don't think that. Sure, I never would have met you if it wasn't for Tony. I'm not glad my husband is an addict, but I am glad I met you.'

Holly nodded. 'Yeah, I suppose . . .'

After a beat, Holly returned to the previous topic they'd been discussing. 'So, go on, you never told me, what exactly happened with Tony? Did he agree to stay over on Christmas Eve?'

'He did,' Allie nodded, smiling as she remembered. Tony had been delighted. A grin as broad as America had lit up his face. 'I asked him as he was leaving. He's staying over on Christmas Eve and Christmas Day. He's heading over to his mother's then on Stephen's day.'

'Wow, two days, I thought you were only asking him to stay over the one night?'

'Well,' Allie shrugged, 'I would have felt sorry for him leaving on Christmas Day.'

'Ya big softie!'

Allie grinned. She guessed she was, but at the same time she reckoned that this Christmas would be special. Just the four of them together and Tony completely clean. She wanted to always remember it, to hold on to it for as long as possible, no matter what happened in the future.

'And are the boys all excited?'

'They don't know, it'll be a surprise.'

'Aww,' Holly sighed at the romance of it all, 'that's lovely. I'm so glad.'

'Yeah, me too.'

Neither woman spoke for the next few minutes, then Allie said, 'It wasn't all Tony's fault the way things were. Some of it was my fault too. He was right that night we fought, it was one rule for him and another for me.'

'Well, you're both making the effort now,' Holly said as she pulled up outside the clinic where the family meetings were held on a Friday night. 'You'll get a lot out of this, Allie. I swear. It's not just people talking about their problems.'

Allie nodded. She didn't even feel nervous, which might have been expected. She just knew that she was doing the right thing. And in time, she thought, she'd even bring Mark and Owen along. They deserved to be part of the journey too.

46

JEREMY WAS PUTTING the finishing touches to his Christmas presents. Last week he'd taken a trip into the city centre for the first time in years and had been amazed at how it had changed. Despite what the news said, he witnessed no drunkenness or stabbings. People had been in very good humour, he thought.

He sat back on his heels and surveyed the array of gifts he'd bought. He was going to Joel's for dinner on Christmas Day and he was surprised to find that he was looking forward to it. He'd bought Joel a gift voucher for a golf shop and Lucy a gift voucher for a clothes shop. He'd bought Jenny a doll and Len a Playstation game. He had been tempted to get them something more educational but had decided that maybe that wasn't a good idea. Christmas was meant to be about what the children wanted. He had also purchased a large teddy wearing a Superman outfit for his newest little grandson, who would be a week old on Christmas Day.

He'd agonised about Adam and Peter's present. Finally he'd decided on a book about the history of television. It was a coffee table book, the woman in the bookshop had told him. It had certainly come with the price tag of a good quality coffee table. He had no idea that books were that expensive. Or heavy. It had nearly taken his arm out of his socket trying to haul it home.

Jeremy turned towards his final two presents. He wasn't even sure he'd get to give them to the children next door.

He put a final tinsel bow on each one and wondered if he should maybe just take a chance and drop them in. Allie could only tell him to get lost, couldn't she? At least he'd have tried. But he wanted to do so much more than just try – the time had to be right, he wanted to be sure of a positive reception. He wasn't certain he'd get that from Allie. And then maybe she'd tell her husband and Jeremy shivered a little. Of all of them, Jeremy felt that Tony would be the most hostile.

Just then, Jeremy's front doorbell rang.

Maybe . . .

Hardly daring to hope, Jeremy hauled himself upright, his knees creaking badly. He hobbled out into the hall and was disappointed to see that the caller was not a little boy, but rather a tall person, not someone he could distinguish through the glass. Opening the door a little, it took him a second to recognise the tarty girl from the park. She looked even tartier out of context. He could only gape. The air temperature was hitting freezing and she was attired in a red mini-skirt and tiny denim jacket. An inch of exposed belly seemed to have goosebumps, though Jeremy tried hard not to look.

'Hiya,' the girl said, sweeping her peroxide hair out of her eyes. 'I was hoping I had the right house.'

'Well,' Jeremy stuttered, 'if it's me you want, then you have.' Half alarmed, he wondered what the neighbours would make of this teenage girl lounging on his doorstep.

The girl shivered a little and pulled her ineffectual jacket around her. Her legs were either plastered in red fake tan or were close to freezing. 'I know it's Christmas Eve and all,' she began, hopping nervously from one goosebumped leg to the other, 'but I was hoping that might make you say yes. You know, good will to men and all that.'

'Say yes to what?' Jeremy held the door a little wider. 'Do you want to come in? You look cold.'

'Eh, no. I just want to ask you something.' She flushed a little. 'It's sort of a secret.'

'A secret?' Jeremy baulked. The last thing he needed in his life was more secrets with kids. 'Oh, I'm not sure. What kind of a secret?'

The girl giggled a little, then stopped. Then started to say something and then stopped. 'This is hard for me,' she mumbled a tad defensively, studying her huge glittery fingernails which were like the talons of an eagle in Jeremy's opinion. 'I hate asking for things.'

'No one likes to ask for things,' Jeremy said matter-of-factly. He wondered if she wanted more cigarettes. 'But you're here now, you might as well go for it. What's the worst that can happen?'

'You could say no,' the girl muttered.

'I could,' Jeremy agreed, 'but that's hardly going to ruin your Christmas, is it?'

The girl thought about it for a second, before taking a deep breath and saying in a rush, 'Well, I was thinking about what you were saying about them grinds and all, well, would you help me? I'm shit at all that stuff.'

Jeremy blinked, unable to answer, he was so surprised. So there was a little ambition in her after all. It was oddly moving. He raised his eyebrows. 'You want me to help you?' he finally spluttered out.

'Yeah,' she glanced about furtively, lowering her voice, 'on the quiet, like. I don't want me mates to know, they'll slag the hole off me.'

'Oh, we can't have that,' Jeremy answered, wincing at her crudeness yet feeling a small thrill start up in the base of his spine. This girl had listened to him. This girl wanted his educational expertise. It'd be so good to feel useful again, to be helping someone. 'You'll have to tell your parents though.'

She tossed her head dismissively, black roots showing through. 'Aw, they won't care.'

'All the same,' Jeremy said firmly. 'I'd feel better if they knew.'

The girl pondered this before nodding reluctantly. 'Fine.' She paused and added, 'Thanks.'

Jeremy was about to thank her, then decided that it wouldn't bode well for a student-teacher relationship. Instead he said briskly, 'Well, I'll give you my number.' He pulled a biro from his cardigan pocket. 'And you can ring me after Christmas and we'll see how we're both fixed.'

'Naw, I'll key it into my phone,' the girl said, pulling out a small silver mobile. 'Shoot.'

Jeremy called out his number, admiring the speed of the girl's fingers on the keypad. A sudden idea struck him and he smiled. 'I'll do a deal with you,' he said, thinking of how Adam would be so surprised. 'I teach you whatever I can, and in return you get me mobile phone literate.'

'Wha'?'

'Teach me how to use a mobile phone.'

'Oh right,' she nodded, 'sure. You should have just said that.' She pocketed her phone and took a step back. 'Thanks.' A pause. 'You're great.'

'Oh, I'm not.' Jeremy waved her admiration away, feeling embarrassed.

'Well, suppose you did come across as a bit of a know-it-all arsehole in the beginning,' the girl said, nodding as if agreeing with him. 'But then, you know, when you got Philo to help that little neighbour of yours, I thought that maybe you were OK. That maybe you wouldn't make me feel stupid when I wouldn't know stuff.'

'Oh, I'd never do that,' Jeremy said hastily, wondering just what he was getting himself into.

She smiled and Jeremy thought that without all the make-up, she might actually look OK. 'Happy Crimbo,' she said. 'Knock yourself out!'

'And you too,' Jeremy called. 'See you in the new year.'

* * *

363

An hour later, Jeremy was bundled up in his warmest coat. In his hand he held a bag containing two brightly wrapped presents, one for Mark and the other for his little brother. Jeremy's heart was hammering and a fine coat of sweat seemed to be trickling down his back from the base of his neck. Still, he'd figured that if that young girl could pluck up the courage to come and see him, well then the least he could do was call into his neighbours and try and make amends for his appalling error of judgement. After all, he was very firmly in the wrong so it was up to him to do all he could to make things right. Though maybe staying away might be the right thing to do. Or maybe not . . . It was all so confusing. That's what happened when you let people into your life, you were forced to make choices and all you could do was hope that the choices you made were the right ones. And Jeremy had never been very good at doing that. Still, nothing ventured, nothing gained. Jeremy opened his front door, stepped outside and froze. There, at his gate, also about to enter Allie's garden, was Tony.

Tony stopped and stared at him.

Jeremy swallowed hard. 'Eh, happy Christmas,' he offered feebly.

Tony nodded and hoisted what looked like an overnight bag higher up on his shoulder. 'You too,' he said back. He nodded to Jeremy's bag, a faint smile playing on his lips. 'Packing the sleigh, are you?'

Jeremy winced. 'Well, eh—'

'Joke?' Tony grinned ruefully. 'Sorry, it was probably a crap thing to say.'

Jeremy blinked, almost weak with relief. 'Oh no, no, I deserve that one, it was appalling what I did. I filled your poor boy with ridiculous hope. I —' Jeremy found that he was babbling. He stopped abruptly. He loosened the top button of his coat, feeling incredibly hot.

'Relax,' Tony said, looking guilty, 'I was only joking.'

'Still though . . .' Jeremy wished he could sit down. His legs had begun to shake a little. Making amends was hard. 'Can I just say,' he said, crossing towards the man, knowing that now was the right time to speak out, that maybe he'd never get the chance again, 'can I just say that, well, lying to Mark turned out to be the best thing I ever did.'

As expected, Tony looked a little incredulous.

Jeremy rushed on before Tony could interrupt him. 'I know what happened afterwards was . . .' He sought for the word and could only come up with 'unfortunate', which was unfortunate. 'Unfortunate, but I'm glad I got to know him. I wasn't a very good father to my own two boys and—'

'Join the club,' Tony said ruefully.

Tony's comment halted Jeremy's speech. He blinked, then shook his head vigorously. 'Oh, no, no,' he reassured him, 'I see you making those boys laugh, you play with them.' He shrugged and admitted, 'I never did that with my boys. I regret that. Very much.' He heaved a sigh, not sure now what he'd been about to say. Instead, he held out his bag of presents. 'If you're going to see your family, can you give them these? It's a couple of small tokens, to say I'm very sorry.'

Tony gazed at the old man, bundled up in his huge winter coat, his hands shaking as he held the presents towards him. A feeling of empathy swept through him. He knew exactly how this guy felt. 'Come on,' he said quietly, as he nodded towards his house, 'give them to the lads yourself.'

'Oh, I don't think so . . .'

'I bet you never hurled cups and glasses on to your kitchen floor, or shouted at your lads so furiously that you made them afraid to speak. I bet you never spent their savings or took the home they loved away from them. I bet you never sat in a chair for hours on end and just ignored them.'

Jeremy bit his lip, hoping he didn't look as horrified as he felt.

'I did,' Tony said quietly. 'So, if I can go home on Christmas Eve, you can pay a visit. Mark was mad about you,' he added.

'He was mad about Santa,' Jeremy stated flatly, hoping his voice wouldn't shake. 'Not me.'

'Naw,' Tony shook his head. 'Santa was just a title, the way Dad is just a title.'

Jeremy blinked, wondering if it were true. He supposed that even if he had called himself Santa, he had still been himself through a lot of it. He'd certainly been grumpy, but he'd helped the boy out too. He'd done things Santa definitely wouldn't have done. He couldn't see a film ever been made of Santa joining a boozing session in a local park in order to drum up help for a little boy or Santa doling out packets of fags by way of reward. Mark, in believing that Jeremy was Santa, had made him into a better person. All someone needed, Jeremy realised, was for just one person to believe that they could be good.

'Well,' he answered wryly, 'I suppose you're correct in that I was never a traditional Santa.'

Tony cracked a grin. 'Come on in so,' he cajoled. 'You can leave if Allie goes off on one.'

'I wouldn't blame her if she did,' Jeremy said. Then added, 'But seeing me, it won't upset Mark?'

'One thing about Mark,' Tony said, 'is that he's a great lad at forgiving people.' He shrugged. 'He's had a lot of practice with me.'

Jeremy gulped. 'Well, OK so,' he said. 'If you're sure?'

'I am,' Tony nodded. 'Come on so.'

Jeremy followed him up the path and stood a little to the side as Tony rang the bell. Inside the house, he heard Allie calling to the boys to answer the door. 'You never know who it could be,' she called out happily.

Next, there was the sound of scampering feet and a struggle to unlock the door. Jeremy smiled at the look of expectancy on Tony's face. He was a nice guy. Decent. Then, as the door opened a crack, Jeremy tried to fix a smile on to his own face, hoping that it didn't betray his anxiety.

Facing Mark was harder than facing his parents, he thought suddenly.

The door opened fully and there was a shriek. 'Daddy!' Mark hurled himself through the door and on to Tony, who laughed and hugged him. Then Mark spotted Jeremy. He straightened up, looked from one man to the other and a slow smile spread across his face.

'Mammy!' he shrieked. 'Mr Lyons has brought Daddy home for Christmas just like he promised!'

'Oh now,' Jeremy rushed to speak but Tony placed his finger on his lips and gently shook his head.

'Mammy!' Mark thundered into the house. 'Come and see, come on! It's like magic!'

Allie appeared a couple of seconds later, being dragged by Mark with Owen holding on to her leg. 'He brought Daddy home,' Mark said, pointing at Jeremy.

'He did,' Tony nodded, 'isn't that great, Al?'

Her gaze flicked from one man to the other, though she was smiling in semi-exasperation at Tony.

'Hello, Allie,' Jeremy said and his voice was a croak. He coughed. 'Eh, happy Christmas.' He held out his presents to her. 'For the boys and to say I'm very sorry.'

Allie eyed the bag, before smiling and taking it from him. 'That's very nice of you,' she said back. Then added, 'And thank you for bringing Tony. We appreciate it.'

Jeremy felt his eyes water. 'And I appreciate your forgiveness,' he gulped. He turned to Mark, 'And I am sorry for telling you I was Santa, it was a terrible thing.'

A fleeting look of hurt passed across Mark's face, before he said, 'Well, you did everything that I asked for in my wish list, so it's OK.'

'There now, it's OK,' Tony nodded. 'Do you think you'd like him to come inside, Mark?'

'Yeah,' Mark said as if it was obvious. 'Sure.'

Jeremy smiled and looked at Allie. She moved away from

367

the door to make room for him to come in. Tony indicated the hallway and Jeremy stepped inside. For the first time in his life, he thought, he was paying a visit to a neighbour on Christmas Eve. It was a very pleasant diversion indeed.

47

A^FTER JEREMY LEFT and the boys were in bed, Allie and Tony sat together in the kitchen. Tony had avoided taking any wine and had instead chosen 7UP. Allie, not wanting to tempt him, was sipping on a cappuccino. They regarded each other across the kitchen table. Allie sighed in contentment – right then she wouldn't have swapped her life for anyone else's.

'You look happy,' Tony remarked, his head to one side, observing her.

'Yeah, I am.' She smiled at him.

'Your dad been in touch then?'

'Nope.' Allie shook her head. Her dad hadn't contacted her at all since that awful day, but she was learning that her mother was right, some men you just had to let go while others you held on to as hard as you were able. 'I'm happy just to be here, with you and the lads.'

'Me too.' His gentle grin took her breath away.

They were quiet for a while as they studied each other. Whatever Tony saw in her expression obviously made him uncomfortable because he stood up abruptly and dumped the rest of his 7UP down the sink. 'Food,' he said without looking at her, 'd'you want me to peel some veg for tomorrow?'

'Yeah, sure, go ahead.'

He opened the fridge and pulled out a bag of carrots and parsnips. He moved with a grace Allie had only ever seen him display when he was playing football with Mark. A confidence he'd never had before. A calm and a purpose.

'I can cook a bit now,' he flashed her a grin as he took a sharp knife from the wooden block on the counter top. 'Ciaran insists we eat proper food.'

'Good for Ciaran,' she smiled back.

He began to peel the carrots. As he did so, Allie took the opportunity to enjoy the great view of his backside as he stood at the sink, legs apart, trainer-clad feet planted firmly on the floor. She loved the long length of his legs, the way his shoulders broadened out, the movement of them underneath his white cotton shirt as he worked on the bag of carrots. She loved his jet black hair, which he'd had cut for the occasion, she loved the curve of his cheek, the dark stubble on his jaw, the way his hair curled into his neck, the brown skin just visible over his shirt . . . Jesus, she just loved him, she realised. She loved this man. This new Tony that she'd glimpsed in flashes through the years and that had kept her hanging on even when things had been terrible. The Tony who had pretended to be crazy so that she could have fun but had still ensured that she wouldn't get into trouble. She was wrong, she realised – he had protected her.

'Remember that night we drove the car home from the NA meeting, me doing the gears and you the clutch?' she asked suddenly.

He turned to her and grinned. 'Yeah.' Then his face softened, his eyes a little pained. 'Yeah,' he said again.

She chose her words carefully. 'Neither of us could have managed without the other.'

'That's true.' He stared at her, his eyes finding hers. 'Not a good way to drive though,' he smiled a little.

'But a good way to live,' Allie said.

There was a silence. Tony turned his back to her. He laid the knife down and sank his hands into the pockets of his jeans, his head bowed.

370

'Without you, I'm going nowhere,' Allie said, realising that it was true.

When Tony spoke, it was so quiet she could barely hear him. 'You're doing fine.'

'Yeah,' she said, 'but I could . . . We,' she corrected, 'could do great.'

He didn't say anything for a second, then, his head dipped even lower, 'I am an addict, Allie.'

'I know, I—'

'I always will be one,' he interrupted, turning to face her. She was upset to see the distress on his face. 'I can only promise you one day at a time. That's all. There is no long term plan for me.'

'We only have one day at a time,' Allie said. Then, indicating her half empty coffee, she added, 'And besides, you make great coffee.'

Tony didn't smile.

'I'm trying to say I need you,' Allie said. 'It's only now, seeing you so well, that I really know it.'

'Any fool can make coffee.' A feeble joke.

Now it was Allie's turn to stay silent.

'Oh God.' Tony ran his hand through his hair and looked anything but happy. 'Al, I dunno.'

'I do.'

He squeezed his eyes shut and massaged his forehead. When he finally looked up, he said, 'I can't give you the perfection you want, Al. I can't give you happy ever afters. The closest I get is that fucking cappuccino.'

'I know that. But you can give me you.'

'Aww,' he groaned softly, closing his eyes again. Unconsciously he rubbed his hand on the back of his neck as he paced to and fro. Allie was reminded eerily of the way he'd get after a high. Edgy. Twitchy. Eventually he paused and asked seriously, 'Are you sure about this? About me?'

'Nope, I'll worry every time you go out. I'll worry each time we row. I'll probably live on tenterhooks for a long time—'

'So nothing will have changed,' Tony said flatly.

'You have,' Allie answered. 'You have changed, Tony, these last few months, you've changed. Grown. Figured out stuff. And I think I've changed. I'm surer of you now than I've ever been of anything in my life. I'm surer of us.'

He held her gaze and stated emphatically, 'I'm not a great prospect, Al. I've no job, I don't even know if I want my old job back, I hated it.'

'So? Get a new job. Work with John. Once you're happy, we'll all be happy.' She stood up and faced him.

'I think about coke most days. I see white flour in the shops and it stops me dead.'

'Avoid that aisle.' She took a step closer to him. 'Just don't do it, isn't that what they say?'

'I'm just letting you know.'

She was in front of him. 'I already know.'

'Your mother will kill you.'

'I know that too.'

They laughed a little. After a beat, Allie said, 'So?'

'I don't want to let you down, Al. I don't want to let the boys down.'

'You're not promising anything, which is great. Before this you'd have said mass.'

He cracked a shamefaced grin. 'I know.'

'I won't mind if you're not ready or if you don't want to,' Allie said, knowing it would kill her but also knowing that it would be unfair to pressure Tony into something when he'd lived all his life trying to be someone he wasn't.

'Jesus,' Tony tenderly studied her before reaching out and brushing some hair from her face, 'I so want to. The old Tony would have agreed like a shot, but I can't. I am a drug addict, Allie. I've fucked up spectacularly in the past. I don't even remember much of it. I now eat five bags of crisps a day and have started to suck lollipops. I will probably be a hundred pounds heavier by this time next year.'

'Me, Owen and Mark can recommend a good diet you can try.'

He laughed.

Allie watched him, her stomach flip-flopping with desire.

'You know I'd love to come back,' he said earnestly. 'You and the boys are the best things I ever had in my life. I just want –' He paused. 'Well, I want to be worthy of you all, I guess.'

'Saying that makes you worthy,' she said.

He dipped his head.

'So?' she prompted.

His eyes met hers. 'You know the answer, Al. You and the lads, it kills me leaving every Saturday, of course I want yez back.'

'Great.' She could barely get the words out, all she wanted was to feel his lips on hers.

He looked at her for what seemed like ages.

'Jesus, will you kiss me!'

He smiled slowly and bit his bottom lip. Allie, not able to wait any longer, reached over and wrapped her arms about his neck.

He groaned and pulled her to him.

Allie melted into his arms, it was like coming home, feeling him beside her, the scent of him, the taste of him, the way his hands held her face between his palms as he kissed her with a passion she loved. The feel of his leg against hers, his chest hard and firm against hers, his arms pulling her closer—

'Mammy, we can't sleep and what if Santa comes and we don't get any presents?' Mark yelled from upstairs.

They both laughed, Tony's forehead tipping hers.

'It's not funny!' Mark sounded indignant as he pounded down the stairs. 'If you were a kid and—' He poked his head into the kitchen and paused as he took in his two parents, his daddy's hand in his mammy's hair. 'Oh, you're kissing! Are you in love again?'

'Yep,' Tony said as Mark smiled. He gave Allie another kiss which made Mark go 'Yuk.' Then, extracting himself from Allie's arms, Tony said, laughing, 'Lead on, Mark, I'll get yez to sleep.' Turning to Allie, he ordered, 'Wait there.'

Allie knew she'd wait for ever if she had to. She thought back to the guarantees she'd wanted at the beginning of his recovery and she realised that there were no guarantees. Not with anyone. Not ever. All there was were hopes and prayers.

And wishes.

Acknowledgements

Thanks to:

All who helped me research this book – you know who you are!
All at Sphere for their help and patience.

My wonderful family.

And finally: if you have been affected by the issues raised in
this book, Narcotics Anon would like you to know that there
is help available at www.na-ireland.org

Second Chances
Martina Reilly

Lizzie Walsh has moved to Dublin to start again –
she has a great job as a fundraiser, a boyfriend she's
crazy about and friends she loves. Until, leaving work
late one evening, she bumps into the one person she
just can't forget.

Ten years ago, Lizzie's teenage sister's body was
found washed up on a beach. A local boy, Joe, was
sentenced to life imprisonment for her murder, despite
always protesting his innocence. Now Joe is back, released
from prison for good behaviour. But Lizzie can't stop
thinking about the pain he's caused her family – it doesn't
seem fair that he should be able to carry on with his life
as if nothing has happened. Then, as Lizzie slowly
inveigles her way into his life, she begins to realise that
all is not what it might seem . . .

'Has all the elements of an excellent read:
mystery, drama and romance'
Woman

978-0-7515-3958-5

Other bestselling titles available by mail:

☐ Second Chances	Martina Reilly	£6.99
☐ The Summer of Secrets	Martina Reilly	£6.99
☐ All I Want is You	Martina Reilly	£6.99
☐ Something Borrowed	Martina Reilly	£6.99
☐ Wedded Blitz	Martina Reilly	£6.99
☐ Wish Upon A Star	Martina Reilly	£6.99

The prices shown above are correct at time of going to press. However, the publishers reserve the right to increase prices on covers from those previously advertised, without further notice.

——————— sphere ———————

Please allow for postage and packing: **Free UK delivery.**
Europe; add 25% of retail price; Rest of World; 45% of retail price.

To order any of the above or any other Sphere titles, please call our credit card orderline or fill in this coupon and send/fax it to:

Sphere, P.O. Box 121, Kettering, Northants NN14 4ZQ
Fax: 01832 733076   Tel: 01832 737526
Email: aspenhouse@FSBDial.co.uk

☐ I enclose a UK bank cheque made payable to Sphere for £. . . . .
☐ Please charge £. . . . . . to my Visa, Delta, Maestro.

☐☐☐☐☐☐☐☐☐☐☐☐☐☐☐☐☐☐

Expiry Date ☐☐☐☐   Maestro Issue No. ☐☐

NAME (BLOCK LETTERS please) . . . .

ADDRESS . . . .

. . . .

. . . .

Postcode . . . . Telephone . . . .

Signature . . . .

Please allow 28 days for delivery within the UK. Offer subject to price and availability.